WHISKEY POISON

VIKTOROV BRATVA
BOOK 1

NICOLE FOX

Copyright © 2023 by Nicole Fox

All rights reserved.

No part of this book may be reproduced in any form or by any electronic or mechanical means, including information storage and retrieval systems, without written permission from the author, except for the use of brief quotations in a book review.

❦ Created with Vellum

MAILING LIST

Sign up to my mailing list!
New subscribers receive a FREE steamy bad boy romance novel.

Click the link below to join.
https://sendfox.com/nicolefox

ALSO BY NICOLE FOX

Orlov Bratva

Champagne Venom

Champagne Wrath

Uvarov Bratva

Sapphire Scars

Sapphire Tears

Vlasov Bratva

Arrogant Monster

Arrogant Mistake

Zhukova Bratva

Tarnished Tyrant

Tarnished Queen

Stepanov Bratva

Satin Sinner

Satin Princess

Makarova Bratva

Shattered Altar

Shattered Cradle

Solovev Bratva

Ravaged Crown

Ravaged Throne

Vorobev Bratva

Velvet Devil

Velvet Angel

Romanoff Bratva

Immaculate Deception

Immaculate Corruption

Kovalyov Bratva

Gilded Cage

Gilded Tears

Jaded Soul

Jaded Devil

Ripped Veil

Ripped Lace

Mazzeo Mafia Duet

Liar's Lullaby (Book 1)

Sinner's Lullaby (Book 2)

Bratva Crime Syndicate

Can be read in any order!

Lies He Told Me

Scars He Gave Me

Sins He Taught Me

Belluci Mafia Trilogy

Corrupted Angel (Book 1)

Corrupted Queen (Book 2)

Corrupted Empire (Book 3)

De Maggio Mafia Duet

Devil in a Suit (Book 1)

Devil at the Altar (Book 2)

Kornilov Bratva Duet

Married to the Don (Book 1)

Til Death Do Us Part (Book 2)

Heirs to the Bratva Empire

Can be read in any order!

Kostya

Maksim

Andrei

Princes of Ravenlake Academy (Bully Romance)

Can be read as standalones!

Cruel Prep

Cruel Academy

Cruel Elite

Tsezar Bratva

Nightfall (Book 1)

Daybreak (Book 2)

Russian Crime Brotherhood

Can be read in any order!

Owned by the Mob Boss

Unprotected with the Mob Boss

Knocked Up by the Mob Boss

Sold to the Mob Boss

Stolen by the Mob Boss

Trapped with the Mob Boss

Volkov Bratva

Broken Vows (Book 1)

Broken Hope (Book 2)

Broken Sins *(standalone)*

Other Standalones

Vin: A Mafia Romance

Box Sets

Bratva Mob Bosses (Russian Crime Brotherhood Books 1-6)

Tsezar Bratva (Tsezar Bratva Duet Books 1-2)

Heirs to the Bratva Empire

The Mafia Dons Collection

The Don's Corruption

WHISKEY POISON

**The hottest man I've ever seen is now my new boss—
and I'm stuck in a house with him...
Until one of us cracks.**

I've got debt—yeah, I know, so does everyone else on Planet Earth.

But the bills I'm paying keep my dad and my grandma alive.

So it's pretty messed-up for Timofey Viktorov to use them as a threat to keep me under control.

Not that he cares.

As a billionaire CEO, he takes no prisoners in the boardroom.

And as the don of the Viktorov Bratva, he takes no prisoners in real life, either.

Which is why he has no qualms about extorting me into taking his deal.

Live in my mansion...

Care for my baby...

Or suffer the consequences.

But he's not the only one with an agenda.

Timofey has skeletons in his closet—and I'm determined to dig them out.

He's just as determined to keep me far away from the secrets of his past.

The longer I'm in his house, the tenser things get.

Every time we brush past each other in the hallway, something sparks.

Every time we cross paths in the night, the ice grows thinner.

Sooner or later, it's going to crack.

***WHISKEY POISON* is Book 1 of the Viktorov Bratva Duet. The story concludes in Book 2, *WHISKEY PAIN*.**

1

PIPER

Thunder rumbles through the ground under my tired feet the moment I step out of work. If I wasn't so sick of hearing my own voice, I'd laugh. Or maniacally cackle. Whichever would more clearly denote that I am losing my ever-loving mind.

The world seems to agree, via brooding cinematic ambiance, that today sucks. A flash of lightning? The patter of raindrops turning into a steady downpour? Sure, why not? All the better to wash away the last of the day's hopes and dreams.

I lean out from under the threadbare awning and glance up at the dark sky. I'm not sure what I expect to see. Maybe a countdown clock in the clouds. Some sign of when the rain will end and I can resume my miserable life.

There's nothing, of course.

Thick clouds cover the waning moon and the streetlight outside the downtown Child Protective Services office is still burnt out, so it's eerily dark. I registered a complaint with the city four months ago, but the person in charge of replacing lights is probably as overworked as I am.

Still, all of that means it is *dark* dark outside.

"Like my soul," I quip quietly to myself.

Apparently, my week from hell hasn't stolen all of my wonderful qualities. My self-deprecating sense of humor is fully intact.

That being said, the guardian I dealt with today wouldn't find my joke especially funny. He'd probably call it accurate, actually.

Dark soul? More like a stone-cold bitch.

That's the thing about working for CPS: you're the face people associate with their child being ripped out of their arms.

It doesn't matter that the face of the child in question is filthy, scrawny, and covered in unexplained bruises.

It doesn't matter that the arms of the parent in question are studded with track marks from dirty needles.

They still think *you're* the bad guy.

Or, to quote yesterday's gem of a birth parent, a "raging bitch with shit for a heart and a bear trap for a coochie." As far as things go, that one was pretty good. I rated it a ten out of ten for creativity and submitted it to the office-wide "Best Insults" email thread.

"You should add that line to your dating profile," my boss, James, responded with a crying-laughing emoji.

What dating profile? I wanted to respond. But at some point, the self-deprecating humor isn't funny… or a joke, even.

Whiskey Poison

I deleted my dating apps months ago, only a few weeks after downloading them post-break up. Hence why I am standing on the doorstep of work trying to muster the courage to ride my bike home in the dark. In a rainstorm.

Because there *is* no one else to call.

I don't have a boyfriend waiting for me at home anymore, Noelle is working tonight, and Ashley's car is the most compact of compacts. She went on a "save the world" kick last year when she got out of rehab and bought a used Smart Car online. Even if she were available, I'd rather ride home in the rain than jam myself into that death trap.

When the claustrophobia starts, it lasts for hours.

"Okay, Pipe," I say to myself, hopping lightly from one foot to the other to psych myself up. "Here we go. Make it home and you can take a shower and put on your pajamas and eat that frozen stuffed crust pizza in the freezer."

And die alone.

I groan at my own intrusive joke and shake out my shoulders. "It's just a ten-minute ride. Then this day will be over and you can relax. Ready, set—"

To try and trick my own brain, I skip "go" and leap out into the rain.

I'm glad I didn't bother with a hat or the cute-but-useless rain jacket I keep in the bottom drawer of my desk for occasions like this. Because this is a soaking rain. The kind that drenches you through and through the moment you step into it.

There is no protection from this.

I keep my eyes down at the ground as I run, making sure I don't trip on the uneven pavement or slip in a giant puddle. Looking around is pointless, anyway—no one is out in this deluge. Even if they were, I wouldn't be able to see them. Every time I lift my head, the rain blurs what little of my vision the dark hasn't already stolen.

I round the corner into the alley next to our building. There's a dingy orange security light attached halfway up the brick facade, but it doesn't offer light so much as a strong sense that I've stumbled into the apocalypse.

I kneel down in an orange puddle to unlock my bike.

"If I'd known it was going to rain, I would have carried you up the stairs," I say.

If maniacal laughter wasn't already a clue that I'm losing my mind, talking to my bike surely is. I fumble with the lock chain in the dark. My fingers are slippery from all the water, and when they slip and I accidentally bend a fingernail all the way back, I want to curl up in a ball and cry right then and there.

Shower. Pajamas. Pizza.

I repeat my evening plans like a mantra as I finally pop the lock free, loop it around the base of the sopping wet seat, and tug my bike away from the rack.

Then the world tips sideways.

Correction: *someone* tips my world sideways.

For a second, the hands around my throat blend in with the pounding rain. My brain is overloaded with things to notice, so when I'm yanked to my left and thrown unceremoniously into the garbage-filled stream of dirty water running down the alleyway, I'm confused.

"What the—"

"You fucking *cunt*," a deep voice hisses.

That was definitely not the wind. Or the rain.

Panic lashes through me. Someone fists the wet material of my shirt and hauls me to my feet like I'm a sack of potatoes. I look back over my shoulder, but rain is pouring down my face and the man is backlit by the orange safety light.

So much for safety—I can't see shit.

I try to scream, but the man slams me against the brick wall. The air in my lungs leaves me in a whoosh.

"Not so tough now, eh?" He pins me in, crowding so close that he blocks some of the rain.

And for the first time, I get a good look at my attacker.

"I know you," I wheeze. "I—I—"

"*You—you—*," he mimics, his voice going unnaturally high. Then he lets out a deep, bitter laugh that isn't mirthful in the slightest. "You took my kid away from me."

The past few days have been a blur of meetings and home visits and filing case reports. The faces that stand out are few and far between. The woman who spat out the word "coochie" with zero humor at all definitely stands out.

This man, with his prematurely wrinkled skin and dark, worn clothes, didn't make an impression. He was just another in a line of parents too deep in their own addiction to recognize the child in their care needed, ya know, *care*.

Until now. Suddenly, he's in Technicolor.

"It wasn't my decision." I hate the way my voice breaks. An unspoken plea wedged between the words. "I make the reports, but someone else—"

"You said I was 'unfit.'" He draws closer. The alcohol on his breath washes over me.

The smell takes me right back.

Back to being five, seven, ten years old. Back to being young and helpless. Back to making myself small, hoping if I stay quiet, it will all go away.

He slicks his yellowed tongue over his teeth. "You wrote in your fuckin' paperwork that I hurt my kid."

The little boy had bruises after every visit with his dad and tiptoed around adults like he was walking through a minefield. It wasn't hard to guess what was happening.

I've seen it too many times.

I've *lived* it too many times.

My heart is racing a million beats per minute, but it isn't blood pumping through my veins. It's panic. Fear. Decades-old trauma like concrete weighing me down.

Fight, I beg myself. *Push him away. Fight back.*

"Not so tough now, are you?" The man grins. One of his front teeth is brown and the other is broken in half. The smell of vodka is so thick I'm going to gag.

Goddammit. Fight, Piper!

But I can't overcome what I was taught as a child: if I stand still and don't fight back, it will be over sooner. The man will tire himself out hitting me. He'll slink away once I crumple to the floor in a useless heap.

I learned all that the hard way. There's no unlearning it now.

The man wraps his meaty hand around my neck, and I close my eyes.

This will all be over soon.

2

PIPER

The man with the broken tooth starts to squeeze. My throat closes up. The world begins to blacken at the edges like someone is holding a match to one corner of my vision.

So this is how it ends. Not with a bang, but with a whimper.

Then, as suddenly as he appeared, the pressure is gone.

A deeper snarl joins the fray. I swear I'm hearing the voice of God.

"Am I interrupting something?"

When I manage to pry my eyes open, I'm positive I'm right. This man is a god, alright—and I'm ready to convert.

The stranger angles his body to shield me from my attacker. All I can see is the thick swell of his biceps and the broad set of his shoulders.

"Who the hell are you?" My attacker sneers. "Her boyfriend?"

"I'm the man who will separate your hands from your arms if you touch her again. Do you understand?"

The guardian who attacked me suddenly doesn't look so scary. As he stands up from where the god threw him to the ground, I see him stumble. He's drunk. I probably could have tipped him over with a good shove to the chest.

But I didn't.

I didn't do anything.

Shame washes over me in a hot wave. I'm surprised the rain on my skin doesn't evaporate in the sudden heat of it.

The drunk gives me one last look. His glassy eyes narrow in distaste before he hunches against the rain and scampers away down the alley. He rounds the corner and disappears.

Relief knocks me back against the brick. I press a hand to my chest and inhale shakily. "Oh my… Holy hell."

"Are you hurt?"

I look up and realize my rescuer is facing me now. His dark hair is short but curly, plastered to his head by the rain. Black-ink tattoos slip out of the ends of his rolled-up shirt sleeves to wrap around his wrists. Sixty seconds ago, I would have been afraid to run into him in this dark alleyway alone. Now, I've never felt safer in my whole godforsaken life.

Our eyes meet, and I inhale sharply. Even in the dark, his blue eyes are luminous. Bright and clear…

And pinned on me.

I swallow down the surge of conflicting emotions rising up in me and shake my head. "No. No, I'm okay. He didn't—You got here just in time. Nothing happened." I roll my shoulders. "Maybe once the adrenaline wears off, I'll be a little sore. But otherwise, I'm perfectly—"

"Stupid," the man growls.

"Excuse me?" I blink at him, a frown working between my brows.

"You are stupid." He repeats the words slowly. "You shouldn't be wandering down dark alleys in the middle of the night if you can't defend yourself."

It takes me a few seconds to process what he's saying. And *how* he's saying it. Like I've personally offended him.

"It's not the middle of the night. It's just after eight. The storm is making it darker than it would be if—"

"You didn't even check to see if anyone was around," he continues, ignoring me. "Your head was down and you don't have a weapon. If you'd spent half a fucking second observing your surroundings, you would've seen that asshole waiting at the mouth of the alley. Fuck knows he wasn't being sneaky about it."

The shame I was already fighting back redoubles and charges at me again. Tears burn in my eyes.

"It was raining too hard to see anything!"

"I saw him from across the street," he scoffs.

I look into his inhumanly blue eyes again and snort. "No wonder. What are you, a werewolf or something? Normal human eyes don't look like that."

His annoyance with me is interrupted for the barest of seconds with something like amusement. Then his full mouth turns down into a grimace. "Get your bike and go."

"Good idea. There are a lot of assholes wandering around tonight, apparently."

"And I won't always be there to save you from them." He turns around and walks away.

Just like that, I'm alone again.

In the dark. Soaking wet. Shaking with a chill that goes far beyond skin deep, and burning up with a single question on my mind.

What the hell just happened?

3

PIPER

My hands are still shaking as I reach for another slice of stuffed crust pizza. I'm showered, in clean pajamas, and eating the frozen pizza I promised myself, but mentally, I'm still in that alley with that man's vodka breath rolling over me in nauseating waves.

"Piper!"

My name being shrieked through the tinny speakers of my phone makes me jump. A dribble of grease drops from my pizza onto my flannel pajama pants.

"Damn it, Noelle. You made me spill."

"Good! Put down the pizza and pick up your phone," my best friend retorts. "You should be calling the police, not stuffing your face."

I drop the pizza on a chipped ceramic plate and wipe my fingers on a paper towel. "I'm not stuffing my face. And what would I even tell the police?"

"That you were attacked by a deranged parent outside of your job! I'd say that's a good starting point."

"It sounds simple when you say it like that, but…"

The beast of the man who rescued me floats in my mind's eye. There was nothing simple about him. He saved me and called me an idiot in the same breath.

Not exactly a knight in shining armor.

"What did you say?" Noelle makes a growly sound in sheer frustration. "Move your camera. What's the point of video chatting if I can't see your face?"

"Ashley has been on a black screen this entire chat," I point out. "You're not yelling at her."

"Ashley also wasn't assaulted tonight, so your situations aren't exactly comparable. Reveal yourself. Now."

I'm a grown woman. I don't take orders from anyone, not even one of my two best friends. Then again, Noelle is scary. If I don't do what she says now, I know she'll show up on my doorstep right as I'm getting ready for bed.

I sigh and grab my phone, giving her an *are-you-happy-now* grin.

"You're pale," she observes without missing a beat. "And is that a bruise on your jaw?"

"No," says Ash, "that's pizza sauce."

"Thanks for finally chiming in, Ashley." I roll my eyes and wipe the sauce off with my forearm. "I'm fine, okay? The guy was drunk and upset. He lost his kid this week. I don't need to make it worse."

Noelle's eyes bug out like they're about to pop. "Who cares about *his* week? What about *you*, Piper?! The guy choked you!"

"He tried," I correct. "He didn't get that far."

"Only because some giant came along and shoved him away," Ashley reminds us.

"He wasn't a giant."

"I distinctly remember the word 'giant' being thrown around."

"Giant biceps, I think," Noelle says. "She said he was a big guy with giant biceps."

"They were proportional to the rest of him," I mutter.

Noelle claps her hands like an elementary school teacher trying to get the class's attention. "Regardless, the fact remains that you need to file a report. He could come back and try again some other time."

I hear the man's deep voice like he's whispering the words in my ear. *I won't always be there to save you.*

Some masochistic part of me is disappointed. Maybe another attack wouldn't be so bad if *he* came back to intervene again.

"Fuck the cops," Ashley blurts out. "Buy a gun. I can get you one on the cheap."

"A gun? Piper isn't getting—she doesn't need a gun!"

Black Screen Ashley is unmoved. "What is a police report going to do if that guy comes back? Piper needs to be able to protect herself."

"Not with a *gun*," Noelle argues. She shakes her head. "If I could see your face, I'd be able to tell if you're joking. What is with the two of you trying to hide tonight?"

Suddenly, Ashley's screen goes white and then she's there. Her dyed-black hair is tucked behind her ears and her eyebrows are as thin as they were in high school, which is to say, almost nonexistent. She raises them and stares at her camera like it's a personal challenge. It takes me a second to understand why.

"Ash," I breathe, covering my mouth, "is that a bruise, or…?"

She presses tenderly at the horrifying black ring around her right eye and gives a humorless chuckle. "Well, it isn't pizza sauce."

Noelle has gone eerily silent. Her nostrils are flared.

"What happened?" I ask, even though I already know.

Ashley has been in an on-again, off-again relationship with her abusive drug dealer for years. Apparently, they're on again. Or they were. I don't know what they'll be after he's punched her fucking lights out.

Before Ashley can even answer, Noelle shakes her head. "I'll kill him. I swear to God I will."

"What happened to filing a police report?" Ashley taunts. "Suddenly, you're Ms. Vigilante."

It's Noelle's turn to be unmoved. "Jason already has several warrants out for his arrest, I'm sure. If the police were going to do anything about him, they would've done it several infractions ago. I might as well take matters into my own hands."

Ashley snorts. "Your boyfriend works for the FBI. You do realize that, right? He's probably recording this conversation right now. Everything you say can and will be held against you."

"He's just an accountant for the FBI, right?" I butt in. "He's not, like, an actual agent."

I've met Wayne plenty of times, but his job is kind of a blur. He has a soft chin, a receding hairline, and a vapid smile. He isn't what television has taught me to think of as someone who works for the FBI.

"He's a forensic accountant," Noelle agrees. "Which is sort of like an agent, but he specializes in white collar crimes. He also is not recording my conversations, so no one needs to know that I'm planning to kill Jason and plant his head on a spike in my front yard."

Ashley gives us a weak smile. "It's fine. I went there to end things and… well, they're ended now. I won't be seeing him again."

I try to toss a dubious look at Noelle, but video chatting doesn't really facilitate body language. I doubt Ashley will ever be truly done with Jason. Mostly because I doubt she will ever be truly clean. She's a third-generation addict and still in deep, despite her latest trip to rehab.

"If you need anything—" I start.

"No," she snaps. "This is why I left my camera off. This is about you, Piper. You had a traumatic experience. A black eye is just another day for me."

Noelle practically screams in frustration. "What is wrong with the two of you? Press charges. Both of you! None of this is normal. This is ridiculous."

"What's ridiculous is you acting like you have any idea what this is like," Ashley says.

There's a beat of uncomfortable silence.

"What does that mean?" Noelle asks finally.

I cover my eyes. "C'mon, you two. Can we not do this?"

I'm the peacemaker. I've always played that role, for my friends and everyone else. Noelle is the boss lady and Ashley is the wild card. The two of them butt heads more often than not, and I'm not in the right headspace to properly referee them tonight.

"No, let's do it," Ashley sniffs, bending closer to her camera. "Noelle sits in a cushy office and lives in a fancy loft apartment with her boyfriend and wants to act like she knows what it's like for *us*."

Noelle rolls her eyes. "Spare me the melodrama. It's not like we're from different sides of the tracks, okay? We grew up in the same apartment complex, for God's sake. But while you were out getting fucked-up with Jason and Mychal and Elijah and I-can't-even-remember-who-else, I got scholarships and went to college and made something of myself. You don't get to be mad at me for that."

"Are you saying I haven't made something of myself?" Ashley snaps. "Are you saying—"

"Stop!" I yell loudly enough that Mrs. Shaban next door is probably going to knock on our shared wall to tell me to keep it down.

Thankfully, it works. I feel both of their eyes flit to me.

"Can I tell you how this is going to go?" I ask. "Because I already know. Ashley is going to accuse Noelle of never really liking her—"

"Of course I like you!" Noelle interrupts.

"And Noelle is going to accuse Ashley of thinking she is stuck-up—"

"She is sometimes." Ashley shrugs unapologetically.

"Then you're both going to cry," I finish. "Then, when you're cried out, you'll apologize and make nice and we'll end the conversation laughing like normal. So how about we skip the drama and go to the laughing? I've had a long day."

They both look like kids who just lost their favorite toy, but I can tell they know I'm right. Noelle is the first to admit it.

"Fine," she huffs. "We're too old for this shit anyway."

"Stop telling Piper and me how to live our lives and we'll be fine," Ashley retorts. "But you know I love you, Ellie Bellie."

Noelle's eyes go watery, even though she's always hated that nickname. "I love you, too, Smashley."

"Great," I conclude. "Now that that's settled, I still have to prep for work tomorrow."

"You're kidding, right?" Noelle drawls. "You need to decompress and handle your personal business. You think you're fine now, but the body keeps the score, girl. You're going to be a mess the moment you try to relax."

Part of me is terrified Noelle is right, but I really don't have time to process this trauma. Besides, I have a lifetime of it built up inside of me somewhere. I've managed that okay.

So far.

I shake my head. "Not kidding, no. The gears of CPS stop for no woman. I have a meeting first thing tomorrow morning about a permanent placement for an abandoned baby. Honestly, it might be a bright spot in my week. Giving a kid a home versus snatching them out of it; could be a nice change of pace."

"Or you could take the day off and get some bottomless mimosas with me," Ashley offers, wagging her brows.

"I thought you were sober."

"I am! California sober," she says a bit defensively. "Weed and alcohol are fine. It's all about moderation."

I watch Noelle zip her lips closed in an effort to keep all of her unsolicited advice inside. We both know moderation is not Ashley's strong suit. Doing the exact opposite of what we advise *is* one of her strengths, though. Most of the time, it's better to stay quiet and let her figure it out on her own.

I give her a thin smile. "Raincheck on the brunch. I have a case file to review."

I hang up to a mini-chorus of well wishes and encouragement. But too quickly, the oppressing silence of my apartment settles over me like a cobweb. No matter how hard I try to fight off the discomfort, I can't seem to shake the tingle of wrongness in my skin.

It was easy to shove my attack into a dark corner of my mind when I had Noelle and Ashley to talk to. Now, it's front and center. The same ninety-second interaction plays on an endless loop in my brain.

Along with the blue-eyed beast who came to my rescue.

That's a little harder to forget.

4

PIPER

After I reread the first paragraph of my case file ten times in a row, I give up and chuck the folder aside.

"That's a tomorrow problem," I mutter, repeating one of my grandma's favorite sayings.

In her world, almost everything is a tomorrow problem. Right now, it sounds like as good a solution as any. Especially when I catch sight of the stack of medical bills on the corner of my desk.

That is *definitely* a tomorrow problem. Maybe a next week problem. Maybe even a next life problem.

I drop down on my bed and drag a pillow over my eyes. I need a sensory deprivation tank. A place to exist without the past, present, and future crushing in on me from all sides. But I guess a pillow on my head will do in a pinch.

Without really meaning to, I fall asleep.

∼

The rain is lighter now. It's a fine mist, more like a fog than anything. It presses in on me, muffling my senses.

Hands plunge out of the haze towards me. Strong fingers wrap around my biceps and jerk me into the mist. I try to scream, but no sound will come out.

I'm frozen. Helpless. Defenseless.

The hands shove me back against the brick wall, but this time, it's spongy against my spine. It's almost comfortable.

Then the owner of the hands steps forward, breaking through the rain to reveal himself. I should have recognized him already. Even through the mist, his eyes glimmered.

"You," I breathe.

The blue-eyed beast smirks. I didn't know his full mouth could do that. I've only seen him grimace. A smile looks good on him.

I feel myself losing focus. But there's danger here. I was being attacked. "Where did the other guy go?"

He leans in close. "It's just the two of us now, Piper Quinn."

The wall behind me is now a bed. Instead of standing upright, I'm flat on my back with the beast looming over top of me. I'm naked, too. When did that happen?

My heart is sputtering and I'm hot all over. Muscles deep inside quiver and tremble as he pins me to the bed limb by limb. I'm like a butterfly on a display board. But so long as it's him skewering me, I don't mind.

"You shouldn't be in dark alleys in the middle of the night if you can't defend yourself," he says. This time, he isn't chastising me. The words curl off his tongue like delicate tendrils of smoke.

"Defend myself from what?" I'm breathless as his lips graze across my neck and over my collarbone.

"Monsters," he whispers, nipping at my earlobe. *"Monsters like me."*

I wake up slowly.

The mist becomes blurry sleep vision. The hands at my waist become what I'm sure is a bruise from my tumble to the pavement last night. I inhale to try and disperse the butterflies in my stomach, but it hurts to breathe.

If the body really does keep the score, I'm definitely losing.

I sit up, wincing at the pain and the disappointment. The blue-eyed beast was an asshole in reality, but he can invade my dreams anytime. That was unbelievably hot.

I dig through the tangled comforter for my phone. The screen is on full brightness and I hiss like a vampire in sunlight while I fumble to darken it. Then I catch the time.

"Shit!" Despite the ache in my shoulder and my hip, I lurch out of bed and dive for my closet.

I'm late. Beyond late.

If I were to arrive at my meeting right this very second, I'd be forgivably late. But I'm still standing in my room with bedhead and flannel pants on.

The next fifteen minutes are spent alerting my boss, texting the number associated with the case file to let the potential parent know I'm deeply sorry but on my way, and then making myself passably presentable.

Whiskey Poison

My bike isn't an option this morning, so I book it to the bus and then dab on some blush and mascara between stops. My claustrophobia doesn't act up so much on public transportation, especially if I find a seat where I can crack a window.

When I reach my stop, I'm so busy double checking the address in my folder and sprinting through the neighborhood that I don't register where I am until the gates are in front of me.

Tall, elaborate metal gates, hedged in by what seems to be acres of thick, foreboding trees.

Behind those, way off in the distance, is a mansion.

"That's a new one," I mutter.

I'm more accustomed to mobile homes on cinderblocks. Studio apartments with four mattresses on the floor and cockroaches climbing the walls. Mansions are uncharted territory.

What a day to skip a shower.

I go up to the gate, expecting to announce myself or something like that. Instead, as I'm reaching for the buzzer button, it sounds before I can touch it. The gate swings inward.

I look over one shoulder, then the other. But the bus is long gone and it's eerily quiet out here now. I'm all alone.

Steeling myself, I slip through the pedestrian gate and half-jog up the long driveway. It takes almost twenty minutes of power-walking, so I have more than enough time to observe and confirm that this place is capital-F Fancy.

Trees after trees after trees. The swirls and spirals in the driveway stones stretch for almost a mile. The front door, when I reach it, is solid wood with a gold spherical knocker. And when the door opens, a man who looks like a Downton Abbey butler is waiting on the other side of it.

His face is dour and disapproving. "Ms. Quinn, I presume."

"Yes. Sorry I'm late. I meant to be here earlier, but—"

"Follow me." He turns and leads me into the house without another word.

I gulp, then close the door behind me and hurry after him.

A lush carpet runs down the center of a long hallway, absorbing the sounds of our footsteps. The arched ceilings should make this place feel like a church, but there is enough rich wood paneling and brass fixtures to keep it warm and cozy. It's beautiful.

I don't like to stereotype, but I can't imagine not trusting the owner with a child. I mean, they probably have enough money to take care of half of my caseload without breaking a sweat.

Even with the rough start, today might turn out to be a much-needed easy day, after all.

The butler stops and pulls open a door. "Mr. Viktorov, Ms. Quinn is here to see you."

"Finally," a deep voice grumbles from inside the room.

It's not a warm welcome, but I can't blame the man. I'm ridiculously late.

I put on my friendliest smile and step through the door. "Hello, Mr. Viktorov. I'm so sorry I'm late. You must be—"

My words dry up as I look past the intimidating desk in the center of the room to the man just beyond it.

His eyes are as blue as they were in my dream.

As blue as they were in the alley last night.

For a few seconds, all I can do is stare. This can't be real. I'm still asleep. Then the blue-eyed beast stands up and fixes me with a frown.

Definitely not a dream, then.

While my body struggles to keep up with my brain, a single word rasps out of me.

"You."

5

PIPER

"Hello to you, too," drawls the man—Mr. Viktorov, apparently. "I see CPS sent their best and brightest today."

Somehow, he looks even more wild sitting behind a desk than he did in that alley. The wide expanse of his shoulders wasn't meant to be contained to an office chair. The tattoos I know cover his arms are hidden by a dark blue suit jacket, but I swear I can still see the outline of them through the sleeves.

"Not their most talkative, though."

His arrogant tone is what gets me to finally lift my jaw off the floor. I close my mouth and take mental inventory of this situation.

This man saved my life last night.

Then proceeded to haunt my dreams.

Now, he's in front of me.

Whiskey Poison

I try to thread these points into something resembling logic, but I come up empty. Instead, I flip open the folder and check the address again.

"You can stop double checking," he advises before I can ask. "You're in the right place." He settles back in his chair, one ankle crossed over the opposite knee.

"How do you know?" I ask. "How did you—do you know me? Do we know each other?"

"We met last night, actually." I don't miss the note of amusement in his voice.

God, he's a douche. I blow out a frustrated breath. "I'm aware of that. But you don't find that a little odd? That we met last night and now, I'm your caseworker?"

Something tickles at the back of my brain. A suspicion I can't fully wrap my head around yet.

"What I find odd is that you seem this surprised to see me," Mr. Viktorov answers. "Have you not read your case file?"

I take a lot of pride in my job. I have to—they sure as hell don't pay me enough to be in it for the money. So I want to argue that *of course I read the file. I'm always prepared.* But as it is… I can't.

"It's been a bad week. You should know—you were there for the worst part of it," I say. "Excuse me for being human and needing to take the night off."

"We all have our weaknesses."

His voice is flat and unreadable. I have a feeling that whatever species he belongs to doesn't have many weaknesses.

He leans back in his chair and points a finger at the chair across from him. "Sit. Read. I'll wait. I've had a lot of practice with waiting this morning."

I clench my teeth together to hold in my retort. *So much for an easy day.*

I settle into the leather chair and open up the folder. It's almost impossible to focus with his eyes on me. Especially since he makes no move to avert his gaze or keep busy. He just stares at me, waiting for me to finish reading.

Luckily—or not so luckily, in this case—it's easy to grasp the highlights of Mr. Viktorov's case. I barely get halfway down the first page before I gasp.

"You assaulted a doctor and kidnapped a baby!"

He doesn't respond. I keep reading in horror. Most files come with one or two "important notes" at the bottom. If a birth parent is a flight risk or if the child has severe allergies, that kind of thing. But Mr. Viktorov's has a page and a half of them, all bolded and italicized and underlined in red several times over.

He is, in fact, allergy-free—what a relief.

On the downside, he is also suspected to belong to an organized crime syndicate.

Like every accusation of that magnitude, it's caveated with the word "alleged" about fifty times. No one at CPS wants to get in a legal war with a violent, criminal billionaire. But I've been in the game long enough to know that "alleged" usually means "pretty damn certain."

If I'd read this last night, I probably would have tried to bring a male colleague along with me for some protection. But the image of James in his sweater vests, sweating and shrinking in the shadow of this giant of a man, is almost laughable.

"Based on your pallor, I'm guessing you've finished the file."

I flinch at the sound of his voice before quickly setting the folder aside and swallowing hard. "Where is the baby?"

"Not your concern."

I frown. "The baby is entirely my concern. That's my job."

"Your job is to determine if I am a proper placement for the child left on my doorstep," he replies. "The child is no factor."

"I don't need you to tell me how to do my job, Mr. Viktorov. The child is a very important factor in a case like this. We like to keep families together."

He shakes his head. "That isn't an option."

I take a deep breath. "Let's start at the beginning. How did the baby get here?"

"I wasn't there for that part, but when a man and a woman—"

"How did the baby come to be on your doorstep?" I interrupt, hissing the question between my teeth. I'm sure Mr. Viktorov knows exactly how to make a baby. If he ever wipes the scowl off of his face, he can probably get as much practice as he wants, too.

His blue eyes sparkle with amusement. Good God, those things are lethal. I do my best to focus on the expanse of the desk between us. It's safer that way. No unwanted flashbacks to my dream this morning.

"He was dropped off."

"By whom?"

"How should I know?"

I arch a brow. "A house this big, this expensive, *with a gate*, and you expect me to believe you don't have cameras?"

"They weren't working that day." He makes no attempt to sound believable. He doesn't need to. He knows I have no way of getting the truth out of him.

"Fine," I grit out. "So a stranger drops off a baby on your doorstep and then what?"

"I took him to the hospital."

I tap the folder. "You *left* him at the hospital. That's what the case report says. You handed him over to a doctor."

His jaw clenches. "Yes. Then I changed my mind."

"You wanted the baby back?"

"Benjamin."

"What?"

"Benjamin," he repeats. "That is his name. I wanted Benjamin back.."

"So you assaulted a doctor. The report says you strangled him, actually."

"Is he dead?" he asks rhetorically, his voice a deep rumble.

"The doctor?" I skim the report again, but surely the man being a murderer would have been mentioned front and center, right? I finally find it at the bottom of page five. "No. He survived."

Mr. Viktorov nods like that proves his point. "If I'd strangled him, he'd be dead. I simply reminded him how much he likes breathing."

For a brief second, I'm back in the dark, wet alley. Mr. Viktorov is standing in front of me again, rain dripping down his neck as he looms over my attacker. *The only thing you need to know is I'm the man willing to separate your hands from your arms if you touch her again.*

He seems to be full of helpful "reminders."

"Why do you even want the baby? Are you the father?"

"I thought you were here to determine that."

"I'm here to determine if you should be granted guardianship, Mr. Viktorov. Right now, I'm asking about Benjamin's birth father."

"Timofey," he says.

"But you said—I thought the child's name was Benjamin."

He nods. "It is. *My* name is Timofey."

A leftover tremble from my dream this morning settles low in my belly. Hearing a name has never been so intimate. "Oh. Sure. Okay. Timofey."

"I'm not Benjamin's biological father," he continues. "That doesn't change the fact that he will live with me, and I'll take care of him."

"Why?"

"Last I checked, babies need a hand here or there."

I blow out a breath and a strand of hair that has fallen out of my haphazard ponytail lifts and resettles on my forehead. I wouldn't be surprised to find steam pouring out of my ears at this point. The man is mashing all of my buttons at the same time.

"I'm asking why a single man like you would want to care for a random baby left on your doorstep? I've been a social worker for seven years and this is a first for me."

"What makes you so sure I'm single?"

The question takes me off-guard. My cheeks heat instantly. "Oh. Well, I—the chart said—I guess it didn't exactly say. I assumed. There was no mention of anyone else. You're alone now, so…are you single?"

There's that flicker of amusement on his face again. It almost gives me hope that the smirking dream version of Timofey isn't completely out of the question. What I'd give to see that smile in real life.

"I have no need for a partner. I can raise Benjamin on my own just fine."

It's an annoying non-answer. Annoying only because I suddenly want to know if there is a woman of the mansion wandering around somewhere. A man like Timofey surely doesn't go too long without a warm, willing body in his bed.

He's right, though. There's no requirement for him to have a partner. It's not pertinent to the case and it would be inappropriate for me to press. That doesn't stop me from wanting to.

"As you've pointed out a few times now, that is what I'm here to determine," I say. "Based on your file alone, it's not looking good."

He folds his large hands in front of him. I mentally measure them against my wrists, assessing how accurate my dream was this morning. How easily I would fit into them. What those fingers would feel like if they—

"What about my file concerned you?"

I blink away the dirty image. "You are a smart man, Mr. Vik—Timofey. You know my concerns."

"I'm sure there's a colorful list of my priors on there. Let's focus on what matters, though: I saved your life last night."

That tickle of suspicion from earlier finally clicks into place. And when it does, I gasp. "Oh my... oh my God. Did—did you stage what happened?"

"Your attack, you mean." It's a statement, not a question.

"Yes. My 'attack.' You did!" I jump to my feet. "You hired that crazy guy to attack me so you could show up and save me. You wanted to get in my good graces so I'd give you Benjamin. You... you..." I fall silent, too stunned to speak.

Timofey fixes me with a stare, the seconds ticking away.

"Well?" I demand. "Are you going to even bother denying it?"

"I'm trying to decide if I'm flattered or insulted," he muses. "I'm going to go with insulted. The fact that you think I need to resort to an elaborate set-up to get what I want... It's beneath me. The theory is beneath you, too. I called you stupid last night, but I didn't actually believe it. Maybe I should rethink."

I glare at him. "So what were you doing there, then?"

"Finally," he breathes. "The fun part."

Goosebumps erupt down my arms at the sinful suggestion in his voice. *Was he there for me? No. No, definitely not. Why would he be?*

"You seem to know a lot about me, Piper."

"It's Ms. Quinn." I try to sound confident, but my voice is shaking.

His eyebrow arches subtly before he continues. "You seem to know a lot about me, Piper. Now, let me tell you what I know about you." He plants his palms flat on his desk and rises to his full height, never once looking away from me. I have to crane my neck back to meet his eyes. "You've been a social worker for seven years, but you still don't make enough money to dig yourself out of the financial hole you're in."

I narrow my eyes. "I'm in debt. Good guess. Me and most other humans on the planet."

"Yes, but your debt is different. It's not even yours," he says. "You have taken on the debt of not one, but two relatives. How are Daddy and Grandma doing, by the way? Talked to them recently?"

The air in my lungs turns sour. My chest burns, but I can't exhale. I can't move. Timofey and I, we're balanced on the precipice of something. One wrong move and it will all go sideways. I'll fall.

And I don't have to ask to know that, this time, he won't help me back up.

"You don't have to answer that, actually. I already know. No one would blame you for going so long between visits. You're a busy girl, what with work and keeping track of your friend Ashley." He clicks his tongue in faux disappointment. "When will that girl get and stay on the wagon?"

"How do you know about Ashley?" I croak. I have the urge to reach for my phone right this second and call her to make sure she's safe.

Timofey ignores me. "You attract addicts, but you aren't one. Good for you for overcoming the statistics. Especially coming from a broken home. The odds were stacked against you, but you came out on top. Is that why you got in this line of work? To help kids like yourself? To give back?"

That's exactly why I got in this line of work. But the way he says it makes it sound pathetic.

"This is illegal," I snap. "You can't—You shouldn't know any of this. You spied on me."

"Are you going to file a police report?" he asks. "I'd be surprised. You didn't file one after your attack last night."

I feel flayed open. Bare naked in front of those icy blue eyes.

"If you think blackmail is going to work on me, you're wrong," I hiss. "There is no way in hell I'm leaving a child in your care. You aren't fit to be around other humans, let alone a child."

He waves a hand like he's shooing away a gnat. "Benjamin is staying here. File whatever reports you want. My lawyers will deal with them."

I stand up, shoving my chair back. "Then why am I here? If your lawyers can handle this, why did you show up at my job last night? There was no point in bringing me here."

"Everything I do has a point," he says icily. His eyes are just as frosty. "You're here because I can save myself the trouble of talking to lawyers and solve both of our problems at the same time."

"Let me guess," I sneer. "Money?"

"You say that like you aren't in desperate need of some."

"I'd never be desperate enough to accept help from you."

"You may think you're above being bought, but that's only because you've never had the opportunity. But suddenly, your state college education and experience with children has some actual value. Rather than turn your nose up at it, I suggest you listen carefully."

Timofey leans forward, and even though he's still a foot away, I swear I can feel the brush of his lips on my skin. A chill races down my spine.

"You make too few pennies working too many hours. Then you come home to a tiny, overpriced apartment and stare at the ceiling while you wonder how you're going to keep making ends meet."

"Are you done, or are you just going to keep insulting me?"

"If you find the facts of your life insulting, that is your problem, not mine," he says. "I'm making you a generous offer. I don't need a woman in my life, but that doesn't mean there wouldn't be benefits to having one around. I'm offering you the opportunity to live here and take on that role."

"You're offering me *what* role?" I drop my voice like I'll be less mortified if I say it in a whisper. "I'm not going to be a live-in call girl. If you want sex, you can get it somewhere else."

Finally, at long last, Timofey's mouth twists into a smirk. It's barely there, just a ghost of a smile, but it's there. Of course it only happens when he's laughing at me.

"You'd be a live-in nanny. To Benjamin," he adds slowly. "The option of a promotion is never off the table, though. Work hard and who knows where it will take you."

I glare at him. "Fuck you."

"I thought you weren't interested in that?"

I ball my fists at my side. "I will never work for you."

"I doubt your pride is worth drowning in never-ending debt. You're in a storm and I'm offering you a life preserver, Piper. Take it."

On some level, Timofey was right: no one has ever offered to erase my debt. No one has ever dangled a life-changing amount of money in front of me. I've never had to decide how much my morality is worth.

But this isn't a generous offer I'm turning down. At best, it's a bribe to let this man raise a child he is obviously not fit to be within a hundred miles of. At worst, it's an outright threat. *Do as I say or be punished.*

I lived that way for long enough, doing whatever was necessary to avoid pain.

I won't do it anymore.

"Thanks for your offer, but I refuse." I snatch his case file off the desk and hug it to my thundering chest. "I'm going to submit my report, and it's going to be the honest version. Whatever happens after that isn't up to me."

I turn and march for the door. Just before I step into the hallway, Timofey's deep voice follows me.

"We all have more control over our destiny than we think," he says. "You're making a mistake. Think about that when you're home alone tonight."

6

TIMOFEY

Akim darkens my doorstep thirty seconds after Piper leaves. He has a way of knowing exactly when I least want to see him.

"Not now."

He ignores me and strolls in. "Good thing I waited. I would've hated to walk in and interrupt you with that fine piece of ass." He whistles long and low. "You really are a lucky man."

"Keep your eyes in your fucking head."

I can't really blame him. Piper looked a bit mussed—probably something to do with why she was running an hour late—but it would take a lot more than a messy ponytail and a wrinkled blouse to make her unappealing. Even in the dark and the rain last night, my body responded to hers with that kind of crackling, carnal need that I rarely feel anymore.

"Down, tiger. I come in peace." He holds up his hands as though to show me he's harmless. "I've known you long enough to know when you've marked your territory. Just tell me who she is."

"My new nanny."

The offer was generous. Beyond generous, really. I didn't need to pay her a dime; I could have kept her here on threats and blackmail alone. Fuck knows I have enough information on her. A girl like that, living in the system all her life? There was plenty of dirt to sift through.

"Seems like maybe she doesn't know that yet," he says, inclining his head towards the hallway. "Considering she told you to fuck off and then stormed out."

I level him with a glare. "Don't ask questions you already know the answer to."

"Don't lie to your best friend, then. It wounds me." He flops down into the chair Piper just left, his legs dangling casually over the side.

Nothing actually wounds Akim. The man is a human golden retriever. You swat him on the nose and he comes back a minute later with an apologetic offering to drop in your lap. If he wasn't the most loyal man I've ever known, he'd drive me fucking insane.

"How do you plan to catch this fly—with vinegar or honey?"

I frown. "The whole point of that phrase is that it's hard to catch flies with vinegar."

"Never stopped you from trying." He grins. "Vinegar is your signature blend. You're a surly bastard, God help you."

I flip him off.

"Case in point," he summarizes.

I'm not in the mood to deal with Akim right now. Piper Quinn set me on edge more than I'd like to admit.

"That woman isn't what I expected," I murmur. "Even last night, I showed up to talk to her—"

"To *threaten* her," Akim corrects. "People don't lurk outside of a woman's place of business in the dark to talk to them. You went to shake her up a bit."

"I went there to make it clear to her that life would be easier if she gave me and Benjamin the stamp of approval and moved along. Call it what you want."

"I call it a threat," he says. "But continue."

"Well, I showed up in time to watch her traipse right into a mugging. I thought women were trained from a young age to be alert and carry their keys between their fingers. She shouldn't be walking willingly into dark alleys. I thought I'd have to lure her into one, but she went in with eyes wide open."

In my mind's eye, I can still see her standing outside the front door of the office, her face turned up to the clouds above. I was going to charge her immediately, but the way her mouth puckered in disappointment distracted me.

It happened today, too. Her pouty lips pursed in displeasure. I've never seen her smile, but if it's anything like her frown, I wouldn't mind a peek.

"So your ambush turned into a rescue mission," Akim summarizes.

"That's overstating it. The *mudak* who attacked her was hammered drunk. I'm not sure why she didn't fight back. She's had no trouble pushing back against me."

"That's true," Akim chuckles. "I heard it firsthand. That woman hates your guts, like, *bad*."

"If you were anyone else, I'd beat your ass for eavesdropping."

"Close your office door then. Your voice carries and these hallways have amazing acoustics. I didn't even have to try."

I sigh. "Then you must've heard that I decided to change tactics. What I saw of her last night taught me two things: she shuts down during violence and she's tough to intimidate."

Akim spins his legs around to the floor and throws an arm over the back of the chair. "And third, you realized she was smokin' hot and you'd like to keep her around."

"Sounds like you're the one who's interested. Should I set the two of you up?"

But even as I say it, the joking suggestion makes my shoulders knot up.

Luckily for him, Akim snorts. "No thanks. I'd prefer to keep my dick attached to my body. You like her. Just admit it."

"I don't like anyone."

"Maybe you've forgotten what it feels like to have a crush. This is your first one in a while." His expression falls and a serious edge creeps into his voice. "Look, man, with everything that went down with Emily—"

My voice comes out crackling with fire. "This has nothing to do with Emily."

Mostly because I don't let myself think about her anymore. I learned a long time ago that grief is a useless distraction.

"Listen, dude, I get it. Really. But maybe it's time to—"

"It's not time for anything," I snarl, shutting Akim down. "I want no part of her. Piper Quinn is fucked-up. Sick and twisted."

Akim's eyes widen. "First, 'sick and twisted' sounds right up your alley. Second, how in the hell do you figure?"

"To spend your days ripping children away from their parents, you have to be fucked up somehow."

My best friend's expression softens. I want to punch it off of him. "Shit has changed since we were kids, man. They have new policies in place. Therapists, that kind of shit. It's all about emotional wellness now, you know? I bet she's nothing like the caseworker you—"

"Go make me some fucking food," I order.

Akim is only my cook because he enjoys it and I figured if he was mooching off my payroll anyway, he might as well contribute a little bit. So for me to bark at him to go fix me a sandwich is condescending as hell. He knows that, but I don't give a shit. I have no desire to sit here and hear about the many improvements made to the child welfare system in this country. I don't need the lecture on how it works.

I fucking lived it.

Surprisingly, Akim stands up and nods. Maybe he's learning to be agreeable after all.

Then, just as he reaches the doorway, he pauses and leans against the frame. "Would you like me to put on my heels and pearls before or after I make the sandwich?"

I roll my eyes. "Don't explain what that means. I don't want to hear—"

"You say you don't need a woman, yet you treat me like a 1950s housewife." He slaps on a cloying smile. "Do you want a corned beef or bologna sandwich today, Timofey dear?"

"You're my chef. I shouldn't need to remind you that making me a sandwich is your job."

He shrugs one shoulder. "Whatever you say. But if I catch you trying to put lipstick on me while I'm sleeping, I'll quit."

I almost laugh at that. But Akim doesn't need the encouragement. "No, you won't. I pay you too well."

He considers it for a moment and nods. "You're right. Fine. Pick the shade and I'll wear it."

"Fuck off."

"That says something, doesn't it? About your girl. Piper."

Her name does something strange to my chest. "She's not my—"

"Right, right. She's not your girl," he says, sounding bored. "I'm just saying, I'm willing to degrade myself to work for you, but she isn't? Either she's got a secret trove of cash somewhere or the woman can't be bought."

I snort. "She doesn't have to be too righteous to outdo you. You don't exactly own property on the moral high ground. I saw you shove Monopoly money in a stripper's underwear at Pavel's bachelor party."

"She was paid ahead of time for being there. It's not like she survives on tips," he mutters. "But the point remains. Things didn't go to plan last night or today. So what's your next move?"

"That's where the sandwich comes in."

He frowns. "Liar. You just want me to leave."

"I always want you to leave. But I also need you to pack me an on-the-go dinner. I'll be eating in the car."

"Dare I ask why?"

"Because," I sigh, tired of explaining myself, "I have an errand to run."

I don't have to elaborate. Akim nods in understanding. "I'll throw in some drinks, too." He steps out into the hall, muttering to himself, "Champagne, candles, condoms…"

"Don't you fucking dare, Akim."

He pretends not to hear me. I know because I can hear him laughing.

7

PIPER

"You look terrible."

I glance over at Andrea's desk, but all I see is a set of bleary eyes staring at me over the top of a stack of paperwork. She's normally a sweetheart, so if she's telling me I don't look good, I can only imagine the state I'm in.

"Thanks for that," I reply wearily. "Really uplifting."

I drop my purse on my desk and flop into my chair. Nothing has changed since yesterday. My magnetic paperclip holder is still perched on top of my dwindling pad of sticky notes. Yesterday's coffee is still half-full like I left it. It's all the same.

But everything *feels* different.

"I'm not trying to be uplifting." Andrea spins her chair out to the side so I can see her properly. "I'm trying to make sure you don't bring that flu that has been going around in here. I can't afford to get sick."

"I'm not sick."

"Well, you look sick."

I fix her with a glare. "Again, very uplifting. I feel the love."

"Well, why do you look like that?"

"I overslept. It's not that bad."

Andrea's mouth twists into a disbelieving wince. "Hon…"

I glance down at myself. Even with the rosiest pair of glasses I can muster, things aren't great. The slacks I grabbed must have been in my dirty pile, because there's a strange brown stain on the thigh and they're badly wrinkled. I avoided the mirror in the office bathroom on my way in, but even in my peripherals, it was easy to tell my hair is a disaster.

"Okay, fine," I concede. "It's bad."

The fact that Timofey saw me like this…

Means nothing, I finish. *It means nothing. He's insane and dangerous. What he thinks doesn't matter.*

"I had a weird night."

I told Noelle and Ashley that I'd let people at work know about the crazy parent that attacked me, but I really don't think the man will come back. He was drunk and distraught. Timofey scared him off easily enough that I doubt he'll try again.

That's the thing about a lot of the parents I work with—they lack follow-through. If they didn't, they wouldn't end up in a folder on my desk. You don't lose custody of your kids by being responsible.

"Did you go to your meeting this morning like that?" Andrea asks. "James said you were meeting with Timofey Viktorov."

I stiffen at his name. "How do you know that?"

"James told me. Apparently, James's twin brother is a contractor or something for the military. He knows all about Viktorov Industries."

I want to ask what that is, but it would give me away. I should know what she's talking about. All of this information is almost certainly somewhere in Timofey's file. I guess I got hung up on the list of felonies on page one.

"He rambled on about it for a while," she continues. "The long and short of it is that the man is loaded. The meeting was at his house, right? Was it huge?"

"Massive," I breathe.

"And what about him?"

"Also massive."

Andrea cackles. "No, you goose! I mean, what was he like? James said he might be a crime boss or something. The truth is never as interesting as rumors, but did he seem like someone who breaks kneecaps for a living?"

The words are right there at the end of my tongue. *Yes. He's dangerous. We need to call the police and get that baby out of his care.*

Instead, I hear myself say, "He actually, uh… wasn't there."

Andrea does a double-take. "He stood you up?"

"It wasn't a date," I say a bit too harshly. "I was running late and he had another meeting to get to. We rescheduled."

I spin to face my desk, hoping Andrea won't sniff out my lie.

I'm not even sure why I told it. Timofey doesn't seem like the kind of man to give up easily. Just because I refused his offer and stomped out of his office doesn't mean he's done with me yet.

Andrea sighs. "Darn. Well, keep me posted."

"Will do." My voice comes out high and tight.

There's a pause before I hear Andrea's chair squeak closer. "Piper?"

I swallow nervously. "Yeah?"

"I don't think you're a liar or anything, but…" I hold my breath before she finishes. "…But if you're sick, please go home."

My heart restarts. *Thank God.* "I'm not sick!"

"Fine. Whatever you say." She slides back into her desk, still muttering. "Sheesh."

I dig the heel of my hand in my eyes. Today is going to be a very long day.

8

PIPER

I thought a run after work would help me clear my head, but as I round each corner, I keep expecting to see Timofey standing there waiting for me.

The run was born of necessity. The last thing a stressful day like this one needs is an elevated heart rate, but I rode the bus into work this morning. Which means my bike is still hanging from its hooks in my living room, and I'm far too jumpy to try and wedge myself into the back of a taxi. Even with the windows down, I'd be trying to claw my way out within a block.

So I dragged out the gym bag I keep in my locker and laced up.

All I want is to get home and double-check all my door and window locks.

I keep my head on a permanent swivel as I run, Timofey's criticisms playing and replaying in my head.

You didn't even check to see if anyone was around.

Your head was down and you don't have a weapon.

You fool. You fucking fool.

I'm still technically weaponless, but I can feel the poke of the mail opener in the side pocket of my leggings. It's better than nothing.

Usually, I use the last two blocks of my run to cool down, but I don't slow this time. Not even when I get inside my building. Instead, I take the stairs two at a time and keep jogging until I slam my door closed and slide the deadbolt home.

Only then do I collapse back against my door with a thud.

"Fuck me," I whisper. Now that I'm inside my apartment, I feel stupid for being so scared.

What was Timofey going to do—lurk behind a trash can and snatch me off the sidewalk? He has no way of knowing I even went for a run. Plus, if he was going to ambush me, he would have done it at his house this morning.

I list off my own rationalizations for why my heart rate should slow and I can relax, but I don't start to breathe normally again until after my shower.

When I get out, I go through the motions of a normal night. I listen to a podcaster I can't stand recap the latest episode of some reality TV show I don't even watch while I make myself a batch of taco soup big enough to last the next three nights. Then I curl up on the end of my sofa and eat while the laugh track to a decades-old sitcom plays in the background.

By all appearances, everything is as it should be in the life of Piper Quinn.

But I barely register any of it. My head is lost in some temporal space just behind my consciousness, torn between replaying my attack last night and parsing through every single word Timofey spoke this morning.

Another part of me is still in that alley, a desperate man's hand wrapped around my throat.

Yet *another* part is standing in front of Timofey on trembling legs while he recounts every detail of my daily existence.

If you find the facts of your life insulting, that is your problem, not mine.

I look at my desk, which is also my side table since my apartment is too small for both. The medical bill on top of the stack has red ink stamped on the envelope.

FINAL NOTICE.

Timofey is right: that is my problem, not his. And I have no idea how I'm going to fix it.

When Noelle and Ashley call me later, I swipe to dismiss the call and quickly text them my excuse. ***I slept like crap last night. I'm already on my way to bed. Talk to you tomorrow.***

It's a lie, but the moment I send the message, I realize sleep is a great idea. My eyes burn with exhaustion and sitting here spinning my mental wheels isn't helping.

The dishes in the sink and the day-old makeup on my face are both a tomorrow problem, I decide as I slip beneath my comforter.

I hear my phone vibrate, but I don't check it. It's probably from Noelle or Ashley. Whatever it is, it can wait.

I close my eyes and fall asleep before I can fully grasp my next thought.

9

PIPER

My eyes snap open and it's like I never slept at all. Between one blink and the next, I'm awake.

With a hand clamped over my mouth.

I claw at the muscled arm attached to the hand even while I'm positive this has to be a nightmare. Then a face leans close to me, and a now-familiar set of icy blue eyes appears like a mirage out of the darkness.

"Hello again, Ms. Quinn."

That's when I realize that this is not a nightmare.

This is very, very real.

I inhale to scream, but Timofey's hand clamps over my lips even tighter.

"Quiet." The word is surprisingly gentle, given the way he's holding me. "Screaming won't do any good. It will only make things harder."

It feels like his palm is vacuum sealed over my mouth. The restriction pushes all the same triggers as sitting in a small room. My skin starts to itch and my chest constricts as the claustrophobia fights for control of my fear center.

I know I'm not going to die. Not right this second, anyway. Timofey isn't actually stopping me from breathing.

But my body doesn't know that.

My lungs are frozen and I jerk upright, desperate for air. It's like I'm drowning in my own fear, thick and black and terrifying.

"I told you refusing me was a mistake." He removes his hand and watches me struggle to catch my breath. "All of this could have been avoided."

"Are you going to kill me?" I croak.

Timofey has the audacity to smirk innocently. "Kill you? What would make you think that?"

"You broke into my fucking house!"

"It wasn't exactly breaking in." He lifts his hand and I catch a hint of silver between his fingers. "I used a key."

"But I don't keep a spare—" The words lodge in my throat when I see the neon pink "A" painted on the top of the key. *Ashley's.* "Where did you get that?"

"You know exactly where I got it."

Without thinking about it, I lunge forward, arms outstretched. Timofey bats me away easily.

"Where is she?" I hiss. "What did you do with her?"

He casually pockets the key. "What did I do with Ashley? Nothing. There was no need."

"I know she didn't give you that voluntarily."

"The way I found her, she wasn't capable of giving anyone anything. She might have a drug problem, did you know?"

"What the *fuck* did you do to her?" I practically scream.

"I kicked in her flimsy front door and she didn't even wake up. Your friend is fine."

I have no reason to trust Timofey, but I believe him. If he hurt her, he'd tell me. He'd rub my nose in it, actually. So if he's saying he didn't hurt her, it must be true.

Still, the thought of Ashley tucked into her bed while Timofey peruses through the key cup next to her front door is enough to make me feel nauseous.

"I could have just broken into your place," he continues. "By the looks of it, your window frames are rotted out and your bolt isn't strong enough to make more than a moment's difference. But I thought this illustrated my point a little more clearly."

His eyes trace over my face and across my shoulder. I'm wearing a tank top from high school. The material is tissue paper thin, and suddenly, I feel vulnerable in more ways than one.

I jerk my comforter up over my chest and do my best to look brave. "What point is that?"

"I know more about you than you think," he whispers, leaning in close. "I know you need the money I'm offering you. Badly."

"You knew that before I even left your house this morning. You didn't need to break in for that."

"True. But breaking in did reveal one thing." He holds up the manila folder I stuffed in my purse on my way out of the office this evening. "I know you didn't fill out your report about our meeting this morning. Do you know what that tells me?"

I honestly don't. I wish I did.

I lied to Andrea about the meeting being rescheduled, but I tried several times today to sit down and write the truth. I tried to capture my experience with Timofey Viktorov in a few paragraphs. To succinctly explain why he is the single most intimidating, terrifying man I've ever met.

It was impossible.

So I brought the file home and hoped being back in my safe space would help. But I couldn't even bring myself to pull the file out of my purse.

Now, Timofey himself is waving it under my nose in the middle of the night.

"It tells me you're still considering my offer," he says. "Somewhere, deep down, you know it's an opportunity you can't walk away from."

"Is that a threat?"

He leans in closer. The dark obscures the edges of him like he's emerging out of a pool of black water. Just the highlights of his nose and lips are visible.

Along with his eyes, of course. No matter what happens from this point on, I'll never, ever forget his eyes.

"That's up to you, Piper."

"None of this is up to me!" I retort. "If it was up to me, you wouldn't be here right now."

"You have more control than you think. What happens next depends on what you choose to do."

He pats his pocket and I remember the key. Ashley's key. Is that another silent threat? He said she's okay, but will that change if I don't do what he asks? As far as I can tell, Timofey Viktorov is capable of anything.

"Why me?" I whisper.

"Why you?" His voice is soft, and I glance up, hoping to see mercy there. Instead, I'm met with a cold, calculating stare. "Because you had the misfortune of being handed my case file. Fate fucked you. There's nothing more to it."

Is it disappointment I feel weighing me down? It would be nice if there was something about me specifically that warranted Timofey's attention. If the reason my life is being turned upside down was more than me being in the wrong place at the wrong time.

"Lucky me," I drawl miserably.

"I'd say so," Timofey agrees. "I saved your life and now, I'm offering to change it. All you have to do is accept."

"And then you won't hurt my friends?" I ask. "I accept, and you won't track down my family and blackmail me?"

He doesn't say anything because he doesn't have to. It's clear we both understand what my options are.

If it was just me at risk, I'd refuse to help him. Timofey could do whatever he wanted to me.

But there are more people to consider.

My grandma took care of me when I had nothing even resembling stability in my life. Noelle and Ashley, too, have been there for me since the beginning. Ashley would pack extra sets of clothes for me in high school when I didn't have a way to wash mine at home. She's had a hard go of things since then, and she doesn't deserve for my bad luck to veer her any more off-course.

"Well?" Timofey snarls. "I'm not a patient man."

"You're really going to pay me?"

"I'm not in the habit of keeping slaves."

"And I have to live with you?"

He shakes his head. "You *get* to live with me. There's a difference."

I huff out a breath. This man really thinks he is God's gift to us all. He probably thinks he is doing baby Benjamin a favor, too. It tracks—most unfit parents have no clue how wrong they are.

Which is why I have to do this. At least long enough to get Benjamin out of Timofey's claws. The fact that I can get myself out of debt at the same time is a bonus.

This doesn't have to be forever. Just for now.

I press my comforter against my chest with one arm and hold out my other hand. Timofey eyes it suspiciously.

"I figured the CEO of Viktorov Industries would know what a handshake looks like," I snap.

His brow lifts. "That's not how I'd prefer to seal this deal."

I start to drop my hand. "Okay, then how do you—"

Suddenly, Timofey snatches my hand out of the air and yanks me towards him. I hit the muscled wall of his torso with a thud. His warm breath coats my skin like honey before I can even catch mine. Then he presses his lips to my cheek.

I can't move. Can't breathe. I'm frozen as he kisses one cheek and then moves slowly and purposefully to the other.

Finally, he presses his cheek to mine and brings his lips to the shell of my ear.

"Pleasure doing business with you, Ms. Quinn."

10

TIMOFEY

Piper Quinn smells like mulled wine, sweet and warm.

I can feel her breasts pressing against me with each of her ragged inhales. She's trembling all over, but the usual urge to squash the weakness out of her doesn't come. The opposite, actually: I want to circle my arm around her waist and hold her to me until the shaking stops. I want to bury myself inside of her sweetness and drain the fear from her limbs with firm strokes.

I'm sure the fact that she is pressed against me in nothing but a threadbare tank top and panties has something to do with that.

I let her go, and she scrambles back under the cover of her blankets. Her back is ramrod straight against her iron headboard, knees to her chest. For a flash of a second, I imagine her hands gripping those bars as I drive into her. The noise they'd make banging against the wall. Her mouth parting in a moan.

"Are we done here?" she snaps, drawing me out of my thoughts. She's still shaking, but her face is etched with a deep frown.

I drag my eyes over her disapproving look and then down… down. Her cleavage needs to be kissed. Caressed. Fucked senseless.

"I'm still deciding."

She yanks her blanket up to her neck. "Then I'll help you make up your mind: we're done. Goodbye."

"I'm not sure what about this situation makes you think you have any control here."

"I may have agreed to work for you, but you don't own me, Mr. Viktorov."

She's wrong—I do own her. The fact she is acting like I don't, however, is strangely appealing.

I had no idea how much I enjoyed a little fight until right now.

I kneel on the edge of the bed. Her eyes go wide. "What are you doing?"

I curl my hand around her wrist and raise it over her head, pinning it to one of the metal junctions in her headboard. When I let go, her arm stays there without me even asking.

Slowly, I trail my fingertip over her skin, watching goosebumps erupt in my wake.

Akim was right about one thing: it's been a long time since I've let myself have anything like this.

"It's interesting," I muse, "the way the body reacts to touch. To desire."

A flush creeps up Piper's long neck. I can see her pulse pounding at the base of her throat. I press my thumb there, feeling her life flutter under my touch.

"You don't have to think about it. No one has to tell goosebumps to appear. You don't have to order yourself to blush." I glance down at the comforter covering her lap. "You don't have to convince yourself to get wet."

"Stop." Her voice is firm, but she doesn't lower her arm. Doesn't shift away from my touch or my gaze.

The little *kiska* stays right where I put her.

I tip her chin up, forcing her eyes to mine. "Control is like that, too. I don't have to tell you that I'm the one calling the shots. Instinctively, deep down, you already know it. Prey doesn't need to be taught to fear the predator. They're born that way."

"I'm not your fucking prey." She jerks suddenly, yanking my hand away from her neck.

In one smooth movement, I reverse the hold so I'm gripping her wrist. I drag her towards me so we're eye-to-eye. The comforter is a puddle around our knees. Our breath mingles, hot and sweet.

"You are," I assure her. "Everyone is. No one controls me; no one questions me. I take what I want, from whoever I want, whenever I want it."

"Like an innocent baby?" she snarks.

I nod. "People, money, power—I can have it all. And when I'm done, they fall to their knees and thank me."

"You'll die before you hear those words from me," she hisses. "I don't kneel to you."

The image of on her knees before me is very fucking enticing. The painful ache in my pants is getting harder and harder to ignore.

But touching her now, before she begs for it, wouldn't serve my purpose.

I rake my gaze over her face before leaning away. "Not yet. You're too busy kneeling for everyone else."

"What does that mean?"

"It means you need a reminder." I slip backwards off the bed and rise to my feet. "Call in sick to work tomorrow. Be at my house at eight."

She frowns. "This nanny job was supposed to be in the evenings. That's what you said. I can't just—"

"You can and you will."

She exhales harshly. "I have responsibilities! I have a life! You can't waltz in and start bossing me around."

"Excellent point. You seem fond of your 'life,' which is why I know you'll do what I tell you."

Her lips press together in a flat line. Piper is a fighter, but she recognizes a threat when she hears one. It makes me wonder how many times she's been threatened. And by whom.

My chest churns with the same feeling I felt the night I walked into that alley and saw a man's hand wrapped around her throat.

I wanted to kill him then.

I still might.

She curls her legs underneath her and rests back on her feet. The smooth stretch of her legs and the increasingly low neck of her tank top sends the ache in my chest downward. Need pulses through my core, and fuck do I need to get out of here.

I move to her door and grip the flimsy wood in my hand. I want to break it, if only because I want to break *her* and I won't allow myself that pleasure yet. "I'll see you tomorrow morning."

"Yes, master," she grumbles.

She's being a brat, but she has no idea how close I am to turning around and ensuring she moans those exact words at the ceiling.

Before I can do anything too stupid, I shove through her door and leave the way I came.

11

TIMOFEY

"Woof. Chilly," Akim says under his breath.

I glance over. It's a relatively warm night, especially given how late it is. He's in a light shirt and jeans, a gun visible in his waistband.

Then I realize what he means. "These handoffs are always like that."

The Albanians are allies, but only in the strictest sense of the word. There is no love lost between my Bratva and Kreshnik Xhuvani's mafia. If he wasn't one of my biggest private customers in the tristate area, I'd avoid him.

As it is, he and his ilk are a necessary evil.

"I'm not talking about this." Akim gestures to the warehouse and the Albanian grunts shuttling boxes from the back of my truck to one of their own. "I'm talking about *you*. You are on edge, man. You're making the guys nervous."

A couple of gunrunners pass by just then. One of them chances a look in my direction before looking away quickly, his eyes wide. They scurry by and keep their heads down.

"What the fuck do you know about 'the guys'? This is only the second time you've ever come with me to a tradeoff."

"Yeah, because Pavel called and told me you banned him from coming with you."

Pavel is fresh out of a bad marriage and preoccupied with screwing everything that moves. The reason I know that is because he can't stop talking about it. The last thing I want after leaving Piper's room is to hear about the inviting pussy of yet another of my lieutenant's sleazy conquests.

"Thank God he sent me a solid backup in his place," I mutter.

"Don't be a wiseass. You know I've backed you up more times than you can count. Remember that brawl on New Years' Eve?"

"*You* started that," I scoff. "You hooked up with the bouncer's girlfriend in the bathroom."

"Yeah, and you defended me. And then, when the bouncer came after you, I backed you up. So, y'know, you're welcome." He clears his throat. "Anyway, it's good to get out of the kitchen occasionally. I know I'm a personal chef, but I can be intimidating, too. Why simply cut off a man's finger when you could julienne it?"

I drag a hand down my face. How anyone could ever take this man seriously is beyond me. "We're not cutting off any fingers tonight."

"Not yet," he tuts. "But it's only a matter of time. You're in a mood. Did things with Piper not go to plan again?"

"Everything went fine." But I speak through gritted teeth. The sound of her name is enough to remind me of the unbearable tension I felt standing next to her bed.

The slope of her thighs.

Her scent in my nose.

The way her hand lingered where I put it, perfectly submissive before she even realized what she was doing.

And then the fire when she did realize it. The spark. The feral growl.

Fuck, my cock is hard again already.

"Your knuckles are *white*." Akim snorts. "Holy shit. This woman is under your skin."

"And you're on my last nerve. Practice a little self-preservation and go help load up. I want this shit over with."

Akim grumbles something about me being a slave driver as he lopes off towards the truck.

"Are you running low on new recruits?" a voice asks.

I turn and see one of the Albanian ringleaders resting against a wooden crate. He's the equivalent of a night manager. Not nearly important enough for me to know his name.

"Excuse me?"

He jerks his chin to where Akim is now laughing with a group of Albanians. Leave it to him to make pals within seconds. "That's your chef, ain't it?"

"What the fuck do you care?"

Akim wasn't just blowing smoke when he said he can be more than a chef. Still, he struggles to be taken seriously in our world no matter how many times he proves himself. I know a fair number of dead men who would argue that he's proved himself just fine. Unfortunately for him, dead men aren't very good at talking.

The Albanian stands up, arms crossed over his chest. "I don't care who you bring with you. What I care about is what you're doing with all the money we're paying you. Is that why this shipment costs almost twice what it normally does? So you can keep your little errand boy on the bankroll?"

"*You* aren't paying me a fucking thing. If you were, I'd know your name."

His face reddens, but he takes a daring step closer to me. A few of his men edge in around us. I think they're mostly curious to hear our conversation, but I have no doubt a few of them might be stupid enough to play hero if things go south.

His jaw clenches. "Just 'cause you're some hoity toity CEO by day doesn't mean shit. You ain't better than me 'cause of that."

"You're right. I'm better than you for many other reasons." I lift my arm and tug my sleeve up, revealing the snowstorm of black dots on the inside of my wrist. "I keep a tally of men I've killed here. It's not quite up to date, but it's close enough."

The rest of the room is getting quieter. I know my voice is carrying in the warehouse, but I don't give a flying fuck. If this asshole wants to make an example of himself, I'm happy to oblige. The more who see it, the merrier.

"You're probably more forgiving than I am, too. More patient, for sure." I give him a flat shark's smile. "Because when people who don't know their place start to run their mouths to me, I get angry. I get very, very angry." I'm pacing closer to him now as I speak, each word dribbling out of my lips like drops of blood. "And when I get angry, I start adding dots to my collection. Do you understand what I'm telling you?"

"Hey, man, easy," he says. He's starting to sense the tide changing. His moment of bravado has passed and a lifetime of regret is about to follow. However much of a lifetime he has left, that is. He shifts back half a step. "I didn't mean—"

"Timofey," Akim interrupts, floating in next to me. "Making new friends?"

"I'm giving our friend here a lesson. I'm almost done, actually."

Akim blows out a breath. "Okay. Great. Well, skip to the end, please."

I can tell by the tone of his voice that he knows what's coming. But he has the good sense to stay out of my way.

"Lastly," I say, reaching into my holster and pulling out my gun, "I'd bet I'm a much better shot."

The blast echoes off the cement floor and metal roof. It's a hollow, grating echo broken up only by the thud of the man's body hitting the floor with a bloody hole where his right eye once was.

For a second, there is no movement. Everyone is too stunned to breathe.

Then chaos erupts.

Shouts bounce off the walls in Russian and Albanian. Some men scatter; others draw closer. I hear Akim curse just as the soldiers in front of me split and Arber Xhuvani comes running through the line.

"What the *fuck*, Timofey?" he bellows. The heir to the Albanian throne looks down at his dead soldier, his nostrils flared and eyes wild.

I pocket my gun. "I hope you brought along some towels, Arber. Bit of a mess there."

"What the hell happened?"

"Your man was out of line," I explain. "I nudged him back into place as an example to the others."

"This is what a nudge looks like?" Arber looks like he is about to burst. This is only the third time he's headed up an arms deal without his father present. Kreshnik has been training his son since he was too small to speak to take over for him, and now that Arber has come of age, they're finally beginning that transition of power.

"If you'd rather use a gentler approach, catch your men before they speak to me. Your father never would have let something like this happen."

"My father isn't here," he snaps.

"Which is the entire fucking problem," I snarl. "Get control of your soldiers before I have to do it for you."

Arber crosses the distance between us in a few strides, bringing his chest to mine. "Is that a threat? Are you looking to overthrow my family? I'll make sure you don't live to regret it if you try."

Only youthful pride could make this idiot believe I'd want anything at all to do with the Xhuvani mafia. Unfortunately, Arber has plenty of that to spare.

In a flash, I wrap a hand around his neck and use the other to press my gun to his temple. He tenses up. His breath is trapped in his throat.

"Hey, Timofey," Akim says, his voice laughably casual. "I think we've made enough friends tonight."

"My finger is off the trigger," I tell him. Then I turn my full attention to the Kreshnik boy. "I just want Arber here to know that if I wasn't in such a good mood, he could be dead right now."

"You wouldn't dare," Arber rasps.

I arch my brows. "I'd advise you not to fuck with me."

He swallows uncomfortably. His throat bobs in my palm. "If you kill me, it will be war."

"A war I'll win. I have nothing to lose."

He thinks about that for a moment and then the fight starts to drain out of him. I release him with a shove and he stumbles a few steps.

"The only thing keeping you from being *that*," I say, pointing from Arber to the dead man on the floor to illustrate my point, "is that I've already killed one person today and it's growing tedious. You may be Kreshnik's son, but you aren't special. Fuck with me, and I'll kill you."

I turn away from him and address my men. "Leave the rest of the boxes in the truck. Arber can explain to his father why he didn't receive the full shipment."

Then I turn and leave without another word.

A few seconds later, Akim jogs to catch up with me. He shakes his head. "And to think things were tense *before*."

12

PIPER

If I could have fallen back asleep after Timofey left last night, I would have thought my interaction with him was some kind of nightmare. It was all too unbelievable to be real.

Unfortunately for me, sleep was non-existent. I tossed and turned hopelessly for hours. Periodically, I flipped on my bedside lamp to check the red welts around my wrist where he held me.

When he pinned me to the headboard and crawled over me, his nearness was a drug. I inhaled him. Got high on Timofey Viktorov.

One hit almost killed me.

Thankfully, time and distance has left me with a clear head. Clear*er*, at least. It's almost fitting that the bruise he marked me with covers the small tattoo of a bright moon I have on the inside of my wrist.

I got it on spring break with Noelle and Ashley. We were seventeen.

"A sun for me because I'm the center of attention, obviously," Ashley had said as she picked them out from the wall of art options at the tattoo shop.

Then she handed a star to Noelle. "A star for the A-plus student. Here you go, Ms. Valedictorian." Noelle rolled her eyes, but accepted her fate.

Then Ashley gave me the crescent moon. "And a moon for the woman who reflects the best of us. The friend who manages the ebbs and flows of our relationship without any of the glory."

"Sure, make her reasoning all cute and thoughtful," Noelle complained. "I'll just be the nerd, I guess."

I run my thumb over the fading tattoo and take a deep breath. It's good to remind myself of the core truth here.

What I'm doing today... *It's for them.*

I leave a message on Andrea's desk phone with a fake cough and an excuse about actually getting sick after all. Then I shower and change.

I opt for something business casual but baggy. I can still feel the way Timofey's gaze dragged over me last night. His attention had a heft that I still can't seem to shake. If there is any way I can avoid catching his eye, I'm willing to try it. I'd wear a potato sack if it meant keeping those eyes away from me.

Before I wheel my bike into the hallway, I stop and look around my apartment. Timofey didn't say anything about me not coming back to my place tonight. Aside from telling me to be there this morning, I know nothing.

But it still feels like a goodbye of sorts.

So I look around at the remnants of my ordinary life—the crocheted blanket my grandma made me tossed over the arm of my ratty couch, the toast crumbs on the counter, my running shoes kicked off next to the door. I catalog all of it, hoping that one day soon, I'll be back here safe and sound and all of this will be a distant memory.

As soon as the thought crosses my mind, I snort.

Yeah, fucking right.

Once you meet Timofey Viktorov, there is no going back.

13

PIPER

By the time I wheel my bike up the stairs of the mansion and lean it against the stone facade, I'm dripping in sweat. So much for my baggy clothes.

"Delightful," I mutter, fanning myself.

Whatever. It's not like I'm trying to impress Timofey anyway. He's seen me looking like a drenched sewer rat once and again with sleep breath in the middle of the night. He can handle my post-bike ride stank.

I go to knock on the door, but it's already cracked open. Voices filter out onto the porch.

I lean in, turning my ear towards the door. The voices are definitely male, but I can't make out what they're saying.

Suddenly, the door yanks inward and I stumble forward slightly. A pair of large hands set me upright.

"Looks like we've got ourselves a Girl Scout. You selling cookies, sweetheart?"

The man in front of me is tall and lean. His face is gaunt, shadows pressed under his cheekbones and his eyes. His lips are stretched into a threatening smile that raises the hairs on the back of my neck.

I pull away from him and frown. "I'm not a Girl Scout. I'm a grown woman."

He looks me over, his eyes taking their time descending my frame. "Indeed you are. But by the look of you, you still might have something sweet for me to taste."

I have no idea who this man is, but I've more than met my asshole quota in the last forty-eight hours. If I have to live in this house for any period of time, I'm going to set a precedent for how I'm treated.

Starting now.

I fix the creep with an overly polite smile. "I'm fresh out, so I'm afraid you'll have to find a treat on your own. I'm sure you're accustomed to servicing yourself anyway."

The other men in the entryway *ooh* and cackle as the gaunt man's face reddens.

Serves him right.

"I'm here to see Timo—err, Mr. Viktorov." I look past the man to the men standing behind him. They're staring at me, refusing to make themselves useful. "Is he here?"

A younger man steps forward, finally prepared to help. Before he can, the gaunt man reasserts himself. "I can help with whatever you need."

I clench my jaw. "I'm sure you'd like to, but I'd rather pluck off my fingernails than talk to you for another second. Get out of my way before—"

"Before what?" His voice is a low hiss. "You think you have rights here, little girl?"

"The right not to get harassed by an asshole, if nothing else."

His lips twist into a nasty smirk. "You gave that up when you stepped through the door. You don't walk into the lion's den and tell a lion not to bite."

I look him up and down with a shrewd eye. "Are you supposed to be the lion in this analogy?"

His eyes flare and he yanks up his shirt sleeve, revealing a black blob tattooed on his inner wrist. "You know what these stand for, Girl Scout?"

It takes a few seconds for me to recognize the blob on his arm is not a blob, but a cloud of individual black dots. There are at least a hundred tattooed dots, maybe more.

"These," he growls, leaning towards me, "represent each person I've ki—"

"Rodion."

A deep, commanding voice I recognize booms through the room. I turn just as Timofey steps through the parting crowd of men.

Considering that the last time I saw him, he was threatening me in the dark of my room, I'm surprised at how relieved I am to see him now.

I suppose the devil you know really is better than the devil you don't.

The man—Rodion, I guess—steps back. "Timofey." He drops his sleeve and his tattoos disappear from sight. "I was just greeting your guest."

"That's not your job for a good reason," Timofey snaps. "Fyodor is better at it. He's also more pleasant to look at."

Rodion holds up his hands and takes another step away from me. "Let's not get mean, *sobrat*. Fyodor might have a face for television, but I—"

"Have revealed enough of yourself already," Timofey growls.

Rodion's jaw clicks, but he nods and lowers his head in deference. "I didn't realize you were expecting a guest today."

"It's none of your fucking business who comes and goes in my house." Timofey walks over to me, standing at my side like a guard dog, hackles raised. "Disrespect me or any of my guests again, and I'll be on my worst behavior."

Rodion swallows. I shudder to think what Timofey's worst behavior might look like. I'm usually anti-violence, but I actually wouldn't mind a little example. Especially if Rodion is the test subject.

"Understood," Rodion mumbles, nodding.

I have to bite back a smile. It's rare in life that you get to witness immediate karma. It's nice to see a creep like Rodion get what he deserves.

Rodion turns and tips his head towards the hallway. All of the other men in the room start to file out. He's clearly some kind of leader to these men, yet Timofey put him in his place with ease. In the hierarchy of this house, Timofey is at the tippy top.

Good to know.

But the relief I felt at Timofey's appearance fades quickly once we're alone. And I'm left thinking, *Maybe Rodion wasn't so bad, after all.*

14

PIPER

I swallow and fold my hands behind my back. "Thanks for—I don't know what his problem was. I walked inside and asked for you, but… Well, anyway, thank you for that."

"You're incapable of completing the most basic task without getting yourself into trouble," Timofey interrupts.

My mouth slams closed. He's staring down at me, his blue eyes narrowed. Every angle of his face is sharp enough to cut glass.

"I don't remember calling for help. I was handling myself just fine."

"That's because you don't know who you were talking to."

I arch a brow. "What kind of dangerous people do you have wandering around your house first thing in the morning? If I needed saving two seconds after walking into your house, that would be your fault, not mine."

"The fact that you're in way over your head is your fault. Don't make me remind you why you're here."

"No reminder necessary. I know why I'm here. It's because I have a moral backbone."

He steps closer, forcing me to tip my head back to maintain eye contact. "You're here because you're too foolish to take the easy way out. You could have agreed to do what I asked in the first place and made things easier on yourself."

"If you keep calling me stupid, I might start to think you mean it."

"I always mean what I say. You should take me at my word."

A laugh that surprises even me bubbles up. "'Your word' means absolutely nothing to me. You're lying to me right now."

His lips twitch, and I can't help but think how wrong it is that a man as rotten as Timofey can have lips like that. Full and soft. Utterly kissable, if we're being honest.

"You aren't upset that you had to save me," I continue. "You're upset that I've spent thirty seconds in your house and already nearly uncovered a damaging secret."

"What secret would that be?"

I tap a finger against my forearm in the same spot Rodion was showing me. "I'm guessing the dots on your man's arm don't represent how many abandoned kittens he's fostered."

"What kind of damaging secret could it be if I let him tattoo it on his body?"

"You *'let him'* tattoo it?" I ask. "You control what your employees put on their own body?"

Timofey moves closer, his blue eyes freezing me to the floor. "I control everything. My business is a body, and I'm the head. The brain. I control everything."

"Makes sense," I retort. "God knows you don't have a heart."

He smirks. "Now, you're starting to understand."

I blow out a frustrated breath. "Of course you would take that as a compliment."

He hedges in closer. Suddenly, I'm aware of how big he is. How good he smells. How alone we are. "Unlike you, Piper Quinn, my emotions don't get in the way of my choices. I wouldn't throw myself to the wolves to protect my friend."

"With friends like those, you wouldn't need to," I say. "You're a wolf; Rodion is a lion, apparently. You all are too busy cosplaying as animals to realize you need serious help. Psychological help. You're fucking deranged."

Timofey presses his shoulders back, his chest straining against the buttons of his shirt. I catch glimpses of golden skin peeking through the material. Instinctively, my heart jolts. Some weak-willed spark flutters deep in my core. I tear my eyes away from him and beat the poor thing into submission.

Absolutely not. We are not ogling our blackmailer.

Maybe just one more peek, though.

I glance back. Timofey has folded his arms across his chest. His biceps bulge. "What are you doing?" My voice comes out in a rasp.

He chuckles. "Watching you pretend not to watch me."

My face heats with embarrassment at being caught. I've never had much of a poker face.

"I wasn't looking at—you're being weird," I splutter. "Besides, looks don't mean anything. I can separate the mask from the man wearing it."

Timofey crosses his arms over his chest. I'm not sure if he's flexing or if he is really just this muscled. This is the first time I've seen him standing up in full daylight. It's…a lot.

"You think I'm wearing this as a disguise?" he asks, gesturing to his face.

"No, but I think the genetic lottery you won has been a big help to you in your life of crime. People expect criminals to look like criminals. They don't expect them to look like…"

My voice trails off as a secret of my own nearly tumbles out.

They don't expect criminals to look like gods.

"Finish your thought. To look like what?" Timofey lifts his chin, and I catch a glimpse of something just under his jawline.

I lean forward to get a better look. "Is that… Is that blood?"

He reaches up reflexively and wipes at the spot. When he pulls his hand away, it's gone.

The building tension between us pops, and I deflate so fast it nearly gives me whiplash. It's all fun and games to trade barbs, to pretend I can hold my own in here. But Rodion was right: this is the lion's den, and I'm just a naive little sheep. Any of the men in here could chew me up and spit me out without a second thought.

Timofey most of all.

"What kind of business is going on here, Timofey?" I whisper. "Why do you want to bring a child into this?"

He rolls his eyes. "You caught me, Ms. Quinn. I don't always clean under my neck the way I should. Is that the kind of offense CPS looks for when snatching children away from their families?"

"I've washed enough blood from my skin to know what it looks like," I say softly. "You may keep calling me stupid, but that doesn't make it true. I'm smart enough to know what kind of person you are."

My imagination conjures Timofey before me, his tall, broad frame dripping in bright red blood. What kind of nastiness did he get into between leaving my room a few hours ago and now?

On second thought, I'm not sure I want to know.

"Then you should know I'm the kind of person who doesn't give a fuck what kind of person you think I am," he says. "I don't need you to like me, Piper. I need you to do as I ask."

"Or else what? You'll have your hitman kill me?"

His lips flatten in frustration, and I hate that my jab landed. I wanted him to deny it. Or be shocked by the accusation.

Instead, he looks coolly resigned.

I knew I was in trouble when I woke up to Timofey hovering over my bed like the Grim fucking Reaper. But this...this is different. I don't just need to worry about Timofey; I need to worry about everyone in his orbit, too.

Timofey closes the distance between us, looking down his nose at me. I've never felt smaller in my entire life. Right now, it feels like he could squash me under his heel and that would be the end of me.

Still, I try to stand tall and meet his eyes. If I'm going down, I'm going down hard.

"No, I won't have a hitman kill you," Timofey promises, his lips moving carefully around each word. "I'll do it myself."

15

PIPER

Before I can say anything else, someone clears their throat from the hallway.

I snap my eyes to the sound, but Timofey doesn't move.

An older man with graying hair and a white goatee stands in the mouth of the hallway. He doesn't look at me, which feels like a conscious choice. His eyes stayed pinned on Timofey's back.

"Everyone is waiting for you," the man says. "Can we get the meeting started?"

"I'm conducting orientation with a new employee," Timofey replies with a sarcastic tint in his voice.

The man sighs. I don't know Timofey well, but he doesn't stand for disrespect. I expect him to whip around and lay into the man who dared disturb him. Instead, he turns and holds out a hand in my direction to coax me forward.

"This is Piper Quinn."

Finally, the older man meets my eyes, though it looks very much against his will. "Welcome."

"Piper," Timofey continues, gesturing to the man now, "this is my father, Sergey."

"Your—You two are—" I look from the older man to Timofey, searching for some resemblance, but there isn't any. Sergey is a good six inches shorter than Timofey. Where Timofey is broad-shouldered with a trim waist, Sergey's mass is consolidated in his bottom half. His legs are thick like tree trunks. Sergey is pale with dark blonde hair where it hasn't already shifted gray, while Timofey is a walking, talking shadow with dark hair and an olive complexion.

"Viktorov Industries is a family business. Didn't you know?" he asks. "I thought you received a folder with all the necessary information."

The urge to flip him off is strong, but I resist.

Barely.

"I guess I have a lot to learn about how things work around here," I say through gritted teeth.

Timofey waves his father on. "Lead the way. We'll follow. Piper should meet the whole family."

Sergey hesitates. "It's a full house today. Might be overwhelming for her."

"She's already met Rodion. It can't get much worse."

The two men share a silent moment that almost makes me feel bad for Rodion. He clearly fucked up by talking to me, and Timofey doesn't seem like the forgiving type.

In the end, their silent conversation ends with—shocker—Timofey getting his way.

He stays half a step ahead of me the entire walk down the hallway, but I can feel his attention on me. He doesn't need to see me to know where I am. I'm intensely aware that if I try to slip away, he'll snatch me up and drag me with him.

We pass by his office en route. It's hard to reconcile that, just yesterday, I was standing in front of his desk, officially meeting him for the first time.

A lot can happen in twenty-four hours.

We stop in front of a set of double doors. The nerves I'm trying hard to squash down begin to rise up.

"Anything I should know before I'm tossed to the wolves?" I gulp. "Not that you have any reason to help me."

"Yet it's all I seem to be doing."

"You and I are operating under different definitions of the word 'help,'" I mutter under my breath.

He shrugs. "So long as we have the same definition for 'obedience,' you should be fine."

"Obedience is for animals. I'm not a dog."

"You're right." He tips his head towards the doors. "*They* are the animals. Without me to intervene, they'll rip you limb from limb."

My heart is pounding, but I stand tall. Timofey is trying to scare me and it won't work. Or, I'm going to do my best to hide exactly how well it's working, at least.

"Is that how you talk about your family? I always thought blood was thicker than water, but apparently you feel comfortable shit-talking everyone in your life."

"They're not my blood."

I frown. "But you said—"

"Given your line of work, I'm surprised I have to explain this to you." Timofey sighs. "I'm adopted."

Sergey turns, his hand still on the doorknob. "Poor Timofey couldn't take after my good looks, so I had to raise him with my disposition."

Two men with Timofey's disposition under the same roof? God help us all.

"How many children did you adopt?" I ask.

"Timofey and his—"

"We're all a family here," Timofey interrupts. "A brotherhood, if you will."

I may not have read Timofey's file as closely as I should have, but I remember a few details. Like his possible criminal connections.

"Like a fraternity?" It's nothing but blind hope that makes me ask.

When Timofey's eyebrow arches in amusement, that hope withers and dies. "Sure," he says with a chuckle. "Something like that."

16

TIMOFEY

My father pushes open the door. The chatter and laughter inside the conference room dies at once. Tension ripples around as we make our way in.

Piper must suspect what she's just stumbled into, because she stays close to my side. Her elbow brushes against my forearm. I can feel her warmth and tremors through my sleeve.

Good. Maybe some of my warnings have sunk in. Coming face to face with Rodion wasn't quite enough to scare her off.

Maybe seeing the whole Bratva will keep her in line.

"Some of you have already been introduced," I begin, drawing all eyes to me. Except for Rodion's. He correctly decides to continue staring at the floor. "For those who haven't had the pleasure, this is Piper Quinn."

"Hi," Piper squeaks out. She raises her hand in a half wave and then tucks herself behind me.

Her weakness ought to be pathetic, but I don't actually mind the feeling of being her human shield. Especially since I underestimated how much I'd fucking hate my men looking at her.

A thought that doesn't belong there races through my head: *she is for my eyes alone.*

It's gone as quick as it came.

"Piper will be living here on the property as Benjamin's caretaker. I don't take his care lightly, as you know—"

I hear a soft snort from Piper's direction that I choose, for her sake, to ignore.

"—so anyone who makes her job more difficult will be removed."

I meet the eyes of my men, ensuring each of them recognize what I'm saying. Thankfully, we all work from the same dictionary.

Translation: *touch her and I'll kill you.*

I'm about to move on when Piper steps around me. Her hand ghosts over my forearm, a remnant of her ingrained training, no doubt. Fuck knows she feels no compulsion to be polite to me.

"I did already meet some of you as I came in this morning," she says, lighting up the room with a warm smile. "As I said then, I'm a grown woman. If anyone is making life difficult for me, *I* will deal with them."

She doesn't need to make eye contact for me to realize that she's speaking directly to me.

If she wasn't such a nuisance, I would truly admire her guts.

Pavel is sitting in the chair across from Piper. His eyes rove over her, and my lip curls in distaste.

I should have given her a uniform. Like a king-sized sheet or a two-person tent.

Instead, she's in a pair of wide-legged trousers that hug her small waist. The shirt clings to her sweat, so I can make out the lacy strap of the bra she definitely wasn't wearing when I saw her last night.

While my men admire Piper, I can feel my father watching me.

I didn't tell him anyone would be coming to live in the house. Before he walked into the entryway a moment ago, he didn't know she existed. I sure as hell don't owe him an explanation, but he'll ask for one. Especially now that she's publicly talked back.

So much for scaring her into submission.

"Wait for me in my office, Piper." I shift in front of her and address the room. "My men and I have a situation to deal with."

She doesn't respond, but she doesn't need to. I feel her leave. It's like the air kicking on in a stifling room. Finally, I can inhale.

When she's gone, I turn to face my men once more. "I meant what I said. I'll kill you all."

There's a nervous chuckle, but my father isn't laughing. "That's why we're here, Timofey," Sergey says. "You're feeling homicidal lately. I hear you murdered an Albanian gunrunner."

"If you want an apology, Otets, you won't get one."

"I don't give a damn about an apology and don't insult me by assuming I have use for one," he barks. "You know better than anyone: I don't want apologies; I want explanations."

"Everything is permissible with the right justification," I say, parroting back something he taught me years and years ago.

When Sergey took me in, I thought he was going to be no better than the string of decrepit foster parents I'd had before. They pretended to want what was best for me, but they were in it for the stipend check. When I proved to be too much trouble for the payment, they sent me packing.

I didn't have high hopes for Sergey as a father, even if his mansion was a far cry from the shacks I was sent to before.

But old habits die hard.

I gave Sergey my worst: sneaking out of my room, stumbling home drunk as the sun came up, and stealing money out of his office to fund all of it.

When he caught me stealing, I expected him to shove my scant belongings into a trash bag and ship me back to the CPS office the way all the others had.

Instead, he stood back and crossed his arms. *"What do you need the money for?"*

"Drugs," I fired back, even though I was just going to buy a case of beer.

"What are the drugs for?" he asked evenly.

"What the fuck do you think *they're for?"*

He shrugged. *"If you're as much of a waste of space as you want me to think you are, then they're probably for you to get high for an hour before you come crashing down to the reality that your life is meaningless and no one cares about you."*

Plenty of people had made it clear over the course of my life that they didn't give a fuck about me. But no one had actually said it out loud. It was a new experience for me. I was speechless.

"But," Sergey continued, *"if you have even an ounce of potential for usefulness, you'll buy the drugs, upcharge some rich frat boy, and pay me back with interest."*

I stared at him, hesitant to respond because it had to be some kind of trap. *"You'd rather I be selling drugs than using them?"*

"You have two options in this life, Timofey: you can be chewed up by life and spit out or you can be of service. Of service to others and to yourself. I only have time for one kind of person. I'll let you figure out which."

Sergey doesn't have a moral code. He has a benchmark. *Have you made yourself useful to me?*

Either you meet it or you don't.

So far in my life, I've met it.

I meet his eyes now. "The man accused me of making an unfair deal for the shipment. He disrespected me openly in front of his men and mine. You wouldn't have let it stand, either."

"You didn't have to kill him, though."

I glance down the table. Pavel already looks uncomfortable. I've known him almost as long as I've known Sergey. He's my brother as much as Akim is, which means he calls me out on my shit. It's why he's a lieutenant, even if it is annoying.

"No, I didn't have to," I agree. "I could have threatened him. Again. Maybe given the Albanian leadership another warning. There's nothing quite as scary as a slap on the wrist."

Pavel holds up his hands and leans back, bowing out of this discussion.

But Rodion takes the opportunity to lean forward. "There is a middle ground between a threat and a bullet between the eyes, Timofey. A shot to the knee could have worked to bring him back in line."

"Excellent idea. Stand up and let's give it a try."

His brow furrows. "Don't equate me with an Albanian."

"I wouldn't. And I don't," I explain. "Because when you stood in front of the CPS worker assigned to Benjamin's case and nearly told her what the tattoos on your inner arm mean, I didn't kill you *the way I should have*."

Rodion's jaw grinds. His eyes cast nervously in my father's direction, waiting to see what he thinks about this reveal.

I don't need to turn around and see. The only opinion I care about is mine. Rodion has been way out of line lately, ever since everything happened with Emily. It's long past time to rein him in.

I continue, pacing back and forth as I speak. "I trust that you have the good sense and loyalty to respect me. To respect my authority. I don't have that same trust in the Albanians."

"It's not so much what you did," Sergey interrupts. "It's who it was."

"The man was a nobody. I'd never even seen him before."

"Not him. Arber."

I sigh. Even the Xhuvani boy's name is enough to evoke a response in me. He was a spineless weasel as a kid and he's an entitled prick as an adult.

"If Arber doesn't want his men to end up dead, he should make sure to control them," I say. Their lack of respect for him made them far too bold in talking to me. That's on him."

"Kreshnik might not see it that way," Rodion suggests.

I spin around, top lip curled back. "Then we'll make him see it that way. He knows his son better than anyone. He knows Arber isn't equipped to lead. It's why it has taken him so long to hand over control."

"You're right. Kreshnik knows Arber is a problem. That doesn't mean he'll take an attack like this lying down."

"Then I'll talk to him."

Sergey arches a brow. "*You* will *talk* to him?"

"You asked me not to insult you, so I'll ask that you don't insult me," I say. "I'm no fool. I've been the go-between for you and Kreshnik since before I could shave. I know how to handle the motherfucker."

He stares at me for a long moment and then waves a hand in the air, ending the meeting with one flick of his wrist. The room clears out, but I don't move. I know he has more to say to me. I can see it in the set of his jaw.

When the room is empty, he leans back in his chair and smirks. "So…who is the girl?"

I frown. "I thought we were here to talk about the Xhuvani clan."

"The man you killed was a nobody, and now, he is a dead nobody. It's done. I want to talk about why you've brought a woman like that into your house."

"Benjamin needs that. A maternal influence."

His brow lifts. I know he doesn't buy a word I'm saying. That's fine—he doesn't have to. I don't need his approval.

"Piper won't be an issue," I assure him. "You won't even know she's here."

"I'm not worried about whether *I'll* see her. I'm worried about whether *you* will," he corrects. "No one would blame you for losing focus. She's a beautiful girl."

I tense at his casual appreciation of Piper. "She's here for Benjamin's sake. Nothing else."

"Ah, Benjamin," Sergey muses. "Another distraction in and of himself."

"Is raising another heir to your empire a distraction, do you think? I could leave everything to Rodion in my will, if you'd prefer."

Sergey almost chokes on a laugh. "He'll be happy to know you think he'll outlive you."

"Do you think he will?"

He shakes his head, still chuckling. "You know Rodion as well as I do." He drums his fingers on the table. "I also know you better than you'd like to think. I can see the way you look at that girl, Timofey."

I feel the cage going up around my chest. The cage I've worn since I was a kid. The cage that keeps everyone at arm's length, protecting the soft parts of myself I can't seem to completely get rid of.

"It has nothing to do with her. This is about the boy."

"You say that," he agrees sadly. "You might even believe it. But I've been where you are now. I met a girl decades ago, and I fell for her. Whatever I told myself when it all started went out the window fast. In the beginning, she was just for fun; right up to the end, I swore she would be the one to help me build my empire."

I keep my face carefully composed. This is a bullshit story, I'm sure; Sergey is full of them. Made-up fables to prove some esoteric point I couldn't care less about. I'm impatient to skip to the ending. "And then what?"

"She played me for the fool I was," he concludes. "She didn't care about me; she wanted my money. When I was away from her, securing our future, she was fucking my brother."

"I didn't know you had a brother."

He meets my gaze. "I don't. Not anymore."

I don't need to ask him what that means. Sergey might be annoyed that I killed an Albanian, but his hands are far from clean.

Where does he think I learned it from?

"Piper isn't the same as…whoever that woman was."

"History may not repeat itself, but it rhymes," he says. "I've only known her a few minutes, but Piper is beautiful and alert. She's going to give you a run for your money, Timo. You may not be my biological son, but you're mine all the same. A woman with that much fire and life? You're going to fall. She'll draw you in and you'll lose sight of everything else. Even Benjamin."

"You don't need to worry about me," I say. "She's only here because she is useful. As soon as she isn't, she's gone."

It's the same for me, too, right, Dad?

That's his real concern here. If I'm busy with her, I won't be able to continue building the empire he has assigned to me. I won't be *useful* to him anymore.

And that's the only thing that's ever mattered.

The only reason I'm standing in front of him today, an army of men at my beck and call, is because he saw potential in me. The life I have, I owe to Sergey. I am grateful for that, despite what he seems to think.

I sure as fuck won't throw it away for Piper Quinn.

17

TIMOFEY

I leave the meeting room to see how well Piper can follow directions. She's supposed to be waiting for me in my office, but I wouldn't be surprised if she's stumbled into some calamity or other in the ten minutes she's been out of sight.

I'm almost to my office when Fyodor hurries around a corner and flags me down. "You have a guest, Mr. Viktorov."

"I fucking knew it. I told Piper to wait in my office. I can handle her from—"

"Not Ms. Quinn," Fyodor cuts in. "Another guest. One who would like to remain…discreet."

Fyodor fixes me with a meaningful look, and I understand instantly. "Where?"

"The south entrance. The cameras are on a loop."

I turn back the way I came and stride away from my office. For all the time Piper has already stolen from me, she can wait a few more minutes. This is important.

Just like Fyodor said, I see a hooded figure standing outside the door to the southern entrance. I open the door and the figure steps inside, head lowered.

"Are you alone?" he mumbles.

"Do you see anyone else here with me, idiot?"

Detective Rooney lifts his face and looks around the alcove at the back of the house. "I can't be too careful. I'm risking a lot by even being here."

"I'm paying you well for it," I remind him. "What's this about?"

His salt-and-pepper mustache twitches in irritation. "A body popped up near the docks this morning. Albanian. A gunshot through the eye."

My expression doesn't change. "And?"

"And I know it was you, Timofey!" he hisses. "Whoever dumped the body did nothing to disguise the person, and I know you met with the Albanians last night."

I nod. "Thanks for keeping the patrols away from the warehouse."

Rooney drags a hand down his face. His under-eyes are baggy and gray. A kinder man would feel bad for him—not only is he a homicide detective in a big, violent city, but he's a dirty one to boot.

I don't feel a goddamn thing.

"Thanks for the warning," he grumbles back, sarcasm thick in his voice. "I could have cooked something up if I'd known this was coming. But I wasn't even the one to find the body."

I cross my arms over my chest. "It wasn't exactly planned."

"You could have called after it happened."

"I was a little busy washing away the blood." The memory of Piper's eyes bulging at the sight of the blood under my chin flashes through me like a cold front. I grimace. A stupid oversight—that's all it was. That's all it needs to be.

Rooney leans back against the wall and shakes his head. "I've done as much as I can, but I don't know if I can shut this one up. Especially with Kreshnik involved."

"Kreshnik won't say shit. This won't look good for him, either."

"He might not press charges, but this man is tied back to his company. He's listed in the employee directory, so this isn't some easy gangland cover-up."

"Pity." I shrug. "He didn't mention it."

"Probably because he was too busy staring at your gun in his face."

I shake my head. "No. He barely had time to process that. I don't like to play with my food before I eat it."

Rooney wrinkles his nose. "I don't know how you do it."

"Which part?"

"Kill people," he says. "And then just walk around like, like… like it's nothing. Like everything is fine."

If he's looking for an introspective answer, he won't find one here. I don't know if it's been bred into me or if it was coded into my cells from the start. All I know is that I kill as needed.

And when nighttime comes, I sleep like a fucking baby.

"Probably the same way you look your brothers in blue in the eyes after you doctor up a crime scene to make me look innocent."

Rooney's face flushes, but I don't let off the gas just yet.

"Or the way you go home after a long day's work and kiss your wife on the cheek," I continue. "The extra money I funnel into your bank account does a great job of quieting that little voice in the back of your head that tells you you're a terrible person."

"I'm not a bad person," Rooney snaps.

"Of course not," I condescend. "You're a man who took a month-long tropical vacation last year on the salaries of a kindergarten teacher and a police officer."

"I don't even know why I agreed to help you in the first place," he mutters. "You're an asshole."

"We're in a symbiotic relationship here, Detective. If one of us stops pulling their weight, the whole thing crumbles."

Rooney looks up at me. "So… what do I do?"

"Get this story shut down and keep the police off my ass. The same as always."

He nods. "Okay. For a price."

I let out a growling exhale and flex my fists at my sides. The crack of my knuckles is the only response needed to remind Rooney who dictates the rules here.

"I didn't mean to—you're dependable. A man of your word. That's all I'm saying." Rooney looks away nervously, and I see the moment his eyes catch on something over my shoulder.

He frowns, his brows knitting together. Then his eyes go wide. "What the f—who is that?"

Before I spin around, I already know.

Only one person under my roof would be stupid enough to eavesdrop on this conversation.

18

PIPER

FIFTEEN MINUTES EARLIER

Timofey's office isn't quite so intimidating without him sitting behind the desk.

The desk chair is warm, worn leather and massive like an emperor's throne. I can see the imprint of his broad shoulders on the back and similar wear and tear in the seat that I do my best not to think about. It's a challenge, though.

The man is a dick.

But he's got one hell of an ass.

"Temptation has to have some sparkle," Grandma used to say. "Otherwise, it wouldn't be tempting."

Timofey Viktorov definitely qualifies as tempting. "Or maybe he's glistening with other people's blood," I murmur to myself.

As soon as the words are out of my mouth, I check the corners of the room for cameras or any obvious recording devices. I don't see anything.

Which I suppose makes sense. Whatever business Timofey is conducting in here, he probably doesn't want a record of it.

Then again, I wouldn't put it past him to keep some personal, secret archives. The easiest way to control people is to have dirt on them. What better way to get dirt than to catch them when they think they're alone?

I pinch my lips closed, silently promising myself I'll control my tongue. Timofey has enough to hold over my head without me offering up more.

I walk around his desk and drop down into the chair. My legs dangle a couple inches off the floor. I reach under the seat and adjust the height to suit me, mostly out of spite. When Timofey sits down later and his knees hit his chest, he'll think of me.

A little thrill wiggles through my chest at that thought. Not that I care what he thinks of me. Or how he thinks of me. Or when he thinks of me.

"God," I groan, dropping my face into my hands. "How am I going to survive here?"

I did my best to hold my own in the meeting with all of Timofey's men sizing me up, but the moment I stepped into the hallway, I wanted to collapse. It took all I had to make it back to this office and close the door.

My entire childhood was me scanning for incoming threats and then knocking them down or avoiding them before they could take me out. It took me years to stop assessing every situation for signs of danger, to stop assuming the worst about people.

Forty-eight hours with Timofey and I've reverted back to my most basic, trauma-based instincts.

Another forty-eight, and I might be in the fetal position on the floor.

Or dead.

I shake my head. "No. No, you won't. You'll be fine. You'll…" I look across his desk in search of something. A weapon or collateral or a secret lever to open an underground escape tunnel.

Even if I had a bazooka, I don't think I could take Timofey in a physical fight. And where would I escape to? My apartment is compromised, he's already broken into Ashley's place, and I'm sure he knows where Noelle and my grandma each live.

There's nowhere to go.

"So I have to stay here and fight in the only way I can." I roll the chair away from the desk and start opening drawers.

Maybe it's a bad idea to fight fire with fire, but I've never heard any adages about fighting blackmail with blackmail. That can't possibly go wrong, right?

But Timofey's drawers are surprisingly boring. Mostly office supplies and sheets full of numbers that Wayne the forensic accountant might understand, but are absolute gibberish to me.

When the drawers prove to be a bust, I shift to the bookshelf. The few books that are there are in Russian, so I amuse myself by pretending they're all on self-help topics.

"*How to Make Friends: Advice for Aggro Assholes.*" I snicker and point to another book. "*Overcoming Your Micro Penis.*"

I'm being childish. I can admit that.

It doesn't mean it's not fun.

There is a crystal paperweight and a gold desk lamp with a green glass shade, but it's all impersonal business-y decorations. Like Timofey hired an interior decorator and gave her the direction, *"Make sure people know I'm rich."*

As if the mansion wouldn't be clue enough.

I climb hesitantly onto the thin ledge below the shelves, stretching onto my toes to see up to the highest shelf. It's probably pointless, but there's no point in leaving a stone unturned. If I have to be stuck in this office waiting for him, I might as well make use of the time.

It's more of the same. Dusty books, a reed diffuser that I can only assume is loaded with the scent of leather, new hundred-dollar bills, man musk, and a gilded cigar box. I reach for the box and tip it out, expecting contraband Cuban cigars or the fingers of his enemies to spill out.

Instead, a gold locket tumbles onto the shelf.

"God forbid he wear jewelry." I grab the necklace and drop down onto the floor. "Can't even let anyone see he owns a necklace. They might take away his man card."

I roll my eyes and flick the locket open. I expect it to be empty, like his heart.

But I freeze when I realize there's a picture inside.

A tiny color image of a young Timofey stares up at me. His hair is shorter, cropped close to his head, and I don't see any tattoos on his exposed arms. Everything about him is leaner, younger, less scarred. He can't be older than twenty.

More than any of that, though, I notice the woman at his side.

She has thick blonde hair that curls around her shoulders and a wide, red-lipped smile. She's gorgeous.

Jealousy I have no right to feel twists in my gut. I snap the locket closed and it flips in my hand, revealing an engraving I hadn't noticed before.

For Emily.

Possibilities fire in my brain one after the other. Emily could be a friend—but what kind of man buys a locket for his (extremely attractive and definitely female) friend?

She's probably a girlfriend. An ex, or…

God, is there any chance they're still dating? Is there a chance they're *married*?

"I haven't done anything wrong," I say aloud, talking myself back from the emotional ledge I feel like I'm approaching. "He showed up in my room in the middle of the night. I'm a victim."

Okay, then why do I suddenly find myself hoping he hasn't seen Emily since this picture was taken?

My decision is swift. Before Timofey can walk in and catch me snooping, I pull out my phone and text Noelle.

Weird request. Use your Google-fu and find out if Timofey Viktorov has any connection to a blonde woman named Emily.

Noelle may be dating an FBI agent, but she's the one with the super sleuth skills. The woman can find dirt on anyone using nothing but her keyboard and a search engine.

She's at work right now, though. Rule follower that she is, she probably won't see my text until her lunch break.

I tuck the locket back where I found it and am about to flop into Timofey's desk chair to wait when I hear his voice in the hallway.

He says my name, but nothing else is clear. I creep towards the door.

"Not Ms. Quinn," his butler says. I think his name is Fyodor, but I've met too many people to keep track. "Another guest. One who would like to remain…discreet."

A guest who would like to remain discreet? What does that mean?

Timofey doesn't ask. "Where?"

"The south entrance. The cameras are on a loop."

My eyes widen. I knew he had to have cameras somewhere. But whoever he is about to talk to, he doesn't even want his own personal recording of that conversation.

That means it has to be something serious.

Something serious—as in, something I could use to get myself out of here and make sure the child in his care is removed as well.

The voices are gone, but I wait for a few more seconds before I crack the door open.

The hallway is empty. I open the door fully and poke my head out, just in time to see Timofey turn a corner and disappear.

Without pausing to think it through, I slip out of his office and follow after him.

Maybe if I walk with my head held high, no one will notice I'm wandering around without permission. Timofey did tell everyone to stay out of my way, after all. If anyone stops me, I'll just tell them I'm running an errand for Benjamin.

In a way, I am. If I can hold something serious over Timofey's head, it could be the key to get me and Benjamin out of here.

This is for him.

I turn the corner and glide down another hallway. It feels like wandering through a maze. I've never been in a house this big. If Timofey doesn't give me a proper tour, I'm liable to get lost.

I'm approaching the end of the hallway when I hear Timofey's voice again. I freeze and press my body flat against the wall.

I can't see who he's talking to and they're whispering so low that it's hard to make out the words. In small, sliding steps, I sneak closer to the hallway intersection, hoping I'll get lucky and their voices will carry.

I hear something about a body, and my heart constricts.

Does that have something to do with the blood I saw on Timofey's neck? Did he kill someone?

My heart is thundering. I blow out a silent breath to try and stay calm. I won't learn anything if I descend into a panic.

Breathe, girl. Focus. This is for him.

I lean closer with my eyes closed like that might help me pick up their words better. Weirdly, it works.

"I don't know how you do it," an unfamiliar voice says. "Kill people."

I swallow down a gasp, biting my lower lip so hard I expect it to split. Timofey kills people. He's a killer. I knew it, and yet somehow, I'm still surprised. That might make me dumb. At the very least, it makes me a sucker.

"Probably the same way you look your brothers in blue in the eyes after you doctor up a crime scene to make me look innocent," Timofey snaps back.

He's talking to a police officer right now. An officer who is clearly working for him.

That's corruption. Or bribery. Probably both. Whatever the name, they could both go to prison for a long time if it was reported. It's exactly the kind of information I need.

I just need to know the man's name.

The men keep talking. I inch closer and closer to the corner of the wall.

One glimpse. That's all I need. One peek at the officer's badge or his face or something that could at least help me identify him in a lineup. I just need one good look and then I'll run back to Timofey's office and pretend this never happened.

Their voices are tense, an argument simmering between them, and it seems like the best opportunity I'm going to get.

I poke my head out slowly and take in the scene.

Timofey is standing with his back to me, facing a man in all black. The cop is fit and well-built, though he's nothing compared to Timofey. He has a hoodie on, zipped up to the neck. If he's wearing a badge, I can't see it.

But I can see his face.

I catalog him, imagining describing this exact man to a sketch artist later. Square head. No chin to speak of. Small, dark eyes…

Eyes that land right on me.

"What the fu—who is that?" the man splutters.

My heart leaps into my throat. I pull back as quickly as I can, but it doesn't matter. I already know it's too late.

19

PIPER

I start running down the hallway. Maybe a miracle will occur and I can outrun Timofey. I lower my head, ready to give that far-fetched escape plan all I've got…when I hear a cry.

A *baby's* cry.

Without thinking, I lunge across the hall for the nearest door and throw it open. The cry fills the hallway, and I duck into the dark room.

There's a crib in the center of the room, and in the center of that crib is a squirming bundle.

"I was looking for Benjamin," I mutter, trying to practice my alibi in the few seconds I have left before Timofey finds me. "I was searching for his room, and I found it. I didn't hear anything. I was looking for Benjamin."

He won't hurt me with a baby in my arms, right?

I don't love the idea of using the child I was sent to protect as a human shield, but I guess I'll find out how serious he was about Benjamin being his main priority.

I pluck the little baby out of the crib and cradle him against my chest. His cheeks are pink and round and he clearly has a wonderful set of lungs because he's screaming so loudly that I don't hear Timofey's footsteps in the hallway until they're on top of me.

One minute, I'm alone with Benjamin; the next, Timofey is darkening the doorway.

"What are you doing in here?" he growls.

I turn around, trying to look calm, but it feels like my heart is going to burst out of my chest. My anxiety is doing nothing to soothe the baby. Benjamin wails even louder.

"My job. I'm the nanny, right?"

His electric blue eyes narrow. "Don't lie to me."

"I'm as honest with you as you are with me."

"You're not half as clever as you think you are."

"Who was being clever?" I ask. "I was telling the truth."

Benjamin is still crying, but with the way Timofey is staring at me, the room feels silent. Each second stretches and warps, and I have no idea if I'm going to get away with this or not.

Suddenly, he steps forward. "Give me the boy."

I tighten my arms around the baby, and I know I'm done for. Timofey knows it, too.

"Piper," he snarls, "give him to me."

"Move out of the doorway first."

I wrap my arms around the wailing child like he's my life preserver. Right now, he is. The police officer in the hall won't shoot me if I'm holding Benjamin. Timofey won't tackle me.

Maybe, somehow, I can get myself to the front door and outside.

To your bike? Genius plan, Piper. Really top shelf stuff.

Fuck, I wish I had a car. I wish I could overcome the fear that is the literal least of my worries right now and ride in one.

But even with Benjamin in my arms and Timofey blocking the doorway, I can feel my claustrophobia wrapping itself around me like an anaconda. It squeezes, reminding me I'm backed into a corner, whispering that there is no way out.

Timofey steps closer until he blocks the door from view. "You aren't going anywhere."

"You can't keep me here. People will notice I'm missing."

He leans his head to the side. "You think I'm going to hurt you."

"You've done it before! You told me just before your meeting that you'd kill me yourself. Of course I think you're going to hurt me."

I pat Benjamin's soft little back. His lower lip is quivering with each cry. He's probably hungry and needs a diaper change. My fingers itch to take care of him. I want to help him.

But getting him away from Timofey Viktorov is the best help I could ever give.

"Why would I hurt you?"

Timofey asks the question in a way that makes me doubt myself. Like it's ridiculous that I'm afraid of him. Like I don't have every reason in the world to run screaming from the mere mention of his name.

Then his expression flatlines. Every emotion drains from his face between one blink and the next. "What do you know that is worth killing over?"

I shake my head. "Nothing. I don't know. You're a criminal, that's all I know. But everyone knows that."

"You didn't know that," he says. "Not before you walked into my house two days ago."

What I wouldn't give to go back to that moment, yank myself away from Timofey's front door, and never go to that meeting. God, would things be different.

Then again, who would help Benjamin if I did that?

I felt an obligation to Benjamin from the moment I heard about him. Now that I'm holding him against me, feeling his tiny chest breathe in and out, there's no way I can leave him behind. He's imprinting on me with every cry and hiccup. I'm a goner, in every way that matters.

But so be it. He's helpless, and I won't leave him behind.

Not the way so many people did exactly that to me.

"Move out of my way," I hiss at the bastard intent on ruining my life. "Let us go. You don't want to take care of a baby."

"Don't tell me what I want. You aren't leaving here with or without Benjamin."

"What do you want with a baby anyway? Whose baby is this?" I ask. "You said he was left on your porch. Why do you care so much about a baby you don't even know?"

"I could ask you the same question."

"And I'd tell you it's because I'm a human being with a working heart. Because I don't want to see a child left in an unsafe environment if I can do something about it," I retort. "I'm sure you can't relate to that."

"You're right." Timofey nods solemnly. "I don't have a heart. I'm cold and calculating. I'm actually keeping Benjamin for a ritual sacrifice later. Regular deals with the devil are how I maintain my peaches-and-cream complexion."

He's joking, I know, but I still squeeze Benjamin tighter. "The sad thing is that I don't know if you're kidding."

Timofey snorts. "Then maybe you really are stupid."

"Or maybe you're a cold-blooded murderer and capable of anything," I fire back. "The truly stupid thing would be for me to underestimate you."

"So I guess that answers the question of whether you were eavesdropping or not." He exhales and shakes his head. "I gave you such a simple, clear instruction. *Wait in my office.* That's all you had to do. Instead, you had to follow me and fuck everything up."

My blood pressuring is skyrocketing, pumping through my body at an ungodly rate. I can hear my heart pounding, the incessant *boom-boom* like war drums.

"What are you going to do to me?" I whisper, even though I don't want to know the answer. Maybe ignorance would be bliss.

"That depends. Are you going to hand over Benjamin?"

I'm ashamed to admit that I consider it for a second, handing over this helpless baby to save my own skin. Exchanging his little life for my own.

But I'd never forgive myself if I did that.

I'd rather die with dignity than live with regret.

"No," I say firmly. "I won't. I'm going to do everything I can to get him away from you or die trying. You're a criminal and the worst possible choice to take care of a child."

Timofey presses a hand to his chest and pretends he has feelings I could hurt. "Then you leave me no choice."

He takes another step closer to me, compounding my claustrophobia and making me feel like a caged animal.

I eye my possible escape routes, but there aren't any. Timofey is blocking the doorway and I can't climb through a window with a baby in my arms. Not before Timofey could stop me, anyway.

"Stop!" I beg, backing up until I'm smashed against the bars of the crib. "Don't hurt Benjamin. Just let us go. I won't say anything to anyone. I'll leave and you won't hear from us again."

Timofey doesn't say anything as he towers over me. I cradle Benjamin's head with shaking fingers and close my eyes, ready to accept whatever is coming next.

Whatever happens, I hope it's quick.

Then Timofey turns his head to the side and bellows, "Rooney!"

Benjamin jolts and starts wailing again. The man I saw earlier appears in the doorway. This time, his hood is up, his face shrouded in darkness.

"What?" he croaks irritably.

"Take your hood down, you idiot," Timofey snaps. "She already saw you."

"You don't know that."

"I do," he says. "It doesn't matter, anyway. Piper won't tell anyone. Will you, darling?"

"*Don't* call me darling."

He smirks. "She's going to learn her lesson. If she doesn't, the people she cares about will have to learn it for her."

Does he mean Benjamin?

Ashley? Noelle? My grandma?

Does it even matter who he means? Timofey is willing to hurt people. Who he hurts is not high on his list of concerns.

Officer Rooney lowers his hood, revealing a worried mouth turned down at the corners. "What do you want me to do?"

In response, Timofey reaches out and grabs Benjamin. I try to hold on, but Timofey shakes his head. "You won't win this one, Piper. Pull too hard and he'll break."

I know he's right. I also know he won't give in.

So, reluctantly, I let Benjamin go.

Timofey holds the baby casually, like he's done it a million times before. It's strange how natural he looks with a child in his arms.

Then he backs away and jerks his chin in my direction. "Okay, Rooney. Go ahead."

I wilt back, but Rooney doesn't move. "Go ahead with what?" he asks.

Timofey smolders. "Arrest her."

20

TIMOFEY

"You're kidding," Piper snorts.

She looks from me to Rooney and back again like she's waiting for one of us to break character and reveal this has all been some kind of practical joke. Even Rooney is standing stock still in the doorway, waiting for... Actually, I'm not sure.

"What the fuck are you waiting for?" I ask him.

"He's waiting for you to make sense," Piper interrupts. "You hired me to be Benjamin's nanny. Being in his room is not kidnapping, or whatever other bullshit accusation you're making up in your head."

"Funny—I seem to remember you saying you'll do 'anything possible' to get him out of my house. I'm no lawyer, but that sounds suspect to me."

"You were here the entire time!" she protests.

I step back, holding Benjamin over my shoulder and patting his back. His wailing has stopped. Silence descends in the room.

The shock is plain on Piper's face. I have to bite back my own smug smile. "And thank God I was," I say solemnly. "Who knows what would have happened otherwise?"

"Stop doing that!"

"Doing what?"

"That!" She circles her finger in my face, her full lips squished into a frustrated slash. "Acting like you're the victim here. That police officer and I both know who you really are. Stop pretending."

I cross the distance between us in one step. Piper jerks back with a gasp, and I tower over her, eyes narrowed.

"Fine. I'll stop pretending," I snarl. "You refuse to accept your role in this little drama. Your job is to do what I say. That is it. You may think I'm the villain, Piper, and you might even be right. But that does not make you the hero."

That little jab might wound her more than anything else I've ever said to her. Angry red splotches color her cheeks.

But I'm not done yet. "You are nothing but a background character, momentarily pulled into the melee. You will make yourself useful to me or I'll rid myself of you. This trip downtown will be a taste of what I'm capable of."

Her eyes widen. "You're serious."

It's not a question, so I don't bother with an answer. I just turn around and gesture for Rooney to go ahead.

He sags with exhaustion, even though the day is young, and unhooks his cuffs from his hip.

"You're serious," she repeats, hysteria edging into her voice. "Timofey, no. You can't do this. I didn't—I didn't do anything wrong!"

When she sees I'm not going to offer her any mercy, she turns to Rooney.

"Please, Officer," she begs, folding in on herself. "I don't know why you're working for him, but I'm sure you're a good person. You don't want to do this."

I can't hold back a laugh. "James is the one who came to me to set up this arrangement. Didn't you, James?"

His jaw clenches, but he nods.

James Rooney is an unfortunate criminal—the kind with a half-formed conscience. The kind who wishes he was a better man, but knows he isn't and never will be.

I don't envy him. This world is much easier when you know who you are.

I offer Piper a cruel grin. "He and I were a match made in hell."

I can physically see the hope drain out of her. Rooney crosses the room, cuffs held out in front of him.

"Come on, sweetheart," he says gruffly. "Don't make this harder than it oughta be."

She jerks her arms away and tucks them behind her back. "No! No. You're not doing this. I'm not going with you."

"I'm afraid you don't have a choice, ma'am."

"Don't talk to me like I'm the crazy one here!" she cries out. "You're fucking deranged, both of you. You can't get away with this. I'll tell someone. I'll report you."

I shake my head. "No, you won't."

"Yes, I—"

"Does Ashley know where you are right now?" I cut in. "Have you told her I'm the one who broke into her apartment last night? Does she know to watch out for me? *Does she even know who I am?*"

Her full lips part in disbelief at my casual cruelty. They're good lips: full and pink. It's a waste, really. If she's going to be as stubborn as a mule, she should look like one, too.

A flash of determination sparkles in her green eyes. "Don't you dare touch her. Leave her alone."

"I will—if you keep your mouth shut." I reach out and stroke a fingertip down her cheek. "Show me you can follow directions, Piper. Prove to me you can be obedient."

She swats me away, her hand shaking in fury. Her nostrils flare. "I already told you: I'm not a dog."

"Call yourself whatever you like, *kiska*. But whatever you choose, know that I will take care of you. I will protect you. All you have to do in return is every single thing I say."

"Oh, is that all?" she snips sarcastically. "Sounds completely reasonable and not at all psychotic."

I click my tongue in disappointment. "We'll talk again later. After you've had time to think through my offer."

Rooney raises a brow, and I nod. No more fucking around. It's clear that this is the only way to get through to the stubborn girl before me.

But when he steps forward, the little bit of calm Piper managed to cling to evaporates. In an instant, she's thrashing like a maniac, throwing herself back into the crib and lunging towards the door.

"No!" she shrieks, her voice breaking with pure fear. "Don't you dare fucking touch me! Get your hands off of me!"

Rooney grabs for her arms. As soon as he manages to get one, she frees the first. They go through the whole routine a few times over. It's a pitiful display of snotty crying, pained grunting, the two of them helpless and hapless against each other.

But she can only hold out for so long. When Rooney finally manages to capture both of Piper's arms behind her back, she collapses forward with a sob.

"Please," she begs me. "Please don't do this, Timofey. Please."

It's a far cry from the way she stepped forward during the meeting earlier, addressing a room full of Bratva lieutenants like she was ready to square up with them right then and there.

"Stop resisting," James barks. He drives a knee into Piper's lower back, taking her down to the floor.

I told him to arrest her, but the sight still sets off alarm bells in my head.

No one should be touching her like that. *Ever.*

It's the same sense of protectiveness I felt in the alley the night we met. I was there to scare her myself—but the moment that drunkard wrapped his grimy, unworthy hands around her neck, I wanted to slaughter him.

"Get her under control and out to your car," I bite out.

"What the hell does it look like I'm trying to do?"

I ignore his tone and step out into the hall. Benjamin is trying to lift his little head to follow the commotion, but he's still too young. I'm grateful for that. He doesn't need to remember this.

A minute later, James walks out with a struggling Piper next to him. She's dragging her feet, but she's not fighting anymore. She's just limp and unresisting. Her breath is coming in quick gasps. Hyperventilating. Fear choking her out from the inside.

"Stand her up so she can breathe, Rooney. We don't need another dead body to deal with."

"Do you want me to arrest her or not?" he complains. "This is how it has to be done."

"It's going to be done the way I say it will be done. Do what I say or you'll be the one in cuffs, *mudak*."

He looks over his shoulder at me, his face twisted into a grimace. Then he releases her and backs off with a huffy sigh.

Piper stands up and sucks in a deep breath. Her trembling eases.

Then she turns and charges directly at the officer.

21

TIMOFEY

Rooney stumbles back against the wall in surprise. Piper takes the opportunity to drive her shoulder into his chest a second time. Air whooshes out of his lungs. For a second, I think Piper might have won this fight. I might have to step in on Rooney's behalf.

Then he grabs her with his left hand, yanks her towards him, and cocks his right hand high into the air.

I see what's coming, but there's no time to stop it. Not with Benjamin in my arms.

Before I can intervene, James cracks his palm against Piper's face. The slap echoes off the walls and sends her head snapping to the side. She crumbles under the force of it.

"Fuckin' bitch," James mutters, shaking out the hand he used to hit her.

On her knees, Piper presses her cheek to her shoulder, trying to ease the red burn in her skin. Her eyes are wide and glassy, tears welling up like diamonds.

That's what does it.

That's what pushes me over the edge.

The sight of her crying is more than I'm willing to take right now.

Cradling Benjamin in my left arm, I snatch the back of James' hoodie with my right and jerk him away from her.

"If I'd known you were incapable of arresting a woman, I would have done it myself."

He wriggles in my grasp like a landed fish. "The hell are you doing, Viktorov? You saw what happened! She fought me!

"I'm sure that was so hard for you," I drawl. "You only have six inches and a hundred pounds on her."

Rooney's voice wobbles as I choke him out with his own hoodie. "If she was anyone else, I would have Tased her."

"You should reconsider how you speak to me, *Officer.*" The title is as close to a slur as I can muster.

He works his lips together nervously. The regret in his face is palpable. "If you don't want me to touch her, I won't touch her," he says at last. "Okay?"

"I want you to act like you've done your job before," I say. I release him in disgust. "Get her in the car and get the fuck out of here. Act like you're capable of that, at the very least."

His face goes beet red, but he turns to Piper, more determined than ever.

She turns her wide green eyes on me, desperate hope etched in every line of her face. If I had a heart, it would break at the sight of her. She's feeble and trembling, pitiful from head to toe. "Timofey, please. Please don't do this. I'll—I'll do what you say. I won't say anything to anyone. I'll do my job. I'll be good."

"Having a sudden change of heart?" I ask.

Deep down, the sudden change in her demeanor is alarming. Something is terrifying her in a way that words can't capture. That's the only reason she'd ever make an offer like that to someone like me.

You don't give the devil a blank check.

She squeezes her eyes closed and takes a deep breath. When she opens them again, she stares at me with complete sincerity. "I'll do whatever you say. I'll do anything."

The dark part of my mind—though that's not saying much, because there is no light part—hears her words and thinks about the many ways I could take advantage of them. What would those full lips look like when they're being obedient to my every command and whim? What sounds would she make at my feet, on her knees before me?

With her hands cuffed behind her, her shoulders are pressed back and her chest is arched forward. The soft curves of her body are even more visible through the thin material of her shirt.

Her offer is tempting.

Very fucking tempting.

I feel Rooney watching me with narrowed eyes. He's as eager to see what I'll decide as Piper is. The man works for me, but I'd be stupid to think he isn't constantly searching for my weakness. He's the kind of man who will go where the wind blows. For the right price, he'll turn on me and the Bratva in a second.

I ought to bury him forever. But right now, I need him under my thumb. I can't let him go just yet.

I look away from Piper to Rooney. "Finish what you started—but carefully, for fuck's sake. I don't need my property coming back damaged."

Piper gasps. "Timofey, please. No!"

He's on her in an instant. He hooks his hands around her biceps and pushes her down the hall. It's easier now than before because Piper isn't fighting—she's just begging.

I turn and walk back to my office with Benjamin asleep in the crook of my arm.

Piper's cries follow me the entire way.

22

TIMOFEY

"Just go get her," Akim pleads with me an hour after Piper and Rooney leave. "You clearly want her back here, so go get her."

I grimace. It's pleasantly quiet without Ms. Quinn screeching in my ear. She's somewhere no one can hear her, locked up in the bowels of the police station with cinderblock walls swallowing up her screams.

It's exactly where I wanted her to be. So why does that mental image grate on me so fucking badly?

"I don't want Piper anywhere."

He snorts. "Not even in a house? With a mouse? Or with a crane on a plane?"

"Fuck off, Dr. Seuss."

"How about doggystyle on the tile?" He laughs at his own stupid joke and then bends his head in apology. "Sorry. I had to."

"I don't want her anywhere, because my life would be easier if she just disappeared."

Akim backs towards the doorway. "Fine. So go get her and then you can kill her if that's what gets your rocks off. But either way, you should go get her. You're in a worse mood than normal and I blame her."

I give him the finger, then leave and get on my motorcycle. I don't have a destination in mind—I just want to ease the roiling knot in my stomach. But I guess I shouldn't be surprised when I find myself riding downtown.

Then winding closer and closer to the precinct.

Now, I'm circling the block.

This shit is getting out of hand.

"It's been almost two hours," I mutter to myself over the purr of the engine. "That's enough to teach her a lesson."

I only wanted to intimidate her, anyway. She needs to understand that I can and will make her life a living hell if she crosses me. A few hours in a cell ought to have done the trick.

I leave my bike at the curb and march up to the building. I'm halfway up the stairs when my phone rings. It's a number I don't recognize.

"Hello?"

"You can't walk through the front doors of a police station."

I check the caller ID. "Why are you calling me from your office phone?"

Rooney curses. "I saw you walking across the street and grabbed the wrong phone. Damn it."

The line goes dead. A second later, my phone rings again. This time, it's Rooney's burner cell.

"You can't be here."

"You are the last fucking person on earth who gets to tell me where I can and can't be." I crack my neck in both directions. "Go get her out of the cell. I'm taking her with me."

There's a long pause before he speaks again. "You're kidding."

"Did you think I was going to have you ship her off to prison?"

"No, I guess not. But—dammit, after everything I went through to get her in the car?" He groans. "You have no fucking idea. She fought the entire way. I thought I was going to have to call a psych unit halfway through the drive."

That catches my attention. "What happened?"

"Your girl is nuts. She was clawing at the windows, screaming like a damn banshee. I thought she was going to break through the partition at one point."

I frown. "How is she now?"

"Quiet, at least. I don't hear her screaming." He sighs. "You can't make arresting her a regular thing. I don't think I can handle it. I've arrested dudes on PCP before and they had nothing on your girl."

"She isn't my girl."

"Sure, sure," he says quickly. "Your nanny. Whatever."

I don't exactly love that descriptor, either. She's more to me than that, isn't she?

When I think about it, I guess not. I barely know her. What should I care if she hated being in the police car or if she isn't thriving in solitary confinement? Why should it bother me if Rooney thinks she's nothing more than my employee?

By all accounts, he's right.

"Just go get her," I say aloud.

He huffs out a pouty breath. "Fine. But meet me in the back."

I hang up and walk around the building. The precinct is in an L-shape that takes up half of the block. The other half is dedicated to a parking lot—most of the spaces are taken up by old police cruisers—and a fenced-in recreation area with rusting basketball hoops. There's a white transport bus parked next to a dumpster. That's where I find Rooney waiting for me. He's propped open the back door with a rock.

"She's right through here." He turns and ducks inside. I follow him in. As he passes a door up ahead, he gestures to his right. That door is propped open, too.

"Through there," he says, not turning around. "The key is on the floor and the cameras are rebooting for five minutes. She didn't get booked on her way in, so no paperwork or nothin' like that. Be out before they turn back on."

He turns the corner up ahead, disappearing from view, and I go through the door he pointed out.

The light in here is much dimmer, so it takes my eyes a few seconds to adjust. When they do, I see a series of cells against the wall. They're all empty.

Except for one.

In the center unit, I see a petite figure curled into a ball in the corner. Piper is rocking back and forth, her head wedged between her knees. Her soft whispers fill the air and echo off the cold stone floors.

Maybe a psych unit would have been the right call.

The key is in the middle of the floor. I bend over and grab it. The metal scrapes against the hard floor. At the small sound, Piper jerks her head up.

I meet her gaze. Her eyes are wide and terrified, her pupils blown so wide I can't even see the green in her irises. She's only been here for two hours, but she looks like a ghost of herself.

"What are you—" She gasps when she sees me, her mouth falling open. "How did you—where did you come from?"

I walk to the bars and slide the key into the lock. "There's nowhere you can go that I can't follow, Piper. Remember that."

The thought should terrify her, but she is far too distracted by the tumblers in the door shifting and sliding.

In one breath, she launches to her feet and throws herself against the door to the cell. "Let me out. Please."

"Why else do you think I'm here?"

"Really?" she breathes. "You're letting me go?"

Up close, I can see tear tracks streaked down her cheeks. Her lips are bloodied and swollen from her chewing on them. Even now, she pulls one between her teeth and bites.

I step away. "That depends. What have you learned today?"

She grips the bars until her knuckles are white. "Timofey… I'll do anything. Anything at all. Please, I—I can't stay in here anymore. Timofey."

Her lips wrap around my name like a prayer. That alone is enough for me to twist the key in the lock and pull the door open.

Piper doesn't hesitate. She lunges through the gap. For a second, I think she's going to try to escape.

Then she throws herself against me, buries her face into my chest, and sobs.

I've faced some of the most dangerous men in the world with my head held high. I've fought my way through a barrage of bullets without batting an eye.

But this? A beautiful woman weeping on my chest, her tears soaking through my shirt?

This is new.

23

TIMOFEY

"Are you okay?"

The question is out of my lips before I can even consider how fucking ridiculous it is. *I'm* the one who put her in here. *I'm* the one who did this to her. So if she's not okay, it's my doing, and I shouldn't give a shit.

But I do care. Way more than I'm willing to admit.

That's the most ridiculous part of all.

Piper pulls away from me and swipes at her eyes. Her fingers are trembling. "Yeah. Yeah, I know. I'm—everything is fine. Can we go now?"

She looks to the cracked-open door like she expects it to slam closed any second. Like she isn't even sure it's real.

I check my watch. "The cameras are only off for two more minutes. Let's go."

I turn to the door and Piper grabs onto my sleeve.

I falter for just a fraction of a moment, glancing down where her hands wrap around my bicep. Then I carry on, as if it's perfectly normal for this woman to be cuddling me after I put her in jail.

We walk out of the room and into the fluorescent light of the narrow hallway.

"This place is suffocating," she whispers behind me. "Have they heard of windows?"

"I don't think the architect was worried about the prisoners' access to natural light."

She grumbles something I can't hear under her breath. When we walk through the back door into the parking lot, she inhales deeply.

"I'm guessing you've never done time before."

She closes her eyes and takes another deep breath. "Never. You?"

The comment was a joke. I have no interest in getting to know Piper Quinn more than I already do. But I suppose this is preferable to her cowering and shivering on the concrete floor.

"A night in jail here or there. Nothing serious. Sergey made sure of that."

She looks over at me. In the sunlight, her green eyes are ringed with gold. "By bribing the officers or by setting you on the right path?"

Piper's hand is still fisted in my shirt sleeve as I walk us back around the perimeter of the building. "You tell me."

"That's what I figured." She sighs. "You all have to be smart people to run an operation like this. You could use your powers for good, you know."

"I could also donate all of my possessions to charity and become one with nature."

"I'm guessing that's a no, then?"

"Bingo. I knew you weren't as stupid as you seemed."

She rolls her eyes, but she stays close to me. I have to admit, I don't mind the warmth of her body next to mine.

Maybe Akim is right. It's been too long since I've fucked. That's all this is. Pheromones. Chemicals. The animal part of my brain going haywire.

We turn out of the alley onto the sidewalk. Piper squeezes my forearm once more, then lets go at last. I swear she whimpers almost imperceptibly as she does. Like she's losing something in the process.

"Thank you," she murmurs.

"For having you arrested?"

"No," she huffs. "For…for coming to get me. You don't deserve a thank you since you're the one who put me in there. But you also could have left me a lot longer. I don't know if I would have… Well, I'm glad you came when you did. So, yeah. Thanks."

I don't respond. Mostly because I didn't go and release Piper for her own sake; I did it for mine.

And that's a thousand times worse.

The thought of her in there with Rooney, with the rest of those corrupt fucks in blue, with any of the slimy bastards they have cuffed up today… I didn't like that shit at all.

Akim would say it's because I want to fuck her hard in the yard or some other Seussian bullshit. But it's more than that. The desire I feel to protect her runs deeper than that.

Maybe it does all go back to Emily.

All I know is, nothing is going to happen to Piper Quinn while she's under my care.

After that, though, she's on her own.

"Wait." Her hand finds my arm again and she jerks me to a stop. I'm surprised at how willingly I let her do it. "How did you get here? What did you drive? *Did* you drive?"

"I didn't walk forty miles in two hours, if that's what you're asking."

Her chest rises and falls as her breathing picks up. "Timofey, I can't."

"A second ago, you were ready to erect a statue to me for getting you out of there. Now, you want to stay?"

Her eyes narrow, but her frowny mask does nothing to hide her obvious panic. "I don't want to stay, but I can't get in your car. I-I'm claustrophobic."

"What?"

"Claustrophobic," she spits, saying the word like it's shameful. "I don't like being in small spaces."

"I know what claustrophobic means."

"Okay, good. So you know that being handcuffed, shoved into the back of a police cruiser with a partition, and then chucked into a jail cell was the trigger of all triggers for me." She licks her lips and looks up at me under long lashes. "I'm barely standing upright here. I'm exhausted and on edge. I can't get back in a car. I just can't. I won't. I—"

"Don't have to," I finish for her.

She blinks. "Huh?"

"It would be pretty hard for you to get in my car since I don't have one."

"But you said—"

I point at the machine in front of us and watch as Piper's expression shifts from confusion to elation.

"Of course you ride a motorcycle." She laughs to herself, part maniacal, part scoffing, mostly relieved. "All the bad boys do."

"You wound me, Ms. Quinn. I'm no cliché."

"Tell me something I don't know." She runs her finger down the shiny black paint of the engine, and I swear I can feel it like she's touching my body instead. "There's no one in the world like Timofey Viktorov."

"I'll choose to take that as a compliment."

I hand her a helmet and climb on.

"I'm getting on the back?" she asks, lingering on the sidewalk.

"It doesn't work as well when you try sitting on the handlebars," I drawl. "So it's either the back, or you're walking."

Piper hesitates for one more moment. I watch her—long, lithe, petite, fucking beautiful. Then she makes her decision.

She throws her leg over easily enough. For a second, she tries to keep space between our bodies. She sits as far back on the seat as she can.

As soon as I start the engine and pull away from the curb, that goes out the window.

Piper yelps and wraps both arms around me. I feel the warmth of her thighs wrapped around my lower back. I feel her breasts squeezed against my back. Every inch of her is held against me, soft and firm in all the right places.

And one thought stands above all the rest of the tumult in my head.

We're both in a lot of fucking trouble.

24

PIPER

With each corner Timofey speeds around, the wind whipping through my hair, I can feel the clutch of my claustrophobia easing. The pressure on my chest lightens.

I can breathe.

"Hang on," Timofey calls over his shoulder as he accelerates through a turn and opens the throttle wide.

He says that like I'm not already clinging to him with every ounce of strength in my body.

Any normal person would be way more afraid of this versus tight spaces. Sitting on the back of an absurdly overpowered motorcycle as it hurtles through traffic with no seatbelt and nothing but a thin layer of plastic around your skull is definitively more terrifying than being in the backseat of a car. Especially when you consider that a known criminal and kidnapper is the one at the wheel. Or, the handlebars, or whatever.

And yet I feel perfectly at peace here.

Ironically, the thought makes my heart race. How can I be perfectly at peace with my arms wrapped around a monster's waist?

How can I find peace next to the man who just had me arrested and tossed in some grimy jail cell simply because he could?

Stockholm syndrome, I think. *I never knew it could kick in so fast.*

This was probably part of his plan all along. He'd hurl me in jail and then show up as the big hero to rescue me. I played right into his hands. I *thanked* him for undoing the horrible thing he'd done.

I snort, disgusted with myself.

"Care to share your thoughts?" Timofey asks.

I shake my head. "Nope."

"Being close to me isn't going to trigger some new freak-out, is it?"

"I'm not going to *freak out*, asshole."

I hate that he knows I'm claustrophobic. I shouldn't have told him. As if he needed one more weapon in his toolbox against me.

There wasn't much of an option, though. He saw me trembling and crying in jail. I had to explain away my behavior somehow. I didn't want him thinking I was weak without a cause.

Now, it's just one more thing he can use to manipulate me.

"My claustrophobia isn't even that bad," I yell over the sound of the onrushing wind. "It was just…a hard day. I'm normally fine."

The lie sits between us, heavy and awkward. I'm not accustomed to lying. There's little reason to be good at it in my life.

"I'm sure that's why you ride a bike everywhere," he chuckles. "Because your claustrophobia is so manageable."

I'm glad he can't see my face because my cheeks burn with embarrassment. "It's good exercise, jerk."

But it's a lame protest and he knows it. He doesn't say anything, but I can feel a laugh vibrate through his chest.

I want to squeeze until he can't breathe. Maybe then he'll understand how I feel during an attack. I could hook my hands around the muscled walls of his chest, tightening until his ribs compress. Until *I'm* the reason he's terrified and trembling.

Maybe then he would understand how I feel now.

I'm not trapped in a small space, but the walls are closing in on me in a new way. If I don't get away from Timofey Viktorov soon, I'll never escape.

It's a funny thought to have when I'm willingly pressing my body against his. The heat of him soaks through my clothes. It's comforting, and I find myself leaning against him more and more. A few times, I even rest my cheek on his back and close my eyes, giving myself over to the rumble of the motor and the vibration of the road beneath the tires.

As we navigate through his neighborhood, though, my guard starts to come back up. The freedom I felt on the road dissipates.

In a matter of minutes, I'll be inside the literal walls of his house again. I have to remember who this man is. What he has done. What he's still capable of doing.

"How often do you find yourself throwing people in jail?" I ask as he downshifts and the engine calms from a wide-open roar to a purring rumble.

"Why? Interested in forming a support group?"

"I just want to know if I should expect it again soon."

He shakes his head. "That's up to you."

"Not exactly. I definitely didn't choose to go to jail the first time."

We're driving slower now, cruising through his rich neighborhood surrounded by ancient, leafy trees and the sudden appearance of a metal gate every so often. I can see a few houses over the stone fences, but they're all set far away from the road and from each other.

Far enough apart that your neighbors would never hear you scream.

"You could have chosen to obey me," he muses. "You didn't."

"Well, with choices like the ones you're offering, I'm sure I'm not the first innocent person you've imprisoned."

"No one around me is truly innocent," he says just as we pull through the gates to his house.

"I am."

"You *think* you are," he fires back. "You're wrong."

I lean forward, trying to catch a glimpse of his face. All I can see is the slope of his jawbone. The long line of his neck. I could frame this view and sell it as fine art. The man is stunning.

He must feel me fidget, because he glances over his shoulder. His blue eyes catch mine, stroking over my face before he faces forward again.

"I've known too many people like you," he continues. "You pretend to be good. Maybe you even fool yourself from time to time into thinking what you're doing is noble. But I know better. Deep down, so do you."

The pieces click together all at once. I'm kind of shocked I didn't already arrive at this conclusion.

"How long were you in foster care before you were adopted?" I ask.

Timofey lifts his chin and parks his motorcycle in front of the house. "Long enough."

That's all he says, and I know it's all I'm going to get out of him.

Communication doesn't seem to be Timofey's strong suit, but that doesn't mean I can't still win him over. He hates social workers? Fine. I'll show him we aren't all bad. I've dealt with enough traumatized victims of the system to recognize one when I see it.

Of course, most of the ones I deal with are children. I bet the same principles apply. One principle above all others: I need to earn his trust.

So I'll obey. I'll do what he asks. I'll go along with his plan.

Until he trusts me enough to give me some space. Preferably, that will be space alone with Benjamin.

Then I'll take the opportunity to get us both as far away from Timofey Viktorov as possible.

25

PIPER

Timofey plants his feet on the ground and hesitates. I'm not sure what he's doing for a second, but then I realize he's waiting for me to get off first.

"Oh. Sorry." I let go of him all at once. The tingle of our recent contact is still buzzing in my skin. "I guess I should get off now, huh?"

I cringe at myself as I awkwardly slide my body to one side and try to shift my leg over the seat. Just as my foot is about to touch the ground, the bike shifts under my weight. I'm not expecting the movement, and I overcompensate in the other direction.

Suddenly, I'm tipping backwards and far too off-balance to stop myself. I yelp and brace to crash headfirst against the concrete step.

Then a strong arm hooks around my back.

It happens as fast as the fall did. In an instant, Timofey has me caught and pinned me against his side.

On the ride, I was behind him. We were still practically zipped together, of course, but I couldn't see his face. It felt...*safe*.

This feels very, very *un*safe.

My breasts are pressed to his shoulder and my lips are at his ear. When he turns his head to look at me, his unreal blue eyes are an inch away. I can smell peppermint on his breath.

"Whoa," I breathe. "Good catch."

His arm is an iron band around my waist. I feel tiny and helpless in his arms. In some ways, that's thrilling. In many others, it's terrifying.

"Feel free to get off any time," he grunts.

"Oh, shit." I slide backwards off the bike and right myself, ignoring the sudden, uneasy warmth in my core. "Sorry. I didn't mean to—"

"Of course you didn't."

He slides off without any trouble. *Like it's that easy.* I want to give him a shove just to watch him be clumsy for one second. I don't, though, mostly because I know that there's no way it would go according to plan.

"Do you think I somehow planned that?" I ask.

He rounds the bike and moves towards me. Rather than wilt away, I face him.

His hands move towards my face. Without meaning to, I tilt my chin back. Ready.

Ready for what, though?

I'll never tell.

His fingers stop short of caressing my jaw and instead hastily unclip my helmet and yank it off my head.

"Ow." I rub my scalp where he pulled out a few strands of hair. "That hurt."

"Can you do one fucking thing without almost dying?" He drops the helmet on the back of the bike and faces me again. His brows are pinched together. I hate that it makes him even more handsome.

The arch of his brows should be studied by scientists. I want to ask him if he gets them waxed. I know women who would die for that brow shape.

"What?" I want him to explain himself, but I also want to make sure I didn't fall too deep into his gaze and miss something.

"It's called survival instinct. Try it sometime."

I blink at him, genuinely confused. Timofey is an asshole, but usually, there's a reason. Me slipping off of his motorcycle seems like a pretty flimsy excuse for this much anger, even for his short temper.

Usually, I'd match his tone and start an argument. But that wouldn't serve my long-term goal. Instead, I swallow down every defense I want to make and nod.

"You're right. I'm sorry."

His brows pinch even harder together. "You're here to make my life easier. If I have to spend all my time saving you from calamity, you won't be worth the trouble."

"That makes sense," I say softly. "I'll try to be more careful."

I can feel his frustration boiling over. The fact that I'm agreeing with him should make him happy. I'm obeying. Isn't this what he wanted?

For some reason, Timofey is looking for a fight. He wants me to push back.

And I have no earthly idea why.

Without another word, he turns around and stomps up the stairs. I follow at a distance, keeping my hands folded in front of me.

Walking back into the house is a relief I didn't expect. Showing up to work this morning, I felt like I was walking to my own execution. After being in the cell for a couple hours, though, I'm thrilled to be back in the mansion.

Again, that was probably Timofey's plan.

I hate that it's working.

26

PIPER

He cuts through the entrance hall and across the hall towards the back of the house. I'm about to stop and wait for direction when I smell something delicious.

My stomach lurches. I haven't eaten since I had a granola bar this morning, so I'm starved.

I jog to catch up to Timofey just as he walks into the kitchen.

The room is spacious with a large island in the center. The black wooden cabinets are modern and flush, no ornamentation except for a carved-out groove to act as a handle. Clear glass orbs float down from the ceiling and radiate warm light.

I can't focus much on the interior design, though, because a tall, thin man is dancing across the tile.

He's wearing a bright red apron and clacking a pair of tongs in the air like a flamenco castanet. I don't hear any music, but that doesn't seem to bother the man. He sways his hips to a silent Latin beat and shakes the tongs every few seconds. I swear I hear him sing-song, "Cha-cha-cha!"

Timofey releases a weary, bone-deep sigh and the man spins around.

Rather than embarrassment, a huge, goofy smile spreads across his face. "Hola, amiga! Welcome back. Did they feed you in the brink or are you hungry?"

It takes me a second to realize he's talking to me, in what appears to be a horrendous Spanish accent.

"Oh… No, they didn't. I'm—" I glance at Timofey, but his face is an indecipherable mask of annoyance. I'm not sure if it's aimed at me, this man, or the both of us. I smile back at the cook. "I'm starving, actually."

He clacks the tongs together again like his own applause machine. "Fantastico! Lunch is almost ready. I'm making teriyaki chicken power bowls."

My stomach growls at the name alone. "That sounds incredible."

He turns to Timofey. "I like her."

"I couldn't care less," Timofey bites back.

The man doesn't seem bothered at all by Timofey's big grumpy act. He just ignores him and talks to me instead. "The other guys who come through this house wouldn't recognize quality food if it walked up to them and gargled their ball sacks. I'm an unappreciated artist."

His vulgarity shocks me, but the man doesn't even slow pace.

"I mean, food is what we need to survive, sure. It's a necessity. But there's no reason it can't also be a treat, right?"

"Uh, yeah. Sure. I guess."

"You guess?" he asks, eyes narrowed.

"Well, the fanciest thing I've eaten recently is a stuffed crust frozen pizza."

He drags a hand down his face. "God help you."

"Somebody needs to," Timofey mutters. I snap my attention to him, but he is already backing away. "I'm not hungry."

"You need to eat," the cook insists. "It'll help keep your energy up. You know, in case you have some kind of high-energy plans later. Tonight, for example."

Timofey glares at him, and I can't help but feel like I'm missing something.

"Bring it to my office then," he says. "I have work to finish."

He doesn't look at me, but I feel the spotlight of attention all the same. Then he turns around and leaves.

The moment he is gone, the man in the kitchen shakes his head. "He gets grouchy when he's hungry."

"He must be hungry 24/7 then."

The man tips his head back and cackles. "It's not for lack of trying on my part. I always make sure there's something around here to eat, but he doesn't often take me up on the offer."

"A man that big can't be skipping meals."

"No. It's even worse than that." He shivers. "Protein shakes. He keeps whey powder and blender bottles in the closet in his room. I swear he snorts the stuff when I'm not around."

I wrinkle my nose. "Those taste like sawdust and chalk."

"Thank you!" He looks over his shoulder. "It's Piper, right? I like you."

"You said that earlier."

"I'm saying it twice so you know I mean it. I'm Akim, by the way."

I take a seat in the white plastic bar stool and watch Akim move confidently around the kitchen. "You're his personal chef?"

"When he lets me be, yes. I end up grilling cod and making bulk batches of rice more than my creative heart would like."

"I'm not surprised. Timofey strikes me as the controlling type."

Akim snorts. "You've got that right. Which of us went to culinary school? Not the one changing all of my meal plans, I'll tell you that."

"If your food tastes as good as it smells, then I'll never tell you what to cook for me."

He spins around and holds out a hand for a surprisingly solemn shake. "No take-backsies."

I shake his hand and laugh. "Wouldn't dream of it."

I'm not sure I'll be here long enough to really keep that promise, but it seems like an easy one to keep. Lunch really does smell amazing.

He spoons a bed of fluffy rice onto a dark green plate and tops it with pieces of caramelized chicken. Then he layers in roasted chickpeas and broccoli, red onion slices, and drizzles some kind of mysterious red sauce over top.

When he finally slides a bowl to me, I grab the fork and dive in.

"Oh my God." I close my eyes and chew, bopping back and forth on the seat in an unintentional happy dance. "This is amazing."

"You really don't know much about food, then. I mean, it's good. But this is the healthy shit. Wait until I cook you something artery-clogging. You'll love it."

I take another bite and then clap a hand over my mouth. "I dinut chay tank yew."

Akim raises his brows. "Pardon?"

I swallow and try again. "I didn't say thank you! I was too busy eating, and I—"

"That is thank you enough," he interrupts. "As a chef, watching people enjoy your food is as much gratitude as you need. Fuck knows I don't get any from the Big Bad Wolf upstairs."

Now that my hunger is more under control, I can see this opportunity for what it is: a chance to make an ally.

I push my bowl away slightly, putting some distance between myself and the delectable smells. I need to focus.

"How did you come to work for Timofey, anyway?" I say casually.

"Oh, you know. In the usual way," he says. "I disappointed my parents by going to culinary school, answered an ad, and all these years later, here I am."

"I don't know what kind of parent would be disappointed in having a child who was a chef."

"The shitty kind."

I nod in agreement. "Your work should be respected."

He gives me a genuine smile, and I'm struck by how handsome Akim is. Not in an otherworldly, godly way like Timofey. But he has a kind face and symmetrically balanced features. Plus, he can cook. That's another point or two right there, easy. Ashley would eat him alive if she could ditch her dealer for long enough to have eyes for another man.

"Do you like working here?" I ask. "I mean, Timofey doesn't seem like the…respectful type."

He snorts. "You can say that again. I am criminally underappreciated around here."

"I think a lot of *criminal* things are going on under this roof."

Akim turns to me, his brown eyes searching. When he speaks again, his voice is soft and serious. "What are you really asking me, Piper?"

I'm not completely sure I can trust this man, but who else am I going to trust? I highly doubt Rodion is going to become an ally anytime soon, if the cloud of death marks on his forearm is anything to go by.

Akim might be my one and only shot.

I lean in, voice low. "I'm asking how you feel about Timofey. My guess is he has plenty of enemies, and I wouldn't mind getting in touch with them."

His eyes dart over my shoulder towards the door. Seeing it empty, he leans over the island. "What are you planning?"

My heart patters nervously in my chest. "I don't have a plan. There hasn't been time for one. Timofey showed up at my house and is forcing me to work here. Then I got put in jail."

"Quite the first day of orientation."

"Is that normal?"

He shrugs. "For Timofey, anything goes."

"That's why I'm worried," I whisper. "A baby shouldn't grow up in a place like this. The lifestyle he leads… It isn't good for a kid. Benjamin will grow up to be a psychopath."

"You think any child growing up in this world will be doomed?"

"Don't you?" I ask.

He considers it for a second and then nods. "I guess you're right."

His words catch the lone, fragile feather of hope I have left, lifting it into the air.

"Would you be willing to testify against Timofey in court? I can write a report and do my best, but witnesses would help. Especially people who have known him a long time the way you have. You've probably seen a lot since you started here."

"Like what?" he asks.

"The criminal stuff. You know, crime and…drugs. Murder, maybe?"

Akim nods. His gaze is distant and unfocused. "Yeah. I've seen some stuff."

"Like what?"

I'm pressing my luck here, but the more I learn, the better. Who knows what could happen to Akim between now and a trial? He could get thrown in jail if Timofey found out he was willing to help me. He might not even make it that far.

"Where do I even start?" Akim shakes his head mournfully. "For starters, I'm here against my will, too. Once Timofey gets your claws in you, it's hard to get them out."

My stomach flips. Suddenly, I'm not as hungry as I thought I was. "You've never had a chance to escape?"

Akim leans in further, his eyes wide with fear. "He's always watching. Every time I've even considered it, he shows up. He's like a ghost. Sometimes, I wonder if he's even human."

I frown. No one will trust Akim's testimony on a trial if he's insane. And he sounds insane right now.

"He probably has cameras up," I say gently. "I'm sure that's how he knows when you've tried to escape."

Akim shakes his head and looks over his shoulder. "No. No, he can hear us. All the time. He's always watching. Always listening."

The hair at the back of my neck still tingles. "He's just a normal human, Akim. We can beat him if we—"

Before I can finish, Akim leans back and guffaws. His laughter is so loud I startle at the sound of it echoing off the high ceilings.

"What the—"

"God, you looked so scared." He wipes tears out of his eyes. "I knew that drama class in college would pay off. Who says electives are a waste of time?"

I blink. "Drama… What are you talking about?"

"I'm kidding, Piper. Obviously."

Obviously. I swallow down the bile rising in my throat.

"You were acting?" I shake my head, unable to believe it. "You didn't look like you were acting. You looked…sincere."

"I've occasionally been accused of having a dark sense of humor." He sculpts the perfect spoonful of rice, chicken, and veggies and takes a bite. "Sorry you got caught in the crosshairs. You'll get used to me, though. Everyone does eventually."

"Akim, if anything you said was even remotely true," I whisper, "you can tell me. I'm not a spy. I can try to help you if—"

"Bagpipes!" A voice yells from the entryway.

A familiar voice. Calling a familiar nickname.

Akim's face screws up in confusion. "Bagpipes? What the hell does—"

I hear footsteps on the tile and turn around just as someone steps into the doorway, wearing a pair of ripped jeans and a dangerously low-cut blouse.

Ashley throws her arms wide, a bright smile on her face. "There's my Pied Piper!"

I'm frozen in shock, unable to move.

Behind me, Akim scoffs. "Oh, jeez. Those are some unfortunate nicknames."

27

PIPER

"Wh-what are you doing here?" I ask when I'm finally able to pick my jaw up off the floor.

I don't trust my legs to hold me up, so I stay seated as Ashley crosses the kitchen to stand in front of me. She plants her hands on my shoulders and looks me up and down.

"Well, you look alright for a jailbird. Are you okay, P?"

"How do you know about that?"

"How do you think?" she asks. "Your boss called me. I guess you chose me as your emergency contact instead of Noelle? Does Noelle know? Is she mad? I bet she's mad."

Too much is happening too fast for me to keep track of it all. "Timofey called you?"

She sighs in frustration. "Yes. Good to see you know your boss's name. Now, who is actually your emergency contact? 'Cause your grandma is here, too. I'm trying to decide where you ranked me on the Phone-A-Friend list."

I angle around her to see the doorway. "What do you mean my grandma is here? *Here* here?"

"She's paying the cab driver. I left my wallet at home."

I highly doubt that's true; Ashley probably just doesn't have the cash to spare. Even if she did, she'd still let a little old lady pay her cab fare. She's kinda shameless that way.

But I still can't wrap my head around the fact that she's standing in front of me.

"What did Timofey tell you?"

"That you were arrested!" Ashley snaps. "What else? He told us you were wrongly arrested and had a panic attack. He was worried about you, so he called us in to check on you. You know, since we know you better than he does."

Did he tell them he was the reason I was wrongfully arrested?

The answer is obvious: definitely not. If he did, Ashley wouldn't be standing here talking to me; she'd be calling in favors with all of her shady friends to have him beat up.

My grandma, on the other hand, would take the beating into her own hands. There's a reason she carries such a heavy purse.

I hear muffled movement from the entryway followed by a prolonged sigh. Everything Gram does is followed by a sigh like that. Whenever I point it out, she does the same things: grabs her wide hips and says, "I've been hauling this body around for five decades longer than you've been alive. I've earned a good sigh."

She sighs again as she walks into the kitchen, her massive purse hooked around an elbow. The fake crocodile leather is cracked and peeling off the straps, but she refuses to let me or anyone else get her a new bag.

"An old bag for an old bag," she always says with a long laugh.

But my heart soars at the sight of that old bag—both of them.

"Gram!" I cross the kitchen in an instant and wrap her in a fierce hug.

She stumbles back on her heels. "You're gonna knock an old lady over. If you break my hip, they'll lock you up again. Jail isn't kind to people who assault the elderly."

I laugh, tears brimming in my eyes. It's so good to see a familiar face after the couple days I've had. "I can't believe you're here."

"I can't believe you didn't call me." She pushes me away and swats my arm. "What in the hell were you thinking, going to jail and not phoning me? I should have been your first call!"

Officer Rooney didn't let me call anyone. I was bustled through the back door of the precinct and straight into a holding cell. But I keep that information to myself.

I look at my feet. "Sorry. I was—I wasn't thinking clearly."

Gram hesitates for only a second before her hand cups my cheek. Her skin is like paper crumpled too many times, soft and dry. I lean into the familiarity.

"No, I suppose you weren't," she says softly. "Are you okay, dear?"

I curl my hand over hers and squeeze. "I am now."

A moment of understanding passes between us.

Gram was there the first time I experienced claustrophobia after I came to live with her, the first time I had a panic attack when I wasn't in any immediate danger. We didn't have money for a therapist, but she did her best to talk me through it. To help me avoid my triggers. She's the reason I can stand being in a small shower or an elevator. Her patience and understanding made all the difference for me.

We never could tackle my fear of being in a car, though. For good reason.

That's where it all began.

"So, Timofey called you?" I ask. "Or did Ashley?"

I hope it's Ashley. I want Ashley to have been the one to call Gram. If she called, it means Timofey might not know where Gram lives. It means she might still be outside his range of influence. It gives me time to figure out how to protect her from—

"Is that your boss's name?" Gram asks. "Timothy? Yes, he's the one who called."

Shit. I do my best to hide the dread pooling in my stomach.

Ashley leans against the counter. I see her sneaking glances at Akim as he cleans the kitchen like we don't exist. "The reason we showed up together is because your grandma called me. She took the taxi to my place and then picked me up and brought me here. I would have driven, but—"

"Gas is too expensive right now for all that," Gram offers kindly so Ashley doesn't have to think up an excuse.

I squeeze Gram's hand again. A silent thank you. She's one of the few people I've confided in about Ashley's issues and how much I want to help her. It's not like Gram can really afford to be here, either, but she still tried to take care of Ashley on her way to take care of me.

That matters.

Overcome with gratitude that she's standing in front of me, I pull Gram into another hug. "I'm so glad to see you." Ashley clears her throat, and I smile back at her. "*Both* of you."

"Yeah, well, it's nice your boss called us since you clearly weren't going to." Ashley picks up my fork and takes a bite of my leftover lunch. "Holy shit. This is incredible."

Akim doesn't say anything, but I see him smile as he loads the dishwasher.

God, how do I tell Ashley to stay far, far away from anyone inside the walls of this house without her doing the exact opposite?

I file that worry away for later perusal. One issue at a time.

"I can't believe Timofey called you. I was going to, but—"

But my life is spiraling out of control and I'm trying to get my bearings and figure out if my new boss is going to kill me.

Can Timofey be so bad if he's bringing my friends and family here to comfort me after a panic attack, though?

I'm hesitant to be grateful towards him, especially after I thanked him for freeing me from the jail cell he placed me in earlier. But I can't help it. My heart has long since stopped listening to reason.

"Whatever. I'm just glad you're both here." I lead Gram to a barstool and wrap an arm around each of them. "Can I get you anything? A drink, or something?"

Ashley opens her mouth to respond, but instead of forming words, her jaw just hangs there. Her thin brows arch and a cross between a shocked exhale and a dreamy sigh wheezes out of her lungs. Her eyes are locked over my shoulder, and I know exactly what she is looking at.

Correction: I know *who* she is looking at.

Sure enough, when I turn around, I see Timofey sauntering into the kitchen. He's undone the top two buttons of his shirt, giving the barest peek of his collarbone and dark chest hair. His hair is tousled from the motorcycle ride.

But that's par for the course at this point. What's weird is that, instead of his characteristic scowl, he's smiling.

Smiling.

I've seen him plenty of times—in the middle of the night, no less—but I'm still floored. I'm half-expecting to see a pig fly past the window any second.

A few changes are all it takes to transform him from surly, intimidating CEO-slash-bonebreaker to a dazzling man of the people. If he was running for office right now, he'd get my vote. Hell, he'd get a lot more than that. I'd start a scandal for this version of him.

Timofey Viktorov is *hot*. I know for a fact Ashley is taking notice.

"Glad the two of you made it safely," Timofey rumbles.

Gram moves to stand up, but Timofey hurries over and grabs her hand. Then the man *bows*, like he is royalty or something. Gram's cheeks turn pink. She's charmed, just like that.

"Thanks for having us," she murmurs in a daze. "Your home is lovely."

Ashley snorts. "Understatement. It's fucking incredible."

I elbow her in the ribs. Timofey and I are far beyond the point of first impressions, but I still want Ashley to be on her best behavior. For all she knows, she is standing in my place of work, talking to my boss. She should know better.

She claps a hand over her mouth. "Sorry. Potty mouth. Good thing I'm not taking care of the baby, right? He'd grow up talking like a sailor."

"Speaking of, where is the little angel?" Gram snaps her fingers together like a greedy crab. "I need baby snuggles."

"Sleeping." There's a hard edge to Timofey's voice that wasn't there a second ago. I think I'm the only one who notices it.

Gram nods in understanding. "And you can't wake a sleeping baby. Everyone knows that. Really, you should be sleeping, Dad. Those are the rules. You sleep when the baby sleeps."

"If only that was possible," Timofey chuckles. "I wouldn't want to be asleep now, anyway. I'm excited to meet a few of the people closest to Piper. I know how much she loves both of you. I'd hate to miss the opportunity to get to know each other."

Timofey's gaze flicks to me for just a second and everything clicks.

Gram isn't here because Timofey was worried about me.

He didn't call Ashley to comfort me.

It's a threat.

I could almost laugh. At myself for being so naive, and at Timofey for being so predictable.

But it's hard to laugh when two of the people I care about most in the world are in danger—because of *me.*

28

PIPER

Anger and panic race through my limbs. I'm fidgety, nervous, crawling out of my skin. I can't stand here for another second.

"Timofey." My voice comes out sharper than I mean it to. Gram jumps in surprise. "Can I talk to you for a second?"

He frowns, feigning confusion. "Everyone just got here. We can sit down and chat together. Does anyone want anything to drink?"

Again, Ashley opens her mouth to respond, but I cut her off. "It'll only take a second. If you don't mind."

Timofey gives me a warm smile, but it doesn't reach his eyes. Those are as cold and distant as ever.

I walk past him into the hallway and keep going until I see an open doorway. I step into what turns out to be a library. I turn to the door just as Timofey pulls it closed behind him.

"It's rude to leave guests waiting, Piper."

I snort. "It's probably worse to threaten them, don't you think?"

"I'm not threatening my guests."

"Aren't you?" I ask, throwing my arms wide. "They're here to remind me what I have to lose, aren't they? You're doing this to scare me into obeying you."

He smirks. "My point exactly. You just proved it."

"Proved what?"

"I'm not threatening them," he says. "I'm threatening *you*."

I'm not sure why I'm surprised he's admitting it. Timofey has done a lot worse than make threats. Officer Rooney confirmed he has killed people. I shouldn't be shocked he's open about the depths of his depravity.

And yet I am.

"Leave them alone. I already told you I would do what you ask."

"That was after I'd made the calls. I didn't want to cancel on them just because you'd finally decided to be reasonable. Plus, in my line of work, I like a little insurance."

"Is that how you view people? Like pawns you can manipulate and sacrifice to your pleasure?"

His chin dimples as he thinks. A shadow of stubble I didn't notice yesterday covers his chin and jawline. "That's exactly how I view people."

"You're disgusting. That's horrible."

He shrugs. "It's better than being broke because I'm too busy bailing everyone else in my life out of trouble. Or has Ashley paid you back for the bail bondsman you hired six months ago?"

I blink at him. No one knows about that. Not even Noelle. I swore to Ashley it would stay between us.

"How do you—"

"Once I knew your friend had some run-ins with the law, I had Rooney look her up. Just like I expected, you had yet another financial dependent."

"I bailed her out once. That doesn't make her a financial—"

"Three times." Timofey holds up three fingers and twists them slowly in front of me, showing me his scarred knuckles. "The adage is 'three strikes and you're out,' but it looks like Ashley is on her fourth. I wonder what kind of fun drugs police would have to find in her car for her to get locked up for good?"

My heart stops.

Time stops.

"Don't."

"How are you going to stop me?" He smiles pleasantly. I swear he's having a good time with this. This is fun for him.

"I… I told you I'd do what you asked."

"And I told you I like a little insurance. Luckily, you come with plenty of weaknesses." He shakes his head. "Why do you keep so many parasites around you?"

"You're confused," I say, brimming over with mock sincerity. "I know you can't understand complex human emotions, but those aren't parasites. They're my friends and family. Maybe you've heard of them?"

He rolls his eyes. "If they stop you from living your life, it doesn't matter if they're blood, chosen family, or anything in between; they're parasites. They're sucking you dry, Piper, and you don't even see it."

"The only one sucking me dry is you," I spit.

He stares at me for a second before amusement creeps across his face. "There's a joke I could make here, but I don't want to be crass while your grandmother is in the house."

I grimace. "In your sick, sadistic dreams."

Suddenly, Timofey closes the distance between us. His chest brushes mine, and I have to lean my head back to look into his eyes.

His vibrant, glowing blue eyes. There's a little extra fire in them now.

If I thought he was capable of such an emotion, I'd almost think it was…*desire.*

"You won't ever have to make that choice," he says softly. His whisper is fine grit sandpaper against my skin. "I'll force you to do a lot of things, Piper, but never that. When it happens, it will be your choice."

When it happens?

When?

I want to call him a cocky bastard and shove him away, but I seem to have lost control of my body. I'm nothing but a heartbeat now.

In my chest.

Between my legs.

The longer Timofey looks down his nose at me, the louder the beating grows.

Then, all at once, he turns and walks out of the room.

29

PIPER

I gather myself with a few deep breaths, then I follow Timofey back into the arena. That's what the kitchen is, after all: a battleground.

When I step into the hallway, I can hear Ashley's high-pitched, flirty laugh.

"Shit," I mutter, breaking into a jog.

Timofey and I walk in together. Ashley is standing at the stove next to Akim, both of their hands wrapped around the same pan handle.

"It's all in the wrist," Akim says, brushing his finger over Ashley's too-pale, too-skinny forearm. "More of a flick than a toss."

Ashley bites her lower lip like she's concentrating, but I know she's trying to make a sexy face. "Okay. Here I go. One, two—"

On three, she and Akim shake the skillet together and flip a pancake in the air. It lands clumsily on the side of the pan and batter sprays across the stove.

Ashley slouches into Akim's chest. "Damn it. I don't understand. I've been told I have very limber wrists."

"By whom?" Akim asks.

She looks back over her shoulder, tucking a strand of hair behind her ear. "Ex-boyfriends."

My eyes practically bug out of my head. Timofey makes a soft snort in the back of his throat.

I stomp around him and grab the pan out of Ashley's hand. "You did not just say that in front of my Gram," I hiss.

Akim turns away, muttering, "She definitely did."

"Say what?" Gram asks.

I look over to see she is doing one of the crosswords she carries around in her purse.

"Nothing, Gram. Do you want a—" I look at what Akim and Ashley were making. "A pancake? Why are you making pancakes?"

"I make them and freeze them for quick breakfast," Akim explains, but I'm not really listening to him. As far as I'm concerned, he can disappear.

Gram nods. "Sure, I'll have one. But you make it, Ashley. I want to taste the love in it."

"I cook with plenty of love." Akim sounds almost offended.

Gram fixes him with a knowing smirk. "I'm worried you've wasted most of your love on Miss Ashley here."

Turns out Gram isn't as much of a prude as I thought.

Akim actually blushes at that. I cannot believe this man works for Timofey. He's the goofiest killer's sidekick I could ever imagine.

"I have some other stuff to do anyway." Akim steps around Ashley and nods in Timofey's direction. "I'd like to talk to you when you have a minute, actually, Tim."

I study Akim. What I wouldn't give to crack his head open and see what he's thinking.

Then he looks at me. Just for a second. A flash of acknowledgement before he averts his gaze.

And I don't need to crack his head open. I don't need to read his mind.

I know exactly what he's going to tell Timofey.

And I have to stop him.

"It's rude to leave your guests," I blurt. In the corner of my eye, Timofey arches a brow, but I plow on. "You said that it was rude to leave guests. I already took you away once."

I can tell he'd put me in my place if Ashley and Gram weren't here. As it is, it goes against his plan to get on their good side.

He smiles so easily and believably that I can't help but shiver. "You're right. We'll talk business later, Akim. Right now, pancakes."

Ashley claps her hands and slides closer to Akim. "You can help me work on my hand-eye coordination."

I still want to make sure the two of them never, ever become a thing, because Ashley's version of hand-eye coordination when it involves a cute man quickly becomes something more like penis-mouth coordination.

More than that, though, I want to make sure Akim can't tell Timofey what we talked about over lunch.

How fucking stupid am I? I told Timofey I would go along with his plan and obey him. Five minutes later, I'm confessing to his cook that I want to get him thrown in prison.

I turn to the stove and scrap the now-burnt bit of pancake Ashley tried to flip. I pour in some more batter and watch the bubbles form as pieces of a plan coming together in my mind.

"What's the upper-left keyboard key?" Gram asks the room. "It's a crossword clue, and I'm not good with computers."

"Delete," Akim answers quickly and incorrectly.

"Don't listen to Akim," Timofey chuckles. "There's a reason I hired him to be a chef, not a tech guru."

"It's because, like you, he also likes the taste of love in his cooking." Akim blows kisses in Timofey's direction, and my stomach drops.

They are good friends. I was talking to one of Timofey's *very good friends* about betraying him. There's no way Akim isn't going to give me up the second he gets the chance.

Timofey waves him off. "The answer is E-S-C."

Gram gasps in delight. "It fits! Thank you!"

I ignore the pang I feel at the realization that Gram let Timofey help her with her puzzle. She never lets me help. She says it's as good as looking up the answers in the back of the book.

Apparently, that's not important in the face of the looming threat that is Timofey Viktorov. Akim is going to tell him that I'm still planning to get Benjamin away from him and report him to the police. When he finds out, he'll retaliate. Maybe against me, but probably through a proxy like Ashley or Gram.

The only option is to get them out of here. Now.

No time for subtlety. I need to get us all out of here before Timofey finds out. We flee, go straight to the police, and hope for the best.

Sure, Timofey has Officer Rooney on his side, but they can't take on an entire precinct, can they?

I hope not.

If anyone can, it would be Timofey. But I have to believe he has some limits. I have to believe I can fight back.

"I hear Benjamin crying," Akim says suddenly. "I should go—"

Ashley grabs his arm. "Isn't that Piper's job? She should take care of it."

I toss her a look, but she's too distracted by the handsome cook to notice.

Akim shakes his head. "She's cooking, so apparently, we've switched jobs today. I'll take care of the wee one."

Timofey slides his stool away from the bar and stands up. "I'll come. Piper's grandmother is too good at this crossword puzzle for me to keep up with her, anyway."

Gram actually giggles, and I grit my teeth.

Timofey has gotten under everyone's skin one way or another. If I don't do something to remove him now, it might be too late.

When he leaves the room with Akim, I'll hustle Ashley and Gram out as quickly as I can. They'll be confused about why we need to run, but we don't have a choice.

I'm in the midst of planning our route out of the house when Akim shakes his head. "You stay here, Tim. I'll handle Benjamin and be right back."

Akim glances at me. It's almost like he's reading my thoughts now.

He knows if they both leave this room, I'll run. He plays the happy-go-lucky sidekick, but Akim is far smarter than he looks.

Timofey scowls at him, probably pissed at being challenged in public. But Akim leans in, and this is it.

He's going to tell him.

Panic like I've never known flashes through me.

Every half-baked plan I've put together in the last few minutes goes straight out the window as I do the only thing I can think of.

I grab the oil dispenser next to the stove, pop the lid, and "accidentally" drop it directly onto the burner.

Instantly, a column of fire erupts in front of me. Flames lick the underside of the cabinets, browning the wood.

My plan was to ruin the pancakes and force Akim to come cook instead. I wanted to buy myself some time, not start a wildfire.

But here we are. Beggars can't be choosers.

"Fire!" Ashley screeches. "Fire!"

Gram is shouting incoherently. Akim jumps over the island and snatches up a fire extinguisher from under the sink. Timofey stands in the midst of it all, beautiful and unmoving.

I back away, trying to escape the mayhem, but the flames follow me.

The entire left side of my body is oddly warm. I keep moving away to get out of Akim's way so he can battle the flames, but I can't seem to escape the heat.

Ashley is safe at the far end of the kitchen, but Gram is gathering her belongings into her purse instead of fleeing.

"Get back, Gram!" I yell. "Leave the crossword book and—"

Gram looks up at me, and her face turns whiter than I've ever seen. She presses her liver-spotted hands to her cheeks and screams. "Help her! Help!"

I look back to Ashley to make sure she's okay when I realize Gram is talking about me.

That's when I look down and see the flames licking up the sleeve of my sweater.

30

TIMOFEY

The look on Akim's face says he has something he wants to share with the class. I'm mildly preoccupied with Piper's friend and grandmother eating out of the palm of my hand, but to be honest, that's child's play. So easy it's borderline offensive.

I can spare a minute for him to unload whatever fucking nonsense is bothering him.

But before I can tell him that he should never tell me to "stay here" again unless he wants his tongue cut out, there's a roar behind me.

I whirl around to see flames shoot up in a solid column of bright orange light from the oven. Piper is lost in the glow. Things crackle and burn.

Akim lunges over the island as Piper stumbles back from the stove. She's watching everyone else, checking on her addict friend and her grandma. She's so busy worrying about everyone but her that she doesn't see that she took a bit of the fire with her.

The flicker takes hold of the sweater. It grows exponentially until it's crawling up to her shoulder in a matter of seconds.

Everyone else is losing their damn minds. Transfixed and screaming and frozen by fear.

But I've spent a lifetime learning to ignore the voice in my head that says to freeze in place. I do one thing: *act.*

I hurtle past Akim and Ashley, who are both arguing over what to do next.

"Fire extinguisher!" Akim shouts, pointing under the sink.

Ashley grabs the sprayer in the sink. "Here's water!"

"You can't use water on an oil fire!" Akim swats it out of her hand and shoves her back. "Move!"

"Put the damn fire out!" I bark over my shoulder.

Piper is still staring at her arm like she's watching a scary movie. Like the action is somehow disconnected from her reality.

In the chaos of Akim spraying the fire extinguisher and Ashley and Gram screaming, the moment crystallizes. Piper is in front of me and nothing else matters.

I grab her and yank her towards me. For some reason I can't imagine, she resists.

"Piper!" I bellow her name, and she looks at me.

It all happens in a quarter of a second. An eighth of a second. Less.

Her eyes meet mine, understanding passes between us, and she follows me.

I drag her no more than a couple feet away from the stove and tear her sweater off of her body. I'm pumping with adrenaline, so the weakened material shreds and rips beneath my fingers like it's made of wet paper.

I stomp out the flaming pieces of fabric on the floor and start smacking out the embers still clinging to her. I feel my palms burning, but it's distant and unimportant. Pain is a signal. Nothing more. I choose to ignore it.

I can't focus on the angry red skin on her arm. All I can think about is getting the fire put out. Removing the danger. *Making sure she's safe.*

I twist her auburn hair over her good shoulder. Somehow, none of the flames touched it. Maybe it's because her hair is like a living flame already. An eternal blaze of gold and red when the light hits it just right.

"Are we good?" Akim asks, turning around with the extinguisher still in hand. Smoke is billowing from the stove and white fog fills the kitchen from the extinguisher.

Then, *finally*, the smoke alarm starts going off.

"Fucking hell," Akim grumbles. "I'm on it."

He hustles around to find a chair and get to the alarm. I move Piper towards the sink.

She's in nothing more than a thin, see-through tank top, but she doesn't seem to notice. I try not to notice, either. I mostly fail at that.

"Arm under here," I order, flipping the faucet to lukewarm. "We need to cool down your skin."

She glances back over her shoulder. "Is my Gram—"

All at once, I grab her face and force her to look in my eyes. "Everyone else in this room is fine. You aren't. Because you were too busy worrying about everyone else."

She frowns. "I wasn't—"

"Get your arm under the water before I have to fucking force you."

Her jaw clenches, but she turns to the sink and does as I ask.

About goddamn time.

As soon as the water pours over her arm, she winces. I can see her jaw quivering from the force with which she's grinding her teeth.

"Does that hurt?"

"It doesn't feel great," she grits out.

"Stay here for fifteen minutes and it will feel better."

"Maybe I should…" She swallows, her eyes darting side to side without ever looking at me. "Maybe I should go to the hospital? My Gram could drive me."

"If you need to go to the hospital, I'll take you."

She frowns. "You don't have to take care of me. I can take care of—"

"Don't finish that sentence," I snarl. "If it wasn't for me, you'd still be standing in the corner with your arm on fire. Actually, if it wasn't for me, you'd be dead in an alley. Clearly, you can't take care of yourself."

"There was a lot going on! I was distracted!"

I nod in sarcastic agreement. "Okay, so you can only take care of yourself when everything is going perfectly and nothing stressful is happening. That's very realistic."

"Why didn't you just let me burn up?" she hisses. "That would have saved you a lot of trouble."

"It would have taken weeks to get the smell of burning skin and hair out of the curtains. I saved you for the maids' sake."

She stares at me for a second, her nostrils flared, a novel's worth of unspoken words hiding behind her full lips. Then she glances down at the water running over her arm. "I don't need to go to the hospital. I'm fine."

"I'm aware. Lucky for you, I put the fire out before it could get through the sweater. You have a nasty scald, but it'll heal up fine."

"Are you a doctor now, too?" she mumbles.

She isn't so far off. With the kind of life I lead, I've been hurt plenty of times when running to the hospital wasn't an option. The police would have put two and two together if someone was killed in a shootout the same night I showed up in the emergency room with a bullet graze.

The point is, I know how to handle fire and blood.

The shrill alarm finally stops. Akim climbs down from the chair and turns to me. "What now?"

"Bandages, antibiotic ointment, and pain medication," I list. "All of it's in the—"

"Linen closet outside the guest bathroom," he finishes, already moving towards the hallway. "I know."

As soon as he's gone, Gram and Ashley step forward to fill the opening.

"What in the hell happened?" Ashley says in disbelief. "How the fuck did you set pancakes on fire, girl? Out of the two of us, you're the cook."

Piper snorts. "Making frozen meals at home doesn't make me a cook."

"It does as far as I'm concerned."

Piper waves her away with her good arm. "I'm fine."

"You were on fire," her grandmother reminds her, as if we somehow forgot.

Piper has to lean forward and arch her back to look over her shoulder and meet the old woman's eyes. "I'm *fine*, Gram."

She's not wrong about that. Her jeans mold to every inch of her long, toned legs. With her oversized sweater in ashes on the floor, I'm convinced she should wear nothing but tissue paper thin tank tops from this day forward. I can even make out the dimples pressed into each side of her lower back.

My mind fills with images of throwing her on top of the island, parting her legs, and devouring her until she screams again and again. She'd taste sweet, I know. She'd taste like fucking honey and sin.

"Fine" is an understatement.

Gram makes a clicking noise in the back of her throat. "Nuh-uh. Nope. You don't get to catch on fire and say you are fine. We're going to the hospital."

"I don't need to go to the hospital."

"I'll call a cab," Gram says. "Or maybe we can borrow a car from you, Timofey?"

"Her burns aren't serious. But if you all insist, I can drive her and the two of you to—"

"No!" Piper jerks upright, pulling away from the sink to face her Gram. "I am fine, Gram. Listen to me: I. Am. Fine."

The woman's already creased face wrinkles even further. "I think you should get checked out just in case. You have no idea what kind of damage this could do. Or scars it could leave. The thought of you in danger...I can't handle it."

"You handled it fine for the first ten years of my life."

The words land like a physical blow. I actually watch Piper's grandma stumble back against the edge of the counter like she's been shot. Her lips move around words she can't give voice to.

"Don't act so surprised. You knew my parents were shit. You knew what your daughter was doing to me," Piper hisses, a venom I've never heard before seething through her words. "And you let it happen. You ignored it until I found my way to your doorstep and begged for help. Until my claustrophobia was so bad I had to sleep on top of my blankets because if I didn't, I'd have nightmares about being choked and smothered. So *now*, when I'm telling you I'm fine, *you should probably listen.*"

The chaos of a few moments ago is sucked out like through a vacuum. The room is void.

Frankly, I'm enjoying the sudden reappearance of Piper's backbone, but I can tell Ashley and Gram are shaken to their core. I'd imagine they would be.

We might've just witnessed the first time Piper Quinn has ever stood up for herself.

"Piper," Gram finally says, her name coming out in a whisper. "Piper, sweetheart, you can't—I didn't—"

"You two shouldn't have come here," Piper interrupts. "This is my job. My place of work. I want to be professional, and I can't do that when you're showing up with crosswords and flirting with my coworkers."

"Hey!" Ashley complains. "We came here because your *boss* asked. Take it up with him."

Piper's spine stiffens. "I will. But *you* should have checked with me first."

"You were in jail! Were we supposed to leave a message with the officer manning the front desk?"

"Just leave," Piper says firmly. She tacks on a "please," but it's pure courtesy.

Her grandma looks deflated. There's no fight left in her. Ashley, however, narrows her eyes. "I'll call you later, Pipe," she says. The promise sounds more like a threat.

Piper nods. "Fine."

The two women pack up and leave, tossing glances over their shoulder as they head toward the front door.

Then it closes, and they're gone.

31

TIMOFEY

The moment the two women are out of sight, Piper sags. All the fight vanishes from her face and she looks sad and broken again, the way she did when I first found her. "They don't have a car. I should get them back in here and—"

"I already texted the driver. He's bringing the car around now."

Piper winces. I'm not sure if it's the memory of what she just said or her burn, but I nudge her back to the still-running water. "You have ten more minutes left."

She bends over the sink again and moans when the water flows down her arm. "Ouch."

I think she's going to say something else, but her lips are pressed so tightly together they're turning white. With every passing second, she's leaning further into the sink, twisting her face away from me so I can't see her.

Then I see her shoulders shaking.

I grab her chin and angle her face towards me. "You're crying."

"Don't touch me." She jerks her chin out of my hand.

"Then don't hide from me."

"I can't!" she explodes, splashing water across the singed remains of the food on the stove. "I *can't* hide from you. That's the problem. I just insulted one of my best friends and my grandma because that was the only way I could get them away from you."

"You didn't need to get them away from me."

"Yes, I fucking did." She nods without an ounce of doubt. "I'm sure Akim will make that clear to you soon enough."

I remember the moments before the fire. When Akim was staring at me, something unspoken in his eyes.

"What happened?" I growl.

Piper scoffs softly. "You're already mad and you don't know what happened. I knew I was right to get them out of here."

"Piper."

"Fine, I'll tell you before Akim can. Maybe it will soften the blow. I doubt it, but maybe." She takes a deep breath and spills. "When I was alone with Akim, I asked him if he'd be willing to testify against you in front of a judge."

I blink at her, stunned by the stupidity of this plan. "And you thought that would work?"

"I thought there was no way anyone who worked for you could find you appealing. What's to like?" she snaps. "But I was wrong. You and Akim are clearly friends, and now, he's going to tell you I was still trying to get Benjamin away from you and have you arrested."

My brows arch as realization sets in. "You started that fire on purpose."

Her face flushes with embarrassment. "I needed a distraction."

"Arson will do that."

"Fire wasn't the plan," she retorts, unable to stop herself from bickering with me. "I was going to ruin the pancakes, maybe cause a little smoke. I'd get my grandma and Ashley out while you were distracted, and—"

"And what? What was going to come next, Piper? Where were you going to go? What were you going to do?"

Her hazel eyes flare nearly as bright as the flames that almost engulfed her. "I don't know."

I bring my hands together in a slow clap. "Marvelous plan. I'm in awe."

"I didn't have a lot of time to think."

"Jail should have given you plenty of time."

"It's hard to think when you're having a panic attack!"

In the midst of our back and forth, we moved closer. She's a breath away from me now. Her green eyes are narrowed to slits. But the longer I stare down at her, the softer her expression becomes. Her indignation fades to something more akin to acceptance.

"Just… don't hurt them," she begs softly. "I won't take Benjamin or turn you in. I won't—I'll do whatever you ask. Just please leave them alone."

Her hair is still twisted over her shoulder, the ends curling against her chest and collarbone. I reach out and twist one lock around my finger.

"I think you're stupid for sacrificing yourself for those people."

She parts her lips to argue, but I tug gently on her hair, pulling her head to the side. Her neck arches, and I wonder what her pulse would feel like against my mouth.

"If you don't look out for yourself, no one will."

"You did." She seems suddenly nervous. "You…you saved me, I mean. A few times now. It's becoming a habit."

"A bad habit," I growl. "Don't count on it again."

Again, Piper parts her lips to respond. And again, I wonder what she would taste like. I pull tighter on her hair, twisting the red strands around my fist.

"If you make any further attempt to betray me, I won't hesitate to retaliate."

"But you said—"

"Not against them," I sneer. One sharp tug and I could snap her neck, yet she's still worried about everyone else. I lean close, my forehead nearly pressed to hers as I whisper. "I'll retaliate against you, Piper. If you cross me again, *you* will suffer. Fire will seem like a kiss on the cheek compared to what I'm capable of doing."

32

PIPER

"I think I got everything," Akim says. "Bandages, ointment, and... wait, what was the third—? Where did everyone go? And what are you two doing?"

Timofey still has his hand tangled in my hair when I look over and see Akim biting back a grin in the doorway.

"Sorry," he continues, not sounding apologetic in the least. "I didn't mean to interrupt. I'll just—"

"Leave the supplies here and fuck off somewhere else," Timofey finishes for him.

I can't find any words. They've evaporated in the sudden heat coursing through my body, a heat that has absolutely nothing to do with the bonfire I created and everything to do with the man standing in front of me.

Akim drops everything on the island, as ordered, but he's stealing glances at us all the while, which I'm pretty sure Timofey is not so fond of.

I want to shove Timofey away, but he isn't in any hurry to extricate himself from me. He slides his hand out of my hair and lets it fall on my good shoulder. He nudges me back towards the sink. "Your arm isn't in the water anymore."

He's right. My arm is hovering over the sink, but it shifted out of the water without me realizing.

To be fair, I was a little distracted.

He gently shifts my arm under the faucet and then moves away to sort through the supplies Akim brought.

He isn't helping you, I tell myself. *He's just fixing the mess he made.*

I swear I'm going to get that phrase tattooed on my forearm so my lady bits don't quiver every time Timofey does something "nice" for me.

All at once, I realize Akim is whispering behind me. Before I can process any of it, Timofey waves him off.

"I know."

"You know?" Akim asks, glancing at me. "She told you? For real?"

Timofey sighs. "I'll take things from here, Akim. Go check on Benjamin."

"Pavel was with him when I was grabbing the supplies." When he sees the look on Timofey's face, he continues, "But I'll go make sure he's not trying to feed him pieces of cereal again."

Akim skips around the corner with an undeserved pep in his step.

"You two are friends, but he's still afraid of you," I observe.

"Everyone is afraid of me."

"Lovely thought," I mutter sarcastically. "You should have that engraved on your tombstone."

Without warning, Timofey whips around and turns the water off. He wraps a linen towel around my arm and directs me to the island.

His gentle touch is shocking enough that I don't resist. Not even when he grips me around the waist and places me on the countertop.

"Take these." He folds two white pills into my hand.

"What are they?"

"Poison."

I roll my eyes. "Hilarious."

"They're Tylenol, Piper. Just take them. You're going to be hurting a lot in a little while if you don't."

I scrutinize the pills as if I'll be able to detect anything untoward. With all the drug addiction I've seen in work and my personal life, I'm afraid to overdose on vitamins. Plus, if there's one thing I've learned as a woman on this Earth, it's to never take the unknown pills a man hands to you.

"Is there a bottle I can look at?"

"If I wanted to incapacitate you, I wouldn't need drugs to do it." He flips my arm over to apply the antibiotic treatment.

Fair enough. If these drugs do knock me out, I'd probably rather be unconscious for whatever sick kind of torture he has planned, anyway.

I pop the pills in my mouth, and Timofey slides a glass towards me.

It's amazing how he can be everywhere at once. He anticipates needs, gracefully solves problems, and always knows what to do. If he wasn't using his skillset for evil, he could rule the world.

On second thought, he might do that anyway.

The notion sends a shiver up my spine.

"You're in pain."

I shake my head. "Not right now. It's just an overflow of adrenaline." And possibly some other "feel good" hormones I don't need to mention. Timofey's calloused hands on my skin are doing strange things to my processing center. He's like a drug in his own right.

"You've had a big day. Started a new job, got thrown in jail, had a panic attack. And now, you caught on fire." He shakes his head. "You'll be dead on your feet tonight."

I narrow my eyes. "Is that a threat?"

His mouth twists into a smirk that twists my insides right along with it. "Are you always on guard like this, or am I special?"

"You're special all right," I murmur. Then the joke fades and reality creeps in. "But this is normal for me. You might not believe me since the first time we met I walked into a dark alley without looking around, but that was a fluke. I'm usually on high alert."

"Because of your shitty parents, I presume." When I look up, his blue eyes meet mine. "Your words, not mine."

I nod. "I know. Either way, they're the right words. Shitty, *shitty* parents."

You'd think that, working in Child Protective Services, I'd see enough terrible situations to feel a little grateful for my own parents. Maybe extend them a little grace.

But no. They rank right up there amongst the worst I've ever encountered.

"And I'm assuming that's why you lived with your grandmother."

My heart stutters. "What? How do you—I didn't say that."

"Yes, you did," he says. "You yelled it, as a matter of fact."

"Oh. Right."

I was so concerned with getting Gram and Ashley away from Timofey that I wasn't thinking straight. I said the first things that came to mind. They were deeply hurtful, which was kind of the point. Still…

Shame coils around my chest, squeezing tight.

I need to call Gram tonight. And Ashley, too. Telling them what is going on here might not be safe, but I have to explain myself somehow. I have to—

"It was good seeing you stand up for yourself," Timofey says, interrupting my thought spiral. "I've never seen that side of you before."

"You're the one who ripped my sweater off. I think you've seen all the sides of me now."

His hand stutters against my skin. It's the tiniest outward sign of a reaction from him, but I cling to it. Somewhere under all the layers of armor, he's a real person.

I think.

"Not all of them." His voice is soft but stable. When he brings a bandage up to wrap over my arm, I flinch so hard I almost fall off the countertop.

If he's looking for a sign I'm a real person, there's yet another one. I'm embarrassingly human at the worst possible moments.

"I'm not actually going to kill you. Relax."

"Easy for you to say. I'm sure relaxing isn't hard when everyone is afraid of you. Isn't that what you said?"

He nods. "I did. But I'm also not afraid of anything. Not anymore."

I snort. "You're such a liar. Everyone is afraid of something."

"Even if I was, it'd be nothing compared to you. Few people fear things the way you fear being enclosed." He opens his mouth to say something more, then seems to rethink it. His gaze softens, but I can still see the tick in his jaw when he does finally ask. "Something happened to you, didn't it?"

I run my tongue over my teeth. It's hard to look in control while I feel like a small child sitting in a therapist's chair. "So what if it did? Am I supposed to be embarrassed?"

"Only if you choose to be."

I shiver. The hairs on the back of my neck prick up almost painfully. "Why is anyone afraid of anything? Who knows?"

"You do. Yet another hint you let slip out when you were on fire."

I chew on my lower lip, turning away as Timofey wraps my arm.

He's right. I did let that slip. I remember it now because I can easily recall the look of shock and pain that crossed Gram's face.

I'm not sure I'll ever forget her expression when I blamed her for my claustrophobia, for leaving me with my parents when she knew they weren't taking proper care of me. More importantly, I'll never forget that I'm the one who put that expression there.

God, I need to call her tonight.

I need to fix this.

"Your mother hurt you," he guesses. "She locked you—"

"It was nothing," I snap before he can finish.

I can't let him keep talking. Somehow, he can guess everything. And if he says it out loud, I won't be able to hide my expression. The truth of it will be written all over my face and it will be yet another thing he can use against me. It will be another fragile piece of my mind and my life that he can hold in his hand and crumple like trash.

"I just said the first thing I could think of to get her out of here," I lie. "She probably doesn't even know what I was talking about."

Timofey doesn't react, but his silence is loaded. He knows I'm full of shit. And he knows I know that he knows I'm full of shit.

Which is why he continues into his own story without preamble.

"I had a foster father who locked us in the broom closet when we were bad."

I go perfectly still. Why is he telling me this? Is it real? It can't be. It's just another trick. Another manipulation.

But when I glance over, the look on his face seems earnest. I see the sharpness in his green eyes. The anger. The pain of authentic memory.

"Being 'bad' in that house didn't require much." He shakes his head and scoffs. "If he was in a mood, anything could set him off. I was locked in the closet for two days once because I dropped a cracker on the floor. He didn't even give me a chance to grab it before he snatched me up and shoved me in the closet. When that lock clicked, I thought I would die in there."

"I thought you weren't scared of anything." It's a low blow, but I don't know how to respond to this vulnerable side of Timofey. I don't want to fall for another trick.

"I'm not now. I was then."

His words are heartbreakingly haunted. My job as a CPS agent is to protect children. It's to give them the best shot at a childhood, at a safe, healthy life. But we don't always get it right. The system has cracks, and sometimes, kids slip through them.

Was Timofey one of those?

My heart shatters at the thought of the frightened little boy he once was. "I'm sorry you went through that," I murmur.

He shrugs. "I'm not special. Plenty of people deal with shit. The same way I suspect you did."

He looks at me straight on, and I can't hide under that gaze. All I can do is look away.

This time, Timofey lets me.

"You don't have to talk about it," he says. "But I get it. Parents don't always deserve to be parents."

I bite back a bitter laugh. That, coming from the least deserving "parent" of all.

Thankfully, before he can read my thoughts, he once again grips my hips. I'm not thankful for that, per se, but it is a nice distraction.

His palms are warm through my thin shirt as he slides me off the counter and back onto my feet.

"I burnt my arm, not my leg," I remind him as I brush his hands off of me. "I can walk."

"Great. Then follow me."

33

PIPER

I'm so focused on putting one foot in front of the other—without fainting from hunger and shock—that I don't realize where I'm standing until Timofey is rifling through a set of drawers in front of me and I'm next to the biggest bed I've ever seen.

"Wait." I spin around, eying the dark curtains, the warm golden floors, and the plush rug. I do my best not to look at the bed, but even in my peripherals, I can tell the duvet is luxurious and there is no shortage of pillows. "Is this your bedroom?"

"You showed me yours. It's only fair I show you mine."

"Since when do you care about fair?" A large painting hangs above the bed. It's a smattering of abstract red flowers. Paint flows down from the petals in thick drips. It looks like blood. "Also, you broke into my room. I didn't 'show you' anything."

"You're showing me a lot right now." He turns around and throws something at my chest. I flail and still don't manage to catch it. It bounces off of me and falls to the floor at my feet.

He rolls his eyes and walks over. He grabs it and then unfurls a shirt in front of me. "This is to cover up."

I'm only aware of my half-clothed state every time Timofey looks at me. The rest of him might as well be stone. He's unreadable.

But his eyes... There's a glimmer of human emotions there. I could swear I catch a hint of desire.

I snatch the button-down out of his hands. It's laughably large. "I wouldn't have pegged you as a prude."

"You probably wouldn't have pegged me for a gentleman, either."

"Definitely not." I snort.

"Then it's in your best interest to keep covered."

I glance up just as his eyes finish their trek over me. Heat blooms in my core, searing and relentless. My fingers fumble with the buttons on his shirt.

"Here." He steps forward and plucks the shirt out of my hands. Like everything, he handles the buttons with ease and grace. When he holds out the shirt for me to step into, I don't even question it.

Timofey Viktorov, for all of his faults, seems like the kind of person you should trust to take care of you.

My entire life, I've watched my supposed protectors fumble and stumble their way through life. Timofey never wavers. He never falters. Even when I should sprint in the opposite direction, I can't quite convince myself to shove him away.

Fuck me for being so weak—but damn, it's nice to feel cared for.

"I know how to put on a shirt," I mumble as I slide my injured arm into the ridiculously large sleeve. "I have my own clothes, too. Ones that fit me. At home."

"Not anymore."

I whip my eyes to his face. "What does that mean?"

"It means your stuff is in boxes on its way here. I had movers pack you up this morning."

"Oh." I can't even muster up the appropriate amount of surprise.

"I told you you'd be living here."

"I know. And I knew when I left this morning, there was a chance I wouldn't go back," I tell him.

Was it only this morning that I left my apartment? It feels like a lifetime ago. So much has happened since then.

"I didn't even like that apartment very much."

"There wasn't much to like."

"Sorry we can't all have mansions," I snap.

"No, *I'm* sorry."

My eyebrows raise. "You're…sorry? Is that the first time you've ever said that?"

He steps closer, grabbing the cuff of my shirt and rolling it up my forearm. His fingers brush against my skin, and my entire body buzzes. "There's a lot about me that would surprise you."

I can feel every beat of my traitorous heart radiating through me.

I'm attracted to Timofey Viktorov.

So what? Who isn't? I'm not alone in that. I'm not special. It means nothing.

I take a deep breath and step away from him. His hands drop away, and I quickly grab the cuff and try to continue rolling it with my bad arm. My burn twinges from the movement, but the pain medication is already starting to kick in.

"I make you nervous," he observes.

"Did you figure that out all on your own?" I chuckle humorlessly. "Everyone is scared of you, remember?"

He runs a hand through his dark hair. His chest strains against the buttons on his shirt. His curls fall in light waves over his forehead.

"You're not afraid of me in the same way as the rest of the world." He dips his head, catching my eyes. "You're not afraid to be honest. Why?"

I set my chin. "Because nothing about you is going to surprise me. I've known men like you. I was raised by one."

"I take it that's not a compliment."

"It's not a compliment or an insult. It's just a fact," I tell him. "My dad gave me the same hot and cold routine. The same way you brought Gram and Ashley here to make me think you cared about me, but then threatened them? My dad would give me candy and then make me feel guilty for spending all of his money on myself. He'd give me love and attention just so he could snatch it away later as a punishment."

"And that's what you think I'm doing."

"That's what I *know* you're doing." I'm speaking to myself as much as to Timofey. I need to internalize this. I need to convince myself that he can't be trusted if I'm going to survive this. "You're mad at me for talking to Akim behind your back and burning down half of your kitchen. I'm just waiting for the other shoe to drop. For this flirty, caretaker schtick to fade away and the truth to come out."

"Saving you from burning alive isn't part of some grand scheme, Piper."

I gnaw my bottom lip between my teeth. "Everything is part of your scheme. My dad was the same way. He could use anything—situations, feelings, possessions. I just…I want to give you as little to work with as possible."

The silence between us stretches until I have no choice but to look up. Timofey is watching me, something unrecognizable in his eyes.

As quick as a blink, it's gone.

"I have to go."

"Why?" I blurt before I can think better of it. "I mean—where are you—never mind. I guess you don't have to tell me anything."

"At risk of being compared to your father, I have to go order dinner for the two of us. The kitchen is out of commission, in case you forgot."

I nod. "Sorry. I didn't meant to hurt your—"

"You can't hurt me, Piper."

Timofey turns and leaves me alone. It ought to feel isolating. But for the first time since we met, I'm positive he's lying.

34

TIMOFEY

She deserves to eat alone.

I know enough about fucked-up fathers to know I don't ever want to be anything like that. Comparing me to her own is spitting in my face. It pisses me the hell off.

Then I remember the way she looked standing in front of me, my shirt drooping off her narrow shoulders and hanging low over her thighs. In some ways, it was even worse than seeing her in the barely-there tank top.

Since the moment she entered the picture, Piper has been one big wrench in my plans.

My phone rings. I answer it without seeing who it is.

"What?" I bark into the phone.

"Sounds like you're in a good mood," James Rooney says.

"All the more reason for you to get to the point so we can hang up."

He sighs. "I'd hope for a little more gratitude considering I just cleaned your house."

Cleaned your house is Rooney's cheesy little code word for "covered up a crime." I don't need to ask to know he's talking about the murder of the Albanian gunrunner last night.

Fuck. Was that really just last night? It feels like it has been days. Weeks. Lifetimes.

"A deep clean?"

"The deepest," he confirms. "You won't recognize the place."

That's good news. Killing one mouthy Albanian will not be what brings this Bratva to the ground.

I honestly haven't even thought about the execution since the meeting this morning. Piper has been a full and thorough distraction. Even now, I can't quite get her off the brain.

"I need you to do something else for me," I blurt.

Rooney sighs. "Why am I not surprised? There's always something else."

"I need you to look into Piper Quinn's background."

"The woman you had me lock up this morning?" he asks in surprise.

"I want to know more about her parents, her early life," I tell him. "I'm sure she's been in the system at some point. I want case files, parent's names, anything you can get."

"Can I ask why?"

"No."

"If she is going to end up dead, I don't want her name tied to my search history."

It's a reasonable question. If Piper were a soldier in my Bratva—or almost anyone else, really—she'd already be cold and buried.

Yet instead of rotting six feet under, she's living in my house now. Working for me.

"She is safe. You will be, too."

"I've risked a lot for you, Timofey, but—"

"Do what I ask and get back to me as soon as you can."

"Yes, sir. Your wish is my—"

I hang up on Rooney mid-sentence and flip back to the food delivery app. Five houses away.

I sigh and push myself to standing. Avoiding Piper will only make things between us more turbulent. If she's going to live here and take care of Benjamin, I suppose I'd better get used to the unique way she gets under my skin.

I left her in my room, but she's not there. She isn't in the room I've designated as hers, either. So I head down the hall to Benjamin's room.

When I peek into the room, Piper is standing in the middle of Benjamin's nursery, cradling him against my borrowed shirt, and singing a soft lullaby to him.

She has no idea I'm watching. I lean against the doorframe and observe.

Her song fades in and out from audible to nothing more than a whisper, but I can tell she has a nice voice. It's soothing, at least. Clearly, Benjamin agrees, because I can see his little head lulled against her non-burned bicep.

"Looks like he's asleep," I murmur.

Piper jolts and spins around, her eyes wide, a scream caught in her throat. When she sees me in the doorway, she doesn't relax. If anything, she stiffens further.

She spins back around and quickly places Benjamin in his crib. He stirs, unhappy with the sudden loss of her warmth and singing. For a moment, he's teetering on the verge of a meltdown. I brace myself for a wail.

Then he settles. The soft sound of his little exhales fills the room.

"Go," Piper hisses, shooing me out of the door. I step into the hallway and she pulls the door closed. "You shouldn't scare someone holding a baby."

"You shouldn't have your back to open doors. You never know who might come through."

She rolls her eyes. "Well, sorry if you were hoping to see him. He is exhausted. He's been fighting a nap for the last hour."

"I told Akim to take care of Benjamin."

"And I told him I was fine to do my job," she fires back. "And I am doing fine. I'm totally fine."

The moment the words are out of her mouth, she stumbles back half a step. I watch her eyes glaze over.

"Piper." I grab her good shoulder and pull her close. "Hey. What the—"

"I'm fine." She blinks and laughs nervously. "I'm a little dizzy. The pain pills with the lack of food and… It's no big deal. I'm fine."

"You shouldn't be holding a baby when you're feeling light-headed."

"I know how to take care of a baby. *I* wouldn't do anything to put Benjamin in danger."

It doesn't take a genius to hear the unspoken accusation in her tone.

"Food," I command. "It's waiting downstairs, so we're going to go eat, and you're not going to have another medical emergency for at least the length of a meal. Can you handle that?"

She jerks her shoulder out of my touch. "Only if you can handle not touching me for the length of a meal. As far as employer/employee conduct goes, we've crossed too many lines to count. I'd like to keep at least a few intact."

I don't mention how I'm not even close to getting my fill of her.

35

TIMOFEY

We walk together into the dining room. Akim has arranged the food on the table and then seemingly disappeared.

I look around, expecting to see him spying on us from the corner of the room. The man is a hopeless eavesdropper and irritatingly invested in my "love life," a misnomer if I've ever heard one.

Sure, I want to touch Piper. Sure, I want to fuck Piper. But I don't want to—

"Oh, for God's sake, Akim," I spit under my breath.

In the center of the table is a lit candelabra. Five flickering candles in a gold fixture, a scene taken straight out of a fairy tale.

The bastard is determined to piss me off.

Piper stops suddenly and wrings her hands in front of her chest. "You looked concerned," I observe. I nudge her forward and pull out a chair. She drops into it and I push her into the table. "Were you expecting hamburgers and plastic containers?"

"You say that like it's ridiculous," she says. "Normal people expect hamburgers and plastic containers. That or, like, lukewarm pad thai. I guess you aren't exactly a 'normal person,' though. You're not familiar with our ways."

"I didn't always live in a mansion." I take the seat opposite her and unfold a napkin in my lap. "And I didn't always eat well. I used to not eat at all, more often than not."

Piper looks down at the creamy seafood pasta on her plate. Seared scallops, a buttery golden sauce, al dente linguine. A basket of fresh bread sits in the middle of the table next to a chilled bottle of red wine.

"How long were you in foster care?" Piper asks suddenly.

She has a bite of food suspended in mid-air as she waits for me to respond. I gesture for her to eat. "I don't need you passing out mid-conversation."

"A conversation would require you to be forthcoming about your life."

"You're the one keeping secrets," I remind her.

She can't argue with that, so she brings the bite to her mouth. Her full lips wrap around the fork, her eyes flutter closed, and a moan starts low in her chest and bubbles up, unable to be contained. It's a uniquely sensual experience watching her eat.

"My God," she sighs. "That's amazing." She drops her fork and stares at me. "I've eaten. Now, it's your turn."

"I've already taken a bite."

She gives me a knowing glare. "How long were you in foster care?"

"It doesn't matter. Long enough."

"It matters to me. It's my job."

"Then you know it's not all rainbows and butterflies," I reply. "I have no interest in anyone's pity. Especially not yours."

Her eyes narrow to slits. Or as close as she can get, anyway. She says she's fine, but I can tell she doesn't have full control of herself. Her movements are slow and sloppy. Her lack of control is unnerving.

I lean closer, ready to make up for her weakness. If she falls, I want to be the one to catch her.

"Then you should know I'd never pity you for something like that." The venom in her voice drains away. "Especially because I didn't exactly have an idyllic childhood myself."

"Shitty parents. I remember."

She pokes at the food on her plate. "Yeah. It's the club no one wants to be in. And the club no one wants to talk about, apparently."

"I'm not part of your fucking club."

"Of course not." She rolls her eyes. "How dare I mistake you for a joiner? You're the handsome man in the dark corner with your arms crossed and a scowl on."

I arch a brow. "So you think I'm handsome?"

She jolts. "That wasn't what I—" Piper stares at me for a few seconds and then blows out a breath. "One thing about you: your time in the system didn't affect your self-esteem. Count yourself lucky."

"Sergey made me earn my keep. I wouldn't still be here if I wasn't worthy."

It's a simple truth, but I know immediately Piper is homing in on it. She's been doing this for years. In my experience, if social workers know how to do anything, it's making something out of nothing.

"So you've always worked for Sergey?" she asks. "Doing… whatever it is you all do here?"

"Since he adopted me, yeah."

It's another truth. A harmless one. But if I play it right, these little truths will pay big dividends. I have Rooney looking into her background, but if I can put Piper at ease and get something out of her now, all the better.

"Sergey needed an heir, and he didn't want a wife," I continue. "Having a bastard was an option, but an inconvenient one. Taking in an orphan solved his problem. There was no one else to claim me."

"An orphan…" she says softly, her voice trailing off. "I guess that means…"

"Dead parents." I hold up two fingers. "Count 'em."

Her face creases into a wince. "Both of them? I'm so sorry. Life isn't easy without your parents."

It's been years. Decades. Still, the question prickles at something sensitive in my chest. The guard I lowered earlier snaps back into place.

"Sergey is my parent," I say flatly.

"Right. Of course he is." Piper sighs and plants an elbow on the table. I can't help but notice she's leaning on it heavily. Her burnt arm is folded tenderly in her lap.

"I don't want to claim my birth parents, so believe me, I get it. They didn't want to claim me most of the time, either." She chuckles darkly, but there is a pain in her green eyes. I've caught a few glimpses of it since we first met. "I guess you could say it was a mutual decision to part ways."

"You mean a CPS agent didn't have to bust into your house and rip you out of your crying mother's arms?"

The words come out with more bite than I expect them to. Part of it is because I can see my own mother, too exhausted to get off the couch, tears soaking her cheeks.

I blink the image away. Piper's face is there instead.

Her auburn hair is frizzy around her face from the chaotic day. The candlelight flickers, drawing out the notes of red.

I know who she is and where she works. I know she wants to take Benjamin away from me.

But it's getting harder and harder to imagine her being casually cruel the way I've seen people in her line of work be.

It's also getting harder and harder to deny the attraction I feel for her. Frazzled or not, infuriating or not…

She's tempting.

36

TIMOFEY

Slowly, her expression softens. I can see her swallowing whatever defense of herself and her profession she wanted to make.

"My dad didn't put up a fight to keep me," she says simply. "We agreed I'd live with my grandma, though we had very different reasons. I knew I was safe there. He knew I'd be out of his hair. The only times he cared was when he needed something from me. Usually, that something was money."

Her eyes go glassy. I think she might cry.

Before the emotion can take hold, I reach across the table and slide her plate closer to her. "Eat."

She sniffles awkwardly, swallowing the emotion. "Someone has a one-track mind."

"I've hired you to be a nanny and so far, I've taken care of you more than you've taken care of Benjamin. At this point, I'm just protecting my investment."

She jabs a finger in my direction. "That's what you get for having me arrested."

"And this is what you get for being a royal pain in the ass." I point to her plate. "Dinner from a five-star restaurant that is soft enough you don't need a knife to cut it. Don't say I never did anything for you."

Piper looks down at her plate with fresh eyes. When she blinks up, there's a small smile on her lips. "I never took you for the thoughtful type."

"Good. I'm not."

"Whatever you say." Her coy smile taps against the iron facade of my guard. I ignore it. "After everything else you've put me through today, I wouldn't have been surprised if you poured me a bowl of dog food."

"After everything *I've* put *you* through?" I hitch a thumb over my shoulder. "Let's not forget whose kitchen is destroyed."

"Let's not forget whose body is destroyed." Piper jerks her injured shoulder up to showcase the bandage, but immediately regrets it. She inhales sharply, her face creasing with pain.

I'm on my feet and moving around the table before I can stop myself. I barely manage to curb my instinct before I actually touch her. "You really can't get through one fucking dinner. Unreal."

She doesn't even try to defend herself. "I was stupid. The pain meds made me feel invincible. I should be taking it easy, but I got caught up in—"

She looks up at me and then quickly away.

She doesn't have to finish her sentence. I can guess how it would go. *Caught up in you. Caught up in this moment.*

Some of the anger in me fizzles at that.

"I should have been more careful," she concludes. "But I'm fine."

"Maybe you haven't noticed, but being careful isn't in your wheelhouse."

She purses her lips. "I'll be fine. Let's just finish dinner."

I start to move back around the table, but I hear another hushed wince from Piper. Her injured arm is still folded against her body. Just the movement of reaching for her plate is causing her pain.

"For fuck's sake," I hiss under my breath. I turn around and snatch her fork out of her hand.

"Hey! What are you doing?" She wants to grab the fork back, but she can't. I'm standing on her bad side and, thankfully, she knows better than to lunge at me with her injured arm. "Benjamin will be up soon. I'd like to finish eating before then."

I drop down into the chair closest to her and twirl the fork in her pasta. I hold it up to her full pink lips. "Then shut up and eat."

Piper stares at the fork like it's a bomb. "What are you doing?"

"Exactly what it looks like."

Her eyes slide over me and a flush ripples across her cheeks. "Oh, so your body has been possessed by a kind, caretaking alien?"

"Start eating or I'll let you starve."

She sighs. "False alarm. It's still you in there."

I wag the fork back and forth in front of her mouth. She's clearly considering the pros and cons of letting me feed her versus starvation.

Finally, she leans forward, lips parted, and takes the bite.

And to think I thought watching her eat was sensual.

Feeding her is something else entirely.

Feeling the friction of her lips across the fork, the warmth of her breath against my fingers… My cock strains against the seam of my pants. I shift in the chair.

With each bite, I find myself staring at her mouth. Watching her throat bob. Her collarbones rise and fall as she chews and swallows.

The collar of my shirt has fallen open across her chest, revealing the barest hint of the swell of her breast.

God, I'm no better than a horny fucking teenager. Falling all over myself at the barest hint of cleavage. What the hell is wrong with me?

Suddenly, Piper's hand shifts over mine. "I can take care of myself." Her voice is soft. She can't even meet my eyes.

I shake her hand off. "I've seen no proof of that."

She rolls her eyes, and her knee brushes against mine. The heat of her body scorches through my pants. It does nothing to ease the ache between my legs.

"I'm not a child."

"I'm aware." Painfully aware. She's a *woman*. Ripe for the taking.

She groans in frustration.

I hold out another bite for her. "If you're scared of crossing the professional line you wanted to maintain, don't be."

Her tongue slides across her lower lip, taunting me. "You're feeding me dinner, Timofey. Right now, we aren't just crossing the line; we're dancing all over it."

Candlelight flickers across her skin. Her expression hides in wavering shadows. But she's blushing. I know that. I can feel the attraction between us burning as hot as the flames this afternoon.

Akim was right. It's been too long since I've been with a woman.

That's all this is. I'm leaning towards Piper, a raging erection between my legs, because it's been months since I've touched anything but my own hand.

"It's only inappropriate if you want it to be."

A nervous whimper sounds from the back of Piper's throat. There's fear in her eyes, but she doesn't pull back. She doesn't turn away.

"Timofey…" she breathes.

I drop my free hand onto her thigh. My fingers slip around the curve of her leg and squeeze. "If you keep saying my name like that, we're going to do a lot more than dance on that line."

Her chest heaves, the inevitability of the moment settling over her. Then Piper looks me in my eyes and whispers it again.

"Timofey…"

I close the distance between us in a heartbeat. I pull her plump lower lip between my teeth and curl my hand around her slender neck.

Piper slides to the edge of her chair, her legs tangling with mine. I drop the fork in my hand, the metal clattering against the hardwood floor, and wrap an arm around her waist.

She whimpers when her injured arm is momentarily pinned between us. But then she slides her free hand into the hair at the back of my neck and moans into my mouth.

Holy fucking hell.

My nerve endings light up like a fireworks display. I feel every brush of her body against mine. Every whisper of breath against my lips. Every tingle of desire down my spine.

I've honed my senses over the years to account for every change in my environment, every possible threat. Never get caught up in the moment. Never let your guard down.

And right now, all I can say is…*fuck that.*

I want to consume every fucking ounce of her. The rest of the world be damned.

I deepen the kiss, swirling my tongue into her mouth. She sighs, and I swallow down every delicious noise she can't bear to bite back.

Forget professionalism. Forget lines in the sand. I'm going to take this woman—right here, right now.

My head will be clearer for it once it's done. I'll be able to focus on what's important. Even though I'm having a hard time thinking about anything beyond how she'll feel wrapped around me.

Piper drags her hand around my neck and down my chest. Her fingers press into my skin like she's looking for some traction. I'm more than happy to give it to her.

I grab her waist and haul her onto my chair. Her hips settle against mine. No sooner is she right where she belongs…

…when a shrill alarm screams.

As if the world itself knows we've gone too far.

37

PIPER

Fire.

That's my first thought. There is another fire in the house. The shrill ring is the alarms going off.

I jerk away from Timofey's warmth, wincing at the sharp pain that tears through my arm and shoulder.

The kitchen is clear. I don't see any flames or smoke.

I frown. "Is the fire alarm…?"

I can't even get the words out before Timofey reaches around my body. His hand slides down my back and lower. He digs around for a second and then comes out with my phone in his hand. It's ringing.

It looks like he wants to crunch my phone in his grasp for interrupting…whatever the hell we were just doing.

"Oh." I reach for it, fighting my own mix of feelings. "I should have recognized the sound. It's the medication, probably. I'm loopy."

I'm high on pain pills. No wonder my inhibitions are lowered.

That's what I'm going to tell myself, anyway. It's easier to think I'm high than to think I have so little self-control that I was going to let Timofey Viktorov have his dirty way with me in the middle of his dining room.

This phone is a sign from the universe. *Go no further. Abort mission before it's too late.*

"Are you planning to take the call?" Timofey dangles the phone in front of me. "Or should I dismiss it so we can pick up where we—"

"I'll take it!" I practically scream.

I swipe up on the call and press it to my ear as I scramble back off of Timofey's lap. He grabs my hips to hold me steady as I find my footing.

I wonder what it would feel like to feel these strong hands on my bare skin. To feel him grip my waist as he drove himself into me again and—

"Hello?" The voice on the other end of the line is quiet, but it snaps me out of my dirty line of thinking.

"Hello?" I parrot back.

"Piper?" I recognize Noelle's voice now, but she's still whispering. "Is that you?"

"Of course it's me. You called me, remember?"

I bite back a sigh. The most intense kiss of my life was interrupted because Noelle wants to tell me about the wrap she made for lunch. Or the latest thing Ashley said to piss her off. It's always something useless with her.

Don't get me wrong—I'm relieved by the distraction. But another part of me is aching to feel Timofey's solid muscles under my fingertips, to settle against the wall of his chest and let his soft mouth devour me whole.

Shame tries and fails to poison my thoughts. I can't blame myself for that fantasy. Timofey may be a monster, but he doesn't look or feel like one.

I'm only human, after all.

"You just don't sound like yourself," Noelle says. "You're all… breathy. It sounds like you sucked down some helium."

I clear my throat and hurry away from Timofey, hoping he didn't overhear anything Noelle just said. "I'm fine. It's me. What's up?"

"Remember what you asked me to do?"

I sort through the last few hours, trying to figure out what Noelle is talking about. It's been *a day.* A certified, trademarked, undeniable, all-caps DAY. I can be forgiven for forgetting the last conversation Noelle and I had.

"Not really. I'm actually busy right now. Could I—"

"Emily is dead," Noelle says suddenly.

A wave of blind panic washes over me. Then I realize I don't know anyone named Emily. "Who?"

"This morning," Noelle pushes. "You texted me to look into Timofey's ex. That's who she was, right? His ex-girlfriend?"

Just like that, it all comes back to me.

The locket. Emily. Asking Noelle for her Google Fu skills.

I turn away from Timofey's watchful gaze. "Sorry. Repeat that. I didn't catch it."

"Emily Anderson is dead," Noelle repeats slowly. "She was murdered."

My heart is thundering in my chest, and I can barely catch my breath. Timofey's last (maybe, maybe not) girlfriend was murdered. But surely he had nothing to do with—

Who in the hell am I kidding? Just look at him! He is guilty as sin. He did it. Lock him up and throw away the key.

I fight back the impulse to scream this very thing in the phone right now, and instead, I do my best to play it casual. "How did that happen?"

Noelle hesitates. "Are you hearing what I'm saying? A woman is dead. Are you—wait. Is he there with you?"

There's a reason Noelle is the smart one.

"Uh-huh," I confirm as though I'm listening to whatever she's saying, encouraging her to go on.

"Shit," she hisses. "Okay. Well, no one was ever arrested. There was a suspect, but he wasn't formally charged. There wasn't enough evidence, I guess."

I don't even want to ask the question. I don't need to. I know who did it. Still, I force the words out. "Who was it again?"

"His name is…" Noelle trails off, shuffling through something on her end of the phone. The seconds pass by torturously slowly. "There it is. Rodion. Rodion Karnovsky."

I'm so shocked Noelle didn't just say Timofey's name that I jolt.

Timofey's chair shifts behind me. Of course he noticed. He notices everything. And now, he's paying even closer attention to me.

I play it off by toeing my shoe into the tile floor. "Right, I remember that."

"You know him?" Noelle gasps. "Are you saying you know Rodion?"

"We met once or twice."

She curses again. "Well, he's been on Timofey Viktorov's payroll for years. Whoever Timofey has managing his PR does a good job of keeping him out of the papers, but it's there if you look hard enough."

"I'm sure," I say. What I really want to say is, *He doesn't have a PR guy. He has a gun and zero inhibitions about using it.*

"Apparently, the police aren't closing the case just yet. They're still asking for tips," she says. "Maybe they'll get caught."

I don't even give myself the chance to feel hopeful. Timofey has probably intimidated every cop and reporter in the city at least once. I'm still not sure why he didn't just hold a gun to my head like he no doubt did to all of them.

It wouldn't have worked. I would have stood my ground. And then Officer Rooney would have been charged with cleaning up *my* crime scene. But still… why is Timofey wasting his time convincing me? Why is he feeding me dinner when he could be burying my body?

I turn slightly, glancing over my shoulder.

Even before our eyes meet, I know he's looking at me. His gaze is icy. I feel it like a drip down my spine.

I give him a wild, uncomfortable smile and spin back around. "Well, I should probably get—"

"I'm not done yet," she says. "Rodion isn't just Emily's suspected killer. Rumor has it he is a hitman. *Timofey's* hitman."

Rodion had a sea of black marks on his arm. *One for every person I've…* killed. I didn't need him to finish the sentence. I can figure the rest out for myself.

Timofey pays Rodion to kill people for him. Maybe even his last girlfriend, if the locket with a picture of Timofey and Emily inside is any indication.

And I was just *kissing him.*

We weren't just playing tonsil hockey and dancing on the line of professionalism; I was playing with my life, risking my continued existence just because the man has a nice jawline and pretty blue eyes.

"Makes sense," I mumble. With every passing second, I'm losing my ability to seem casual. I feel nauseous. The five-star pasta in my stomach is turning into a five-star brick.

"She was killed a couple months ago. Recent. Not like that matters, I guess. Murder is murder no matter when it happened. But still. Whoever did this to her, Rodion or whoever, they're more than capable of doing it again."

"I know." The words lodge in my throat, but I choke them out. "Thanks."

There's a long pause before Noelle speaks again. "Be careful, Piper."

I feign a smile and turn back to face Timofey. "Will do. Talk to you later!"

The forced cheer in my voice sounds beyond fake to me, but I hope Timofey doesn't know me well enough to realize I'm speaking several octaves higher than normal.

My screen turns dark and I shove my phone back in my pocket. Having Noelle on the line made me feel less alone.

Now, there's nothing to hide behind. No one to cling to.

It's just me and the monster in front of me.

"That sounded important." Timofey watches me walk back towards the table carefully.

"Nothing Noelle says is important."

Can he hear my voice shaking? Is it actually shaking? My entire body feels like it's vibrating. It's making it hard to judge how well I'm pulling this off.

"Noelle is the third member of your trio," he says flatly.

I arch a brow. "Is that a question or a statement?"

He ignores my question. "She didn't answer when I called her earlier today."

It feels like I'm being interrogated, but I don't know why. I try to follow the track of his logic, but I'm tired and in pain and panicked. My mind is a muddle even I can't puzzle my way out of.

"She's a hard one to pin down. Busy lady." I give him a tight smile and then quickly let it fall away. No smile is better than a fake one.

Timofey refuses to look away. *Why won't he look away?* I want to throw my cloth napkin at his face just to get a break from his scrutiny.

He tilts his head to the side, brows lowered. "So whatever she called you about, it's more important than you being in jail. More important than you catching on fire."

Shit, shit, shit. I finally pick up the trail of Timofey's logic, but it's too late. He's cornered me, and he knows it.

"Tell me what she said." The mouth that was soft against mine only a couple minutes ago flattens into a threatening slash.

"You're nosy."

"And you're a shitty liar," he snarls back. "What did she say?"

I want to lie, but he's right. I'm no good at it. I've never been a good liar. Great liars are kids who had to lie to their overprotective parents to get out of the house. Teenagers who had to fib to get drunk with their friends or swear up and down that they have no clue who scratched the passenger side door of the car when they took it out.

I never had to tell those lies. My parents didn't care enough to know where I was or who I was with. They certainly didn't care what I was doing, so long as I wasn't bothering them.

I'm a terrible liar, and so now, the truth is sitting inside of me like a jack-in-the-box, dying to be released.

I do the only thing I can do: I turn the crank.

38

PIPER

"Who is Emily?" I hurl the truth at him like a weapon. "I found a locket with a picture of the two of you inside. Her name was engraved on the back."

Timofey stands up. He's so much taller than me. So much bigger in every way. It's strange to think we fit together as well as we did, my body curled into his lap. A man as big as him should dwarf me.

I peel my eyes away from the broad set of his shoulders and try to make myself look strong. It's hard when my arm is pulsing with pain and tucked into my chest like I'm a bird with an injured wing, but I do the best I can.

"You shouldn't be snooping through my office."

"And you shouldn't be killing your girlfriend," I snap. "I guess we all make mistakes."

His jaw works side to side. "I don't have a girlfriend."

"Not anymore."

"Not ever."

"Bullshit!" My heart is thundering in my chest, but the adrenaline is making me courageous. Noelle told me to be careful, but here I am, thirty seconds later, poking the beast. "Fine. She wasn't your girlfriend. Titles aren't important. What is important is that she is dead and you did it."

I've seen Timofey frustrated and upset. But something about the calm way he is glaring at me is even more unnerving.

"I didn't do a damn thing to her."

"Oh, that's right. Rodion did. He's your hitman, right?"

If Timofey is surprised I know about Rodion's job title, he doesn't show it. He doesn't reveal anything. His expression doesn't change one iota as we stare at each other, the uncomfortable truth sitting between us.

"You don't know what you're talking about," he says finally.

"Screw you. Yes, I do, and you know it."

At that, Timofey's control snaps. He lunges towards me, towering over me. I feel his hot breath on my face as he leans impossibly close. "You don't have a single fucking clue what I know. Don't pretend you do. Trust me, Piper Quinn—you're safer being clueless."

I swallow down the terror crawling up my throat and meet his eyes. "I'm sure you'd love it if I was some clueless ditz. Just another human chess piece you could move around the way you wanted. That would make things easier for you, wouldn't it?"

"If you cooperated? Yes."

"No, if I was as stupid and blindly loyal as every other person on your payroll," I fire back. "But I'm not. I've spent my entire life protecting myself from dangerous people like you. I'm not going to let myself be steamrolled over now. I'm not going to end up like Emily."

Suddenly, Timofey's fist is in my hair. He jerks my head back and stares down the long line of his nose at me. I struggle to swallow with my head at this angle, but I won't give him the satisfaction of begging to be let go.

"Listen to me," he demands. "You don't know what you're saying. Rodion didn't kill Emily. Even if he did, walking around shouting about it is a good way to get yourself killed."

"So you admit it. You'll have me killed."

"Of course I will," he says easily. "I made that clear the first time we met. I've never claimed innocence. I've killed plenty of people, and I'll add you to the list if need be. But where Emily is concerned, my hands are clean."

I don't know why Emily matters so much to me. I don't know the woman. Maybe she was Timofey's girlfriend; maybe she was just a fling. She shouldn't be important…

But she is.

It's probably because I can tell she's important to Timofey. He tenses at the sound of her name. I want to know what woman could have that kind of hold over him.

I want to have that kind of hold over him.

I bury that last truth down deep. Into the dark shadows at my core where no one will ever find it. Not even me.

"If you didn't kill Emily or have her killed, then who did?" I ask.

Timofey stares at me for one second. For two. The tension from earlier wraps around us, now tinged with anger and violence.

The part of me desperate to lose myself in his touch doesn't mind so much. I can only imagine what Timofey would be like unrestrained…

The sane part of me knows I need to run as fast and as far from this man as possible.

All at once, he lets go of my hair and shoves me back. "Tread carefully, Piper."

"What does that mean?"

He grabs his drink from the table and tips it back. His throat bobs as the alcohol in the glass disappears. When he finishes, he doesn't even wince. "If you turn against me now, I'll ruin you."

Without another word, Timofey turns away and leaves me standing there.

I'm too terrified to ask what he means.

39

PIPER

I've been swaying side to side with Benjamin for what feels like hours.

Maybe it has been. I'm not sure. I've lost track of time.

Since Timofey left me in the dining room, my mind has been too full to keep track of something as trivial as the passing of the seconds.

Except now, my good arm is sore from cradling a squirming baby and exhaustion burns the backs of my eyes.

Benjamin woke up only a few minutes after Timofey and I parted ways, and he hasn't been happy since. I changed him, fed him, burped him. I did everything I was supposed to do, but he's been somewhere between a whine and a cry for ages, and I'm at the end of my rope.

I would ask Timofey for help, but…

I shake my head, dismissing the thought before I can even consider it. The less I see him, the better.

I'll ruin you.

Financially? Physically? What did he mean?

Probably both, I decide. God knows Timofey has that kind of power. It wouldn't take much, anyway. I don't have much of a life left to ruin.

Benjamin lets out a sudden pitiful wail, and I pat his back.

"There, there. Things aren't so bad." I'm not sure if I'm talking to him or myself. "Everything will be alright."

He settles back into the crook of my arm.

"At least one of us buys my bullshit," I mumble.

Eventually, his little eyes grow heavy and close. I rock him for a few minutes longer before my arm is trembling too hard for me to hold him another second longer. Gently, carefully, I settle him into his crib.

Instantly, Benjamin's arms and legs jolt outward. It's a newborn reflex. A built-in response to being startled. It means Benjamin is healthy.

It also means he's crying again.

"No," I whimper. "No, no. It's okay. It's alright." I collapse into the chair next to his crib and press a gentle hand to his warm tummy. "It's okay, buddy. You're alright."

The slow rocking of my touch slowly eases him back to a dozing sleep. But every time I try to pull my hand away, he jolts awake again.

Finally, too exhausted to fight it, I rest my cheek against the bars of his crib and fall asleep with my palm over his little chest.

I don't know how long I lie like that, but when my eyes blink open, my body is riddled with pain.

The burn on my arm is stiff and pulsing, my cheek aches from being smashed between the wooden rail and my teeth, and my spine is screaming for me to fix my posture and sit up straight.

As slowly as possible, I pull my hand away from Benjamin. His sleepy breathing is a constant whirr of noise in the nursery, and I fall back into the chair, ready to doze off again to the easy rhythm of it. Maybe when I wake up, I'll have the energy to pry myself out of this chair and get to bed.

Before I can slip back into sleep, though, a deep voice slices through the quiet.

Initially, I jolt because I don't want Benjamin to wake up. I did not work this hard to get him to sleep, just for one of Timofey's careless, obnoxious cult members to stumble by and wake him up.

Then I hear it. The familiar rumble of Timofey's baritone voice.

"I called you two fucking hours ago. Where have you been?"

All at once, I find the energy. I ease out of the chair, wincing when a spring somewhere deep inside creaks at the loss of my weight. Benjamin doesn't stir.

Thank God.

I tiptoe across the plush blue rug and press my ear to the barely-there crack in the door.

"You're always on duty. Your life is duty," he barks. "You have the goddamn word inked into your skin."

Light from the hallway spills into the room through the open door, though it's hardly enough to see by. It certainly doesn't allow me to see where Timofey is in the hallway. But it sounds like he's further down the hall and retreating.

I peek out. When I don't see Timofey, I step into the hall and pull the door closed again so the light doesn't wake Benjamin. I follow the sound of Timofey's voice.

"Maybe I could relax if I wasn't the only one paying attention to the shit that actually matters," Timofey snaps. "We call an all-hands meeting for one dead Albanian, but I'm the only one with an actual ear to the ground."

Timofey goes quiet. I'd kill to hear who he is talking to. What are they saying? What's going on?

Maybe I don't need to hear the other end of the line, because they seem to be asking the exact same questions I am.

"You'd already know what's going on if you'd answered the first time I called."

I make it to the end of the hallway and peer around the corner. In the center of the hallway, not six feet from me, there he is.

I jerk back and press my good hand to my mouth. It takes a few seconds for my brain to recognize that Timofey's back was to me.

He didn't see me.

"Emily's murder is being investigated again," Timofey snarls. There's a pause before he curses under his breath. "If the police are reopening the investigation, it doesn't just concern you; it concerns all of us."

He's talking to Rodion. He has to be.

No…he's *warning* Rodion.

Because of me.

I panicked and blurted that I knew about Emily and the locket, about Rodion being his hitman. Now, Timofey has a leg up on the police.

I'm an idiot.

"Come tomorrow to talk strategy," Timofey says, confirming my worst fears. "If Rooney can't handle this, then we'll have to figure it out ourselves."

Can he do that? If he doesn't have someone working for him on the inside, can he sway an investigation?

Who the hell am I kidding? He probably has an entire squadron of officers working for him. Based on this mansion alone, Timofey can afford to buy off almost every morally gray officer in the city. Then he can cover up the murders of every officer too ethical to join him.

It's been quiet for a bit too long, so I chance another peek around the corner. Timofey is gone.

I lean my head against the wall and blow out the oxygen that has been burning my lungs. It doesn't make me feel better. Instead, I feel hollow. Scraped dry.

"It's what I get for kissing the devil," I mutter. "He probably stole my soul."

My lips tingle, my body remembering the way Timofey felt against me. Of course the first guy I kiss in months turns out to be a monster. It's just my luck. The people in my life can't be normal and healthy. They have to be unbalanced. Fundamentally broken. Skewed far, far beyond the grotesque.

I tap a finger to the center of my forehead like a cartoon character trying to focus. It's the only way I can orient my thoughts. It's the only way I can ground myself in this moment. Here and now—if I don't force myself to stay right there, I'm going to die.

"What am I going to do?" I whisper. "What do I do next?"

Don't kiss him. That's step number one, obviously.

Definitely do not, under any circumstances, kiss Timofey Viktorov again. No matter how lush his lips look. No matter how good he smells. No matter how strong his hands feel around my waist.

I bite my lower lip hard between my teeth. This calls for a little negative reinforcement, I think. Timofey, bad. Kissing Timofey equals pain.

That way lies trouble.

"Okay, next," I say, trying to keep myself on track. "What next?"

Again, the answer is obvious.

Get the fuck out of Dodge...

And take Benjamin with me.

40

TIMOFEY

Sergey leans back on the sofa with a groan. When he meets my eyes again, he rolls his own. "Don't look at me like that. I made it here, didn't I?"

I gesture towards the setting sun. "Barely."

"I had more important things to do."

More important than this? What kind of father has more important shit than this? I want to ask. But that's what *he* wants. That's who he is to me right now—just "Sergey." Not my father.

I learned early on that the father who adopted me and the man who once ran the Viktorov Bratva are not one and the same. Sergey has sides to him, masks he puts on and takes off as it pleases him.

"We need to talk about how to handle the investigation," I say, shifting to the matter at hand.

"No, we don't," Sergey counters. "They don't have anything."

"We don't know that."

He levels his gaze at me. There are more wrinkles around his eyes and across his forehead than there used to be. Age has dragged down his jawline and turned his ever-present frown into an unintentional droop. But I still recognize the stubborn set of his mouth.

"Rodion didn't kill Emily."

I grimace. "You know damn well that—"

"He has slaughtered plenty of people," Sergey interrupts. "You know his signs as well as I do. His cutesy little calling cards. Emily was a clean kill."

"Nothing about that was clean," I grit out.

Scenes flash before my eyes. Blood. Screams. Nightmare fuel.

"Pah! You know what I mean. Whoever did it didn't delight in death the way Rodion does."

I do know what he means, as much as I wish I didn't. I've killed people; it comes with the job. I don't feel guilty about it, either. But the thought that Rodion genuinely enjoys the slaughter will never not skeeze me the fuck out.

I drag a hand through my hair. "So he didn't string up her bowels like streamers. That doesn't mean he isn't guilty. He knows we'd expect something like that from him."

"He wasn't even in the country, for fuck's sake," Sergey snaps. "He was in Russia. You know this."

I do. That doesn't make it any easier to believe. Very few people could have killed someone close to me and gotten away without leaving a trace.

Rodion is one of those few.

Sergey leans forward, elbows resting on his knees. "You need to let this go, son."

"Let *her* go, you mean."

Sergey takes a deep breath and nods. "If that's what it takes, then yes. You are alive. Do what you need to do to keep it that way."

"Is that a threat, Otets?"

"You aren't a child anymore," Sergey says by way of an answer. "I don't need to threaten you to get you to comply. You know I'm right."

"I know you *think* you're right."

"Then that should be enough."

We stare at each other for a few seconds. The constant push and pull of our relationship vibrates between us.

Finally, I stand and pace to the window. I can see Piper standing outside just beyond the stone patio with Benjamin in her arms. She's pointing at the garden and talking to him animatedly.

I glance back over my shoulder at Sergey. "Your opinion is enough for me to focus elsewhere. *For now.*"

His face warms into a broad smile. "This is why I chose you to be my successor, Timofey. You always see reason. You aren't driven by your emotions."

"Of course I'm not. You raised me to ignore them."

I don't miss how bitter those words sound on my lips.

I turn my attention outside again. Piper is walking across the grass, pointing out things as she goes. I haven't seen her since last night at dinner, but Akim has kept me filled in on her movements. He'll never admit it, but he's jealous that someone else has taken over his caregiving role. Every time I've seen him today, he's been watching Benjamin's nursery cameras like a hawk.

"I usually play peek-a-boo with the new diaper before I put it on him," he whined earlier. "It makes it a bit more fun. But whatever. She's doing fine, I guess."

She looks comfortable enough now, with Benjamin cradled in her arms. But I notice the way she keeps glancing back at the house. The way her eyes dart for the far end of the property line.

She's nervous.

I have a good guess as to why.

"Like I said, I hope you're not being driven by your emotions." He steps forward and joins me near the window. His eyes narrow in on Piper. "I just have to wonder if your sudden interest in Rodion being involved in Emily's death has anything to do with the new…presence in your life."

"There is no new anything in my life."

"Don't forget, I've seen her," he says, his voice low and suggestive. "She's beautiful."

If he was anyone else, I'd shove him out of the window. Instead, I fist my hands at my side. "She's Benjamin's nanny."

"Interesting you waited until now to hire one. Benjamin is… how old?"

"Six months. Which is old enough that I can't depend on Akim and whoever might be around to hold him," I snarl. "He needs a designated caregiver."

Sergey continues on like he hadn't heard me. "In the girl's case, maybe emotions really aren't involved. There are lots of other very human urges that could drive you to keep someone like her around."

I can't even deny it. Less than twenty-four hours ago, those human urges were at the helm.

There was no reason to kiss Piper. I wouldn't gain anything from it. It wouldn't benefit the Bratva in any way.

I *wanted* to. Simple as that.

And I always get what I want.

Piper is venturing further and further from the house. It would be smart to look away and feign disinterest, but I want to see where she's going.

"She's useful to me. I'll keep her on so long as she remains useful. I'm sure you can understand that."

Sergey nods, unconvinced. "Certainly I do. Women can be useful in many ways, can't they? You can find some way to put her to work."

"Let it go, Otets."

He bites back a smug smile. "For instance, we have that wedding coming up. The Marine Corps Commandant. I believe the invitation came with a plus-one, as a matter of fact."

"Are you asking me to be your date?" I drawl viciously.

He waves me off. "I might not even go. But one of us should. And if you do, you might as well enjoy yourself. Strap some pretty little thing to your arm and try to relax."

My entire life, Sergey has pushed me to focus on the Bratva. To work harder. To stay devoted. Now, suddenly, I need to relax?

Unlikely. Even before meeting him, I was never built for it. I need to be in constant motion. When you pause, that's when the thoughts come in. That's when the memories crop up.

That's when the nightmares return.

"It would be hard to relax, knowing an event like that would be the perfect place for whoever took Emily out to strike again. The last thing I need is my date showing up dead. Bad press."

"You're going to skip it, then?"

I shrug. "I'll decide later."

The smile is gone from Sergey's face as he leans forward, his head dipped low to catch my eyes. "Sometimes, you forget how well I know you, Timofey."

"I don't forget anything."

He smirks for a moment before it falls away. "I knew you'd say that. I also know that, after what happened, you are obsessive about protecting the women in your life."

"I want vengeance against those who hurt the people close to me. That's not unique," I say. "That's the Bratva way."

He nods. "It is—unless that vengeance comes at the expense of the Bratva. No woman is worth risking what we've built together. Remember that, son."

Down on the ground, Piper turns. Her profile is in sharp silhouette, sunlight glinting off her auburn hair.

I'm still watching the sway of her hips as she walks away when I realize Sergey has left the room. I'm alone.

41

TIMOFEY

I step onto the back patio and pull a cigarette from my pocket.

Emily would slap it out of my hand if she was here. I would pull out another one without hesitation.

"Old habits die hard," I always said when she complained.

She'd inevitably wrinkle her nose in disgust. "So do smokers."

I light up and lean against the brick column. Piper is no longer visible in the yard. Not that I expected her to be. I know she's trying to escape. I could tell she was trying to slip away from the house without drawing notice.

But I noticed. I know what she was trying to do.

What I don't know is when she'll return.

Because she *will* return. People don't walk away from me that easily. Especially when I want them around. And despite all the trouble she's caused, I do want Piper around.

What I told Sergey is still true: Piper is useful to me. She can take care of Benjamin. More than that, she can help ensure I keep guardianship of him.

It would be a lie to say there's nothing else to it, though. Especially after the kiss we shared yesterday.

Maybe mutual hatred is the best foreplay in existence. Something about wanting to tear each other limb from limb might feed into the desire, heighten it in some way. Kissing her was better than fucking anyone else has ever been.

There's just something to the way she stands up to me, while at the same time barely being able to stand at all. The woman is a walking juxtaposition. She's fiercely vulnerable.

Sergey wasn't so wrong: I feel protective over the women in my life. I don't like to see them hurt unless I'm the one doing the hurting.

But Piper isn't in my life. She's a tool I'll utilize to get what I want.

It would serve me well to remember that.

I take a long drag from my cigarette. The smoke tickles through my lungs before I blow it out in a haze around my head.

For now, Piper stays. At least as long as she continues to live inside of me just like this smoke does. But as soon as I figure out how she's doing it, I'll be able to ensure it never happens again. And as soon as *that* happens, she'll be gone.

Until then…

Tires crunch over gravel. I walk around the side of the house just as a black car pulls to a stop. The windows are tinted and rolled up tight. I curse under my breath and toss my cigarette to the ground.

The moment Rooney steps out of the driver's side, I meet him at the door.

"I told you to roll down your fucking windows," I bark.

He jolts at my sudden appearance and slams his door closed. "I didn't want another escape on my hands. I child-locked everything."

"Fucking *mudak*." I drag a hand over my jawline and shake my head. "Just open the doors. Now."

Rooney hops to it, moving around the car and pulling open the back door.

Instantly, Piper catapults out of the car.

Benjamin is dozing on her shoulder, but I'm not sure how. Piper is pale and breathing heavily. Based on the tear tracks running down her cheeks, she was crying, too.

Her green eyes meet mine, but they are glassy and unfocused. She's still in a panic. Her body doesn't realize she's safe again.

"Fucking fantastic," I hiss, turning to Rooney. "You brought me a basket case again. I told you she's claustrophobic."

"And I told you I'd get her back to you. Here she is. I don't see the problem."

I take three huge steps to stand in front of Rooney. "The problem is you don't know how to follow directions. It makes me think you can't do anything right. It makes me think you aren't trustworthy."

Rooney lifts his chin in defiance. "You know I'm trustworthy."

"I don't know a goddamn thing," I snap. "Not when you can't crack a window. Maybe your days of being useful are done."

His eyes bug out and his mouth flops open and closed.

"You know what I do to people I have no use for, don't you, James?" I ask. "You've cleaned up enough of the aftermath to take a stab at it."

He swallows and nods. "I know."

"Then don't let it happen again."

Piper is sucking in breath after breath next to me. It's like she can't get enough oxygen to fill her lungs. Still, she pats Benjamin's back, calming him with gasping, erratic shushes.

She's halfway to dying and she still cares for him. It's remarkable.

The moment my attention is on Piper, Rooney takes the opportunity to slip away and duck inside the car. He returns with a file in his hands, then thrusts it at me. "Here. The information you asked for," he explains. "I found everything there was to find and compiled it here. Some of it is in my own handwriting to avoid using the printers."

The file on Piper's background. I almost forgot I requested it. So much has happened in the interim.

"Maybe you can still take direction after all." He starts to grin, but before he gets too far down that road, I add, "Now, show me you can understand what I'm saying by obeying this very simple instruction: get the fuck out of my sight."

Rooney's jaw clicks under the strain of his teeth grinding together, but after a second, he slips into his car and drives away.

I turn to Piper.

Her attention is split between watching Rooney leave, taking care of Benjamin, and keeping an eye on me. None of it seems to be on regulating her breathing and taking care of herself. Nothing new in that regard.

"Stop worrying about everyone else and breathe," I order. "None of it will matter if you hyperventilate and die."

Her pink lips pucker into an "O" as she draws in air and then pushes it out slowly. Still, she finds the energy to scowl at me.

"I'll take your annoyance as a sign that you're going to survive. Can you walk?"

"Of course I can walk," she spits.

"That's true. You were just about to walk off of my property, so I guess your legs work fine."

"I wasn't—" She shakes her head, auburn waves falling around her pale face. "I wasn't escaping. Benjamin needed some fresh air. It was a walk. A *normal* walk. Your friend showed up and blew things out of proportion."

I turn away from her, expecting her to follow. "Don't lie to me. It wastes your breath and my time."

Piper doesn't argue or try to defend herself again. I'm not sure if it's because she's relenting or because getting up the stairs without falling backward requires all of her energy. She may be able to walk, but her legs are shaky.

I reach back and grab her elbow. She tries to twist away from me, but I hold her firmly.

"You look like a newborn giraffe mounting these stairs," I tell her. "You're no help to me if you crack your skull falling down them. I'm not going to let you put yourself and a baby in danger."

"You aren't going to let me do anything," she mutters. But she lets me lead her up the rest of the stairs and into the house.

I don't hesitate in the foyer. We cross it quickly and head down the hall towards my office. The whole way, I feel Piper tensing beneath my touch. With every step, she draws further away from me.

By the time we're in my office, she's shaking again.

I close the door and Piper promptly presses herself into the corner. Like maybe if she flattens herself against the shelves, I'll forget she's in here.

"Fine," she says before I can even begin to ask, "I was trying to escape. Is that what you want to hear?"

"I didn't ask you anything."

She presses her lips together. "But you're going to. I'm being interrogated, right?"

I lean against the edge of my desk, legs crossed at the ankle. "You tell me. Does this feel like an interrogation?"

Piper ignores the question and squares her shoulders. "Before you do whatever you're going to do to me, Benjamin needs to leave."

Benjamin is drooling on Piper's sleeve, his chubby cheek squished against her arm.

"But he's so riveted in the conversation," I drawl.

She doesn't laugh at my joke. "I don't want him here for whatever is about to happen."

"You don't know what's going to happen."

"I can guess," she hisses. "I'm not stupid."

I bob my head back and forth. "Agree to disagree on that one. You walked out my back door with Benjamin in your arms and thought you would just keep walking? To where? Don't bother trying to fumble up some bullshit answer. You didn't have a plan. You have nowhere to go. No one who can protect you. Unless you planned to rough it in the acres of forest around my property, I'm not sure where you thought you'd go to escape me."

"Anywhere!" she shrieks.

Benjamin jolts, and Piper instantly starts to console him. She shushes in his ear and rocks him side to side.

The moment he's calm again, she turns her venom on me. "I wanted to go anywhere else. Anywhere you weren't. Feeling desperate made me stupid, I'll admit. But I won't apologize for it. I don't regret it. In fact, I'd do it again."

Her chest is heaving again, but it isn't with panic or fear—it's rage. The fire that took down half of my kitchen yesterday has nothing on the fire burning in her eyes right now.

Piper hates me. She despises every inch of me.

Yet all I want to do is wrap her auburn hair around my fist and watch her bend under my touch.

I stand up, adjusting the front of my pants as I go, and take a step towards her.

"Wait!" she gasps, fear creeping into her act. "Benjamin. He can't—I don't want him to see this."

"He's an infant. He won't remember."

"It doesn't matter. Kids shouldn't be around when their parents are doing anything unsavory."

I arch a brow. "Unsavory?"

"You know what I mean," she snaps.

I do. And I admire it. There may be a lot of reasons not to hire Piper as Benjamin's nanny, but the woman cares for him. I know she'll protect him.

That's reason enough for me.

She turns, positioning her body between me and Benjamin. "Do what you want with me, but get him out of here first. Please."

I swallow down the desire that rises up at that invitation. Oh, if she only knew what I wanted to do with her.

"That won't be necessary."

Her shoulders sag. "Timofey, please. I don't want him to see—"

"He won't see anything."

"I know he's sleeping," she says. "But still. It's the only thing I'll ever ask from you. Get him out of here."

"I've warned you about lying."

"I'm not—"

"It doesn't matter," I interrupt. "He doesn't need to leave. You and I will be the ones leaving."

She frowns. "Where are we going?"

"Dinner."

42

PIPER

The chandelier hanging over my head feels like a threat. Any moment, Timofey is going to pull a cord and it's going to come crashing down on me, I just know it.

Honestly, right now, that doesn't sound so bad. Death would be preferable to watching our bottle blonde waitress shoot "fuck me" eyes at Timofey all night.

This restaurant is supposed to be fancy, for God's sake. Can't she keep it in her pants?

"And for you?" the waitress asks. She's talking to me, but her eyes are too busy perusing Timofey to look in my direction.

I don't know why I'm here. Not just here, as in, in this moment, jealous over a waitress I don't know making eyes at a man I wish I didn't know.

But here as in *here*. At this restaurant. With Timofey.

I asked a million times on the car ride over, but he refused to say anything. I'm sure he has a reason, of course. He has a reason for everything. And I'm sure that reason is infuriating. It always is with him.

"Chef salad," I say, folding my menu closed and sliding it over to her. "No dressing."

At that, the woman finally glances in my direction, surprised. "You want a… dry side salad? For your entree?"

I give her a smile with all my teeth. "You got it."

Timofey may be trying to wine and dine me—for what purpose, I don't know—but I can simply refuse to be wined and dined. There's nothing tempting about a bowl of lettuce and one grape tomato.

Let that be a lesson to you: don't try to buy Piper Quinn, people, because she can't be bought.

I cross my arms confidently over my chest, though I have to bite back a wince when my burnt skin twinges. I'm feeling much better today than yesterday, but I still have to move cautiously.

Timofey reaches out and encircles my wrist in one huge hand. Goosebumps erupt across my skin. "After the couple days you've had, you should eat something more substantial."

From the outside, it sounds concerned. Maybe even caring.

I hear it for what it is: a command.

"I'm fine," I grit from behind a tense smile.

He studies me, understanding sparking in his eyes. He knows what I'm doing. Of course he does.

"Actually, she'll have the milk-braised pork shoulder with mascarpone polenta and charred apples." Timofey picks up both menus and hands them to the waitress. "And another bottle of wine for the table."

The waitress beams at him, practically melting when her hand brushes over his fingers as they exchange menus. Then she's gone.

"She didn't even check to see if that's really what I wanted," I grumble. "She just took your word for it."

"She's smart. You could learn something from her."

I narrow my eyes at my dinner date. Timofey is sitting next to me, conveniently outside the range of the chandelier should it come tumbling down. One hand is on the back of my chair, the other wrapped around the stem of his wine glass.

He is effortless charm and sex. No wonder the waitress doesn't give a single fuck what I think.

"Relax," he says, leaning in to whisper the words in my ear. "We're having a nice time."

"Why does it feel like you're saying that with a gun pointed at my back?"

"Because you're always looking for the catch," he says. "For the real reason someone is showing interest in you. Your entire life has been a lesson in never letting your guard down, so when someone is being genuinely nice to you, you don't recognize it."

I blink at him in shock. Timofey sips his wine, unbothered.

"Are you familiar with that feeling?" I finally ask.

He shrugs. "I was. For a time. I've grown out of it by now."

"Must be nice."

"Even with shitty parents, you're too young to sound that bitter," he scolds. "Besides, you're where you are in life because you're too stubborn to get out."

I snap my attention to him so quickly my neck pops. "What does that mean?"

"Exactly what I said. Instead of looking out for yourself, you've spent all of your time and most of your money taking care of everyone else. Life shit on you, and you decided to scoop as much of the stuff as possible off of everyone else in your vicinity."

I grimace. "Charming analogy."

"The problem is that you're scooping everyone else's shit onto your own pile," he continues. "You're burying yourself alive to save them."

I want to deny everything he's saying, but the words hit a little too close to home.

Six months ago, I got a bonus at work for being "Social Worker of the Quarter." Two hours after clocking out for the day, I spent the entire thing plus an extra hundred I couldn't really spare on Ashley's bail.

Every time I get ahead even an inch, I hand it off to Ashley or Gram or my dad. I don't see him often, but when I do, his hand is out and ready.

There is a lot of shit I deal with in my life. And Timofey is right: most of it isn't mine.

"What would you suggest I do?" I snap. "Should I start a crime syndicate and have my loved ones murdered when they bother me?"

"I'd suggest not having 'loved ones' to begin with," he replies coolly. "That has always worked for me."

"What about Emily?"

He freezes. It's not the flinch of prey in headlights. More like he turns to stone. The only motion is him running his finger over the rim of his glass again and again. The only sounds are the soft wail it emits and the quiet murmur of the restaurant around us.

"What about her?" he says at last.

"You know what I'm asking. Who was she to you?"

Timofey angles himself towards me. It feels ominous. Like I'm the suspect on a cop show, as the searingly bright light swivels onto my face and the bad cop cracks his knuckles and gets ready to take his pound of flesh.

"I'd rather know who she is to you," he rumbles. "You seem to care a lot about her."

"Did you love her?"

My voice wobbles but doesn't break. I'm proud of that part, although I'm mostly ashamed of the rest of the question. *Did you love her*—that's the root of my concern, isn't it? I want to know whether or not Timofey was in love with another woman.

As if it matters. As if his answer will change anything for me.

Spoiler: it won't.

Timofey inhales and exhales slowly. Every second that passes feels like it takes fifty years. "I don't love anyone. I never have. Not in the way you're asking."

"The locket in your office would beg to differ."

"You know what else would beg to differ? The fact Emily was dating Rodion after I introduced the two of them." He must see my face fall, because his lip twitches up in a subtle smirk. "Pity. Did I ruin your 'jilted ex-lover murders his soulmate' theory?"

"Emily and Rodion were dating?" I shake my head. *Did I misidentify Timofey as the man in the locket?* No. Definitely not. Even as young as he was in that photo, he's hard to confuse with anyone else. "I don't believe you."

"Suit yourself. I have no reason to lie."

I snort so loud the woman at the table nearest us turns her head. I cover my mouth with a dainty hand and scoff at Timofey from behind it. "Of course you do! You have every reason to lie. The most important one being that you may be *responsible for her murder.*"

Timofey's brow pinches as some unreadable thought passes through his head. Before he can say it, the waitress returns with our food.

"Here you are, sir. I hope everything is absolutely to your liking." She leans much further than necessary across the table to slide Timofey his plate of miso-marinated black cod. It also looks like she's undone a button or two on her uniform. Absolutely shameless.

My plate, on other hand, is dropped in front of me without so much as a word.

"Is there anything else I can get you?" she asks Timofey exclusively.

Without looking up, he waves her away. "No."

I hate the zing of pleasure his curt dismissal sends through me. I shouldn't care. In fact, I don't. So what if he flirts with a waitress? It doesn't matter to me. Nope. I could not care less.

And yet I bite back a smile as the woman's face falls and she turns dejectedly towards the kitchen.

The moment she's gone, Timofey turns to me. His ice blue eyes on mine are a reminder of who I'm dealing with.

I just accused him of murdering his ex-girlfriend—or Rodion's ex-girlfriend, if Timofey is to be believed. I don't want his attention on me any more than is necessary. I should be grateful for the distraction of the bimbo waitress.

"I don't waste my time lying to people who hold no power over me," Timofey says. His eyes sweep over me like he's double-checking to make sure I'm as harmless and unthreatening as he thought. And that little twitch of the mouth again confirms it. "I'm primarily interested in why you care more about what happened to someone who is already dead than you seem to care about what happens to you right now."

"Is that another threat? You've issued so many that I'm starting to lose track."

The words are barely out of my mouth when fire erupts to my right.

Between one blink and the next, flames several feet high roar to life no more than three steps away from me. I shriek and lunge instinctively towards Timofey. My sore arm plows into his chest, but I ignore the scream of pain in my shoulder and plow on. Anything to get away from the flames.

He's not moving. Why isn't he moving? The place is burning. We need to run! We need to get the hell out of—

"Piper."

His hands grip me tightly, keeping me from charging across the restaurant.

"Let me go!" I cry out. "It's a fire! There's a—"

"Flambé." Timofey grabs my chin and turns it towards the table next to us. "Someone ordered Baked Alaska."

The couple next to us are gawking over, their eyes wide, mouths hanging open. Sticking out of the now-caramelized meringue coating the Baked Alaska is a flaming candle. *Happy Birthday, Rhonda* is piped in gold frosting along the edge of the plate.

I nod and gulp. My mouth tastes like acid. "Right. Okay."

The information permeates my mind, but my panicked body isn't responding. The communication between the two has been severed. Despite knowing I'm no longer in danger, I can feel my torso compressing like an aluminum can. My lungs can't expand. I'm suffocating.

"Breathe," Timofey commands. "Piper, breathe."

Even his stern voice isn't enough to break through the fear strangling me. To drown out the thought running circles in my head.

I'm going to die here.

43

PIPER

"Get up." Timofey doesn't give me the chance to refuse him. He hooks an arm around my waist and hauls me against his body.

Distantly, I recognize how muscular his arm is around me. I acknowledge the burning heat of his chiseled chest pressed to my side. But I can't enjoy it.

Not when it's the last thing I'll ever feel.

Timofey walks me around the edge of the dining room. As we pass by the kitchen, our waitress steps out.

"Is everything okay? Do you need—"

"I need you to get the fuck out of my way," Timofey barks.

The woman stumbles back against the door as we plow past her. A second later, Timofey shoves open the door to the women's restroom.

A woman is inside washing her hands and he holds the door open for her. His voice is the crack of a whip. "See yourself out."

She takes one look at him and sprints for the door. The moment she leaves the room, Timofey locks it behind her and turns to me.

"Breathe," he orders again.

"That isn't how this works." I suck in a shaky inhale that does nothing to soothe me. "You can't order me to stop having a panic attack."

"Seems as though I can. Look who can speak in full sentences again."

I bite my tongue. He's right. I hate that he's right.

He smooths a heavy hand down my uninjured arm, squeezing as he goes. It's strangely grounding. I want to tell him to stop, but it would be a lie. The firm pressure is doing wonders to loosen the iron band around my chest.

"I thought you were claustrophobic."

"I still am," I gasp. "This bathroom is microscopic."

He just keeps massaging my arm. A few times, his hand dips lower, brushing over my hip before traveling back up.

I close my eyes and focus on the movement. On the human contact. On what is real and right next to me, not the irrational fear thrumming in my mind.

My heart rate decreases bit by bit. I lean deeper into Timofey's chest. I let his scent swallow me up.

It happens slowly, the way we fall together. I press my forehead to his shoulder. Then my cheek. I can hear the steady drum of his heart, and I time my breathing to the even rise and fall of his.

Eventually, I'm lying against his body, more relaxed than I can remember being in months. Years. *Ever.*

Timofey starts to move his hand away, but I squeeze him hard. "Don't stop. Please."

A low sound like a growl rumbles through his chest, but he brings his hand back to my bicep. He massages my slackened muscles. Then he shifts and our bodies fit together like puzzle pieces. Like I was made to fit between his arms, to rest my cheek in the hollow of his chest.

Touching Timofey Viktorov shouldn't feel this good.

Our hips align. I freeze when I realize this feels good for him, too. I try to slide my body away, but we're wedged together so tightly and I'm so off-balance that I end up shimmying side to side against his hard length.

Timofey releases a breathy growl.

"Sorry," I whisper. The word is muffled against his warm chest.

He chuckles softly. "I'd tell you not to stop, but, I actually like this restaurant."

"What does that have to do with anything?" I ask. My lips are putty. Barely functional.

"The owner is rather conservative," he says. "Loudly fucking my date in his bathroom might land me on the 'Do Not Serve' list."

"Are you—" I clear my throat. "Are you saying you're loud in bed?"

He rubs his thumb in a delicious circle just below my neck and my entire body goes slack like I'm a robot and he just smashed my Off button.

Instinctively, I tip my head up to look at him. The blue in his eyes is almost gone, eaten away by the black of his pupils. He's looking at me with such raw desire that I almost think it's a trick.

He can't want *me* like that. It doesn't make sense.

"No." He lowers his head until the tip of his nose brushes against mine. "But you will be. You won't be able to help it."

My body quivers at the thought. Need floods my nerve endings and pulses between my thighs.

I've been with men before, but no one has ever held me like this. Textbook "good guys" have stood by while I suffered alone through a panic attack brought on by a stupid compact car.

Yet, somehow, Timofey is the man who takes me to a private room to calm down. He's the man who strokes my over-sensitized body until I can relax. Who tells me to breathe and, miracle of all miracles, it actually *works.*

He turns my brain off and my body on, and I can't think of a more intoxicating feeling than the one coursing through me now.

I want him.

He's still staring at me as I press onto my toes. As I watch, stupefied, he leans down. He licks his parted lips, but I wish he wouldn't—because I want to do that for him.

I want to taste them on my own tongue.

I let my eyes flutter closed and the rational part of my mind go to sleep.

Maybe this will be the first step to learning how to take care of myself. Letting myself indulge in Timofey—just for a moment—can be the watershed moment I've been waiting for.

Just as I feel the warmth of his lips on mine, however, reality comes knocking.

44

TIMOFEY

The knock on the bathroom door sends Piper shooting off like a firework.

She knocks against the stall door behind her. It swings open, and the only reason she doesn't tumble into the toilet is because I grab her hand and reel her back against my chest.

"Hello?" a male voice from the hallway calls. "Is anyone in there? The door isn't supposed to be locked."

"Wait," I order him.

I'm going to need at least a second, maybe several, to get rid of my raging hard-on. Based on the way Piper is looking at me, horrified and filled with shame, I assume sex is off the table.

There's a pause. "This is a *women's* restroom, sir. If you don't come out, I'll have no choice but to—"

Frustrated in several ways, I reach back to flick the bolt and yank the door open.

The middle-aged manager barely reaches my elbow, but he's high on power. "Please retake your seats or I'll have to ask you both to leave."

"I had no clue using the bathroom was a crime," I drawl.

He isn't amused. "Public restrooms are still 'public.' If the police are called, you'll be fined with lewdness and public f—"

"Fucking?" I finish for him.

His eyes narrow. "Fornication."

"It's called fucking when you do it right." I grab Piper's hand and walk past the red-faced manager, pulling her along behind me.

"So much for avoiding the 'Do Not Serve' list," she whispers.

I chuckle. This is one of my favorite restaurants, but I have no regrets. I'd do it again a million times over just to see that heat in her eyes.

Back at our table, our food is cold, but Piper doesn't seem to mind. She digs into her plate with a utensil in each hand.

"You eat like I'm starving you," I remark.

"Panic attacks use up a lot of energy," she explains. "I'm always hungry afterward."

The pork shoulder falls apart as she slices into it. When she places it in her mouth, her eyes flutter closed. The same way they were in the bathroom. Ecstasy. An orgasm on her tongue.

She sighs, and I can still feel the imprint of her against my chest, the warmth of her pressed to my body.

She looked like she wanted it. I know she did.

But that doesn't mean anything. I've learned by now to never trust anyone.

"I want to know why you're really so concerned with Emily's murder."

Piper lowers her fork and stares at me. "Because an innocent woman was killed and—"

"I also want to know why you looked so shocked when you found out she was dating Rodion." I tighten my grip on my fork until the metal digs into my palm. The pain helps me focus.

"I thought maybe you and her were…" She blows out a frustrated breath. "It doesn't matter."

"I'll decide what matters," I reply. "I want to know why you asked your friend to look into Rodion for you."

"I didn't. I asked her to look into who Emily was."

That could make sense. It doesn't mean I believe her. Not yet.

"Jealous, are we?" I ask, eyebrow raised.

Her cheeks flush, confirming my half-baked theory. Then she flips the script. "No more jealous than you are right now."

"I don't get jealous."

"Oh, really?" She shrugs. "Then you won't mind that Rodion asked me out."

I'll fucking kill him.

"Maybe you haven't noticed, but he's not good company."

"Neither are you," she retorts. "But here I am. How much worse could he be? I'm sure he wouldn't risk me getting charged with... what did the manager call it? 'Public fornication'?"

The thought of Rodion's hands anywhere near Piper, in public or otherwise, has me teetering on the very edge of my self-control.

"No, but you might become an accessory to murder. I hope you don't mind him taking out a hit between entrees and dessert."

Piper's eyes widen. She wasn't expecting me to be so forthcoming. Truth be told, I wasn't expecting it, either.

"Don't give me those doe eyes," I scowl. "It's nothing you don't already know."

After a second, she nods. "Yeah. Rodion showed me his tattoos."

An image flashes in my mind of Rodion pulling his shirt over his head. Of Piper dragging her smooth hands over his body, tracing the tattoo on his inner arm. Of her looking at him the way she just looked at me.

I'll kill him. I'll kill him, bring him back to life, and kill him again to make sure of it.

"The one and only time I've spoken to him, he showed me how many people he has killed." Piper's voice is bitterly sarcastic. "It wasn't exactly a turn-on."

The green fire of jealousy dims to burning embers. "Maybe you have some survival instincts after all, Ms. Quinn."

She gives me a half-smile. "Were you worried about me, Mr. Viktorov?"

My name sounds different on her lips. It's a seductive roll of syllables. I don't mind it at all.

I stab my fork into a bite of the cod and eat without tasting it. "I was looking out for myself. I've had enough bad press lately. A dead nanny wouldn't help matters."

"I'd hate for my death to be an inconvenience for you." She rolls her eyes and turns back to her plate. "I live to serve."

"That's great to hear. Because there's a reason I brought you to dinner tonight."

Piper goes perfectly still. Then she looks up at me beneath lowered brows. "I knew it."

"No, you didn't."

"Well, I suspected," she snaps. "There's a reason I always look for ulterior motives. Usually, there is one."

"When you're done playing the sad, manipulated victim, I'd love to get to my point."

She subtly flips me the bird behind the candles in the center of the table, and I have to force myself not to laugh. She may be afraid of it, but the woman has fire.

"I have a wedding coming up."

"You're getting married?" she practically guffaws.

I press a finger to the headache forming between my eyes. "I'll be a *guest* at a wedding soon. You will be my plus-one."

"Oh," she says, relief obvious in her tone. Then she stiffens. "*Oh*. No. No way."

"It wasn't really a question."

"Then ask your not-a-question to someone else," she fires back. "The waitress tonight would love to go with you. Actually, she would love to do lots of things with you."

I set my silverware down and fold my hands in front of me. "There's that jealousy again."

"You're confusing jealousy for disgust."

"You didn't seem disgusted in the bathroom."

Her mouth flattens into a grimace. "Take someone else."

"I could," I admit. "There are plenty of women I could ask. But after what happened with Benjamin at the hospital and the news running with the story that I attacked a doctor, I could use some good publicity."

"And you think kidnapping a woman and forcing her to be your date will help?"

"I think taking a poor, homely social worker as my date might garner some sympathy for me, yes."

I'm being intentionally cruel, but it's all bullshit. There is nothing homely about Piper. She's a fucking vision, all the more beautiful for how much she tries not to let me see it. She leans her face to the side, her green eyes flickering golden in the candlelight.

"Whose wedding is it that you think it'll make this much news? The pope?"

"The pope marrying would certainly make a headline or two."

"You know what I mean," she grumbles.

"It will be a well-publicized wedding. That's all you need to know for now," I tell her. "And taking you as my date will look less fabricated if we're seen out together a few times before the event."

It takes a few seconds for that to sink in. Then Piper sits tall and glances from side to side, scanning the half of the room she can see. "Is that what this is right now? Is someone watching us?"

"A woman in the waiting area took a less-than-subtle photo of us half an hour ago and the waitress tweeted that she was serving me five minutes after we arrived," I say. "Congratulations, princess. We've just made our debut as a couple."

Her cheeks flame red. She leans in, hissing between her teeth. "You are a…a narcissist. A twisted, sick, entitled narcissist who—"

"Brings you to fabulous restaurants and pays for your meals and keeps you from having a panic attack," I finish for her. "You're right, I sound awful. How monstrous of me."

"Dragging me to dinner as a prop in your P.R. scheme makes you an asshole. Using people like that is the mark of an entitled narcissist."

"'Using' implies you don't want to be here."

"Here's a headline: I'd rather be cold and dead than here with you," she spits, nostrils flared.

I give her a winning smile just as the woman from the front of the restaurant takes a second, much less discrete photo of us. "That can be arranged." Piper's face pales. I lean in. "But we both know you're lying. You felt the exact opposite of 'cold and dead' in the bathroom."

She fists her hands on the table, staring straight down at her plate. "I'm not going with you. There's nothing you can say to change my—"

"I know Noelle is the person who called you tonight."

Piper doesn't move except for her eyes, which flick in my direction and tremble.

"It was easy enough to track who the call came from. Even easier was to track where she lives and who she lives with." I release a bored sigh. "She's dating an FBI agent, did you know?"

Her shoulders sag, and I can see the fight draining out of her as easily as if I pulled the plug in a bathtub.

"The only reason you aren't 'cold and dead,' as you so elegantly put it, is because I know you aren't working for the FBI. That's good news for you. But it could mean bad news for your friend and her boyfriend."

"L-leave them alone," Piper stammers. "Leave them out of it. The only reason Noelle looked up anything is because I asked her to. She'll stay out of this if you just—"

I hold up a hand and she goes silent immediately. That's progress. Maybe I can teach an old dog new tricks after all.

"I'll stay out of her life if you cooperate. It's that simple, Piper. Do as I say and the leeches you insist on loving stay safe. Do you understand?"

She nods slowly.

"Good. Then you'll be my plus-one for—"

"No." She releases a shaky breath and meets my eyes. "I said I understand. I never said I agreed."

"I knew things with you wouldn't be that easy," I sigh. "When will you learn, Piper?"

She lifts her chin up in defiance. "When I'm cold and dead."

45

TIMOFEY

It's late, but I can hear Piper talking softly in her room.

"It was a stressful day." There's a long pause while whoever she is talking to responds. "I love you, too. I've just been busy."

Who the fuck is she talking to? I asked her about Rodion, but I apparently should have made sure there wasn't anyone else in her life.

"You're right," she sighs. "I should have called sooner. You and Gram both deserved a prompt apology. I didn't mean anything I said."

My hackles lower as I realize she's talking to Ashley. One of the leeches.

"I really didn't mean it. You are one of my best friends, Ash. You mean—" She stops, groaning at whatever Ashley says. "Yes, you're *one of* my best friends. I love you and Noelle the same. No, no tiebreakers."

I roll my eyes. Ashley is a leech financially *and* emotionally, apparently. Fucking pathetic.

"Where are you?" There's a tension in Piper's voice that wasn't there a second ago. "I hear voices, and you…you don't sound like yourself. What's going on?"

Some emergency, I'm sure. Something just bad enough to make Piper feel guilty for ever being honest with her. Something that will make Piper rush off to save her.

"Where are you?" Piper demands. "Ashley, tell me right now. Please."

I push open her door just as Piper curses into her phone. "Ash, goddamm—"

"I hope I'm not interrupting."

Piper jumps at the sound of my voice and then scowls. "Get out of my room."

I lean against the frame. "No."

She waves me away and reaches for her purse at the end of the bed. "Fine. Then I'll leave."

"Wrong again."

"This isn't a debate, Timofey."

"You're right," I agree. "It isn't. You're not going anywhere."

She rifles through her purse for a second and then her entire body droops. When she turns around, there are tears welling in her eyes. "Ashley is in trouble."

"What else is new?"

"Stop it," she snaps, sniffling. "After our fight the other day, she kind of fell apart. She went off the radar, and I thought everything was fine, but she sounded messed up on the phone."

"So?"

She gapes at me. "*So,* as a good friend, I have to go help her."

"You've helped her again and again. It doesn't seem to take."

"What do you suggest I do then?" she argues. "Just let her fall off the face of the earth?"

I shrug. "Sounds fitting to me. No one will miss her."

Piper shoots lasers at me. "I think you're mistaking Ashley for yourself. No one would miss you because you're manipulative and cruel. Ashley is different."

I give her a sarcastic slow clap. "So eloquent. So persuasive. *'Different.'* You've really changed my mind about the woman who uses you as a permanent bail bondsman and then forces you to confirm how much you love and adore her at every opportunity."

"Shut up."

"I heard you on the phone, comforting her, assuring her she's your very bestest friend. It's pathetic."

"Shut. Up," she repeats, acid in her voice now.

"The truth can be uncomfortable."

"What's uncomfortable is that you think you know everything!" Piper cries out. "You don't. Ashley is going through a hard time, but she was there for me when I needed someone. She was a good friend to me. She was loyal and caring. She was dependable."

"*Was.*"

Piper shakes her head in confusion. "What?"

"Past tense," I say. "You said Ashley 'was' all those things. You and I know better than most that relationships change. Someone who used to be your parent suddenly isn't. Someone who used to be worth your time is now a drug-addicted parasite sucking you dry."

Piper mashes her lips together, trying to drum up a response to refute my incredibly solid point. In the end, she can't.

She spins around and keeps digging through her purse. "Leave me alone. I'm going to go help my friend and then I'll be back. Benjamin is asleep and I'll ask one of the maids to keep an ear out for him. Don't worry—your nanny will be back before work hours begin."

"I'm not worried."

"How sweet," she says sarcastically. "It's good to know you care about your employees."

"I'm not worried because you're not going."

She twirls around, green eyes wide. "I'm not a prisoner here. You can't chain me up and throw away the key."

I arch a brow. "I can do whatever I want with you. I've made that perfectly clear."

Piper flicks her auburn hair over her shoulder defiantly. "I'm going."

"No, you're not."

She grunts in frustration. "One of my best friends is sitting in a fucking crack house right now! She's vulnerable and alone. You can't expect me to leave her there."

God, this woman and her bleeding heart. It must be exhausting.

"I expect you to take care of Benjamin. That's what I'm paying you for. Ashley doesn't factor into my plans at all."

She turns away from me and drops her phone in her purse. "I don't care what you say. I'm going to go get my friend."

I'm across the room in a second. Piper gasps as I toss her back on the bed and loom over her. "I'm not going to stand aside and watch you throw away your life for a woman who would never do the same for you."

She frowns. "You don't know—"

"I do know," I interrupt. "The second you stop being useful to Ashley, she'll drop you. She'll find someone else to manipulate. You don't see it, but I do. So yes, I'll chain you up if I need to."

She exhales. We are so close I feel the warmth of it across my lips. Like a dog recognizing a scent, my body remembers the feel of her. Hardness grows between my legs. There's an inch of space between our lower bodies, but at this rate, it won't be there for long.

I shove away from the bed and pace back to the door.

Piper sits up slowly and folds her hands in her lap. "I didn't realize you cared so much."

I grab the door frame. My fingers turn white gripping the wood. A little more force and I could rip it clean off. "I don't want to search for another nanny."

We both know that's not even close to the whole story, but Piper is smart enough not to press. "Okay," she says finally.

I look back. "Ashley is grown. If she can't take care of herself, she'll never learn."

She nods. "You're right. I'll stay here."

She sounds dejected. Surprisingly soft-spoken.

Our eyes meet, and I might as well still be on top of her. Her legs might as well be wrapped around my waist with the connection I feel from just a momentary glance.

"Stay in your room." I swallow down the desire and turn away. "She isn't worth your life."

46

TIMOFEY

I head in the direction of my room, but when I reach it, I keep walking. I take a side hallway, looping back around to the back staircase, and then I go outside to the patio beneath Piper's room.

I can see light from her window splashing across the grass. I lean against a wooden banister and pull out a cigarette. If I'm lucky, I'll get through the whole thing before I'm interrupted.

But a few puffs later, I see a shadow cross the square of light in the lawn. I hear the rattle of metal against stone as someone climbs out of Piper's window and shimmies down the trellis.

Blyat'. Just once, I wanted to be wrong.

I sigh and drop my cigarette to the ground, smashing it down with the toe of my boot. Then I stroll to the edge of the patio with my hands in my pockets and wait.

A minute later, Piper drops to the ground. The damp grass squelches beneath her feet, and she's already breathing heavily. She's so focused on catching her breath and scanning the lawn that she doesn't even look my way.

She doesn't see me coming until it's too late.

I reach out just as she looks over. Her eyebrows shoot up, and she tries to stumble away, but I snatch her arm. My hand wraps around her bicep, my finger and thumb overlapping.

"I thought I told you to stay in your room."

"Let go of me!" she screams, flailing wildly.

I pin her arms to her side and back her against the house. "Scream as loud as you want. No one is coming."

She narrows her eyes and then arches her head back to unleash a truly impressive scream. The sound echoes off the trees and leaves my ears ringing for a second. But I don't even flinch.

"Feel better?" I ask flatly when she's finished.

She tries to kick me, but I pin her legs down with my knees. We're entirely sealed together. I can feel her chest against mine with every ragged inhale. She's trembling.

"You can't be reasoned with," she spits. "This was my only choice."

"Or you could fucking listen!" I release her and take a cautious step back, ready to step in and grab her again if need be. Piper stays put. "I've never met someone so eager to get themselves killed."

"I'm not going to get myself killed. If Ashley can survive there, so can I."

I scrutinize Piper's outfit. Her straight-legged jeans and knit green sweater. Her white sneakers are scuffed and worn, but they aren't the only thing straight-laced about her. "You look like you're off to knock on doors and talk to people about your Lord and Savior Jesus Christ."

"I do not!"

"It's obvious you've never stepped foot into a drug house. It would be obvious to everyone there, too. They'd assume you were with the police. Or the neighborhood watch, at least."

"So they'd get out of my way." She shrugs. "That sounds like a good thing."

I drag a hand down my face. "They'd gut you before you got a toe through the door."

"What do you know? You don't even know where she is."

"A tumbledown, two-story shithole that used to be painted blue, with a faded 'For Sale' sign in the overgrown lawn." I would ask Piper if I'm correct, but I can tell by the widening of her eyes that I'm on point.

She gapes at me. "How do you—"

"Your friend has been in trouble since well before you yelled at her the other day. I tracked her there after the night you and I met. She had a black eye at the time, if that helps with your timeline."

Piper closes her eyes. "I knew she was involved with Jason again, but I hoped she wasn't—I didn't know she was back in this deep."

"Of course you didn't. Which is why she tried to manipulate you into thinking it was your fault." I shake my head, anger building into a dark cloud inside of me. "She wants you to feel bad enough that you'll come yank her out of that house and pay off whatever she owes. It's as predictable as it is pathetic."

"Pathetic for her?" Piper asks.

"For both of you. You're better than this."

She looks up at me with wide, pained eyes. "You keep saying stuff like that. *She isn't worth your life. You're better than this.* How do you know? You don't even know me."

"I know enough."

Piper stares at me long enough that the sadness and frustration in her expression drain away into an exhausted kind of acceptance. "Then you have to know that I'm not going to stop until I can help her." I grimace and Piper shrugs again. "I know you think I'm pathetic. I know you think my friends are leeches. I know you probably think I'm the dumbest woman alive—"

"That depends on what you decide to do now."

"But," she continues over my interruption, "at the end of the day, I don't care what you think of me. The only thing I care about is how I feel when I climb into bed at night. If I don't try to help my friend and something bad happens to her, I'll never forgive myself."

There's an earnestness to the way she's talking to me. Each word out of her mouth is a travesty, but I have no doubt she means every single one of them.

"You can't really believe you had any chance of saving Ashley anyway," I finally say. "Were you going to hotwire one of my cars, or what?"

She chews on her lower lip for a second and crosses her arms. "My bike is still here."

I stare at her for a second before I tip my head back and laugh.

"Shut up," she grumbles.

But I can't. This is the hardest I've laughed in a good long while, and I'm enjoying it.

Piper slaps my arm. "You're an asshole."

I stop laughing and grab her wrist. Gently, I twist her arm. Her entire body moves with it. I spin her around until her back is against my chest, my lips pressed to her ear. "And you're incapacitated. That's how easy it would be for someone to take control of you."

"Let go." She squirms, her ass grinding against me. My cock twitches, but that's not what I'm doing here. I have a point to make.

"You're not prepared to fight," I explain. "And on a bike? Fuck, Piper. It's laughable. The thought of you peddling away from the crack house with Ashley riding on your handlebars... I mean, come on."

She huffs, but doesn't say anything. Because she knows I'm right.

Finally, she turns her head and looks at me. Her lips are less than an inch away. She's so close that I can't take all of her in at once. My eyes flick from her full lips to one green eye and then the other. Her eyes stay focused on mine.

"Then drive me there," she pleads. "You can fight. You're intimidating. You have a car."

"I'm not wasting any of my resources on Ashley. The woman needs to learn how to take care of herself."

I release Piper and walk away. She follows after me, her footsteps heavy across the damp ground. "Please! Timofey, I can't do this without you."

"So you're finally starting to see reason. About time."

"Don't be smug," she snaps. "I'm admitting that I need your help. Doesn't that mean anything to you?"

I spin around. Piper has to slam to a stop before our bodies collide. "I don't do anything unless I benefit. Picking your friend up from her drug den doesn't help me in any way. I gain nothing."

"Okay, then I'll… I'll…" Piper's mouth twists into a knot as she thinks. "I'll do whatever you want. I'll go to that wedding with you."

"Regardless of what you thought, you were always going to that wedding with me," I inform her. "You didn't have a choice."

She rolls her eyes. "I'll go *willingly*."

"I don't give a fuck whether you're willing or not."

"But this wedding was supposed to be a place where people would see us as a couple, right?" she asks. "You wanted it to be a coming out for us as a couple to help your image?"

"I need you to be breathing, that's all."

In one instant, Piper's expression shifts. She lowers her chin and cocks a brow. Her mouth twists into a seductive smile, and she crosses one leg in front of the other as she moves towards me. She trails a finger over my shoulder and down my arm. "It would be more convincing if I really played the part, wouldn't it?"

I know she's putting on a show, but it's a damn good one. "What part is that?"

"The part of your adoring girlfriend." She drags my arm around her waist and slides my hand lower so I'm cupping the curve of her ass. Her body arches into mine. "No one will doubt that we're a couple if I give it my all."

"You're no actress."

Her brow flicks in obvious annoyance at my doubt. Then she stretches onto her toes and breezes her lips across my throat. "Could've fooled me."

I swallow. "You won't do anything. Your annoying moral high ground is miles above a stunt like this."

Slowly, Piper drags her hand over my chest and lower. Her hand heads directly for the crotch of my jeans, but at the last second, she veers to my thigh. She works a delicious pressure up and down my thigh as her lips graze my neck without quite touching me.

She's absurdly close to exactly where I want her, but without the relief that would come with it.

"I don't need to do anything to sell the story," she whispers. "If we get close enough to the real deal, people will buy it."

Fuck. Under different circumstances, I'd shove her away and hire a high-class escort just to prove a point.

But I'm not in different circumstances. Right now, the police are looking into Emily's murder again, and if I'm right— which I always am—it might all lead right back to the Bratva. Plus, tensions are high with the Albanians. My public image is so tarnished right now that a little shove from either of those two things could spell more trouble than I want to deal with.

A devoted girlfriend in the form of a wholesome-looking social worker could be just what I need.

I sigh. "You do realize your friend is firmly in Albanian territory, don't you?"

"No," Piper says, pulling away from me. "I don't even know what that means."

I reluctantly remove my hand from the curve of her ass and grip her chin. I force her eyes to mine, making sure she is paying attention. "Which is why you had no business hopping on your bike and going over there. They would have fucking killed you, Piper."

"Does that mean you're going to go get her?" she asks hopefully.

"I'm not going to drag her out of there kicking and screaming," I tell her firmly. "Either she wants to come with me or she doesn't. If she refuses, I'm not getting myself killed for her. Whichever the case, the agreement still stands."

Without hesitation, Piper thrusts out her hand. "Deal."

47

PIPER

Timofey's mansion is huge, but there isn't enough square footage in the world to handle my pacing.

I can clearly see the path I've worn in the plush rug in my room. It's been two hours since he streaked out of his driveway in one of the black sports cars from his fleet of vehicles, but it feels like a lifetime.

"They're fine," I tell myself, inhaling and exhaling in an even measure to settle my heart rate. "Ashley is fine. Timofey will take care of her."

I want to laugh at the absurdity of my own pep talk. In no world did I imagine I would be depending on Timofey for the health and safety of one of my best friends. Or for anyone, for that matter.

Then again, he's saved me almost more times than I can count. At some point, I will have to reconcile the two sides of him, but I don't know if I'm capable of it now.

She isn't worth your life.

Those words have replayed in my head too many times to count since Timofey said them. It's stupid, but there's something there, right? He must think I'm worth something. Maybe I'm more than just a nanny to him. Maybe I'm…

What? What do I want to be to Timofey Viktorov?

"Nothing." It seems like a sentiment worth saying aloud.

The butterflies in my stomach are not a valid way of judging a person's character. The only thing that getting butterflies around Timofey tells me is that it has been too long since I've been with a man. It's chemical nonsense, that's all. Nothing worth throwing my dignity away over.

"Focus," I breathe. I squeeze my eyes closed as I pace. The path is as well marked in my head as it is on the carpet, so I don't need my eyes open to see it. Plus, I need to purge thoughts of Timofey pressed against me from my heart and soul.

Right now, I need to be focused on Ashley.

I hear tires squealing across the pavement in the front of the house, and my eyes pop open. I don't bother looking out the window to see who it is—I just take off at a run for the entryway.

As soon as I slide to a stop on the wood floor, the front door slams open.

But it isn't Timofey and Ashley standing in front of me.

It's Sergey.

"Where is he?" he growls, not even looking at me.

I actually don't think Sergey has even seen me yet. That's just the way he enters a house: throw open the door and shout a vague, demanding question to whatever lifeforms are unfortunate enough to be in his vicinity.

"Who?" My voice comes out in a tiny squeak. I clear my throat and try again. "Sorry, who are you looking for?"

Sergey turns to me and my guess was correct. This is the first time he's seeing me.

His hooded eyes slide over me with all the joy someone would have inspecting a festering wound. "I'm looking for my son. Where is he?"

"Oh. He's—" I stop.

Am I supposed to tell anyone where he went? Timofey doesn't answer to anyone. He's the leader of the criminals, as far as I can tell. Still, he might not want his movements—

"Well?" Sergey barks, interrupting my panicked thoughts. "Are you as dumb as my son says you are or can you answer a fucking question?"

There's the reminder I needed. I'm nothing to Timofey except for the stupid nanny he is using to get his way. None of these people care about me at all. Why should I care about them?

I give Sergey a smile bordering on a grimace. "I'm not sure where your son is. Even if I did, I wouldn't tell you. Timofey is the boss, so I report to him."

Sergey's nostrils flare as he stalks across the room towards me. "Timofey may be the don now, but I built this place. If you know where he is, tell me."

What part of "even if I did, I wouldn't tell you" does this man not understand?

"Sorry. I don't know where he is."

Sergey stares at me for a second and then, with no warning, swipes an arm toward the table to his right. Some kind of decorative bronze horse and a leather folder go flying across the room. Papers flutter in the air as the statue takes a chunk out of the wood floor and then bounces into the hallway.

I take a cautious step back. "I can take a message for you if—"

"I'm not leaving a message with a fucking secretary," Sergey spits. His eyes are glowing with rage. All the hairs on the back of my neck stand straight up. "I understand why Rodion confessed to you."

"Confessed what?" I ask, even though I don't want to engage Sergey in any kind of conversation right now.

He taps his forearm. "I hear you know his role in the family business. Or maybe Timofey told you. If he's letting you walk around his house un-fucking-supervised, then what the fuck do I know?"

Timofey must have told Sergey that Rodion showed me all the tattoos he had representing the people he's killed. Is that why he's so upset?

"You're looking for Timofey?" I ask. "Not Rodion?"

His top lip curls. "I said 'my son,' didn't I? You don't think I know my own goddamn son?"

I'm not sure if he means to, but he keeps moving towards me. With every step closer he takes, I feel the need to retreat two. Sergey is unhinged.

"I'm just—" I shake my head. "It doesn't matter. I don't know where either of them are anyway."

"Figures," Sergey mutters, stomping over to the bronze horse statue and kicking it again. "He brings you in here and runs shit into the ground. A distraction. I warned him, but he didn't listen. Now, he's making decisions that put us at risk."

"Is this about the Albanians?" The moment the words are out of my mouth, I want to reel them back in. I wave my hands. "Never mind. I don't need to know. Forget I said anything."

But Sergey isn't going to forget anytime soon. He spins on me, his back hunched as he closes in on me. "What did he tell you about the Albanians?"

"Nothing. I swear. I just—" I think I hear a thud somewhere outside, but it might be the beating of my own heart. Am I in actual danger? Would Timofey's father kill me?

Apparently, I'm a distraction. Maybe he knows about Timofey going after Ashley. I don't know what it has to do with anything, but Sergey is livid, and I'm the only person nearby for him to use as an outlet.

I have to get out of here.

"I think I hear Benjamin crying," I lie. "I need to go."

Sergey grabs my arm and holds me in place. "I don't hear anything. Now, what did you say about the Albanians?"

My mouth is dry, and I can't find the words. Anything I say will only make things worse.

He shakes my arm. "Speak!"

I yelp in fear and surprise—just as the front door bangs open again.

Sergey spins around as Timofey and Ashley slouch through the door, one of Ashley's arms thrown over Timofey's neck.

I use Sergey's distraction to ease around him and then run for Timofey and Ashley.

"Everything okay?" I ask as calmly as I can.

I still don't know if Sergey knows about Timofey's excursion into Albanian territory tonight. Clearly, it could be a sore point, so body language will have to do for now.

I give them a wide-eyed greeting, scanning them from head to toe. They both have blood on them—splatters and spots on Timofey's shirtsleeves and a bit across Ashley's stomach—but I don't see any wounds.

"Everything is amazing!" Ashley squeals. She doesn't sound like someone who just came out of a life or death situation. "What a night!"

"Yeah, big fun," Timofey mutters. He shakes Ashley off gently, but with clear intent.

Ashley wavers, and I step in to fill the role of her crutch. She drapes herself heavily across my shoulders. "I'm glad you didn't listen to me and sent in the big guns, Bagpipes."

"Don't call me that."

She reaches over and squeezes my cheek. "Come on, Pied Piper. Cheer up. All is well."

"No, it damn well isn't!" Sergey's voice shatters the relative calm. I was so relieved to see Timofey and Ashley that I almost forgot about him.

Timofey walks straight up to him with his shoulders pinned back. "What are you doing here?"

"What am I—This is my fucking house!" he splutters in outraged disbelief. "If I want to be here, I don't need to sign the guest book."

"It *was* your house," Timofey corrects. It's not cruel, but it is drawing a clear and obvious line in the sand.

Sergey's face purples with rage. "I'm here to talk about—"

"In my office." Timofey cuts off his father and waves him down the hallway. "We'll talk there."

The old man is practically vibrating, but he storms down the hallway. With one last blank look over his shoulder, Timofey follows.

48

PIPER

"Draaama," Ashley whispers a bit too loudly as soon as the men are out of sight. "What did I interrupt?"

Everything. Ashley inconvenienced everyone here—Timofey most of all—and I'd bet everything I own that she never even thanked him.

Instead of saying that, I shrug. "I don't know. Sergey showed up pissed. He didn't fill me in on the details."

"Who is he to you?"

"Sergey?" I ask. "He's nothing to me. He's just Timofey's dad."

Ashley lowers her chin, wagging her brows suggestively at me. "What about Timofey? Who is *he* to you?"

No one.

My boss.

The man who makes my insides flutter and burn with anger at the very same time.

I shake my head. "I'd rather talk about why you have blood on your shirt."

Ashley gasps and pinches her shirt, pulling it away from herself so she can see. "I do? Where is—shit! I liked this shirt."

It's a threadbare shirt with a graphic of some rock band I know Ashley doesn't listen to. The way the collar hangs off her shoulder and the sleeves drape down to her elbows, I'd guess it belongs to Jason. I hope it does. The asshole deserves blood on all his favorite shirts.

"Actually, the blood is kind of a look." Ashley tips her head from side to side, studying it. "If nothing else, it's a good story."

"A story I'd love to hear," I say impatiently.

She drops her shirt and nods. "Right. Sorry. Tonight has been… wild. Unexpected. I mean, have you seen Timofey fight? If he is someone special to you, tell me now because I'm about to wax poetic about how sexy he looked clearing that room out."

My heart leaps into my throat, making it hard to breathe. "A room? He fought an *entire room*? How many people?"

"Ten? Twelve?" Ashley guesses. "I don't know. Maybe it was more than that. He could have taken on a hundred, though. The guy was unstoppable."

I wish Timofey was here so I could give him another look over.

No. He can take care of himself. You don't need to worry about him.

The internal pep talk does nothing to assuage my concerns. Is he okay or was he playing tough? How much of the blood belonged to him?

"These guys came up to him speaking in whatever language they were speaking. Eastern European or something. Whatever it was, Timofey knew it. I have no clue at all what they were saying, but it sounded tense," Ashley says. "Next thing I know, Timofey shoves me out of the way and fists start flying."

"But how did he find you? How did he get inside?" I ask. I need a million more details. "Was he fighting the people holding you hostage?"

"I wasn't being *held hostage*." Ashley rolls her eyes. "You're so dramatic. I told you on the phone I was fine."

I gape at her. "No, you didn't. You told me, and I quote, 'Just leave me here. It's not like you care what happens to me anyway.'"

Ashley waves me away and leans back against the wall. "I was mad at you. I didn't mean anything by it."

"Well, I thought you meant something by it, *because that's what you said*. I made a deal with Timofey so he would go pick you up. I was scared for your safety, Ash. I thought you were in trouble."

"What deal?" Ashley asks saucily. "Was it dirty?"

My cheeks warm, and I hope to God I'm not blushing. I didn't barter sex or anything, but it was close enough.

Seducing Timofey, even for pretend, felt way too close to the real thing. I'm not sure how I'm going to pull a routine like that off for hours on end for the wedding, but I better figure it out.

"No, it wasn't dirty!" I snap. "But I went out of my way to help you. Timofey did, too. He got in a fight! You were reckless and it put him in danger."

"He wasn't in danger, believe me. Your man can fight. I mean, if he wasn't clearly in love with you, I would be asking permission to jump his bones."

My brain wrinkles while I try to figure out which part of her sentence to respond to first.

Fighting ten men is inherently dangerous. Timofey was absolutely in danger.

He's not my man. Don't call him that.

And Ashley doesn't need my permission to "jump his bones," even though the thought of it makes me want to drop her ass right back in that crack house.

But those all feel less important to mention than the utterly ridiculous bit she wedged in the midst of all of it.

"Timofey is not in love with me," I say clearly. "Like, not at all. In any way. At all."

"Well, he sure spent a lot of time talking about you for a man who isn't in love."

I chew on my cheek but say nothing.

Ashley sees right through it. "You're dying to know what he said," she laughs. "I can tell!"

"It doesn't matter what he said. Nothing will change the fact that—"

"He bitched about you the entire way home," Ashley drawls.

"He complained about me?" It figures. I'm not sure why I expected anything different.

"Nonstop," she says. "But in a flirty kind of way. Boys are always mean to girls they like."

"In the schoolyard, maybe."

Ashley gives me a look. "All love is a schoolyard, Pipes. He even complained that you're always sacrificing yourself to save me. Isn't that ridiculous?"

I bite my cheek even harder. Telling Ashley the truth wouldn't do any good right now. Especially since I can't tell if her boundless energy is because she's high or because of adrenaline.

"He said the only reason he came to get me is so you wouldn't get hurt trying to do it yourself. It was so sweet!" She clutches her hands to her chest. "I wish I had a man who loved me like that."

"He doesn't love me!" I snap. Something about hearing the impossible repeated over and over again makes me wish it was true.

Not that I want Timofey Viktorov to love me. I don't. I don't care what he thinks about me.

But if he *did* love me...wouldn't that be something?

The fantasy carries me away for a second before Ashley brings me crashing back down to earth. "Like I said, I'd love permission to take a running jump at that man and land on his dick. If you don't mind."

"No." The word is out of my mouth before I can stop myself.

Ashley raises her brows. "Oh, really? Are his feelings reciprocated?"

"I can't reciprocate what doesn't exist. It's just that Timofey is…"

"Ridiculously handsome?" she offers. "Even more ridiculously rich? Adorably protective?"

I lean forward and look straight into her eyes. "*Dangerous.* He's dangerous. You shouldn't have anything to do with him."

Ashley's lips curl in a smile, and I know I've said the entirely wrong thing. When it comes to danger, she's like a moth to the flame.

And Timofey Viktorov is a bonfire.

49

TIMOFEY

The second my father walks into my office, he spins around, red-faced and spitting. "You had no fucking right to pull Rodion off the mission I had him on."

I knew this would come around to bite me; I just didn't expect it to be so soon. I never would have left Piper here alone if I suspected Sergey would charge in.

I close the door and step around him. "I had every right. He's my soldier."

"He was carrying out a high-risk hit for me," he argues. "You interrupted and put the entire thing in jeopardy. Just so you can talk to him about Emily's murder—again. It's reckless."

"What was reckless is sending Rodion out to kill your gambling buddy."

He hesitates for a second. The soldiers are mine to control, but Sergey has kept a hold on a few of them. He uses them for his own purposes from time to time, assuming I have no clue.

Idiot. Nothing happens in this Bratva that I don't know about.

"Igor is not my 'buddy,'" he says finally. "The man is a thief and a crook. I warned him not to cross me, and now, he has to pay."

"He isn't going to pay with his life. At least, not at the hands of my hitman who is already under scrutiny for Emily's murder."

He clenches his fists until his hands tremble. "You didn't even talk to me before pulling him from the job. I had to find out from a lieutenant."

"The last time I wanted to talk about Emily's case, it took thirty-six hours to even get you here. Then you defended Rodion. Now, you bust down my door the second I talk to Rodion about it. It all makes me wonder if you have a good reason for wanting me to let go of what happened to her."

"Are you questioning me?" he growls.

"Tit for tat. You've done nothing but question me for days."

"Since that girl came along," he says, flinging his arm towards the door, "your head has been up your ass. There's suddenly a beautiful woman around and you're ready to throw away everything I built."

"I'm not throwing anything away. Certainly not for Piper. This has nothing to do with her."

"It has everything to do with her!" Sergey bellows. "Rodion showed her his tattoos and she figured out he's killed a few people, so you're ready to get him charged with Emily's murder. It's lunacy. Sheer fucking lunacy."

I grit my teeth together until my jaw aches. "Rodion flaunted his crimes in front of a woman who works for the state."

"A woman *you* brought here! The only reason their paths crossed is because you planted her in this house."

"To ensure Benjamin has a home here. I did the right thing by him."

He snorts. "You did the right thing for yourself. Your cock made the decision for you this time, son. The moment you get that bitch in bed, your head will clear. You'll realize what kind of mess you made. And all for a whore."

I blink at him. My vision is red and pulsing.

"You are my father. But if you talk about Piper that way again, I'll kill you."

My father stares at me. "You choose her over me?"

"I choose myself over you," I correct. "I am the one who took your motley collection of half-assed side businesses and turned it into a monolith. I am the one who turned this family's finances around. The Bratva is thriving because of me and my leadership, and I won't let you stand in my house and question my choices. Especially not when you are benefitting from them."

His anger cools, but doesn't dissipate. He's a volcano rumbling between eruptions. I know more will come, but I head him off.

"You've taught me well, Otets. But now, it's my turn to make the decisions. You need to make your peace with that or we will have problems."

His nostrils flare as he exhales, his eyes hooded and pinned on me. Finally, he speaks. "I never should have given you a home."

The words cut straight to my core, but I don't waver. "It's too late for that. It's my house now. But you're free to go whenever you like."

Without another word, my father turns and leaves.

50

TIMOFEY

The interaction with Sergey hangs over me as I search the house for Piper and Ashley. I expect to find them in Piper's room, but I don't hear voices until I make it back to the sitting room off the kitchen.

Ashley is cackling while Piper repeatedly tries to shush her. "It's late. You're going to wake everyone up."

"Who cares?" Ashley asks. "This is your house, isn't it?"

"No! I just work here. I'm a live-in nanny, not a wife."

For a brief second, I can see it: Piper lying in bed next to me. Piper under the spray of my shower, her auburn hair dripping wet down her exposed back. Piper clinging to my shoulders as I thrust into her again and—

"There's the master of the house," Ashley calls even louder than before. She stands up on the end of the sofa and gestures to me with both arms like a model on a game show. "The fearless fighter himself. Welcome!"

I tuck my dirty thoughts away for later perusal and step into the room. "Someone is still excited."

"I thought it might just be adrenaline, but maybe not." Piper glances at her friend dubiously. "It's been over an hour."

When I showed up to get Ashley, she was in a blissed-out haze. I didn't have to worry about her fighting me because she was barely able to stand. Clearly, she's moved into the next phase of whatever drug she took.

"Have you had any water?" I ask.

"I'm hydrated and ready for anything." Ashley bounces lightly on the sofa. Her back is arched, and I can tell she wants me to look at her chest.

Great. A junkie *and* an attention whore. Winning combination.

"You should be ready for bed," Piper grumbles. "I have to go to the office tomorrow and then come back and take care of a baby."

"Just go to bed then. I'm sure Timofey and I can keep ourselves busy."

I have no intention of being alone with Ashley. There will be no point to me saving her tonight if I end up killing her out of sheer annoyance.

I decide not to say that, though.

I want to know what Piper will do.

Her jaw clenches for a second, then she jerks to standing and yanks Ashley down off the sofa. Ashley yelps in surprise.

"That's it. It's time for a shower," Piper grits out. "You need to relax."

Ashley groans. "Showers wake me up. I need a bath. A hot, soapy, sexy bath."

"Okay, fine. A bath, then." Piper starts dragging Ashley towards the hall. "Say goodnight to Timofey."

Ashley bites her lower lip and lifts her hand in a finger-curling wave. Before she can say anything, I shift into their path.

"Slight problem, ladies. I don't have a bathtub."

Ashley laughs like I just did a special in Madison Square Garden, but Piper sags in obvious exhaustion. "Fine. I guess we'll just go lie down."

"I do, however, have a hot tub." I hitch a thumb over my shoulder towards the patio doors.

Piper starts to shake her head, but Ashley starts jumping and clapping her hands. "Hot tub! Hot tub! Hot tub!"

"I only have one swimsuit here, Ashley, and it won't fit you."

Ashley is a good foot taller than Piper, but Piper is curvier. She's fuller in all the right places. Anything that fit her would slide right off of Ashley.

"That's fine. I'll wear my clothes," Ashley says. "My shirt has blood on it, anyway. Come on!"

Ashley takes off across the room and throws the doors open. They bang off the walls, and Piper winces at me on her friend's behalf. "She's a wreck."

"If we're lucky, she'll drown in the hot tub."

Piper gasps and slaps my arm. "That is not funny!"

"I wasn't making a joke. You're the one who wanted her here, not me."

"I didn't want her *here*," Piper says. "I just wanted her…not there."

"Next time you make a deal, you should be more specific. I could have dumped her off at the police station instead. She would have sobered up faster in a jail cell."

She rolls her eyes. "Can I trust you to watch her while I go change? Or will I come back and find her at the bottom of the hot tub?"

There's a splash outside and Ashley squeals. "This is ohmygoshsofuckingincredible! Hurry up, guys!"

"That won't be a problem. You have at least five minutes before she starts to crash." I wave her on. "Better hurry."

Piper gives me a nervous glance over her shoulder and then dashes to her room, her hips swaying like a pendulum.

I linger by the window to watch Ashley from the sanctity of the living room. The last thing I want is to have some desperate, drugged-out woman draping herself all over me. If I'm alone with Ashley for any amount of time near the hot tub, that's what will happen.

Thankfully, Piper is back in record time.

Not so thankfully, she's wearing the tiniest scrap of a black bikini I've ever seen.

It absolutely, without a doubt, never would have fit Ashley. It barely fits *her*.

"What the *fuck* are you wearing?" I ask.

Piper pulls a towel in front of herself self-consciously. "My swimsuit."

"I doubt you can swim in that. You can barely touch your toes in that."

She glares at me. "It's not like I'm going to the Olympics. I just like to float and tan."

I can tell. Her skin is bronzed everywhere. Every perfectly proportioned, tantalizing curve of her is the same shade of caramel. I want to take a bite of her and see if the taste matches.

"I never would have guessed this was hiding under your clothes."

"This wasn't hiding under my clothes. Nothing was under my clothes."

Heat coils low in my belly. "You're not serious."

She shrugs and walks past me, moving purposefully slowly so I have plenty of time to watch. "Maybe I am, maybe I'm not. You'll never know."

She's wrong about that. She just doesn't know it yet.

51

TIMOFEY

I follow Piper outside and pull my shirt over my head with one hand. Ashley whistles as soon as I'm bare-chested. "Is Mr. Boss Man going to join us? Does this place have an HR department? Because this can't possibly be kosher."

It's Piper's turn to stare. Her green eyes are wide as saucers as I shuck off my jeans and undress down to my boxer briefs.

"I make the rules. If I say it's allowed, it's allowed." I hop over the edge and slide beneath the warm, bubbling water.

"What if we don't want you here?" Piper asks.

Ashley taps the surface of the water and splashes Piper. "Of course we want him here. We needed a little sausage in this taco soup."

"Oh my god. Ew, Ash!" Piper wrinkles her nose, but she's fighting back a smile. "You're disgusting."

"Just saying what we're all thinking."

"Literally no one was thinking that." Piper looks over at me like she wants to apologize, but her eyes drop low over my chest before she jerks them away. Her cheeks flush.

Just like I predicted, within a few minutes, Ashley is lolled back against the back of the hot tub. A grating kind of snore erupts from her once every thirty seconds or so.

"We should take her inside, right?" Piper peers across the hot tub at her friend. "She's going to drown."

"Not on your watch. You'd never let that happen."

She sighs and sinks lower into the water until it bubbles around her chin. "I'll give it a few more minutes and make sure she's good and asleep. I don't want her to perk back up."

The night is quiet without Ashley's constant yammering. It's not cold out, but there's a haze of steam in the air that makes it feel like we're in our own personal bubble.

"I'm not going to be able to lift Ashley out of here by myself," Piper says quietly.

I sigh. "Fortunately for you, my altruism knows no bounds."

"You'll help?"

"Considering all the shit I've done for you, you shouldn't sound so surprised."

There's a pause before she nods. "You're right. It's just… you're not what I expected. Not entirely, anyway. You can be caring. When you choose."

"It runs in the family." I saw the way my father was holding her arm when Ashley and I walked through the front door. It's the first time in my life I've genuinely wanted to hurt him.

"After my run-in with your dad, I'm going to confidently say it was nature, not nurture. Your mom must be really nice for you to have even a sliver of it left once Sergey was done with you."

"My mother is dead."

There's a beat of hesitation before she lays her hand lightly on my bicep. "I'm sorry."

I pull away from her. "She died a long time ago. Sergey is the only person I ever had to depend on."

Despite it all, that throughline of loyalty Sergey planted in me all those years ago is still there. He may regret adopting me, but my impulses are still the same. *Close ranks. Protect the Bratva. Family above all else.*

"I'm sorry I said anything about him. He just scared me tonight." She sits up so the water laps around her narrow waist. The blue light reflects off the swell of her breasts. "I'm not feeling very charitable towards him right now, but he's still your father. I shouldn't have said anything."

Ashley lets out a sleepy snort and slouches further into the water. Her chin hovers just above the surface. I make no move to help her, but Piper hurries over. She stands with a foot on either side of Ashley's legs, hooks her arms under the unconscious woman's armpits, and heaves. It's almost comical, watching Piper's petite form struggle with Ashley's long limbs.

Then I notice the way the lean muscles in her back shift and pinch as she works. As she hauls Ashley up, I can see the dimpled impressions just above the black line of her bikini bottoms. My thumbs would fit nicely there, my fingers wrapped around her hips. It'd be so easy to manhandle her exactly the way she deserves.

"You really aren't going to help, are you?" Piper looks over her shoulder at me, and I'm glad for the coverage of the water. It hides the hardest erection I've had in years.

I recline back against the edge of the hot tub. "You're handling things fine on your own."

Piper gets Ashley situated so her head is pillowed on her arm. A line of drool flows out of her mouth and puddles on the wooden deck.

"The one time I don't want to handle something on my own is the time you let me," she grumbles. "Figures."

She takes a step back away from Ashley, but her foot slips off the bench. Suddenly, Piper is falling sideways.

The scene plays in my head in a flash. *Piper bashing her skull against the hard rim of the hot tub. Fractured bone. Blood.*

Usually, I'd let it play out. I don't owe anything to anyone. If they can't stand in a fucking hot tub without cracking their heads open, that's no trouble to me.

But before I really think about it, I'm up and wrapping an arm around Piper's middle.

She lets out a yelp, but it cuts off with an exhale as she lands in my arm. My hand cradles the back of her head just an inch from the edge of the hot tub. A millisecond away from disaster.

I hold her there for a second, letting the gravity of the moment hang.

Piper twists to look at me. Shock is etched in every line of her face. She swallows. "Thank you."

I tighten the arm around her waist and bring her to standing. I'm standing in the center, which is a foot lower than the rest of the hot tub. We're as close to eye level with one another as we'll ever be.

Still unsteady, Piper leans against my chest. Her breasts brush across my rib cage. Her fingers trail over my biceps.

The entire time, her eyes haven't left mine. Not for a second.

Ashley or not, I will take Piper right here. I'll wrap her legs around my middle, shove her tiny scrap of a bikini to the side, and fill her with my throbbing cock until she screams my name.

Because I want to hear her scream my name.

Instead, I hear my father's voice in my head.

The moment you get that bitch in bed, your head will clear. You'll realize what kind of mess you made.

Piper is a distraction. Fucking her now won't serve my overall goal. The only thing I need from Piper is to pretend. I need her to pretend for the sake of my reputation, for the sake of Viktorov Inc.'s reputation. I need her to pretend so the Bratva I've built for Sergey doesn't fall apart around us.

All at once, I release Piper and sit on the edge of the hot tub. She's still frozen in the center, her chest heaving from the intensity of the moment.

"Sit down before you kill yourself," I bark.

A myriad of expressions cross her face at once. She blinks in surprise then frowns in annoyance. Finally, she smooths her flushed face into a mask of indifference and sits down, choosing a spot further from me and closer to Ashley.

"You're no good to me dead," I add.

"Being dead wouldn't be so convenient for me, either," she says coldly.

"You probably can't afford anymore sick days at work."

She narrows her eyes. "Yes, that's exactly why I can't die. I don't have enough sick days."

She's laying the sarcasm on thick, but I ignore it.

"You know, I think I'll go to work with you tomorrow," I remark, draping my arms over the rim of the hot tub and sinking lower into the water.

Piper sits up straight. "To the CPS office?"

"Unless you have a third job I don't know about, then yes."

"You…you can't."

"The only person who matters says I can." I point to myself. "I'll give you a ride."

She swallows nervously. "But I thought—I'm only useful to you as a social worker, right? My image as a civil servant is going to boost your reputation. I won't be any good to you if I get fired. That's what you told me."

"You won't get fired."

"It will look unprofessional if I bring my supposed 'boyfriend' to the office," she says. "Especially if that boyfriend is one of my cases. It is going to look really bad."

I dismiss her with a flick of my wrist. "You'd be surprised how a little money thrown at a situation clears up problems like that."

"You're going to pay off my boss?"

"If I have to." I smile and arch a brow. "Or I'll woo her with my God-given looks and charm."

She worries her teeth along her lower lip, nibbling the skin until it's pink and plump. "I don't know. I could lose my job. I worked hard to earn their trust, and I don't want to throw it all away."

"You aren't throwing anything away," I say. "No matter what happens there, you have your job here. I'll make sure you're taken care of."

Piper looks up at me, and I watch as realization settles in.

I control her now.

For as long as she is a pawn in my game, she's mine to manipulate as I wish. If she doesn't cooperate, I'll cut her off at the knees. I'll bend her to my will whether she wants it or not.

Piper, proving once again she isn't as dumb as she first appeared, lifts her chin and nods. "Fine. You'll drive me to work tomorrow."

I nod back solemnly. "Looking forward to it."

52

TIMOFEY

"No one is here." My voice echoes off the creaky hardwood floors and bare cinderblock walls of the CPS office. "We didn't need to get here this early."

Piper plants a hand on her cocked hip and glares at me. "*You* didn't need to be here at all. I could have come alone."

"No, you couldn't have. Because I told you I was coming with you."

She rolls her eyes. "I needed to make up hours, anyway. I am drowning in cases right now and being 'sick' the last couple days hasn't helped matters. I would've worked overtime the last two days, too. So I did need to be here two hours early."

Now that she mentions it, Piper's desk is overflowing. Folders and files spill out of stackable paper sorters on the corner of her desk. She can barely wedge anything else into the pull-out drawer underneath. In comparison, the other desks in the office look tidy.

"Lots of children to kidnap, so little time."

She huffs out a frustrated sigh. "Let me get some things in order and then I have an on-site visit."

There's a long bench in the back corner with a few stuffed animals and a long pillow. It's situated next to an office with window blinds. It's the room where kids recently removed from their parents' care sit and wait for a temporary placement.

I've sat there too many times to count. In that room, on that bench, or in rooms and on benches similar enough for the difference not to matter. I want nothing to do with them now.

I opt for the rolling chair of the desk across from Piper's.

"Andrea will hate you sitting at her desk," Piper says without looking up.

"Thankfully, we're here in the middle of the night, so Andrea isn't here to care."

Piper smashes her lips into a hard line, but doesn't respond. The silence continues for the next hour as she reads through files, organizes them into three piles I don't know the significance of, and drops a few into the recycle bin. I watch her the whole time.

Finally, as I'm finishing the last of my coffee, she shoves a file in her purse and turns to face me.

"I have an on-site visit. You can wait here or head back to the house. I'll meet you there when I get off later."

I grab the keys to my motorcycle and stand up. "No need. I'll come with you."

"Timofey, please," she sighs. "Whatever point you're trying to make, you've made it. You have the upper hand. I'll do what you want. I'll play the role you want. Just let me do my job."

"I'm so glad you've seen reason."

She frowns. "Does that mean you'll let me finish out the day on my own?"

I snap my fingers in an *aw shucks* motion. "Damn. Maybe you haven't seen reason, after all."

She levels me with a glare and stomps towards the door. I follow after her at a slow stroll. I have the keys. She isn't going anywhere without me.

Besides, the view from back here is pleasant. Piper is in a knee-length wool dress today. It's modest enough when she's standing up, but when she mounts my bike and straddles my hips, there is nothing modest about the long stretch of thigh wrapped around my body.

It suits me more than it ought to.

~

This part of the city is a shithole. As we near the address Piper gave me, we veer around potholes and roadkill. Trash clogs the gutters and more houses look abandoned than not.

Piper presses herself against my back, her mouth close to my ear. "This is going to be a tough case. I know you're here to punish me or annoy me—maybe both—but I don't want to make things worse for these kids."

I didn't process until now that she would be dealing directly with the children involved. It doesn't change anything for me. Because my motives here are not purely malicious like she might think.

"This is research. It's been almost two decades since I had any contact with a CPS agent."

I swallow down the resentment boiling inside of me at memories I do my best to never touch. Maybe things have changed since I was a kid.

I hope they have.

I pull the motorcycle along the curb of a rundown duplex. The small square of lawn in front is dried and brown. Aluminum foil is pressed into the upstairs windows to block the sun. Where a garden might have been along the front facade, there's instead a graveyard of faded plastic toys.

Suddenly, I'm back in the trailer my mother moved us to after Dad died. I see the dark-haired CPS man with the mustache blocking all the light from the front door, his shadow stretched long over our empty living room.

He haunted our house like a demon. Every time he showed up, a little more of my mother disappeared.

"Are you coming inside?" Piper asks from the sidewalk.

I blink back to reality. I didn't even feel her get off the bike.

I see the blinds in the front window move. A little head pokes out for just a second to watch us in the street. Then it disappears.

I prop the kickstand up and sit down on the leather seat. "I'll stay here for now."

"But you said—" Piper shakes her head and backs away. "You know what? Never mind. I'm not going to look this gift horse in the mouth. I'll be back soon."

Her heels tap up the cracked front sidewalk. After only a few knocks, the front door swings open. A little girl no older than seven stands barefoot in the doorway. Her dirty hair is falling out of a lopsided braid.

Piper bends down to the girl's level, shakes her hand, and then steps inside.

Staying out here was the right call, I tell myself. I don't want to play any role in what those kids are going through. I'm the lead figure in many people's nightmares, I know that, but I'm not going to unintentionally terrorize a bunch of kids.

I'm outside for a few minutes when I hear a raised voice.

It's male.

Coming from inside the house.

And *angry.*

53

TIMOFEY

I hop off my bike, jog up to the front door, and shove it open without knocking.

"You tricked a little girl into letting you inside!" the male voice screams. "I never would have opened the door for you. You're not welcome here! We don't need you!"

"I'm sorry you feel that way," Piper says calmly. "That's actually what I'm here to determine. I need to speak to your mom. She scheduled this meeting."

The living room is small and square, with a sagging plaid sofa under the window and an ancient television sitting on the floor in the corner. Toys and blankets cover the scratched hardwood floor. I can smell the spoiled food in the dishes stacked on the table. The sickly sweet scent of rot is strong.

"She isn't here!" the voice barks back. "So leave and never come back."

"I can't do that," Piper says.

I follow the sound of her voice to the hallway just behind the living room wall. Piper is standing in the middle of it, her foot wedged into a wooden door.

The yelling kid can't be older than fourteen, but he's standing in the middle of his room with his arms crossed and a scowl that makes him look a decade older than he has any right to look.

His eyes skirt past Piper and land on me. His expression hardens. "You can't threaten us to do anything. This is private property."

Piper looks back at me and then gives all of her attention to the kid once again. "He isn't here to threaten you. I'm just here to talk to your mom."

"She isn't home. I already told you."

I know Piper can hear the television playing low from the closed bedroom at the end of the hall just as well as I can. It's coming from the same room with the aluminum foil on the windows.

I glance that way, and the kid doesn't miss a thing. He can't. Because he may only be a teenager, but he's running this entire house. It's all up to him.

"There's no one back there," he says quickly. "The baby sleeps with the TV on for white noise. That's all."

"The baby is in the dining room." I can see the bassinet from here. The little girl who opened the door for Piper is sitting on the floor next to it, her legs tucked into her chest.

"Right." His eyes dart around. He's panicking. "I left it on… from earlier. It's nothing. Come back later."

Piper takes a half step forward. "Grant, listen... I'm not here to punish you. I just need to talk to your mom and see how she's doing."

"She's great," Grant says. "She has a job now. That's where she is right now. At work."

He's lying through his teeth. It's confirmed when the little girl walks in front of me and pulls on Piper's dress. "Mama is sleeping."

Piper points at the door at the end of the hall. "Is she in there?"

The girl nods, and Grant's face turns red. "Leave her alone, you...you bitch!"

The curse feels clumsy on his tongue. But when he steps towards Piper, I don't care how much he reminds me of a younger version of myself. I tuck Piper behind me and block the kid's path.

"Don't do anything stupid, son."

"Or what?" he hisses. "You'll take me away? It's a little too late for that."

God, it's like looking at a picture of me at his age. I was right to stay outside. I shouldn't have come in here.

"No one is taking you anywhere," Piper says.

I turn my head to her, my voice low enough so only she can hear. "Don't lie."

Her attention snaps to me just as Grant turns around and kicks the hell out of a lawn chair sitting in his room. The plastic bends and deforms under his foot, but he whales on it a few more times until it's limp and useless in the corner.

When he turns to face us, he's breathing heavily. "You're not taking us today, but you will. Get out of my room."

Piper looks at him with her eyes pinched together in sympathy. She might as well toss acid at the kid. He doesn't want her sympathy. Fuck knows I didn't want any from the man with the mustache who yanked me out of my home.

"Get out!" Grant screams. "You're not welcome here. Leave!"

The moment Piper steps back into the hallway, Grant kicks the door closed in our faces.

"That went well," Piper mumbles. She shakes off the interaction and looks down at the little girl standing next to her. "Where is your mom's room?"

The girl points to the end of the hall. "Is Mama in trouble?"

"No, honey." Piper kneels down to the little girl's level. "I just need to talk to your mama about how she takes care of you. It's boring, grown-up stuff about her job."

"Mama doesn't have a job," the girl says. There's an innocence to the way she says it. No judgment or understanding of what it means. Talking to her is a manipulation. She doesn't know what she's saying or what it could mean for their case. "Grant takes care of us. He taught me how to make bottles for Olivia and—"

"Enough," I growl.

The little girl shrinks away from me. Good.

I grab Piper by the shirt sleeve and drag her towards the back door. "You're here to talk to the mom."

"I'm here to talk to all of them," she hisses. "It's my job. You're just watching. Let me do what I need to do."

"They don't want to talk to you." I rap my knuckles hard on the wooden door. No one answers, so I throw it open. A woman is lying in bed, her hair matted against her head. Her pajamas are dingy and almost transparent from constant use. The room smells like sweat and must.

The scent, more than anything, takes me back.

I see myself standing in my mom's doorway, begging her to get up. To do something. It didn't work. It never did.

If I don't leave now, I'll walk into this strange woman's room and shake her. I'll try to slap some sense into her, even though I know it won't do any good.

I push Piper through the door ahead of me. "Talk to her."

Then I walk away.

54

TIMOFEY

I pace in the hallway for a few seconds before I realize the little girl is trembling at the idea of being left alone with me. With nowhere else to go, I push open Grant's door and step inside.

"Get out of here!" He jumps up, on the defensive even though I can tell he's terrified.

"Sit the fuck down," I order.

He does, dropping into his chair with wide eyes.

I blow out a long breath as I lean against the wall. "Relax. I'm not going to hurt you."

He squints at me, trying to decide if I'm telling him the truth. I can only imagine how many adults have lied to him in his short life. I won't be joining that list.

"Do you work with the Department of Child Services?" he asks. "Or are you an off-duty police officer, or—"

"I'm not with the police. I'm not with anyone," I tell him.

Whiskey Poison

"You're with her, though. Ms. Quinn."

I shrug. "I guess I am. For today. I drove her here."

"She usually comes alone," he says softly.

"How many times has she been here?"

He shrugs like he doesn't know, but I know better than that. After a few seconds of purposeful silence, he sags. "Five. She took us away once. For a little while."

"Your mom earned her privileges back?"

When I was in group foster homes, some kids were able to see their parents once per month and then once every week. Then they'd progress to weekend trips home or a week at a time if their parents showed signs of improving the situation.

I loathed those kids.

"She held down a job for three months." He sounds like a proud parent himself. He wants me to understand that his mom tried. That she did her best, at least for a little while. "Until our car broke down. It was too expensive to fix and her stupid ex-boyfriend blew the money on drugs and left."

"Where's your dad in all of this?"

He chews on the inside of his cheek, and I know the answer before he speaks. "Dead." Before I even have the chance to respond, he blurts out, "And don't say you're sorry."

"Why should I say sorry? I'm not the one who killed him."

Grant blinks. "Everyone says sorry."

"Everyone is stupid."

He huffs out a laugh. "Yeah. Well…he isn't even dead."

"He must be close to it if you'd rather live here than with him." I look around his room. At the sparse decorations, if they can be called that at all. Most of them look like pictures drawn by the little girl.

"He isn't an option," Grant grits out. Rage practically bubbles off of him. "He left after Tiana was born. Even before that, he was in and out. My mom is more dependable than him. At least she's here."

He glances towards the back of the house.

Fuck. I really should have stayed outside with the bike. I feel nauseous and light-headed. Caught between a past I hated and a present I should walk away from before it gets worse.

"How long does she stay in there?" I ask.

It seems like Grant might not answer. Then he crosses his arms over his chest. "Days at a time. A week, maybe."

"Who takes care of the baby?"

"Me and Olivia split it up when she's not in school."

"Are you in school?"

He wrinkles his nose in distaste. "I don't need any of that crap. What I need is a job. But I'm too young. I pick up money doing maintenance stuff around the neighborhood. It's barely enough for formula."

I look in his eyes and I see the same psychic scars that I bear. I know the bone-deep chill of shoveling driveways in the dead of winter. I know the searing pain of hot summer sun, the sting of sweat in your eyes as you slave away to make too little money to change a goddamn thing.

I know his pain.

Whiskey Poison

It made me.

There's a soft knock at the door and then Piper pokes her head inside. Grant spins away from her and faces the wall.

"I'm done for today," Piper says. "I'll see you later, Grant."

"I'd rather not," he mutters.

As we're walking through the house, Piper drops her business card on the table.

"In case they need anything," she explains to me, even though I didn't ask.

I hang back for a second. Just long enough to drop all the cash in my wallet on the table next to her card.

In case they need anything.

55

TIMOFEY

I toss the motorcycle helmet in Piper's direction. It hits the center of her chest with a thud, and she winces.

"Ow."

I straddle the bike. "Get on. We're leaving."

She spends what feels like ages struggling with the straps and buckles of the helmet. Finally, I snatch it out of her hands and hold it up for her to step into.

"Thanks," she mutters.

The sun paints golden rays in her wide green eyes. She just walked into that house—into those kids' hell—and she still looks radiant. Perfectly fine. Almost as if nothing happened.

"It's not for your sake," I growl.

"Right. Sure. God forbid you be polite."

"I don't have time for you to trip and tumble your way through every task. I have other shit to do today."

"Then go do it!" She steps out of my reach and fumbles with the buckle under her chin. "I thought you wanted to observe what I do every day. Wasn't that the point of this? You're acting like I made you come here."

"You made me go inside. You couldn't handle that kid without it blowing up."

"I could have handled Grant," she snaps. "I've met him plenty of times before."

"Even worse," I retort. "If he's met you before, he has even more reason to want to knock you flat on your ass."

Blood rises across her chest and neck. Anger colors her pale skin. "You don't make any sense, Timofey. If you hate me so much, why am I pretending to be your girlfriend? Why not go find someone you can stand?"

"This isn't about whether I hate you or not. It's about the fact that the boy in there absolutely does."

"He doesn't hate me. He's just... He's going through a hard time," she says. "I'm here to help him. You saw what it was like in there. His mother isn't doing anything to take care of him and his siblings."

"She's doing her best."

Piper takes a step back and blinks at me. "You're kidding."

I shift the kickstand up with the back of my heel and balance the bike under me. "Get on."

"No," she says firmly. "I'm not going anywhere with you while you're treating me like I'm the villain here. I'm not the one forcing a fifteen-year-old to parent his two younger sisters. I'm not the one rotting away in bed while my baby cries."

"Right. You're the noble one ripping that family apart."

"*She* is ripping them apart!" Piper flings a hand towards the foiled-over windows on the corner of the duplex. "She isn't doing her job as their mother. I don't have a choice."

I don't have a choice here, my caseworker would say to me every time he came for a visit. Mom would be back in her room, lying in bed. He'd rub two fat fingers over his mustache and shrug. *There isn't another option.*

"There's always another choice," I snarl. "If you take those kids away from that woman, she's as good as dead."

"She might as well be, for all the help she is to them now."

I snap my head to her. "Say that to Grant. See if he agrees with you."

Piper's expression softens. "He doesn't know what he needs."

"He'd rather have a depressed mother than a dead one," I bark. "Those kids would rather have each other than be split up in the system."

"We try to keep siblings together."

"You try and you fail. Do you know how fast a baby will be adopted? Instantly. Maybe even Oliva will get scooped up in a few months. But Grant? He's fifteen fucking years old, Piper. You know how long he'll sit in some foster home or a group home. You know what happens when he ages out."

She casts her eyes to the empty box of cigarettes and energy drink cans smashed in the gutter. "I have to hope for the best."

"You must be blind to what you're actually doing here."

Whiskey Poison

"I can't operate in the unknowable future! I have to make decisions on the here and now. And right now, she is unfit. She can't care for them properly."

I wave her off. "You were in there for fifteen minutes. You don't know."

"There's no food in the cabinets and there were buckets of water in the bathroom in case the utilities get shut off. I can't leave them there!" Piper shouts. "How are we even arguing about this? You'd never let this happen to Benjamin, so why do you think these kids deserve it?"

"The mother doesn't deserve it."

"It's not my job to take care of the parents," she fires back. "My job is to focus on the kids. It's to do what is best for them. She should be able to take care of herself. If she can't, that's not my problem."

"Then whose problem is it?" I lower the kickstand again and toss my leg over the bike. Piper takes a step back as I face her and climb the curb. I'm being propelled by a force beyond myself. One I don't want to stop, even if I could. "Who is going to be held responsible when you take those kids away and that woman fucking kills herself?"

"That almost never happens, Timofey. But kids *do* starve. They end up in unsafe situations because they're trying to survive when their parents don't take care of them. That happens every day. I'm going to focus on that. And if Trish kills herself, I'll feel bad. I'll have to live with that. But I'll do it knowing I made the right choice for—"

"For yourself." I bend over her, talking down into her confused face. "You'll do the best thing for *yourself*. Because you'll forget about Trish and those kids, but Grant will blame himself for the rest of his life. He'll feel responsible for leaving his mom even though it wasn't his choice. He'll carry that guilt to his grave."

"Why are we talking about this? I didn't even make a choice today. It's just one report in their case file. Why do you care so much about these kids?" She tips her head to one side, her brows pinching together. She might as well be peering through a magnifying glass, inspecting every pore of me for evidence. She sees more than I would like her to. "Timofey, last night, you said... How did your mom die?"

I take a step back. I reel in my loosely controlled anger, bringing it back within my command. "Get on the bike. We're leaving."

I turn around, but Piper is there in a second. She whips around me, blocking my path with her glassy-eyed sympathy and trembling lip. "Is that why you were talking to Grant while I talked to Trish? You relate to him, don't you?"

"His dad abandoned him."

"And yours died," she says. "It's not so different, when you think about it."

Grant would agree. To him, his dad is as good as dead.

Piper lowers her chin and her voice. "How did your mom die?"

I mount the bike and start it. The rumble of the engine almost drowns Piper out, but she draws closer. "Timofey... did your mom... after you were taken away, did she...?"

"You can't even say it, but you want to do the same thing to those kids in there." I swallow my rage. I don't know why I ever expected anything different. I speak through gritted teeth. "Get on."

Piper reaches out. Her hand brushes across mine for the briefest of seconds before I jerk it away.

"Get on the bike, Piper. Now. I swear to God, I'll leave you here."

"Timofey," she breathes. "I never would have brought you here if I knew. I'm so sorry."

That single word—*sorry*—smashes through the locked box where I shove thoughts about my mother. All of the guilt and anger I don't have time for explodes out of me in a torrent I don't expect. It paints a new world on top of the real one. Or rather, an old world. A world I thought I left behind.

Right now, I'm not seeing Piper Quinn, petite and red-headed and naive; I'm seeing a six-foot-tall man with a mustache and a collared shirt. I glare at her, and she shrinks back from the hatred I'm sure she can see written all over my face.

"My mother needed help. She didn't need someone to take her only reason for living away. She didn't need yet another reason to give up."

Piper shakes her head. Tears are welling in her eyes. "I'm so sorry, Timofey. I'm so—"

If my caseworker was standing in front of me right now, I'd kill him. There wouldn't even be time for him to get an apology out.

But he's not.

It's just Piper.

"None of it matters anymore. It's too fucking late for apologies."

"I can still be sorry you went through that," she insists.

I fling an arm towards the shabby duplex in front of us. "You're sorry, but you're going to turn around and do it to another kid right now. What happened to me is exactly what is going to happen to Grant and Tiana and Olivia."

"Maybe. But what will happen to them if they stay?" she asks softly. "What kind of future will they have then?"

"They'll figure it out. Kids are resilient."

She shakes her head sadly. "Not always. I've seen too many cases where they aren't. Am I supposed to just hope these kids beat the odds?"

"You're supposed to *help*. That's your job. And a dead mom doesn't help anyone."

Her arms hang limp at her sides. The fight has drained out of her, but my engine is still revving. I want to hash this out. I want to roar and punch walls and burn this anger out until it's a simmering heap. I'm not ready to let go of it.

I jab a finger at Piper's stunned face. "Her death will be on your hands."

Her brow pinches for a second. I see a flicker of frustration. But it's lost in a wash of sympathy. She gives me the sad eyes I've seen too many times in my life.

"I never would have brought you here if I'd known your history," she says again. "I'm sorry this was triggering for you. I can't imagine how you must feel."

"Don't pretend like you understand what I feel!" I bellow. "You don't know me or my life. You and I came from similar circumstances. We were both in the system, but I got out. You opted to become it."

She lifts her chin, shoulders back. "That is not what happened! I became a social worker so I could—"

"Repeat the mistakes of your predecessors," I interrupt. "Yeah, I know. I've witnessed it."

She exhales sharply. "I know you're hurting."

"I'm not hurting."

"Your mom's death must have been traumatic," she presses on. "But I'm not going to stand here and let you make me out as some storybook villain. I haven't done anything wrong."

"I had Officer Rooney look into your past," I say suddenly.

Confusion settles between her brows. "What does that mean?"

"You have a long paper trail. Your mom, too. I know how many times people reported her for neglecting you. For leaving you sitting on public park benches for hours at a time. Teachers said you showed up hungry and dirty. Weird that she couldn't afford clothes or food, considering how many times she was arrested for prostitution."

Piper is breathing heavily now. She's trying to stay calm, but I see the storm walls inside of her failing under the punishing weight of her anger and shame.

"If you read everything, then you should know exactly why she couldn't afford it."

"Addiction has a genetic component. Have you ever wondered if you have it, too?"

"Being hurt doesn't give you the right to be an asshole," she says softly.

"No," I continue, "I'm sure you've steered well clear of all that nastiness after her overdose. The last thing you'd want is to end up like her, right? Out of all the adults in your life, your caseworker was probably the most stable. Is that why you became one?"

Her face is a rainbow of hate. Red, purple, pale. "So what if that is the reason? It doesn't change anything."

"There is a difference between what your mom did to you and what is going on in there." I point at the house. "Don't punish those kids because of your own baggage."

Her eyebrows arch up. "*My* baggage? We are talking about *my* baggage? I'm not the one defending a woman who can't even get out of bed to feed her own baby! You're the one who can't let go!"

"Oh, I let go," I tell her. "You can't make it to the top carrying all the shit from our terrible childhoods. I dropped all of that and sacrificed everything to get to where I am today."

"Including your humanity," she mumbles.

"Better that than sacrifice the rest of my life," I snarl. "No one was on my side when I was a kid. But now, I am in charge of an entire Bratva. I have an army of men who are loyal to me. Men who will die to protect me. Meanwhile, you practically kill yourself to please everyone else."

Shock blanches the color from her cheeks. Piper's mouth flops open. She's too stunned for words.

If she hasn't figured out I'm the don of the Viktorov Bratva by now, maybe she really is as dumb as I've been telling her she is. I haven't exactly kept my title a secret.

But maybe I've been overestimating her from that start.

I use her silence to my advantage. I yank her towards the bike and rev the engine as she climbs woodenly onto the back.

Without another word, we roar down the street and away from the duplex.

And when I glance in the mirror, for the briefest of moments, I could swear I see something: a mustached man raising one thick hand in a goodbye wave.

I twist the accelerator, until he's gone like the rest of it.

56

PIPER

I don't know how long I've been sitting at the dining room table, staring unblinkingly at the open file folder with another child's heartbreaking life story splayed across the pages, when a plate of food slides in front of me.

I look up to see Akim standing just behind my shoulder. He's holding a napkin and a bottle of wine in his arms.

"What is this?" I ask.

"Has it been so long since you've eaten that you don't remember what food is?" He points to the plate. "This is roast beef. It's from a cow. Then there are mashed potatoes, which come from the ground. Asparagus is also—"

"I mean," I interject, rolling my eyes, "where did this come from? The kitchen is still under construction, right?"

I don't even need to ask. From here, I can see the charred burn marks up the side of the cabinets and the melted top of the oven.

"Obviously. If my kitchen was open, I would never serve you dry, reheated roast beef. This shit was dry when it arrived. One Michelin star, my ass." He wrinkles his nose at the gourmet food on my plate. "If you want something done right, don't let a guest burn down your kitchen."

I wince. "I really am sorry. Have I said that yet?"

"No. But I accept."

I chuckle. "Wow. You and Timofey really are nothing alike."

"Yeah, well, holding grudges is bad for one's digestion." He folds a cloth napkin into a little pyramid and sets it on the table. "Enjoy your rehydrated astronaut food. I'm gonna go make sure Benjamin is still asleep. Then I'll check the shipment tracking on my new oven. Heads will roll if I don't get that shit, like, *yesterday*."

I start to push away from the table and the work I brought home with me and spread out all over the table. "I should check on Benjamin. It's my job."

Akim quickly hip checks the back of my chair and slides me back into the table. "No, I'll do it. I can't do my real job right now, anyway. Watching that little bread loaf of a baby is the only thing keeping me from spiraling into a deep, dark depression."

The last few hours of catching up on case files and diving into work helped get my mind off of Timofey. But Akim's words bring it all right back.

Timofey's mom battled depression. In the end, it is what took her away from him.

I know he blames the caseworker who removed him from her care, but I've been in that same position before. Being forced to decide between taking care of the children or helping the adults is not an easy place to be in. At the end of the day, though, I work in Child Protective Services. The job description is right there in the name. My duty is always to the child.

I'm sure Timofey's caseworker felt the same way, whether Timofey can recognize that or not.

Still, someone failed Timofey along the way. For him to end up in Sergey's home, to be forced down the road he's still walking… It's the worst-case scenario.

Which is why I've made my choice: I can't let Benjamin stay in this house. Timofey may not be outright abusive or neglectful, but there is more than one way to abuse a child. In the long run, Benjamin won't be safe here.

We have to get out.

"Speaking of spiraling," Akim elbows me lightly in the shoulder, "don't think so hard. You'll pull a muscle."

I blink out of my thoughts and laugh. "I guess the lack of food has me feeling foggy."

I stab the roast beef and take a bite.

"Well?" he prods.

I give him a grin full of roast beef. "I can't wait for the kitchen to be up and running again so you can make me something better than this."

"Oo, don't talk dirty to me, Piper Quinn. There is nothing I'd rather do."

Suddenly, there are footsteps across the hardwood floor and Timofey walks in carrying a large box in his arms. "Who is talking dirty?"

"Piper and I are flirting," Akim says without hesitation. "I think our relationship is headed somewhere serious."

Timofey drops the box on the end of the table, rattling my water glass. He arches a brow at Akim.

"She wants me to *cook* for her." Akim says it like it's the nastiest sex talk that has ever passed someone's lips.

Timofey shakes his head. "As long as she can still fit into these dresses when you're done, cook away. It'll keep you from annoying me."

"Oh, I'll always make time for that."

"Make time for watching Benjamin," Timofey grumbles. "Piper is going to be busy."

He may be my boss, but I don't appreciate the insinuation that he controls my time. I mean, he does, but I still don't appreciate it.

"Actually, I'm not busy right now," I tell Akim. "I'd love to watch Benjamin for—"

Timofey interrupts. "You're busy. I need you."

Before I can respond, Akim leans in. "You *need* her? For what, precisely?"

It's not hard to miss the insinuation. Which was entirely Akim's point.

"I need her to earn her paycheck by following my orders." Timofey gives Akim a pointed glare. "It's the same expectation I have of everyone on my payroll."

"Message received." Akim holds up his hands and backs away. But as he turns, I hear him talking to himself. "If he wants me to do everything he wants her to do, then I'll quit. I don't swing that way."

If he wasn't talking about me, I'd laugh. Instead, a blush burns my cheeks. I'm sure I'm red all the way to my hairline.

Timofey picks the box up off the table and turns. "Come with me."

"I'm eating."

"I don't care."

"I'm not going to starve myself to work for you," I tell him. "Akim would never let that happen."

He waves a bored hand over his shoulder. "Fine. Bring the food. Just stop wasting my time."

I stare down at the plate of food and debate disobeying him. It would feel good to stand up to him.

Then, of course, he would show me I'm powerless to resist him, and I'd feel every bit like the caged animal I am.

With a bitten-back sigh, I grab my plate and carry it down the hallway. I'm so focused on the way Timofey's butt looks in his trousers that I don't realize I've walked through the door into his bedroom until he kicks it closed behind me.

The room is all warm wood and soft textures. It's masculine, painted in a moody navy blue that matches his eyes, but it's cozy, too. Very unlike the occupant.

"What are we doing?"

I can't stop staring at the massive bed against the wall. Part of me wants to dive into the mound of pillows and see if I can pick out his woodsy scent in the sheets.

The survivalist part of me knows that would be equivalent to wearing a bear trap as a hat. I'm vulnerable enough around Timofey. There's no need to lay down and give him an advantage.

"*We* aren't doing anything. *You* are trying on clothes." He drops the box on his bed and rips back the cardboard flaps. "Dresses, to be exact."

I'm relieved for a second. So this isn't some kind of weird seduction technique. The box isn't full of whips and chains and skimpy leather harnesses.

Then I understand what he means. "I repeat: what are *we* doing? You don't need to be present in order for me to try on clothes."

"As your wedding date, I disagree. I get final say on what you wear."

"As a woman in the twenty-first century, *I* disagree. I've agreed to go with you, but I never agreed to give you fashion power."

He turns around, bored indifference oozing off of him. "I know you'll be disappointed, but beige wool dresses and shapeless pant suits aren't part of the dress code."

"Hey! I work with children. It's not like I can show up to work in cocktail dresses and backless crop tops."

Plus, I opt to spend the little bit of money I have on nice basics. I go for quality neutrals so I can wear them again and again. The wool dress he's making fun of has seen me through every single season for two years thanks to a rotation of tights and cardigans.

"No, but you could bear to wear something that hinted at you having a human-shaped body."

I want to argue with him, but the pink oversized sweater I'm currently wearing would be one easy, slam dunk score for Timofey. Instead, I narrow my eyes. "Apparently, shapeless works for me. I've seen you staring. What's your excuse?"

He lays an armful of colorful, glittery dress options on the bed in a heap. "It's hard to look away from a trainwreck."

Timofey is good at that: turning any jab I make right back around on me. No matter how hard I swing at him, I'm always the one who gets hurt.

I cross my arms defiantly. "If I go to this wedding with you, I'll wear whatever I want, regardless of what you say."

"Keep going," he says, circling his hand in the air.

"Keep what?"

"Keep talking back. Keep disobeying," he says. "It will give me a good excuse to do what I've wanted to do since the moment we met."

There's dark amusement in his blue eyes. They trail over me again, and this time, I'm not sure it's in any way romantic. He looks every bit like a lion admiring a zebra's hindquarters.

"How will it look if your girlfriend shows up to the wedding covered in bruises?" I challenge.

He bites back a smirk. "I won't leave any bruises."

Goosebumps break out across my skin, and now, I just want to get this over with as soon as possible. I've changed in front of men before. Only when I was dating them and only after we'd had sex, but still, that was different. I cared what those men thought of me. I wanted to look attractive and appealing. I wanted them to think I was sexy and mysterious.

I don't give a shit what Timofey Viktorov thinks of me.

That's what I tell myself, anyway, as I grab the hem of my sweater and pull it over my head.

"Are you going to pick out Benjamin's clothes, too?" I snap. "Or, hey! Maybe you could call up the bride and suggest a neckline for her wedding gown. I'm sure she'd love that."

Timofey reaches for an emerald green dress on the bed and drapes it over his arm. "Benjamin won't be going."

I feel his eyes on me as I fold my sweater over the back of the armchair next to me and reach for the buttons on my jeans. With each sliver of skin being exposed, I feel more vulnerable. Both physically and emotionally.

Even though I told myself I don't care what Timofey thinks, I can't help but wonder if he likes the shape of me.

He's been with a lot of women, I'm sure. How do I stack up?

I shove the thought away and shimmy my jeans down my hips. *This is all fake. None of it matters. This is purely business.*

I try to focus on the conversation instead of the cool air of the room washing over my bare skin. "Kids aren't allowed at the wedding, then?"

"I didn't ask," he says. "And when we're at the wedding, you're going to forget Benjamin exists."

I glance up at him, trying to discern something from his flat expression and failing. "What do you mean? Like, you want me to relax?"

"I meant exactly what I said. At that wedding, Benjamin doesn't exist," he bites out. "I don't want anyone knowing about him yet."

"If you're worried about women being concerned you're a single dad, you should be more worried they'll think our ruse is serious and you have a girlfriend. If you'd rather I not go with you so you can prey on some jealous bridesmaids, then by all means—"

"I'm keeping Benjamin away for his own safety."

My jeans puddle around my ankles as I jerk my attention back to Timofey. "Are you thinking the wedding will be dangerous?"

"In my life, there's always the threat of violence."

I kick off my jeans, and I'm so focused on what he's saying that I barely recognize I'm down to my bra and underwear. A small, vain part of me wishes I'd known this was happening so I could put on a matching set. Or at least a pair of underwear that aren't saggy from too many washes. My whole body is one hot blush.

"With a sales pitch like that, it's easy to see why you needed a fake girlfriend. I'm not going if there's any chance I won't come home."

He rolls his eyes. "Cool it with the dramatics. You'll be fine. Benjamin is my heir. You're no one."

Ouch.

"And what does that mean?"

"As my sole heir, life will be dangerous for him. I want to make sure I have full legal custody of him and every protection put into place before anyone beyond the Bratva knows about him."

"You're saying people might want to hurt Benjamin? But he's just a baby!"

"In your line of work, I figured you'd be used to the idea by now. People hurt their own kids for a lot less."

"Yeah, but the last time someone told me their kids were in danger, it turned out she'd been diagnosed with schizophrenia and wasn't taking her medication. She thought secret agents were trying to brainwash her children through their breakfast cereal."

"This is no delusion. The threat is real," Timofey says with all seriousness. "If the right person takes out Benjamin, they could stand to inherit everything I'll leave behind."

As if I needed more motivation. I have to get Benjamin out of here.

I have to get out of here.

Timofey chose this life for himself. He walked in with eyes wide open. But Benjamin is a baby. He never had a choice. And if I don't get him out of here, he won't stand a chance.

I just need to get away from Timofey, and then I can start to formulate a plan.

"Can you handle that?" Timofey asks. "If you can't keep your mouth shut about Benjamin, I'll take someone else. I need to know you'll act to keep him safe."

"Of course I will," I snap. "I can't believe you even have to ask."

As far as I can tell, I'm the only person in Benjamin's life trying to keep him safe.

"Good." Timofey nods and holds out the green dress. "This one first."

I hold it up to my almost naked body, grateful for the coverage. It's strapless and, even without putting it on, I can tell it's skin-tight.

"This looks like I'm going to a strip club, not a wedding. I don't need to put it on. I can already tell I can't wear this."

"Not with your bra and those underwear on." He eyes my saggy granny panties, and I shift further behind the scrap of satin fabric in my hands. "Take those off."

My mouth falls open. "You can't be serious."

"I was going to say the same thing about that underwear. Really, Piper. Have some standards."

There's nothing else to throw, so I grab my sweater and hurl it at him. He snatches it out of the air easily.

"Give that back."

"You need less clothes right now; not more."

"I'll need it back eventually," I argue. "And I'll… I'll go change in my room and then come back in here to show you each dress. If we want to avoid being unprofessional, that would be the right thing to do."

He arches a brow. "We are way past being professional. Besides, lying isn't professional."

I frown. "I'm not lying."

"I guess it makes sense," he says, striding closer to me. "The woman who can't dress herself also can't wear a mask to save her life."

"I don't know what you're talking about."

Timofey grips my chin and forces my eyes to his. I can smell his peppermint breath and see his pulse thrumming in his throat. "You're a terrible liar."

"I'm not."

"You don't want to leave for privacy," he interrupts. "You want to leave so you can grab Benjamin and flee. *Again*. How many times are we going to have to go through this before you realize there is no escape?"

Internally, I panic. How easily can he read my thoughts? Is anything a secret from him? Does he know I stared at his ass as we walked down the hallway?

Externally, I do my best to prove him wrong. I lift my chin and narrow my eyes at him. "Stop acting like you know what I'm thinking. You don't."

Timofey looms large over me, blocking out my view of anything except for him. "I know you think I'm the worst person to take care of that little boy. I know you think you can find a way to get him away from me and escape. But you can't. And at the end of the day, I don't care what you think— so long as you do what I say."

"Blind obedience. How original," I drawl.

His grip on my chin tightens, and I hold back a whimper. I'll never let him see me crack. Not if I can help it.

"You should understand this next part better than anyone," he rumbles. "Family means everything to me. I didn't have one growing up, but I want that for Benjamin. Whether you like it or not, Benjamin is as good as my son. Which means I'll do anything—hurt anyone—to keep him with me. There is no law I won't break. No line I won't cross. If you take him from me, you're as good as dead."

I can feel my body trembling, but I clutch the thin fabric in front of me as tightly as possible to try and contain the fear coursing through me.

Timofey jerks my chin up, looking straight down into my eyes. "Do you understand?"

His body is pressed to mine. I can feel his heat through the dress.

I want to slap his hand away, but I also recognize the look in his eyes. The look of a father who, misguided as he may be, cares for his son.

It's as admirable as it is terrifying.

"I understand," I grit out.

He holds my gaze for a few more seconds and then lets go of me all at once, backing away. "Good. Now, put on the dress."

57

PIPER

"Another one." Timofey flicks his hand lazily at me like he's scrolling through a slideshow instead of gesturing at a human being.

I groan. "This dress is fine! It's…it's…"

I glance down at the disco-ball-like gown ballooning around me and try to drum up something positive to say. Truth is, though, I hate it. It's showy and gaudy and makes me feel like a princess in all the worst ways. But I'm so tired of trying on dresses.

"Preposterous," Timofey finishes. "Next."

"If you want to catch attention, this is the way to go," I say. "I think it's unique."

"It's terrible. Take it off."

I spin around and face him. "You've had a problem with every single dress so far."

"That's why we're trying them on. To get the right one." He snaps his fingers. "Put on the next one, Piper."

Usually, I'd jump at him for snapping his fingers at me, but I already tried that. The first time he snapped, I told him I wasn't a dog.

He replied he'd chain me up like one if I couldn't behave.

He may have scored that point, but I'm about to score this one.

I pull down the zipper along the side of the shimmery bodice slowly. I feel each tooth of the zipper releasing. The material slides further and further down. Then, with a whisper, it lands in a puddle at my feet.

For the first time in half an hour, Timofey perks up.

Every other time I've undressed, I've covered myself. I held up another dress in front of me or hid behind a partially opened closet door. Somehow, I've managed to keep myself at least partially covered during every outfit change.

Not this time.

"If you're doing this just to see me naked, then take a good look." I hold out my arms and spin. "Take it all in."

To my surprise, that's exactly what he does.

Timofey leans forward, icy blue eyes not missing a single inch of me. But as he trails over my breasts and around the curve of my hips, I'm starting to have regrets. The moment of frustration that led to this burst of confidence is being burned away in the heat of his attention.

Without looking away, Timofey grabs the purple gown next to him and walks over to me. I want to shrink away, but I force myself to stay put. He's already seen it all now, anyway. There's nothing left to hide.

He walks until we're less than a foot apart. I'm positive he can hear my heart thundering in my chest.

"If I wanted to see you naked, I wouldn't have needed to spend thousands of dollars on dresses." He looks between us, admiring the shape of my chest with his lower lip between his teeth. Then he holds up the purple dress. "Cover yourself."

I snatch the dress out of his hands and hurl it on the floor. "No."

Before the dress even hits the ground, Timofey pins me against the wall. One hand is curved around my waist, the other is at my neck. He's not holding me tightly, but it's obvious who is in control here.

I swallow, my throat bobbing against his palm.

"I warned you," he whispers, drawing close. His thumb traces over my hip bone. "I warned you again and again, Piper. I told you that if you kept talking back, I'll do what I've wanted to do since the moment we met."

A chill races down my spine, but I'm so tired of being afraid. I'm so tired of feeling small.

"If you want to kill me badly enough, you'll find a reason eventually," I tell him. "So do it. Go ahead. Kill me."

He looks at me like he's considering it. Like he's imaging exactly how he'd tear me apart, limb from limb.

Then his hand curls around to the back of my neck. He leans his head to the side and casts his eyes down to where his thumb is still caressing my hip. "What does this tattoo mean?"

His touch on my naked body is more than enough to scramble my brain. Throw in the fear of being pinned against a wall and entirely at his whim, and I am beyond incapacitated. It takes me several full seconds to even comprehend what he has asked.

Then I look down.

First, I notice the way his golden skin looks against mine. The way we complement each other. The way I fit perfectly in his palm almost like we were made for this.

Then I see the tattoo on my hip. It's a mountain scene with a wall of dark, impenetrable trees along the bottom.

"It doesn't mean anything."

He holds me tighter, his thumb digging into my soft flesh. "You're lying."

I look away over his shoulder. "No, I'm not."

Timofey shifts so he's in my line of sight once again. "Why won't you tell me the truth?"

"Why do you care?" I snap back.

He holds my jawline tenderly. When his thumb traces over my bottom lip, I can't hold back my moan.

It's not fair that his touch feels this good. I know too much about him to give myself over to his hands, but here I am, putty in his palms.

"The only thing that matters is that I do care," he says. "Tell me."

Timofey's pull is magnetic. It's overpowering. If I let him pull me under, I'll never reach the surface again. I'll never make it out of here.

When he leans closer with his lips parted, I can't help but stretch towards him. It's a natural response. Like a sunflower angling towards the sun.

"I want to know everything about you, Piper." Timofey's voice is a purr in my ear. It's a rumble deep inside, sending shockwaves to the traitor between my legs.

I want to be known. More than anything.

But this is a trap.

Anything I tell Timofey gets turned into a weapon he can throw back at me. He doesn't want to know me; he wants to know how to break me.

The more I tell him, the deeper I dig my own grave.

My eyelids flutter closed. It would be so easy to kiss him right now. To tell him what he wants and then take what I need. One sliver of my shattered heart for a second of bliss.

It seems like a fair trade.

But like Timofey said earlier, I need to understand what's at stake. A kiss from him isn't worth my life.

All at once, I shrink back against the wall.

Timofey's hand slips away from my face, leaving me cold from the lack of him.

"I need…" I scramble for something, anything, to say to give myself five minutes. "I'm thirsty. Can I go get a drink?"

Timofey labors through a sigh. Am I imagining things or is he actually… disappointed?

"I'll go." He drags a hand down the back of his neck and turns away. "You stay here. And, for fuck's sake—put on the purple dress."

He walks away so fast that I start to wonder whether he needs a few minutes to himself just like I do. But there isn't time to wonder.

I only have a short window of time here, and I need to make it count.

How many times are we going to have to go through this before you realize there is no escape?

Timofey was right. Again and again, I tried to grab Benjamin and run. Run where, though? Timofey has threatened every person I love. He's told me he'll kill me if I take Benjamin from him.

So the only thing I can do now is get my family away from him.

I drop to my knees next to my jeans piled on the floor and pull out my phone. As fast as I can, I type in "flights to Mexico." I click on the cheapest link and buy two tickets.

I just got paid, so I have enough in my bank account to afford them. Whether or not I can afford my rent is another story, but so long as I'm living with Timofey, that won't be a problem. As far as I can tell, I'll be living with him for a long while.

I shakily type in Gram's and Ashley's information and enter in my card number. I'm amazed I can remember anything.

My hands are trembling, and I keep pausing to listen to the hallway.

Is he coming back? Do I hear footsteps?

I'm still naked, and he asked me to put on the purple dress when he left, but I'll deal with that later.

Right now, I have to take care of my family. I have to make sure they are okay. That way, I can stay here, gather evidence against Timofey, and have his murderous ass thrown in prison where he belongs.

Deep down, some part of me balks at the idea. *Does Timofey really deserve prison? Is that what you want?*

I shake the thought away. It doesn't matter what I want. Right now, it's all about needs. Mine and Benjamin's.

As soon as the confirmation goes through for the tickets, I clear my history, shove my phone back in the back pocket of my jeans, and step into the purple dress.

I just get the gown pulled over my pounding heart when the door opens and Timofey comes in. He has a bottle of wine and two glasses in his hands.

I turn around, showing him the undone zipper along my spine. "Can you zip me up?"

58

PIPER

Timofey places the wine and glasses on his bedside table. A moment later, I feel his fingers on my spine. He doesn't need to touch me to zip up the dress, but I'm too busy trying to keep my legs from buckling to question his methodology.

An electrical current zips through me. A shiver follows. As if trying to warm me with his hand, Timofey presses his entire palm to my exposed back.

"Sit down," he orders. His voice is quiet but firm.

"But I need—" I lift my arm weakly over my shoulder to gesture to the zipper. "I need to be zipped. I need—"

"You need to sit down," he repeats, directing me towards his bed. The armchair is covered in discarded dresses. "You're about to pass out, and I'm tired of saving you."

I'm shaking. Adrenaline and deception are a lethal mixed cocktail in my veins. Timofey can probably see right through me.

He knows what I've done.

He knows I'm trying to escape.

"I'm just tired, I guess." I let him push me down on the edge of the bed. The unzipped back of my dress opens even wider. Cool air skirts across my exposed skin all the way to the very top of my butt. If I wasn't currently trying to play off the fact that I just panic-ordered two tickets to Mexico, I'd be worried about plumber's crack.

Timofey opens the wine bottle more gracefully than I've ever done anything in my life and pours us each a glass.

"I asked for water," I say, even as I take the offered glass.

"Your inability to know what's best for yourself continues."

He sits at the top of the bed and leans back against the headboard. He looks every bit as confident as he sounds. I want to believe it's an act, but no one could pull off this level of conviction for this long without slipping.

Timofey really believes he knows everything.

Though if he does know literally everything, he's doing a good job of pretending he doesn't know about the plane tickets.

Hell, maybe he doesn't. Maybe for the first time ever, I'll pull one over on him.

And maybe pigs will fly.

"You're saying I don't even know what I want to drink?" I shake my head and take a sip. "It's a miracle I've survived this long."

"My thoughts exactly."

I purse my lips. "I was being sarcastic."

"I wasn't." He lets his head rest against the tall wooden headboard. His throat bobs as he swallows. "You aren't tired; you're anxious. You need to relax. That's what the wine is for."

I make a show of tapping a finger against my chin as if deep in thought. "Here I thought the forced, naked fashion show would have been relaxing for me. How bizarre."

"The sarcasm is getting old, Piper."

"Fine. I'll go for honesty then." I turn to face him, eyes wide open. "Changing in front of you makes me nervous. I felt vulnerable and uncomfortable. Hence the trembling."

"I don't know why that would be the case."

"You don't know—" I stop and shake my head. "Of course you don't get it. You probably love being naked in front of people. Why wouldn't you love showing everyone your twelve-pack, cheese grater abs? When you could be on the cover of a men's fitness magazine, there isn't really much to be stressed about."

He twirls his glass absently, immune to both my vulnerable feelings and my assessment of his undeniable good looks. It's annoying that I can't seem to ruffle him the same way he ruffles me.

"I've seen the whole spectrum of what human bodies are capable of—the sexual and the vile alike."

"Charming."

"If you're worried you've somehow made it to the vile end of the spectrum, rest easy. I've seen the inside of a human skull while its heart was still pumping blood. Your naked body doesn't compare."

I blink at him a few times, waiting for the punchline or the "gotcha!" moment. It doesn't come.

"If that was supposed to make me feel better, you need to work on your bedside manner."

He arches an eyebrow. "Don't forget, Piper: you were naked earlier. I know exactly how well my 'bedside manner' was working."

He glances down at my chest, which is thankfully covered by the dress I'm half-wearing. Still, I feel my nipples pebble again at the mere suggestion that Timofey is talking about them.

Traitors.

"I could care less what you think of my body," I lie. "I'm more concerned with the kind of graphic things you've seen the human body do."

"You'd be scarred for life if I told you everything I've seen."

"Because I'm weak?"

I want to challenge his perception of me. I want him to think I'm tough and can handle anything. But the truth is, he's probably right. I can't even watch a cheesy slasher movie without covering my eyes every time the knife comes out.

"No. Because you're *normal*." He looks up at me, and in that moment, I feel more naked than I have all night. The way he's seeing me sends goosebumps racing up and down my arms. "Not everyone can be what I am. Not everyone should. I was born for it."

"What about Benjamin?"

His eyes harden. "What about him?"

"He's your heir, right? You expect him to take over for you. But what if… what if he's normal?"

Timofey shakes his head. "I'll train him. I'll teach him how to handle it. He'll be strong."

"You really think you'll be able to run the Bratva *and* raise him? Parenting isn't easy."

"Nothing worth doing in life is easy," he growls.

I don't want to press Timofey too hard. I've worked with enough foster kids in my life to know that they can shut down if I'm too heavy-handed. So I lower my head and speak softly. "Like giving Benjamin up to people who could give him a normal life? That wouldn't be easy. It might be the hardest thing you'll ever do."

"If you think an emotional goodbye is the hardest thing I could ever go through, then you really don't know a single fucking thing about my life."

Maybe he's right—there's so much I don't know about Timofey Viktorov. Apropos of absolutely nothing, I want to ask him about Emily. How did it feel when she was murdered? Did he cry? Did he shed even a single tear?

But I keep the question locked up tight.

"I'm not raising Benjamin because it would be too hard to say goodbye," he continues. "If I didn't want to care for him, he would have been gone within the hour. He's here because I want him here. That is reason enough. I'll be his father because I want to be. And if I want it, I'll succeed."

I exhale in frustration. "How? You just told me you can't even let people know Benjamin exists because it would put him in danger. Your enemies want to kill him."

"And you were attacked outside of your office by a drunk, angry parent," he fires back. "Does that mean you can't have children?"

"That's not the same thing. That guy had too much to drink and was upset. He isn't a murderer. The people you interact with are way more dangerous."

"There is nothing more dangerous than a parent on the brink of losing their kids," he says matter-of-factly. "Which makes me the most dangerous man in the world."

I open my mouth to say something. Anything.

But I can't argue with that.

Even if I wanted to, I don't have the energy. Timofey was wrong: he said I just needed to relax, but I really am exhausted. My body—physically and mentally—is spent. Being around him is like living atop a minefield. There's danger around every corner, and it never, ever ends.

"Benjamin's mother must have been special if you're willing to raise him on your own," I remark.

I study Timofey's face for any sign of weakness. For any hint as to how he feels about the mysterious woman who gave birth to Benjamin.

His mouth tightens and his finger drums on the side of his glass.

On anyone else, it would mean nothing. On Timofey, it's like a flashing neon sign: **Weakness this way! Emotional pain, sharp and fresh!**

I thought it would feel good to see him feel *something*. Remembering he's a human being and not some programmed killer robot on a mission to destroy me is difficult sometimes. When I catch a glimpse of his beating heart, it makes it easier to empathize with him.

Instead, my own troublesome feelings rise up.

What must this woman be like for Timofey to care about her? How could anyone else ever compete?

"Things are rarely that simple," he murmurs.

"Love never is."

"Which is probably why you continue footing the bill for your deadbeat dad and your grandmother, even though it's draining you dry."

Boom. Boom. Boom. More mines in the emotional minefield blowing sky-high.

I swallow hard. "You said yourself that family is important. After the way we grew up, I know you can understand that."

"I can understand wanting people around you that you can trust. In my life, that's the difference between life and death," he says. "But wanting the same family… that's the stupidest thing I've ever heard."

"Being loyal is stupid now?"

"Being loyal to people who will never return it is stupid," he says. "Once someone has betrayed you, you cut the cord. No second chances. No mercy."

I raise both brows. "That's harsh."

"That's how you get to the top. But with people clinging to you and weighing you down, you'll never rise beyond where you are now. So long as you have people like Ashley in your life, you'll remain stuck in the mud."

"There have been points in my life where Ashley was the only person I could count on."

"I doubt that," he snorts.

I turn to him. "Oh yeah? Remember that tattoo on my hip you asked about earlier? I got that because of her."

He leans forward, eyes dragging down my body to my hip. I'm wearing a dress, but I could be convinced that he can see straight through the material to my skin beneath. "Are the two of you fucking or something?"

I barely manage to swallow my next drink of wine without spraying it across his room. "What the—No! Of course not! Why would you even say that?"

"Friends get matching tattoos on their forearms or on their shoulder blades. You don't let a friend brand you with a hip tat. That's… sensual."

My skin burns. I can feel the tattoo, hot and tingly at the very edge of where my hip transitions to groin.

"You're right," I say. "Ashley didn't brand me there. Someone else did."

Timofey goes eerily still.

I laugh at my own nerves. "I shouldn't have brought this up. You already think I'm stupid. This will cement it."

"What happened?" he asks in a low voice.

"I think I've bared enough of myself tonight." I wave him away. "It was nothing. Forget it."

Timofey snatches my hand out of the air. His fingers are firm around my wrist, but his touch is gentle, too. He brushes his thumb over the webbing of blue veins under my skin. "Tell me what happened to you, Piper. Tell me who touched you. Tell me who hurt you."

I'm trembling in his hold and there is no way to hide it.

It's not as if his opinion of me can stoop any lower, so I take a deep breath and let it rip. "There's a reason why abused people tend to end up in abusive relationships again. There's a vulnerability we carry. Or, at least, that *I* carry." I correct myself because I can't imagine anything about Timofey being vulnerable. "Abusers can sense it. When I met my ex, I didn't stand a chance. He knew exactly how to draw me in."

"Tell me." Timofey is staring at my hip like his eyes are the laser that might be able to remove the ink embedded in my skin.

"He gave me everything I wanted." I laugh at Past Piper's naivete. I thought Josh was perfect. I really, truly did. "He treated me like a princess. Always said the right thing. He told me how beautiful and talented I was. He lifted me up and made me feel like the luckiest girl in the world."

"And then?" Timofey asks. I'm not surprised he sees where this is going.

"And then… he pulled it all away." I fold my hands around my nearly empty wine glass, trying to stop the shaking in my fingers. "He withdrew and got cold. I thought it was my fault, so I tried hard to connect with him and get back to the warm, loving place we were in before. But nothing I did was good enough. That didn't stop him from enjoying my efforts, though."

I heard once that sex isn't a simple activity; it's a destination. It's a journey.

Whiskey Poison

When things got bad with me and Josh, there was no escaping the oppressive walls he'd built around us. The sex was lifeless. I could never get out of my own head long enough to enjoy it. I was so worried he wasn't having a good time even while he grunted and thrusted. Then, the moment he finished, he'd tell me how his ex did it better.

Timofey plants a fist in the mattress. The comforter twists under the pressure from his knuckles.

Is his anger for me?

Definitely not. Don't be stupid.

"He got really possessive. He was convinced I must be cheating on him since... since I wasn't as good in bed anymore. I swore I wasn't cheating, but he didn't believe me. So when he suggested I get his name tattooed in a place where any man who touched me would see it..."

My chin wobbles. I take a deep breath to calm the emotion welling up inside of me.

"He fucking branded you," Timofey growls.

I nod, shuddering. "And I let him. I rushed out to do it because I thought it would help. I thought if I just did what he said, things would go back the way they were. But they didn't."

"He wouldn't have been happy until you were dead."

"No. No, it wasn't like that. Josh wasn't violent."

Timofey reaches out and touches my hip bone. His fingers wrap around my thigh, tracing over the place where my tattoo is. "He branded you. That's a kind of violence. He wanted to own you, but instead of earning it, instead of letting you give yourself to him, he stole it. He wouldn't have stopped taking until you were dead."

I stare at Timofey with wide eyes. What would it feel like to be earned by Timofey? To have him slowly softening the hardest parts of me? If I gave myself to Timofey, would it feel like something had been taken from me? Or would I find pleasure in the giving?

I already know the answer.

Which is why tears are rolling down my cheeks.

"Anyway." I swipe at the tears quickly and shove my hands under my legs. "It didn't come to that—because of Ashley. She convinced me to leave him. She helped me load up all of my stuff while Josh was at work and found me a place to crash with a friend of hers. Then, when the breakup wasn't as fresh, she took me out and we got the tattoo covered."

Timofey is watching me, but he looks distant. Like his eyes are focused on something else. "A mountain," he says, recalling the tattoo. "A snow-capped mountain with trees beneath."

"Standing on top of a mountain is the freest feeling I could imagine."

"No small spaces up there," he says, understanding perfectly what I was going for.

I nod. "Exactly. The trees at the bottom are to remind me of the darkness I overcame."

Timofey's hand tightens on my body. His square jaw is clenched with barely restrained rage. "I hate that his name is still on you."

Why? The question burns on the end of my tongue. *Why* does Timofey care whose name is on me? *Why* does it bother him so much?

I can't bring myself to ask it, though. I have no clue what his answer would be, and there are at least a thousand different ways he could slice me open. I don't want to risk that.

"His name isn't still there," I say. The back of the dress is still unzipped and cut low enough that I can pull the fabric down and over my hip until the black and white tattoo is visible. "You can't see it at all. See?"

Timofey's fingers are on my bare skin. He brushes the pad of his finger over my tattoo like he's worried the ink will spread. It's the gentlest I've ever seen him. He walks his fingers up to the top of the mountain before he looks up at me.

His blue eyes are stormy. "How many men saw that tattoo?"

I should be offended by the question, but I don't think Timofey is trying to shame me. "The mountain or—?"

"The bastard's name," he grits out. "How many men saw that asshole's name on you before you got it hidden? How many times have you had to tell a man this story?"

I let my finger trail over Timofey's hand. The heat coursing through him sears my skin. "The answer is the same for both. Just you, Timofey. You're the only man I've—Well, the only man who has seen me. Since him."

The answer is shameful in a way I didn't expect. I feel pathetic that I haven't been with another man in years. Especially when Timofey has probably been with countless women.

"Being close to another man wasn't exactly appealing after all that," I explain, rambling nervously. "The closer I get to people, the more they can hurt me. So I've kept my distance."

But then Timofey leans close, his breath hot against my neck. This moment alone is enough to sear Josh from my skin and my memory. Every hurt he ever caused is gone in one exhale from Timofey.

"Being close with someone… being *intimate…* can be a risk." His words curl around my neck like a serpent. I can feel his hold on me tightening, but I'm powerless to escape.

My body angles towards him. There is no one but Timofey. There has never been anyone else.

"How many women have you dated?"

"I don't date," he says without hesitation.

"But—" *Benjamin's mother. What about her? What about Emily?*

The ghosts of women I don't even know are hovering over this moment, casting long shadows.

"I'll brand you if you let me, Piper," Timofey whispers, his teeth grazing my earlobe. "I'll mark you in ways that no one else can see and that can't be undone. Just say the word."

"What word?" I mutter.

I'm not sure what is more intoxicating: Timofey's body pressed to mine or the wine swirling through me. I feel dizzy from his presence and there's a heat in my core that no alcohol could cause.

His teeth nip at my jugular, and I've never wanted to be devoured more in my life. "Timofey, what—"

"There," he growls, going rigid against me. "Just like that."

"But I didn't say anything."

"My name, Piper." His mouth sketches my jawline. "Say my name."

Oh. Is that all he wants? I'll say it. I'll scream it. I'll sing it opera-style with a pair of Viking horns on my head. Whatever it takes for this moment to stretch into eternity.

I turn and catch his mouth with mine, sucking on his lower lip. Then I pull away for half a second and gasp out what he ordered me to give him.

"Timofey…"

His hands curl around my lower back and mold me to his body. I'm not sure where Timofey stops and my body begins. He tips me back, and I fall into the mattress willingly. The tissue paper from the box of dresses crinkles underneath us, but I can barely hear anything beyond the thrumming of blood in my veins and the sound of our breathing.

What am I doing? The logical, moral part of me is screaming for me to slow down, but I'm feral now.

"Touching you feels good," I whisper as I trace his shoulder blades and luxuriate in the pinching and stretching of his muscles. "I want to feel good. It's been so long."

His hands slip and slide down the smooth fabric of the dress. It's my favorite piece of clothing I've ever worn, and I never even got it on all the way.

He rucks it higher around my hips until his hand slips beneath the slit in the side. My body is pulsating for him. My need is a second heartbeat between my legs, and there is no room for doubt or questions.

"You're so soft," he growls, juxtaposing the tender words. "Are you this soft everywhere?"

"Find out," I beg, opening my thighs wider in invitation.

His hand slips up my leg almost all the way to the aching heat at my center. Almost, almost, almost…

Just as a shrill ring cuts through the moment.

59

PIPER

Timofey freezes with his fingers half an inch from heaven. "For fuck's sake. You need a new ringtone."

"Oh." I blink out of the lusty haze and look around. "That's my—my phone. That's my work ringtone."

I start to get up, but he pushes me back into the mattress. "Ignore it."

"It's from my desk. It means someone called me and then asked to be redirected to my personal number. It could be important."

Is anything more important than tamping the fire currently roaring inside of me? I want to say no, but my good sense is gaining more and more traction with every shrill ring.

Finally, Timofey stands up and I climb out of the bed and rummage for my phone. It's in the jean pocket where I left it after I bought the tickets to Mexico.

Tickets I bought because I'm so afraid of Timofey that I have to get my family and friends as far away from him as possible before I even try to take him down.

I mentally curse myself for being so stupid. Thank God we were interrupted. Who knows what sort of mess that could have caused?

I answer my phone, half my mind still pinned to the mattress beneath the man intent on ruining my life. "Hello. This is Piper Qu—"

"Kidnapper!" A voice roars through the phone. "Where is she? What did you do with her?"

I hold my phone away to protect my eardrums from the screaming. "Who is this?"

"It's Grant! You were at my house!"

"I remember you, Grant. I know who you are."

Timofey stands straighter at the mention of the boy's name. I turn away from him so all of my brain power can be devoted to the young kid screaming in my ear.

"What did you do with Olivia?" he screams. "I know you took her! Where did you—"

"Wait!" I yell, interrupting him. "What are you saying? Is—is Olivia gone?"

"Yes! And you took her! She's gone, and—"

"Grant, stop," I say firmly, already stepping out of the purple dress. I can't even be bothered that Timofey is staring at my naked butt right now. There are more important things to worry about. "I don't have Olivia. I don't know where she is.

But I'll be there as soon as I can. I'm going to help you find her."

Grant yells something else back, probably warning me not to come. But I hang up before he can finish.

I yank on my jeans and turn to explain things to Timofey, but he's standing behind me with my sweater in hand.

He tosses it to me. "Get dressed. I'll drive."

60

TIMOFEY

I can feel the dampness in the air the moment I open the garage door. The sky is darker than usual. Gray clouds hang low and heavy, swollen with rain.

I grab the motorcycle helmet I've come to think of as Piper's and roll my motorcycle into the driveway.

While I wait for her, I pull out my phone and dial Rooney's cell number.

"Detective Rooney." The greeting is short and clipped, as far as greetings from James usually go. It lets me know someone else is within earshot. He wants this to sound like a professional call, which works for me.

"Missing kid. Seven years old, give or take. Blonde hair."

"Did you—" He cuts himself off and clears his throat. "When did she go missing?"

"I'm not sure."

"How are you not sure?" he hisses.

I realize all at once what he's asking. "Because I didn't fucking kidnap her, *mudak*."

"Oh. Okay. Good." Rooney sounds relieved, but I don't know why. I've never hurt a child. Ever.

"No, not good," I growl. "A little girl is missing, and no one knows where she is. You need to get up and go look for her."

"I'm off-duty."

"Not anymore."

He sighs. "Do you know this girl?"

Not really. But Rooney doesn't need to know that. "I'll text you the address where she went missing. Call me when you find something."

He starts to respond, but another voice snatches my attention away.

"You called the police?"

I spin around. Piper is standing on the lowest step of the porch, once again wearing her jeans and sweater. On top, she's added one of my jackets from the hall closet. The sleeves are rolled at least three times and the bottom hangs down to her knees.

She looks better than any woman has a right to.

I end the call and slide my phone in my pocket. "I called Rooney."

Her brow wrinkles at the mention of him. "I don't want him around those kids. Grant has been through enough."

"It's your choice."

Her eyes widen in surprise. "It is?"

"Yes. You can decide whether you want to find Olivia or whether you'd prefer to hold a grudge against Rooney for arresting you and let Olivia fade into memory."

Her shoulders sag. "Finding Olivia is obviously the most important thing."

"Okay, then. That's settled." I hold out her helmet, and she steps forward to let me place it on her head. "He's going to start a search and let me know as soon as he finds something."

"She'll be okay, right?" The helmet is pushing down some hair over her forehead and eyes. I swipe a finger across her face to push the locks out of the way. Her breath hitches, and she looks up at me.

Her green eyes are vibrant in the otherwise gray night. I know we are both remembering the position we were in less than ten minutes ago.

I'm not usually one for false promises, but for some godforsaken reason, I want to tell Piper everything will be fine. I want to assure her and ease the crease between her brows. I want her full lips to curve into a smile, and then I want to be back in my bed with her soft body underneath mine.

But I won't lie to her.

Instead, I pull out my phone again.

"I'll text Pavel, too," I inform her. "He'll rally the soldiers. There will be fifty men out looking for her within thirty minutes."

I start tapping out the message, but then I feel her hand curl around my knuckles. Her touch slides down my wrist and squeezes softly. "Thank you, Timofey."

Once I send Pavel everything he needs to know, I climb onto the bike. Without hesitation, Piper climbs on behind me. She almost seems comfortable there, her arms wrapped around my middle and her chin pressed against my back.

It's getting hard to remember what it felt like to ride without her curled around me.

61

TIMOFEY

"Someone took her!" Grant insists for the tenth time since we walked through the front door five minutes ago. The kid is a pacing, frantic mess. "Olivia wouldn't leave. She knows she can't leave the house without me with her. She wouldn't go out on her own. The dark scares her."

I don't need to look out the window to know it is dark and rainy. Drops splatter against the windows and the roof. Based on the large water spot in the dining room ceiling, rain will be dripping into the bucket below in just a few minutes.

Piper has been flipping through the case file she has on the kids and calling every contact listed to see if anyone has talked to Olivia. Between calls, she keeps reassuring Grant.

"I didn't take her. That isn't how my office works," she tells him. "We wouldn't come in and take her in the middle of the night."

"Well, someone did!"

"Or she walked out the front door," I suggest coolly.

Grant turns to me. His eyes narrow like I've betrayed him in some way. "I'd know if she walked out the front door."

"If that were true, you'd also know who walked through the front door and took her."

His face turns red and his hands are shaking. Suddenly, he pounds a fist into the wall. The drywall buckles and cracks. Piper yelps and jumps up to stop him, but I hold out an arm to keep her back.

"Where were you when she disappeared?" I ask.

Grant's shoulders rise and fall with every breath, but he doesn't turn to face me.

"No one blames you, Grant," I add. "Mistakes happen. But it would help to find her if we had some idea of when she left."

"I was right here," Grant grits out, gesturing to the couch. It's the story he's repeated since we showed up. "I was in the living room."

"You said you turned around and Olivia was gone and the front door was open," Piper says. "So you would have seen who came or went."

Grant spins around, his eyes wild. "I'm not lying."

"No one said you were lying," I say.

"She's trying to trick me," he spits, jabbing a quivering, accusatory finger at Piper. "She wants to write this up in her stupid folder and use it as a reason why we should be taken away."

Piper drops the folder on the desk and holds up both hands. "I'm not writing anything down. I'm here off the clock and unofficially. I just want to help."

Grant doesn't look at all convinced. "I've been here all night. I didn't leave. I never leave. I'm always here in the house."

His words carry the weight of his responsibility. He's a fifteen-year-old kid. He should be out doing stupid teenage shit with his friends. He should be talking to girls for the first time and playing video games.

He shouldn't be raising two other children. Not when he's still a child himself.

"Were you awake?" I ask.

The question seems to hit the teenager square in the chest. His breathing hitches like he might cry, but he swallows it down quickly. "Tiana didn't sleep last night."

"Babies can be exhausting," Piper says softly. "Especially if you're taking care of them all alone."

Grant nods. "It was just me. I was up all night and then Olivia woke up early this morning, and… I never went to sleep last night. I guess tonight I… fell asleep." He runs his hands through his hair, sending strands sticking straight out. "I don't remember when I fell asleep. Olivia was watching a movie when I closed my eyes. When I opened them, she was gone. The door was open. I guess she walked out, but I don't—I don't know. Maybe she didn't. Someone could have taken her."

Piper steps forward. This time, I let her. She lays a hand on Grant's shoulder and squeezes. "None of this is your fault, Grant. None of it, okay?"

"We have fifty men out looking for your sister right now," I add.

He snaps his attention to me. "The police? You called the police?"

"No, we didn't. They aren't police."

"They're...friends," Piper says. "Timofey called in some favors. They'll find your sister."

With the truth finally out, Grant sits down for the first time since we showed up. He drops down into the sagging, faded sofa and lowers his face in his hands.

He's only fifteen, but the weight of the world is on his shoulders. It's no wonder he's cracking under the pressure.

"I'm going to go talk to your mom," Piper says. "Does she know what is going on?"

Grant looks up for a second and shrugs. "I think so. I talked to her, but...I don't know. She barely looked at me. She probably didn't hear."

Earlier today, Grant was nothing but defensive of his mother. Now, I can see the cracks in that relationship, too.

"We'll be right back, okay?" Piper gives Grant a smile he doesn't see. Before she heads down the hallway, she waves for me to come with her.

"You don't trust me alone with the kid?" I drawl in her ear.

Piper hesitates outside the bedroom door at the end of the hall. She sags back against my chest, letting me hold her weight. "It's not that. I just... I don't want to do this alone."

My arms stay by my side, but a few quiet seconds pass that way. The two of us nested together. Breathing in rhythm.

Then I reach around her and knock. A voice on the other side beckons us inside with a hollow croak.

Piper lifts herself back to standing as I turn the knob. When she walks through the door, I'm just half a step behind.

We were just in this room earlier today, but the smell of sweat and dust is still a shock.

"Trish?" Piper calls softly to the lump on the bed. "Hey, Trish? It's Piper Quinn. With Child Protective Services."

There's a faint rustle of blankets as Trish turns her head. Her eyes are heavy-lidded and puffy. She squints against the light from the hallway. I wonder how long it's been since she has seen the sun.

"You're still here?" Trish mumbles.

"No, I—that was hours ago," Piper says. "I came back because… Did you know Olivia is missing?"

Trish blinks and, for a second, I swear I can see a flash of understanding. It's like a ray of sunlight breaking through a sky choked with clouds. She sits up a little straighter and frowns.

"Olivia," she repeats, nodding. "Yeah, she's…she's not here. She went with… Where did she go?"

"That's what we're trying to figure out. Do you know of anywhere she might have gone?" Piper asks. "Do you have family in the area? Or maybe she has a favorite store?"

Trish opens her mouth to say something, but no words come out. She shakes her head, her face twisting into grief. Suddenly, a loud, wracking sob echoes off the low ceiling.

It's an animal sound. It's the cry of a weak, dying animal who has nothing better to do. Nothing else to give.

Piper jolts in surprise. I hook an arm around her waist and pull her close to me.

"Go back with Grant," I whisper in her ear. "Tell him everything is fine."

I can tell she wants to leave, but she feels like she shouldn't. "She is upset. I should—"

"I'll talk to her," I say. "Go."

Piper hesitates, but then Trish lets out another wail. It's obvious Piper is in over her head. She has never dealt with anyone like this.

But I have.

Piper slips through the door. I move to the edge of the bed. The sheets are dingy and sweat-stained. They need to be washed, but that would require Trish getting out of bed for a few hours. I have a feeling she hasn't done that in a long time.

"Stop crying," I say flatly.

The woman keeps wailing like I haven't even spoken.

I lean forward and snap my fingers in front of her face. "Now."

She blinks and looks over at me, snorting and sniffing. "My b-baby girl is g-gone. Will they put me in jail?"

"I don't know," I tell her honestly. "Probably. If Olivia dies, then almost certainly."

Her chest hitches as she whimpers and gasps. "I didn't mean for anything to happen to them. I just get so tired when I'm taking care of them. I left for a few minutes…"

The Trish-sized dent in the mattress speaks to a lot more than "a few minutes." She should be beside herself worried about her daughter. Part of her is, I think. But the rest of her is mired beneath a black ocean of depression so deep that she can no longer sense which way is up.

I look down at Trish, but it's not her I see. For a flash, I see a dark-haired, blue-eyed woman tangled in the dingy blankets in front of me.

I see her cracked smile as I walk through the door.

I hear my name, rasped through dry lips.

"My Timmy," Mom always said.

Then I look again and she's gone. Trish is back. Her blonde hair is limp and greasy on her scalp and tears stream down her cheeks.

"Stop crying," I bark again. "It won't help."

She sniffles. Her chin curls and dimples as she fights back more useless wails. "Are you going to take them?"

"Who?"

"The kids!" she says. "My babies. They're too little to be away from me. You can't take a newborn from her mother."

"Olivia is without her mother right now. No one knows where she is." She starts to cry again, but I clap my hands in front of her in one loud crack. "Stop crying."

"You don't understand," she sobs. "You don't have children."

"I do, actually. A baby boy."

She looks over at me, and the misery on her face lifts. She smiles. "Congratulations. Children are a gift from God."

Finally, I see it. There's nothing Grant can do to make his mother better. He can't coax the mental illness out of her with gentle nudges or harsh rebukes. He can't make the house run smoothly enough that Trish will get up and rejoin their family.

Grant can't fix his mother, in the same way I couldn't fix mine.

As much as we both may wish that wasn't true, it is.

Which means Piper is right.

"Children are a gift," I repeat back to her. "They're a responsibility, too. A huge responsibility. You have to be able to devote your entire self to taking care of them and raising them. It's exhausting work."

Trish rearranges the blankets around her. In the yellow light coming from the lamp behind her, I see a cloud of dust rise from the blankets. "My kids are good kids. They don't give me any trouble."

"Except Olivia," I say.

Trish frowns, and I watch as reality washes over her again. There's a pattern here. She breaks through the fog of confusion for a handful of seconds at a time before descending back into its murky hold.

I have to catch her in one of those clear-headed windows.

My phone buzzes. I pull it out. It's a text from Rooney. ***Found the girl. Bringing her to you now.***

I breathe a sigh of relief. There's one crisis averted.

I pocket the phone and kneel down next to Trish's bed. I reach across the ripped patchwork quilt for her hand. She seems confused by the gesture, but she accepts it.

"Your son loves you, Trish. From where I'm standing, you don't deserve it. But there's no denying that he does. That's why he lies to stay here."

Her lower lip juts out in the beginning of a cry, but I keep talking before the waterworks can begin.

"Grant works hard to make you proud and take care of his siblings. He does it all because he wants to protect them and you. But maybe it's your turn to protect him."

She swipes at her eyes. "What does that mean?"

"It means you're going to do the right thing and give the kids up."

She instantly shakes her head. "No! No, I can't. They're mine. They belong with me."

I see the panic in her unfocused eyes. Even though she doesn't know how to do it properly, Trish really does love her kids.

Sometimes, though, love isn't enough. I know that truth all too well.

"Your kids aren't with you, though," I counter. "They're out there. Alone. That's how Olivia ended up sneaking away. That's why Grant does yardwork for neighbors to keep the heat on. Because you aren't there for them."

"Times are tough right now!" she whines. "They'll calm down. They'll go back to normal."

She tries to pull her hand away, but I squeeze even tighter. "How many times have you made that promise to yourself? How many times have you sworn you'd get out of bed and make breakfast? That you'd be there for them the way you know they deserve?"

Her chin dimples as she tries not to dissolve into tears again. "A lot."

"I know." I pat her hand. "And since you can't keep that promise, you have to do what's right for them."

Her eyes widen again. "You're going to take them?"

I shake my head. "No. I'm not going to take them. I won't have to. You're going to give them up. Because you know it's the right thing to do."

She stares down at the nest of dirty blankets around her. "How…how did things get this bad?"

"Because life is hard. Right now, you need to focus on getting out of this bed and taking care of yourself. Let someone else care for your kids."

She bites her lip and nods. "Okay." She nods again. I can see exhaustion moving over her like a shadow. "I love them very much."

"I know you do."

"I need to know they're safe," she whispers.

"I'll personally make sure I know where they are and who is taking care of them," I assure her. "I won't let anything bad happen to those kids out there. They will be under my protection."

She looks over at me, a sad smile pulling on her pale lips. "Thank you."

Then Trish leans back against the headboard and, within a few seconds, falls fast asleep.

Her trust in me leaves a warmth I've never felt before. People respect me for what I can do: make money, wage war. I know what it feels like to have people revere me and fear me and throw themselves in awe at my feet.

But this—having a woman be grateful to me for protecting her children—it's different.

There is absolutely nothing in the world Trish can give me. I don't gain anything by looking after her children and making sure Grant, Olivia, and Tiana are safe.

Yet, it feels like work worth doing. They feel like people worth protecting.

Fuck if I know what that might mean.

62

PIPER

I'm frozen in the hallway, rooted to the spot by the appearance of a man I don't recognize.

Outwardly, he has Timofey's broad shoulders and narrow waist. The amber light of the room shines off the dark black strands of his hair. The same hair I had my fingers buried in only a couple hours ago.

But the words coming out of this man's mouth are so beyond the kind of behavior I'm used to from Timofey that I can't make heads or tails of them.

I won't let anything bad happen to those kids out there. They will be under my protection.

Who is this man and what has he done with the vicious Bratva don I know?

I'm so stunned by his tenderness that I don't register that he is standing up and turning towards me until it's too late.

Timofey's frame swallows the small room. I stand stock still as he stomps towards me and slams the door closed behind him.

"I told you to stay with the kids," he growls.

This gruff, grouchy version of Timofey I'm used to has never felt more like a facade than in this moment. I don't buy it for a second.

I gesture towards the door. "What did you just do?"

"Nothing."

I shake my head. "I heard you, Timofey. You… you got Trish to agree to sign over her rights to the kids."

"She was wailing. It was annoying. I did what I had to do to make it stop."

"Don't do that," I say sharply. "Don't try to make me feel stupid."

He sighs wearily. "Move out of my way or I'll do it for you."

I place a hand on his chest. "Don't act like you didn't just do something amazing, Timofey. You comforted her."

"I lied," he hisses, leaning down so I feel his exhale on my face. "I told that pitiful waste of a woman what she wanted to hear so she'd shut the fuck up and I could leave."

He's lying. Not to her, but to me. I know he is.

"It was quite the performance then," I insist. "You should take up acting. Kneeling by her bedside and holding her hand was a really great touch."

His dark eyebrow arches as he studies me. "Since you liked this performance so much, how did you feel about my performance earlier?"

"What performance?" I ask.

He curls his finger under my chin and lifts my face to his. "The one where I made you believe I wanted you. What about that one? Did I have a *'great touch'* then?"

I narrow my eyes and stretch up onto my toes. He has to pull back slightly to keep our lips from meeting. Part of me wishes he hadn't.

"Yeah, you really sold it," I say effusively. "You were so believable I was almost certain I felt your dick on my thigh. I bet that was just you 'getting into character,' huh?"

I start to turn around, but Timofey grabs me by the waist and pins me to the wall.

In the other room, I can hear the baby cooing and Grant whispering soft words to her. They can't see us or hear us from here, and I bite back a yelp to make sure it stays that way.

"Stop looking for the good in me," Timofey snarls, holding my jaw with a vise-like grip. "Don't expect to find some heart of gold buried beneath the tattoos and scars. You'll only end up hurt."

I want to tell him that it's too late. *I'm already hurt.*

It kills me knowing that Timofey was once a warm, loving little kid who was turned cruel by the world.

It kills me that the sweet boy he once was still exists in there, but his life is so dangerous that he can't let it show.

More than anything, it kills me that he won't show the soft side of himself. Not even to me.

I want to tell him all of this, but before I can, Grant yells out from the other room. "Olivia!"

I gasp and look at Timofey, wide-eyed. He doesn't look surprised at all. "Rooney texted," he explains. "They found the girl."

I push him away, and he lets me go without a fight. I run into the living room just as Grant drops to his knees in front of the newly returned Olivia and curls her into a bone-crushing hug.

"I can't breathe," Olivia complains, grinning the entire time.

Grant holds her at arm's length. "Where were you? Why did you leave?"

The little girl's toothy grin spreads even wider as she reaches into her back pocket and pulls out a bag of gummy candies.

Grant stares down at it, speechless.

"I wanted candy." She presses the bag into Grant's hands. "If you open it for me, we can share."

Behind me, Timofey chuckles, but I'm too busy fighting back tears to turn around and see what that's about.

Grant squeezes the bag of gummy worms in his fist until his knuckles are white. Then he drops to the floor again and pulls his sister into a hug.

"Grant," she complains, "I can't breathe."

He squeezes harder. "I don't care."

63

PIPER

Timofey is silent on the ride back to his house.

For the first time, I wish we were in a car. I'd have a panic attack, but it would be worth it to be able to glance over at him in the passenger seat and read his expression. I wish I could talk to him without needing to yell and my hair whipping around my face under the helmet.

Usually, I like the wide-open freedom of the bike. I like being able to cling to Timofey's strong body and feel the wind against my skin. It's easier when we aren't face to face. I can hold him from behind and pretend he's a different man. A better man.

But after what I saw tonight, I think Timofey might already be that better man.

I want a closer look to be sure.

The garage door opens as we approach. Timofey glides the bike gracefully past his fleet of parked vehicles to the back wall. He kills the engine as the door closes automatically behind us.

I'm so lost in thought I don't realize I should be moving until Timofey says something.

"Whenever you're ready."

"Oh. Right." I slide off the seat and unbuckle the helmet. My fingers are cold from the night air and it takes me a few tries to get the buckle off. It doesn't help that I'm shaking.

When the clasp is free, Timofey lifts the helmet off my head and places it on the back of his bike. The gesture feels comfortable and intimate. Like, somehow, through the tangled mess of drama we're in, something akin to an actual relationship is forming.

Right now, when I'm away from my family, my routine, and my apartment… this moment with Timofey feels like home.

He turns to walk past me towards the house, but I grab his arm. My hold isn't enough to keep him here. We both know he could blow past me without even trying.

But he stops and waits.

"What?" His voice is a growl, but it doesn't frighten me the way it used to. It's a tactic. He's trying to push me away.

I turn to him, my hand sliding up his forearm to wrap around his elbow. "I don't know yet."

"Piper…" He sounds exasperated, but he always sounds that way when he's talking to me. I'm starting to think I might not exasperate him as much as he lets on.

I shift in front of him and draw close, arching my body against him so I can look up into his face. He keeps his eyes pinned above my head, focused on the wall behind me.

"Look at me." I slide my hand up and cup his jaw. "Please."

Slowly, he tilts his chin down. His blue eyes are silver in the dim light, and I want to take a dip below their surface. I want to know what is going on inside of his head.

"You said you were just pretending to want me," I whisper.

His jaw clenches. He doesn't say anything.

"Was that the truth?" I don't know if I want to hear his answer. Right now, I'd be okay with his pretending.

Tonight was hectic and stressful. Timofey comforted Grant when he felt guilty about losing Olivia. He eased Trish's worries about giving up her children.

Now, it's my turn. *I* need comfort. I need him to hold me and make me forget for a few seconds that everything in my world is a complete fucking mess.

"I'm not the man you saw tonight," Timofey says suddenly. He's looking directly into my eyes like he's trying to make sure his words find their mark. "If that's the man you want, then you should turn around and go inside right now."

Part of me wants the tender side of him. The soothing words and gentle voice.

Then again, I kissed him earlier tonight before I knew that side of him existed.

"You're right," I whisper, looping my hands around his neck. "I never know what I want."

"What do I do with that, Piper?"

I press my hips into him and lick my lips. "What you always do. Show me."

The words hang in the air between us for a few seconds. I'm not sure anything is going to happen. I convince myself he's going to shove me aside and disappear into the house.

Then, in a heartbeat, he spins me around and slams me against the side of a black car.

The air whooshes out of me, but I don't need it where we're going. His hand curls under my thigh and hooks my leg around his hip. He presses into me so I can feel every single inch of how much he wants this, too.

That's more than enough.

"I'm not going to be gentle with you, Piper," he warns.

I claw at his shirt, wishing I could rip it off of him. "I'd hate it if you were."

He lifts me higher, hooking my legs around his midsection as his mouth slants over mine. He swallows my moans, sucking on my lower lip and nipping at my jaw. I tip my head back against the car and give myself over to him. To every kiss, every lick, every bite.

I hook my ankles behind his back and roll against the sizable length of his erection. My body is pulsing with anticipation.

I could not be less interested in foreplay. With Josh, I practically begged him to touch me. To kiss me. I faked it more times than I count.

Now, I'm having the opposite problem. If Timofey doesn't hurry, I'm going to explode.

"You said you weren't going to be gentle," I remind him.

"Funny that you think foreplay is gentle." He gives me a devilish smirk. "It's going to be torture. When I'm done with you, you'll be begging for release."

He drags the flat of his tongue along the side of my neck and goosebumps erupt over every inch of my exposed skin.

Timofey is a universe of contradictions. He is a mysterious dichotomy I can't seem to unravel. He's gentle and cruel. He's passionate and cold. I can't make sense of him, especially when his hand slides between our bodies, pushes inside my pants, and cups my aching center. Any attempt at logical thought goes right out the window.

"Fuck," he growls, his teeth scraping against my earlobe with every word. "You're more than wet. You're fucking soaked."

He swipes low with the pad of his finger, and I practically shoot up the wall. Every muscle in my body contracts, and the sensation is too much to handle.

"I can't," I gasp. "If you do that, I won't last."

Timofey tightens his hold on me and swipes over my clit again, moving in deliciously painful circles. "You don't need to last, Piper."

"But what about you?" I ask even as I arch and grind against his hand. I can't help myself. I'm being selfish, but I need this.

"Don't worry about me. Let me worry about you."

Those words alone almost push me over the edge. It's been so long since I've been like this with anyone. More than that, it's been so long since anyone has taken care of me. Like this or otherwise.

Timofey's warm hand slides deeper between my thighs. The heel of his palm massages me while his fingers slide into my wetness.

I drop my head onto his shoulder and cry out. The only reason I haven't fallen to the floor is because he's pinning me to the car. My body is limp, so unaccustomed to this kind of pleasure that I'm not sure how to function.

"Timofey," I cry, hugging his neck as I ride his fingers, "I'm going to—I can't—"

"Come." It's a single command spoken in my ear.

I obey.

64

PIPER

My muscles clamp tightly around him, and I dissolve into a puddle of ecstasy. Heat pulses through my core and flows to the very ends of me. I'm on fire, and I've never been happier.

"Oh my god," I moan again and again.

He lets me ride out the waves, then slowly pulls his thick fingers from me. I feel every inch, every brush of skin on skin, and it's as good as anything I've ever felt.

He lowers me to the concrete floor on shaky legs, and a wild laugh bubbles out of me. "You said I'd be begging for release."

"I did," he says flatly.

My body is buzzing, and I am drunk on the feeling. I drag a hand over the points of my nipples and lower. I twirl my fingers over the place in my belly where I feel warm and loose. I sigh. "You said that would be torture, Timofey. I think you oversold. That wasn't torturous at all."

My eyes flutter closed, and I could fall asleep standing up.

Then the world spins. Timofey's hands are on my hips, yanking me towards him and bending me over the hood of a silver car.

"Hey! What are you—"

His hand cracks across my ass before I can get the words out. Pain lances through me, but before I can complain about that, he yanks my jeans down and presses a kiss to the tender flesh.

His words are a dark, breathy snarl. "I'm nowhere near done with you yet."

I'm shaking as Timofey rips off my clothes piece by piece. Part of it is the orgasm still vibrating inside of me. But the slow, methodical way Timofey stands me up and peels me down to my bare skin is definitely the other part of the equation.

It's nothing he hasn't seen before, but this feels uniquely vulnerable.

Still, he couldn't pay me to put my clothes back on. Whatever is coming, I'm going into it with eyes wide open.

Timofey stands behind me, and I spread my legs wider. I lean across the hood of the car and arch my back for him. I realize in a sudden jolt how badly I want him to want me. I want him to think I'm sexy and beautiful. I want him to reward me when I'm a good girl, to punish me when I'm bad. I want to give myself over to him in every way a person can be given.

But before I can express any of that, he drops to his knees. I start to stand up, confused, when I feel his hot breath against my very center.

"Wait," I gasp. "Timofey, I already—"

Then his soft lips part me. When his tongue thrusts into me, I have to fight to stay standing.

Like he can tell I'm on the verge of collapse, Timofey grabs my thighs and pins me against the chrome grill of the car. I don't even mind the metal biting into my skin. I welcome the bruises so long as he keeps licking me.

"Yes," I pant. "Right there. Please don't stop. Please."

I can feel the familiar tremble starting deep in my belly. It's almost overwhelming, the way it rides the edge of earlier tremors. I roll myself against his mouth, seeking out more of his touch.

I'm so close.

So painfully close.

And then Timofey pulls away.

The feeling I've been chasing fizzles out, and I whip around, my face knit into frustration. "What are you doing?" I practically scream.

Timofey wipes his mouth with his forearm. Even though it's one of the sexiest things I've ever seen, I still hate him right now.

With a rough twist, he forces me to turn around and then pins my back against his chest with the band of his arm. "Whatever the fuck I want to do," he hisses in my ear.

His other hand slides up my stomach and cups my breasts. His fingers tweak my nipple, rolling and pinching until it's taut and sensitive. I lean back into him as his other hand rises up to hold me, too. He's palming me and grinding himself into my ass.

Timofey's heavy breathing against my neck is hot. Knowing that he's like that because of me is intoxicating. It's maddening.

Pretty soon, I can't resist. I reach around and slide my hand beneath the waist of his briefs.

"Piper," Timofey warns, his hands stilling on me. It's like a warning. *Do as I say or you'll be punished.*

But I don't care. Whatever happens next will be worth it. Hearing him fall apart at my touch would be worth anything.

I wrap my hand around him, and gasp when I realize he's so thick that my thumb and finger don't meet. Then I slide my hand down and down… and down.

"Oh, Timofey," I gasp, squeezing as I slide my hand back up his endless shaft. "I can't wait. I want you."

Timofey has been frozen while I touch him, but he drops his hands and thrusts into the circle of my hand. "I don't care what you want. Keep going."

With my back to his front, I continue stroking him. He slides his pants and boxers down to give me better access, and I work his length until he is rock hard and twitching in my palm. Until I'm pulsing with every stroke, hungry for him in a way I've never known.

"Timofey," I whisper, bending forward so I'm spread in front of him.

"No," he barks as he lays a hand on my hip.

I arch my back and stroke him, working the very tip of him against my opening. "Timofey. Please."

A growl rumbles through Timofey's chest and his hand tightens on me. "I said *no*."

I can hear his breathing growing labored, and simply knowing I'm the one pushing him towards the edge is enough to take me there.

"I don't want to come again without you inside of me."

He blows out a shaky breath. Then, without warning, Timofey yanks my hand away and slides himself into me.

I'm wet and beyond ready, but I still cry out at the size of him. He stretches me wide and pulses shallowly a few times before he pushes in even deeper.

He hits the very deepest part of me, and I spread my arms wide on the hood of the car. "Don't move. Stay right there. I can't—"

"You'll do exactly what I tell you to do," he commands, sliding out inch by unbelievable inch before sheathing himself in me again.

"Fuck!" I pound a fist on the car, and I kind of hope I dent it. That way I can come out here again and again to remind myself that this happened.

"You're so tight, *kiska*," Timofey growls. "You feel so fucking good."

He retreats and then presses forward until the slide of him inside of me feels natural. Until I never want to be without him in this way. Until I forget what it was ever like without him buried all the way in me.

My legs are shaking and trembling. My muscles are exhausted from my two previous orgasms, but I need another one. I need to come again with him inside of me, and I need it now.

"Please," I pant, reaching back to stroke his muscular thighs. "Take me. Fill me."

He curses under his breath and lifts me to standing. My back is arched, my shoulders against his chest while he pounds into me.

I lay my head back on his shoulder, whimpering with every thrust.

Timofey wraps his hand around my throat, and he was right, it's torture. I'm so close, but I can feel him holding back. He's moving with even, practiced strokes. I need wild. I need feral.

I need the blue-eyed beast.

"Maybe it won't happen, after all." My voice is high and breathless. It's obvious every word out of my mouth is bullshit, but I tell it anyway.

"Liar." Timofey squeezes my throat tighter. I can feel his teeth on the back of my neck.

I shrug. "It's okay. You finish. I'm fine with two."

"Piper," he warns, "don't play with fire."

I don't just want to play with fire; I want to be consumed by it. I want to burn.

"I'm just being honest. This isn't doing it for me anymore."

He cries out suddenly, and then he is everywhere.

Timofey drills into me from behind as his hand wraps around my hip. He flicks and circles my clit, and I scream into the empty garage.

"C-come with me," I beg, fighting off the pleasure building in me. "Please. Come with me, Timofey."

His breathing is ragged. A string of Russian words I don't understand pour out of his mouth.

For some reason, that is what does it for me.

I come for a third time, this one so powerful that the first two feel faint and distant in comparison.

Heat erupts inside of me, and I pulse around Timofey's thrusts again and again and again.

"I feel you," he groans, tightening his hold on my throat until I see black at the edge of my vision. Somehow, it adds to the pleasure. I feel euphoric. That feeling only grows when Timofey goes rigid behind me. Then I feel him twitching deep inside.

I gasp his name again and again. Until he stops thrusting into me and collapses on top of me.

I'm content under the weight of him, happy to be crushed.

If this is torture, I never want it to end.

65

PIPER

Timofey pulls up his jeans and leans against the hood. It's the perfect position to watch me hunt for my clothes.

"You could help," I say, snatching my panties off of a side mirror and finding my shirt under a workbench in the corner.

He shakes his head. "I'm fine here."

Honestly, I'm fine here, too. The world feels manageable in this garage. The two of us make sense in here. But the world out there is complicated. The longer we can stay in this sexy, sweaty bubble, the better.

"I'm not even going to bother with the panties." I hook them around my finger and fling them in his direction. Then I step slowly into my jeans and shimmy them up my legs.

It's a cheap trick, but based on the way Timofey crushes my underwear in his white-knuckled fist, I think it might be working.

If we only had sex once, but I came three times, would this next round be number two or number four? I'm trying to solve that philosophical riddle when I hear a loud rumble.

It takes me a few seconds to realize it's the garage door.

It takes me a few seconds more to realize I'm commando and still naked from the waist up.

"Shit!" I hiss, diving behind the black car Timofey fingered me against. The thought still sends warm fuzzies through me, even as I start to hear distant shouting. "What is going on?"

"I have a visitor." Timofey is standing between the cars, staring at the door.

"Did you open that door?"

He nods.

"Asshole!" I yelp. "I was naked. Someone could have seen me."

"Then I suggest you hunker down and be quiet or someone still might." He takes a step forward and waves his hand. "I'm right here, Rodion."

My eyes are so big they're bulging. *Rodion* is here?

I duck behind the hood of the car as Rodion's voice gets closer. "Don't fucking wave at me like we're friends."

"Fine. I'll wave at you like I'm the last face you're ever going to see," Timofey fires back. "Which I will be, if you don't calm the fuck down and tell me what you're doing here."

In a flash, Timofey ducks down just as something explodes on the back wall. Tools and bits of corkboard fly everywhere. Is he *shooting* at Timofey?

But no, I realize as something comes skittering to my feet. It wasn't a bullet. It was a whole gun. He chucked it right at Timofey's head.

"Don't waste your breath threatening me now. I already know you want me dead," Rodion snarls. "I swiped that gun off the hitman you sent to take me out."

Timofey is standing eerily still. His body is tense, and I can see his mind churning. "Someone tried to kill you?"

"Tried and failed. I saw him coming from a mile away. How fucking stupid do you think I am?"

"If you really came here to accuse me of arranging your death, then you're much stupider than I realized."

My shirt is too far away, but I manage to grab my bra and ease it on. I can't quite get the clasp, but now that my nipples are put away, I can focus on what the two men are saying.

Someone tried to kill Rodion. It might've been Timofey. *Huh?*

He was with me all night in his bedroom and then across town, helping the kids. But if he hired a hitman, he wouldn't need to be there in person to have Rodion killed.

I don't need to ask myself if Timofey is capable of something like that. I know he is. I just hope he didn't do it. I'd like to think he wasn't murdering someone at the same time we were… *occupied.*

My thoughts scatter when footsteps slap across the concrete. Timofey dodges to one side as Rodion flies past him and slams into the car.

If he looks closely, I'm sure he'll see the outline of my handprints on the hood. If he turns around, he'll see my entire body hunkered in the corner.

I silently pray he doesn't notice either one.

Timofey glances in my direction only once, to make sure I'm hidden. Then his gaze locks on Rodion, drawing the man's attention away from me.

"Don't be stupid, Rodion. If I wanted you dead, you'd be dead."

Rodion shakes his head. "No. Because I'm the best killer you have. You can't hire someone to take out the best."

"I wouldn't hire anyone. I'd do it myself," Timofey snaps. "And I'd relish it, too. You're a pain in the ass more often than not."

Rodion rears back and spits hard at Timofey's shoes. He barely misses, his saliva splattering across the concrete. "You're fucking coward, *Don Viktorov*. Look me in my eyes and tell me the truth."

"I didn't hire anyone to kill you, Rodion. That might change if you spit on me again. Murder attempt or not, I don't take kindly to disrespect."

Even from behind the car, I can see Rodion's hackles raise. His entire body seems to inflate with rage. "Before I killed the man who tried to take me out, I tortured him. I'll give you three guesses whose name he gave when I asked him who sent him."

"Right, because hitmen are notoriously trustworthy," Timofey says sarcastically.

"I've always been loyal to you."

"As I've been to you," Timofey says. "I'm telling you: I didn't send anyone after you."

Rodion folds his hands behind his back. His arms barely move. Timofey probably can't tell he's reaching into his pocket. He definitely doesn't see the knife Rodion tucks into his palm.

But I do.

"And I'm telling you," Rodion says, slipping the handle into his shirt sleeve, letting the blade hang down into his palm, "I don't believe you."

It happens so fast I don't have time to think.

Rodion charges across the garage and lifts the arm with the knife.

Timofey starts to react, and he might respond in time. He might knock the blade out of Rodion's hand. He might save himself.

But he might not.

With my bra clasps flapping in the wind and no shirt on, I jump to my feet and run straight at Rodion.

It's not what anyone would call graceful, but I have the element of surprise on my side. I slam into the arm holding the knife, and the blade clatters across the floor.

Rodion reacts quickly, turning his shoulder and sending me ricocheting over towards Timofey.

Timofey wraps an arm around my waist and pulls me behind him. "Fix your fucking bra," he barks.

I quickly kick the knife the rest of the way under the black car and then adjust my bra. "You're welcome, by the way."

Rodion snorts. "You had your girlfriend hiding as backup? No wonder your hitman failed. You're obviously scraping the bottom of the barrel."

"Shut the fuck up and leave, Rodion." Timofey keeps shifting in front of me to keep me and Rodion separated.

Rodion leans to the side and wags his brows at me. "Afraid I'll see something I like?"

"I'm not afraid of anything. But I will cut your eyes out if you look at her like that again."

"Careful, Timo." Rodion wears an easy smile now, but I can see the tension rippling through him. He's not masking his rage as well as he thinks he is. "Keep talking like that and your little lady here might figure out who you really are."

"I already know who he is," I snap.

It would probably be smart to keep my mouth shut, but the words spewed out of me before I could stop them. It was the suggestion that I don't know Timofey that triggered the word vomit.

I've learned a lot about him in the last twenty-four hours. *Like the way he sounds when he comes.*

More to the point, I've seen a side of him I know Rodion hasn't seen. I've seen Timofey passionate and gentle and caring. I've seen him hold a sick woman's hand and convince her that her kids will be okay.

I know exactly who he is, in all the ways that matter.

Rodion snorts. "You think so?"

"I know so," I spit. "I know he's your don. And I know he could have you killed by your own Bratva brothers if he wanted."

Rodion raises his brows and looks at Timofey. "Wow. I was in hot water for telling her I'm a professional killer, but now, you've told her you're the professional killer's boss? Sounds like a double standard to me."

"I get to make the rules and you get to follow them," Timofey says. "Leaving now would be a good start."

Rodion holds up his hands and edges towards the door. Timofey moves with him, maintaining his position between me and his hitman.

Just before Rodion walks through the open garage door, he turns back to me. "In case no one has told you, you ought to start updating your will. The women Timofey loves have a bad habit of turning up dead."

I should be focused on the "dead" part. That's the important piece of the puzzle. Still, my heart and mind are snagged on the idea that Timofey has been in love. There have been women in his life that were close to him. Women who knew him maybe as well or even better than I do.

Those kinds of thoughts are still muddying the waters of my mind when Rodion leaves and I see Timofey lunge for the nearest car.

He digs around in the glove box for a few seconds. When he stands up, there is a gun in his hand.

"Timofey," I gasp, reaching for his wrist. "No!"

He shakes me off and stomps towards the garage door. He's moving like he can't even hear me. Like I'm not even here.

"Timofey!" I move in front of him and plant two useless hands on his chest.

He keeps walking, plowing me backward.

I wrap an arm around his waist and raise my other hand to touch his face. "Timofey. Don't do this. Please."

And there it is. He looks down at me.

I keep talking, trying to use the moment wisely. "You don't want to do this right now," I tell him. "Don't let him get a rise out of you."

His blue eyes are impossibly dark. They narrow to slits. "I'm not doing this because he goaded me into it. He disrespected me. I have to answer in kind."

"He thought you sent someone to kill him!"

"And I told him I didn't," Timofey growls.

"Just like he told you he didn't kill Emily." The woman's name is bitter on my tongue. I hate bringing her up now when I'm still flushed from what just happened on the hood of the car. I want to be the one who brings him back to himself, not this mysterious woman he once loved. Still, I'm desperate enough to use whatever cards I have at my disposal.

He shakes his head. "It's not the same."

"Maybe not," I concede. "But shouldn't you figure out who tried to kill him? Maybe that will be important."

Timofey stares after Rodion's dark figure disappearing down the drive. His grip on the gun loosens and his arm goes slack.

My body sags in relief. "Thank you."

"It wasn't for you," he snaps. "Now simply isn't the right time to kill him."

"So… you're going to kill him later?" I ask.

Timofey turns to me, and I almost don't recognize him. For a few blissful minutes, I felt cared for in his hands. Now, he looks at me like he doesn't even know me.

"Whether I do or not, that is Bratva business. *My* business." He replaces the gun in the glove compartment and turns towards the door. "It has nothing to do with you."

66

TIMOFEY

I should have fucked Piper in a linen closet.

Or the tool shed out back.

Or one of the countless, identical, anonymous guest rooms in the east wing of the house.

The point is, it should have been somewhere random. Somewhere I never go. A room where I'd never have to walk in and imagine her naked in front of me, confident and wet and willing. A place where the imprint of her curves wouldn't be left on the hood of one of my favorite cars.

Because now, every time I walk through the garage, I think of her.

I glance at the smudged print Piper left behind on the shimmery, silver surface. My body tenses with the memory of how perfectly she fit into my hands.

When I think about it, I can still hear Piper panting. I can feel her warm hand wrapped around my length, stroking and pulling with a toe-curling pressure. She was on the brink of orgasm without me even touching her.

You don't have to do anything, she panted. *This is enough.*

Twice now, I've almost grabbed a rag and some cleaner to wipe the smears away, then put it right back up. I can't bring myself to clean it. Not yet.

That imprint might be the only proof I have that it happened. Because I sure as hell shouldn't be stupid enough to let it happen again.

Too much is at stake.

The women Timofey loves have a bad habit of turning up dead. The echo of Rodion's voice in my head is grating, but his words still ring with an unfortunate truth.

My mother.

Emily.

Now, Piper's name threatens to join the list.

I can't afford to let that happen. She needs to last until Benjamin belongs to me. After that, I don't give a damn what happens to her.

Or so I tell myself.

I climb out of my car and slam the door closed. As I pass my motorcycle, I swat her helmet off the back of the seat. It smacks against the cement floor with a satisfying thud. I barely resist the urge to kick the entire bike over.

I haven't spoken to her since the night with Rodion. It's been two days of burying myself in Viktorov Industries board meetings, Bratva business, and legal paperwork.

All so I can stop thinking about burying myself in her.

As I walk to the door that leads into the house, I'm determined to keep my eyes straight ahead. I'm not going to look at the evidence of what we did. I'm not going to think about Piper's perfectly tapered waist and long legs. I'm not going to think about the smell of vanilla in her hair and the way her pulse felt under my fingers.

I look over. But to my credit, I don't think about any of those things.

Only because, instead of the outline of Piper, I see an envelope sitting on the hood.

"Who the fuck was in my garage?" I growl.

I swipe the envelope off the hood. Inside are three photos. One of Piper standing at her desk in the CPS office. She's wearing the outfit I saw her leave in yesterday, a pair of navy blue trousers and a pink sweater. A coffee cup sits on her overflowing desk, and she's smiling at the male coworker sitting next to her. I have no clue who he is, but I want to pluck his tiny head from his shapeless body and throw both out the window.

The second photo is of her walking into a rundown home with a manila folder tucked under her arm. It's clearly a house visit, and she's so focused on doing her job that she doesn't notice she's being followed.

The third photo is Piper wheeling her bike down the sidewalk. Akim told me she wanted to ride her bike to work this morning, and I allowed it.

Fucking *stupid*.

The photos crease in my fist. They're a warning, that much is clear. Or, at the very least, this is meant to look like a warning. For all I know, it could be a distraction.

"Rodion," I breathe.

The son of a bitch might want me to spend more time watching Piper so he can attack me from another angle.

Benjamin.

"I should have killed him when I had the chance."

I would have, too, if Piper hadn't stopped me. Rodion mentioned Emily, and I was blind with rage. Piper is lucky I didn't put the gun to her head for standing in my way.

In the end, she was right. I didn't have anything resembling an alibi. If anyone came sniffing about Rodion's death, I wouldn't have had a convenient explanation.

But I should have dealt with him immediately afterward. Instead, I've spent the last two days distracting myself and steering clear of Piper.

No more. This is my house. I won't hide from anyone.

She and I need to have a talk.

67

TIMOFEY

For the first time in two days, I go looking for Piper.

Usually, at this point in the evening, she's working at the kitchen table or curled up with a book on the sofa.

But the living room is empty and the kitchen and dining room are too littered with remodeling equipment and supplies for anyone to sit there.

Akim is overseeing the repairs to the kitchen after the fire so, naturally, it has gone wildly over budget and is taking far too long.

"The kitchen is my office," Akim argued. "When my office is nice, better things come out of it. That means you eat better food. It's a win-win."

Akim could make a five-star meal over a trash can fire, and we both know it. Still, I've been too overextended to argue with him. If a ridiculously expensive stove keeps him off my back right now, then so be it. God knows I have the money to spare.

Sighing, I head up to Benjamin's room.

His door is closed, which isn't surprising. It's late, and he's finally started going down at a reasonable time every night now that Piper is in charge of his schedule.

I crack open the door. He's lying in his crib, arms tucked into a swaddle blanket and a pacifier hanging out of his open mouth. I watch his chest rise and fall to the rhythm of his quick breathing.

Once things calm down, I'm going to be around for him more. Once he is officially, legally mine, I'll make sure he has the childhood I never had.

Convinced he's fine, I close the door and head down the hall to Piper's room.

I push her door open without knocking and prepare to see her scowling over at me, annoyed by the intrusion. I figure I'd prefer her annoyance to her wide-eyed surprise. Or worse, excitement. A smile from her would undo the last two days of avoidance.

Instead, the room is empty except for the warm vanilla scent of her shampoo.

That's when I hear the shower running. Water splashes on the tiles, and Piper is humming off-tune. It might as well be a siren call.

I close the door behind me and step further into her space. Steam swirls through the crack in the bathroom door like a finger beckoning me forward.

There's a lot at stake. I know that.

But what would one more fuck hurt? It'll soften her up before I tell her about her new stalker.

Maybe, every time I deliver bad news, I make her orgasm first. It can be part of the business arrangement. An extension of our professional relationship.

I've almost convinced myself that whatever complications come afterward will be worth it if it means holding her tight, supple body against mine one more time.

Then I see her purse lying at the end of her bed.

A few folders and a small book spill out of the wide mouth onto the comforter. One folder has Trish's name at the top. The first page inside is her intent to relinquish her parental rights, with her illegible scrawl at the bottom. I nod in grim satisfaction. Grant won't like it, but it will be best for him in the end.

The next folder has my name printed on the label. I crack it open and see Piper still hasn't written a single word in Benjamin's case file.

It's not the glowing recommendation I'd like, but blank pages are better than a recommendation for removal. This means Piper still has time to make the right choice. An empty document means I don't have to eliminate Piper as a threat to my end goals.

Yet.

I slide the folders back into her purse and grab the book. Except the book isn't a book at all. It's a planner.

I flip through the monthly and weekly trackers. She writes down meetings and calls she needs to make, and she keeps a running to-do list in the margins. I skim a few of them, but it's all boring, useless shit.

Pay rent

Lunch with Noelle

Buy stamps

Check in on Ashley

I flick the planner closed, but as the last pages flutter shut, something catches my eye.

I have to thumb through the lined "note" pages at the back to find what I saw. The writing is in the middle of a section of blank pages, almost as if Piper hoped anyone who found her planner would think the end pages were empty. Once I read it, I understand why.

She's written a series of dates in the left-hand column with shorthand, barely legible writing in the right. Things like "E on Insta" and "R Mos." It doesn't click in until I see the date Emily was murdered in the column on the left. Next to it in large, underlined letters are the words "TV IN TOKYO?"

TV. Timofey Viktorov.

I was supposed to be in Tokyo the day Emily died.

The rest of the code cracks easily. E is Emily. R is Rodion. "R in Mos" is "Rodion in Moscow." Sergey insisted Rodion was out of the country the night Emily died. Apparently, Piper believes it, too.

Piper is looking into Emily's murder and compiling evidence.

Against *me.*

68

TIMOFEY

The shower turns off, and I can hear Piper moving around in the bathroom. Her wet feet slap against the tile floor and she continues humming as she towels off.

When she finally comes out, she yelps in surprise when she sees me sitting on the end of her bed. She scrambles to tighten her towel around her chest. Her auburn hair hangs in a dark, wet tangle over her shoulder.

"Timofey!" she gasps, hand still pressed to her chest. "What in the hell are you doing?"

"I'd like to ask you the same question."

She frowns in confusion until I lift the planner and wave it in front of her. Her eyes widen. "That is for work."

"That can't be right. Because you're a social worker, not a private investigator."

She clenches her jaw. I know she knows what I'm talking about. But she isn't going to reveal anything until I do.

"Don't tell me you're one of those pathetic, do-it-yourself, true crime sleuths, Piper. A good government gal like you, I figure you would leave the investigative work to the police."

"I don't know what you're talking about."

"Does that mean you do or don't want to know why I didn't go to Tokyo a few months back?" I ask.

Piper stares at me blankly, and I take it all back. Any emotion would be better than the flat way she is staring at me now.

I hurl the planner at the wall, and she jumps in surprise. It's a second of genuine emotion before she lowers her completely transparent mask of neutrality. Below the surface, she is terrified.

"I have a right to know if a woman was murdered in your house. The house where I am now living."

"You don't have a right to anything. Living here is a *privilege*."

"A privilege I was forced into! I don't get a choice. If I'm in danger, then I deserve to know the details."

I scoff. "So this is about Rodion. About what he said."

Her skin is flushed from her shower just like it was when I pinned her against the passenger door and dropped to my knees in front of her. I shove the memory away, but it leaves reluctantly. It doesn't help that Piper is wearing nothing but a tiny towel.

"You beg me to fuck you hard," I spit, "but you still trust Rodion over me. He says you're not safe here, and you believe him. Forget what I have to say about it."

"That's not fair."

"No, what's not fair is you accusing me of Emily's murder."

She shrugs without making any attempt to deny it.

"But you know what's strangest of all? You think I murdered a woman and yet you still spread yourself open for me. What does that say about *you?*"

"I didn't know two days ago what I know now," she snaps. "Like the fact that Emily gave birth right before she was murdered. If I did my math right, her baby would be a few months old."

I stare at her, refusing to acknowledge the dots she has obviously connected.

"Benjamin is Emily's child, isn't he?" she asks.

"You've come to enough conclusions without my input."

Too many, honestly. I've made a lot of cracks about Piper's intelligence, but the woman pays attention.

"Timofey…" she breathes. She's holding her towel to her chest with white knuckles. Her eyes are pleading with me. "Just tell me what's going on. I've already agreed to lie to CPS for you. This doesn't change anything."

"We both know how tenuous your word is."

"You want to talk about *my* word?" she spits. "What about yours? I know you were supposed to go to Tokyo the week Emily was killed. But you didn't. You canceled the trip. Why?"

Because a baby was left on my fucking doorstep.

The excuse is there on the tip of my tongue. It would answer so many questions. But I don't owe an explanation to Piper or anyone else. Especially since Emily swore me to secrecy.

"Rodion has an alibi," Piper says. "Do you?"

The mention of his name lights a fuse in me. I'm not sure what will happen when it burns down.

I stalk towards her, backing her into the corner of her room. She's trembling. It could be from fear, though she was trembling that night in the garage, and she certainly wasn't afraid of me then. My guess is it has more to do with the fact that she is damp and practically naked.

"If you think I'm guilty of a crime, call the police."

"Like it would matter. You own the police."

"Not nearly as many as you must think," I admit. "You're bound to find someone who is all too happy to bring down the Viktorov Bratva. You'd be a star witness."

She swallows, her throat bobbing nervously. "Like you'd let me."

I throw my phone on her bed and wave for her to grab it. "Go for it. Be my fucking guest."

Piper looks from me to the phone and back again. I can tell she isn't going to make a move for it, but she is trying to decide how serious I am. What my angle is.

"Call them and get me locked up if you want," I continue. "But see who will protect you when I'm not around."

She frowns. "Protect me from what?"

The insinuation is plain enough. I'm the only threat she is worried about right now. With me gone, what would she have left to be scared of?

I pull out the photos that were left in the garage and fan them in front of her face. She takes them in, one by one. Her green eyes narrow and then widen, confusion shifting to horror.

"Who took these?" she whispers.

"The person who will end your life the moment I'm no longer standing guard over you."

I throw the photos on the bed. Piper follows them, her bare arm brushing past me on her way to get a better look. She doesn't even touch the phone lying right next to her.

"This is me at work," she whispers, rifling through them. "And on my way home. This is... Someone was following me?"

"And you had no idea," I bite out. "Because you don't understand this world, Piper. You have no idea what you're dealing with."

She tosses the photos onto the comforter and turns to me. "I get it, Timofey. I'm stupid. I'm an idiot. I'm useless. Okay?"

No, Piper, you're none of those things.

You're vulnerable.

She has no idea how fragile her life is right now. And I can't make it clear to her without revealing far, far too much.

"Turn me into the police if you want," I tell her, walking for the door. "But the moment you do, you're as good as dead."

69

PIPER

I can't look at the photographs anymore.

Seeing myself going about my day, unaware I was being watched… It's too unsettling.

Is there any way that Timofey actually took these photos to scare me? I wouldn't put it past him to try cornering me into doing what he asks, i.e., not going to the police.

After all, I'm more convinced than ever that he has some role in Emily's murder. He has good reason to want me scared and dependent on him.

But no. There's no freaking way. He couldn't have gotten that close to me without me noticing. Every time he's close, I feel it like a static charge.

For better or worse, I'm drawn to him. There's no way he did this without me noticing.

"Which means I have *two* psychos out to get me."

I shove the photos in my bedside drawer and stand up. I'm still wrapped in the towel from my shower, even though my skin has long since dried. My hair is dry, too. It hangs in unbrushed tangles around my shoulders.

Walking into the bathroom and cleaning myself up feels like a monumental waste of energy. There's too much to sort through. Too much to unravel to spend any bit of energy that isn't completely necessary.

I walk over to the corner of the room and grab my planner. There's a scuff on the wall from where Timofey threw it.

"Stupid," I whisper, flipping to the notes I made in the back. I can't believe I thought my silly little code would fool him. E for Emily. R for Rodion. TV for Timofey Viktorov. I did his entire initials, for God's sake. What was I thinking?

I wasn't. And I can't afford to do that again.

I'm going to need to do a lot better than some scribbled dates in the back of a planner if I want the police to take my case against Timofey seriously. Especially since he has Detective Rooney and who knows who the hell else on his side.

Not nearly as many as you must think, he said.

Lies. He probably owns the entire police department. It would bring him immense joy to get a call from one of his Bratva Brothers in Blue that I tried to bring charges of murder against him. Then he'd snap his fingers and have me thrown in a dungeon with no key.

Like always, the deck is stacked in Timofey Viktorov's favor. My evidence against him for Emily's murder is circumstantial at best. Nonexistent at worst.

I want to call Ashley or Noelle and talk this all out. Processing verbally is my thing. It's how I make sense of the noise inside my head.

"Are you aware you narrate your entire life?" Noelle said once. "Like, just a running commentary of what you're doing and why."

They were both waiting in my living room for me to get ready to go out. But to afford a night out, I needed to have a plan for the rest of the week.

Ashley cackled and dropped into her pitiful attempt at an impersonation of me. "'I, Piper Quinn, am going to defrost this chicken to cook tomorrow night. Then I'll have leftovers the night after when I have to work late. I can also shower while the chicken is defrosting, so I don't have to do it the next morning when I have an early meeting.'"

"Excuse me for trying to organize my life!"

"Ever heard of a planner?" Noelle teased.

I bought one after that conversation. It helped. For a time.

But no more. The mess inside of my head needs to stay there. At least until I know it can't get me into any trouble.

Slowly, I flip the page Timofey was looking at to the very next page. The one he thankfully didn't see.

My handwriting fills the page from top to bottom. At first glance, it looks like some kind of crazy person's manifesto. The frantic, sloppy writing of a person whose brain is bursting with bad ideas.

__Life would be easier if I stopped trying to collect evidence against Timofey. I could do what he's asked me to do, recommend he raise Benjamin, and then walk away. Except, I__ *don't think there is a way to walk away from this. From him...*

I grab the corner of the page and start to rip. Maybe if I tear the page out, the feelings associated with it will disappear, too.

But I hesitate, letting myself scan further down the page.

Being with Timofey is thrilling, if I'm honest. I don't know if that makes me a bad person or not. It probably does. I don't even think I care anymore. When we were in that garage tonight, I would have done anything to stay there forever. I've never been touched that way before. I've never wanted someone so much before. Is it possible he wants me, too?

My face burns with shame so powerful it makes me nauseous.

"He made it very clear what he thinks of me," I remind myself.

"That is Bratva business. My business," he said when I asked him about whether he was going to kill Rodion. "It has nothing to do with you."

Timofey ghosted me after we had sex. There's no other way to put it. I didn't even see his shadow in the hallway for two days. All of our communication took place with Akim as the middleman.

That's why I did a deep dive into Emily's murder. Because Timofey's indifference to me wasn't enough of a reason to give up my romantic fantasies. But if he's a murderer? Surely that would be the ticket to forgetting about him once and for all, right?

And it worked. It really, truly did.

Until I came out of the shower and saw him sitting on my bed.

All it took is one glimpse of him to release all of the feelings I'd squashed down and pent up.

Timofey is like a vine planted deep in the dark depths of me. It doesn't matter how many times I tell myself it's wrong to want him or that I can't be with him. Until I rip him out of me, roots and all, he will always have a hold.

Clearly, he didn't like me looking into Emily's murder—which is exactly why I can't give up now. Rodion was right: the women in Timofey's life don't tend to live long.

So the only solution is to make sure I'm not in Timofey's life.

70

PIPER

Akim is in the living room when I find him. He has a bowl of popcorn on his lap and the remote in his hand, furiously flipping through channels faster than the television can keep up.

"What are you doing?" I ask.

"Counting how many channels Timofey subscribes to," he says, not slowing his clicking or looking in my direction.

"Just go to the guide page."

"Channels aren't numbered the way they used to be, you know? 1, 2, 3, on and on. Now it's CineDine 1 and CineDine 2 or The Game Channel and The Game Channel Late Night. I just want a straight-up number. Why is that so hard?"

I sit on the far end of the couch and reach for his popcorn. "Why does it matter?"

"It doesn't," he says. "I just want to know how much money he's wasting. Cable is basically a scam. Only the boomers still have it. Plus, he never even watches television. What does he need 1,349 channels for?"

I whistle. "That's a lot."

"And I'm still counting. When would he have time to watch the Travel Channel in French?"

"Never?" I guess. "But I don't know. Maybe he has a lot of free time. I never actually see him do anything except for work."

"And you," Akim says. He stops his channel flipping just long enough to play the pretend drums. *"Ba-dum-tss.* I'll be here all night, thank you very much."

I throw my handful of popcorn at the side of his head. "Asshole."

"Hey! That is cheddar ranch popcorn. It's too good to waste and it will stain the sofa."

I take a bite of the kernels still in my hand and beam in appreciation. "Wow. You weren't joking. That is really good."

"Good enough that you'll forgive me for making that joke about you and Timofey and all the loud lovemaking you did in the—"

"I'll only forgive you if you shut up right now and never mention it again."

He pulls an imaginary zipper across his lips and continues his channel flipping.

The word "lovemaking" hangs in the air like a cloud of gnats. I can't ignore it, as much as I'd like to.

"You have to be capable of love to make love," I mumble.

Akim partially unzips his lips. "Since you brought it up, am I allowed to speak on it or...?"

"We aren't speaking about *that*," I say, giving him a stern warning look. "But you can talk about him if you want."

He peeks over at me, eyes narrowed in suspicion. "Do you want to talk about *him*?"

"No!" I blurt on instinct. Then I shrug. "Yes. Maybe. I don't know."

I do know. If it wouldn't put Noelle and Ashley in danger, I'd be upstairs in bed telling them everything right now. But the less they know, the better.

Akim is my only option.

"He's just so frustrating. I don't feel like I know what is going on in his head."

"Some people are easy to read. They're an open book. Others, like Timofey, are a book that is chained closed, shoved into a safe, and dropped into the deepest part of the ocean."

I snort. "That about sums him up."

"But some of us are really good scuba divers. We have all of our qualifications and know how to dive that deep without getting the bends and dying... or getting eaten by a giant squid or something."

I wave him on. "Enough with the analogy. Get to the good stuff."

He sighs. "You two are more alike than you know."

"I highly doubt that. For instance, I have a heart and people in my life who love me without needing to earn a paycheck from me."

If Timofey were here, he'd contest that point. But Ashley doesn't get a paycheck from me. She just occasionally needs my entire paycheck to stay out of jail. But that's different. That's completely and totally different.

"I was friends with Timofey before he paid me," Akim says. "I liked him from the moment I met him. Of course, I met him when Emily was there. She had a way of softening him."

My entire body goes rigid at the mention of her name.

Of course Akim knew Emily. Why didn't I think of that before?

Maybe because you were too busy getting bent over the hood of Timofey's car to use your brain?

"What was she like?"

I'm not sure why I even asked. There is no answer Akim can give that will make me feel better.

If she's exactly like me, then I'll feel like some kind of sick replacement for the woman Timofey lost.

If she's nothing like me, then I'll feel like I don't have a shot in hell of being with him.

Not that I want to be with him. Or that I should be with him. That isn't my goal here…

Is it?

Akim sighs, drawing me out of my pathetic, frantic thoughts. "She was… she was really amazing. Such a sweet person. Incredibly beautiful."

Yeah, this isn't helpful. I want to go back in time and withdraw my question.

"That makes sense," I say. "Timofey is ridiculously handsome."

Akim frowns. "I mean, they aren't related. So I don't see what that has to do with anything."

I wrinkle my nose and turn to him. "Obviously, they aren't related! Gross."

He stares at me for a second, looking confused, and then shrugs. "Anyway, she was amazing. Timofey was always more at ease around her. They'd known each other for a long time, so he was more himself with her than with most people. It was good to see."

What did it look like when Timofey was being more like himself? Was he the gentle version I saw the other day? Maybe he even smiled when he was around her.

Jealousy twists in my gut, hot and foul.

"Then they had a falling out and things changed," Akim continues.

That's right—Timofey may have killed her. I was too busy being jealous to remember how things turned out for Emily. Her position isn't exactly enviable.

"Oh. That's too bad. Was it a serious argument?" I ask. "Were they able to sort it out before she was killed, or…?"

Akim opens his mouth to respond. Then, all at once, he lowers the remote and turns to me. The usually lighthearted chef is suddenly serious. "What are you asking me, Piper?"

I feign innocence as best I can. "I'm not asking anything. I just wondered if they put their differences aside before she was—before she died. Were they still together?"

He shakes his head. "Have you talked to Timofey about any of this?"

I snort. "You said it yourself: he isn't exactly an open book."

"Right." He clicks off the television and stands up. "Maybe I should follow his lead then."

I reach for him. "Wait! Don't go. If you can't talk about it for whatever reason, then don't. If it wouldn't be safe for you, I won't press."

"Ask Timofey whatever you want, but I should probably keep my mouth shut from this point on."

Before I can say anything else, Akim hands me his bowl of specialty popcorn and hurries out of the living room like I've started another fire.

71

PIPER

Benjamin is awake when I open his door to check on him.

It's not so strange. He usually wakes up sometime around midnight to eat. The only difference is, he isn't crying. He's just lying in his crib, staring up at the perfectly still mobile hanging over his head. Tiny wooden airplanes floating beneath a white cloud.

Did Timofey order that for him? The thought of Timofey standing in the infant section of a store, picking out mobiles, is laughable.

Also, adorable.

If Timofey wanted, he could have any woman in the world. All he'd need to do is take Benjamin on a walk down the street. Handsome men with adorable babies are catnip to single women.

Myself included.

"Hi, bud," I whisper, peeking over the edge of the crib of the adorable baby in question. "Are you hungry?"

He won't respond, I know, but he doesn't even act like he can hear me.

I pluck him out of the crib and move him to the changing pad strapped to his dresser. As I undo his swaddle, the usual pocket of warmth I find between the layers of his clothing is noticeably absent.

"Is it too cold in here?" I ask, sticking a foot out to feel warm air flowing out of the air vent near the floor. It seems normal. "Maybe I'll turn up the heat. What do you think about that, huh?"

His chubby arms are limp at his sides. When I pick him up, they dangle behind him, his fingers loose rather than curled into dimpled fists.

The beginnings of panic curls in my chest, coiling like a snake ready to pounce. I ignore it, though. I'm being dramatic. I'm worried over nothing.

"You're just hungry," I coo against his round cheek. "We'll get you something to eat, and you'll be right as rain."

I hold onto that hope until I step into the butcher's pantry and flip on the light.

Usually, Benjamin blinks at the brightness or recoils, but he doesn't react at all to being bathed in harsh white light. Even worse, I look down and see a blue ring around his lips.

The snake in my chest goes wild.

"Oh my god," I gasp, stroking his face. Suddenly, he feels cold. Was he always this cold? Or is it me?

My heart is racing, but I feel like I'm not getting any blood to my extremities. My hands and feet tingle, and I feel lightheaded.

I sink down to the floor, Benjamin lying across my knees. I press my palm to his tiny chest to assure myself his heart is still beating.

"You're okay," I whisper when I feel the faint, fluttering thud against my hand. "You're going to be okay."

I take a deep breath and do the only thing I can think of. The only thing that makes sense.

I call Timofey.

For a second, I worry he won't answer. Maybe he thinks I'm calling to explain myself or apologize. I'm sure he doesn't want to hear that any more than I want to do it.

Then I hear his voice, deep and firm. I grab onto the lifeline.

"What?" he barks.

"Timofey. Benjamin." So many words and explanations are running through my head, but that's all I can get out.

There's a beat of hesitation before he responds. "What are you saying?"

"Benjamin," I try again, working hard to slow the racing of my heart. "He's not crying or… or fussing. He is quiet and—and—he's blue. His lips are… Something is wrong with him. We need to—"

"I'll be there soon."

The line goes dead.

I drop the phone and cradle Benjamin in my arms. "It's okay. Everything will be okay. Your daddy will be here soon. He's going to help us, okay? He'll make sure you're fine."

I'm shocked to realize I'm not lying to make him feel better. I believe every word out of my mouth.

Timofey is going to fix all of this.

72

TIMOFEY

I fly around corners and speed through as many lights as I can. The thought of getting in an accident isn't nearly as terrifying as the thought of losing Benjamin.

Piper must feel the same. She isn't complaining at all that she's wedged in the backseat with Benjamin and his car seat. Her claustrophobia should have her clawing at the windows, but when I glance in the rearview mirror, all of her attention is on the boy.

Even in the dark, I can tell her eyes are glassy with unshed tears. "His eyes are starting to close. I don't know if he's sleeping or—"

"We're almost there," I interrupt. "Two more minutes."

She pokes at him, whispering sweet assurances in his ears to keep him awake.

The moment Piper called, I knew I had to be the one to get them to the hospital. An ambulance would take too long. And if something happened to him on the ride, I'd have no choice but to kill the EMTs in retaliation.

No, it had to be me. Piper didn't fight me on that. Nor did she hesitate to jump in the car with us.

"The emergency room is over there," she says, leaning into the front seat to point out the passenger side window.

I'm already careening through the parking lot towards the brightly lit red sign.

"Get him out of his seat," I tell her.

"But we're still moving. It's not—"

"Now," I order. "I don't want to waste another second."

I hear the straps being loosened and by the time I slam the car into park and climb out, Piper is handing Benjamin's small body to me through the back door.

He looks worse than he did when I first got to the house. His usually rosy cheeks are pale with a gray pallor. His wide, bright eyes are flat. He looks like a badly made baby doll, a poor reproduction of the happy boy I'm used to.

I hold him in the warm crook of my arm and sprint towards the front doors.

I hear the rumble of an engine and turn just as Piper waves to me from the driver's side window. "Go on ahead. I'll park the car."

Stepping into the artificially bright emergency room is disorienting, but I don't slow my pace. I weave around rows of uncomfortable plastic chairs and miserable people to the nurse's station along the back wall.

Without looking up, an older nurse slides a tablet that is chained to the desk towards me. "Sign in and we'll get to you when—"

"Right fucking now," I growl.

She looks up, lip curled and ready for a fight. But when she sees Benjamin, her eyes widen. "What's wrong with him?"

"He's turning blue, not crying, not eating," I say, listing off everything I can remember Piper saying. But this woman is smart. She can tell as well as I can that something is seriously wrong.

She presses a button on her desk and hustles around, plucking Benjamin from my arms and placing a stethoscope against his chest.

I was ready to tell her that I've donated millions of dollars to this hospital and she needs to show Benjamin the best care they have or I'll burn the entire place to the ground. But it seems Benjamin is doing all the heavy lifting for me.

"What wrong, sweet boy?" the nurse murmurs. She frowns as she runs a thumb over the back of his hand.

The entrance doors slide open and Piper rushes in, her head turning frantically before she sees us standing at the front desk. She skids to a stop next to me. "Are you taking him back now?"

The nurse gives Benjamin one more look and then nods at us both. "Come with me, Mom and Dad."

I meet Piper's eyes. The labels hang in the air like the universe taunting us. In a split second, we silently agree not to correct the woman. Whatever gets us both back into an exam room with him is fine.

We follow the nurse through the labyrinth-like halls, collecting more nurses as we go. Every single one lights up at the sight of Benjamin coming their way and then grows concerned once he's close. It's not exactly encouraging.

We're taken into a room where he's stripped down to a clean diaper and poked and prodded.

"He should be crying," I snarl, the words hissing out between gritted teeth. "Why isn't he crying?"

"That's what we're going to find out," the nurse says.

Silently, Piper reaches over and takes my hand.

The anxiety in my chest doesn't ease, but it doesn't get worse, either. It feels like someone else is here to carry the load. My fears are just as big as they were, just as dense, but feeling the warmth of her hand in mine grounds me.

When the nurse tells me she needs to take Benjamin for some tests, Piper's hold on me is the only thing that keeps me from demanding I go with them.

Then the space clears and we're alone.

The white box of a room is sterile and lifeless. My eyes bounce from medical chart to medical chart, seeking anything to distract me for even a second.

"What I wouldn't give for some terrible dentist's office art," I mutter.

Piper, who has been standing perfectly still since the nurse closed the door behind her, jumps up and begins pacing the two steps back and forth across the room. "Maybe we should have gone with him."

"Are you a doctor?"

She ignores me. "Did they put a tag on him or anything?" she asks. "How do they know he's ours—I mean, yours—how do they know where he belongs?"

"They put the wristband on him and scanned it into the system when we first got in the room."

She drags a hand through her auburn hair, her eyes shifting at the pace of her thoughts. "Right. Okay. Good."

I can feel the frantic energy like a forcefield around her. It's impossible to imagine that just a minute ago she was the one being strong for me. Now, she looks like her nerves are almost fried.

"Piper," I say softly.

"What if I hadn't gone to check on him?" she whispers, still ignoring me. "He wasn't even crying. I just peeked in to look at him because I—Because I wanted to see him. Because I—"

"You love him," I finish for her.

She looks up at me. For the first time since I walked into the house and saw her on the floor with Benjamin in her lap, I feel like Piper is seeing me.

For the first time, she can see beyond the haze of fear and panic that has been surrounding her since the moment we met.

Tears fill her eyes and she nods. "I really do. He's perfect." Then she remembers why we're here, and she starts to break down again. "He's perfect, but something is happening, something is wrong with him, and it happened on my watch. I was watching him and I almost missed it and—"

"But you didn't miss it. You noticed and you called me. Now, we're here."

"You're supposed to be mad at me," she says in a weepy voice. "It would be easier if you were mad at me."

"There's nothing to be mad about. You saved him."

She shakes her head, refusing to accept my words. "Not yet. We don't know what's wrong. We don't know anything yet."

"I do," I tell her.

She blinks up at me, her eyes as wide and pure as a child's. "You do?"

Suddenly, I want nothing more in the world than to take care of this woman. I reach out and stroke her cheek, cradling her quivering chin in my palm. "I know everything, remember?"

A surprised laugh huffs out of her. She fights off a watery smile.

"Benjamin is going to be fine," I tell her. "He's going to be perfectly fine. Just wait."

She exhales, her warm breath gentle against my skin. Then she nods. "Okay."

I open my arm, and Piper curls into my body easily. Like we've done it a million times before.

73

TIMOFEY

Piper's head is on my shoulder and her eyes are closed when the door opens again.

We're both on our feet before we can even process who is walking inside. And that Benjamin isn't with them.

"What's wrong with him?" I demand. "Where is he?"

She gives me a smile that I want to slap off of her face. It's a useless waste of time. I don't want platitudes; I want information.

"Benjamin is still getting some tests done," she says. "He's with our nurses and is in great hands."

"What's wrong with him?" Piper asks, echoing my question.

That's when the nurse's smile shifts into a grimace. Her lips turn down at the corners, and I realize how powerful this little boy is.

How loving him can and might bring me to my knees.

"Do either of your families have a history of congenital heart defects?" she asks.

"Nothing is wrong with his heart." I snarl it as if I might be able to make it true.

"Is that what it is?" Piper asks. Her chin wobbles. "Oh my god. His heart."

"We're still testing things. It's just a possibility," the woman says. "Now, do either of you have a family history of heart issues? They can be genetic."

Piper shifts behind me, shying away from the question. After a second, I remember why.

"We aren't his parents." The nurse looks alarmed before I clarify. "We aren't his *biological* parents. And his mother was adopted, so we don't have any family history on her."

"And the father?" she asks, making a note on her clipboard.

"Unknown."

Her frown tightens, but she gives us a quick nod. "Someone will be back soon to give you the results of the tests."

The moment the door closes, Piper is in front of me. Her green eyes are electric. "His life is in the balance, Timofey! Fuck your secrets."

It's such a turn from a moment ago that I'm taken aback. "You're hysterical."

"I'm not hysterical; I'm terrified. And still thinking more rationally than you! If you know something, tell it. Whatever secret you're trying to keep isn't more important than Benjamin's life."

"My secrets have nothing to do with whether Benjamin lives or—" I stop myself, not wanting to even voice the possibility. "They have no bearing on this situation."

"Of course they do! You know more than you're telling." Her finger jabs me in the chest twice, enunciating each word. "Tell. Them."

I grab her wrist and twist it away, controlling her movement without hurting her. Once she's out of my way, I drop down into one of the plastic chairs. "I have nothing to tell."

"Tell them you're his father!" she practically screeches.

Ah.

I cross my ankle over the opposite knee and lean back. "Apparently, your investigative work wasn't as thorough as I thought."

She crosses her arms. The expression on her face is one I've come to recognize. Defiance mixed with a heavy dose of disdain. "It was thorough enough."

"No, it wasn't. Not if you think I'm Benjamin's biological father."

She throws out her arms. "Get fucking real, Timofey! Why else would a woman choose to leave her newborn child with the leader of a Bratva?" At least she has the presence of mind to lower her voice. The last thing either of us needs is an eavesdropping nurse calling the cops.

I touch my fingertips to my chest. "Are you saying I don't radiate paternal instincts?"

"This isn't a game, Timofey. Don't give me some little performance. Tell me the truth."

I want to be annoyed with her, but underneath it all, I see her concern for Benjamin. She loves him more than I could ever ask any nanny off the street to. She wants to take care of him as her own, and I don't want to punish her for that.

If she can overcome her own fears and obstacles to get Benjamin to the hospital as quickly as possible, then I can overcome mine, too.

"Emily left Benjamin on my doorstep because she mistakenly believed I would be a good father to him. Not because he's actually mine."

Piper frowns. "But why? It doesn't make sense. We both know you aren't the fatherly type."

"Well, Emily thought so," I say. "Because I was like a father to her."

The crease between her brows deepens. Something like disgust curls her upper lip. "You were like a father? But the two of you—"

"Were siblings," I finish. "Foster siblings. We lived in the same house after I was taken from my mother."

Piper's mouth falls open. "But I thought… The locket I found had a picture, and…"

I click my tongue in mock disappointment. "That's what you get for assuming, Piper. You were so ready to think of me in a certain way that you jumped to all the wrong conclusions."

"It didn't make sense that she'd leave her baby with you. Actually, it still doesn't make sense," she admits, shaking her head. "So did Sergey adopt her, too?"

"Emily never got adopted."

Her face falls. She's heard this story too many times to believe it has a happy ending. "Oh. Oh… Oh no."

"She was thirteen, but not very many people want to take on a troubled teen, do they?"

Piper winces. "Like Grant."

I nod. "I saw a lot of Emily in him. The way he cared for his sisters and stood up to you. Emily was fierce like that."

"Something the two of you had in common, then."

I shrug. "I guess so. But Emily stood up to our abusive foster parents one too many times. I stopped her from getting beaten, and we ran away together. We took care of each other as well as two kids could. Then the police picked us up and we got dumped at Sergey's."

After the police picked us up, Emily swore we could have made it on our own. She went on and on about the life we would have built for ourselves. But I was hours away from dragging her to CPS myself. She'd lost so much weight. Looked so sick. The streets weren't treating her well, and I was scared I wouldn't always be there to save her.

"Why didn't she get adopted?"

"Sergey isn't exactly sentimental." It's the understatement of the century. "He didn't see two needy kids on his doorstep; he saw two potential investments. Apparently, he saw something in me worth investing in."

"That's so cruel," she gasps.

"I wasn't in a position to refuse. Especially when living with Sergey gave me the opportunity to pass my good fortune on to Emily."

Her eyelids flutter. "You stayed in touch?"

"When Emily let me." I nod. "Once she aged out of the system, she got good at dodging the radar. Whenever she popped up, I gave her food and money. I took care of her as well as I could before I was running things."

"And after you were running things?" Piper asks.

"She was the first person I hired. I brought her on as an… an assistant, I guess you could call it. She had everything she could have ever needed. I thought…" I sigh and drag a hand through my hair. The late hour is starting to catch up with me. I'm weary down into my bones. That exhaustion is probably the only reason Piper manages to drag this story out of me. "I thought things were going to start looking up for her."

Piper lays a hand on my elbow and squeezes gently. "I'm sorry."

"Yeah. So am I."

There's a beat of silence before Piper steps back. "But wait. If you hired her, then you must know who the father of her baby is. You were back in her life. She would have told you."

I stare at her, watching, waiting. I've called Piper dumb plenty of times, but I know she isn't. I know if I wait a few seconds, she'll put the pieces together. Three, two—

She gasps. "Rodion."

Ding, ding, ding.

"Oh my god." Her eyes go wide. "That's why he said—So much makes sense now!"

"Hindsight has that effect."

She ignores me and laces her hands around the back of her neck. She's pacing again. Finally, she faces me and snaps her fingers. "So you know who the father is! You can call him and see if his family has a history of congenital heart disease."

"No." The word is out before she can even finish. And before she can ask me why, I say it again. "No. Absolutely not."

"But Benjamin is in trouble. The nurses could use that information to help him."

"Rodion could use that information to hurt him," I say with as much gravity as I can. "I need you to understand that Rodion can never, under any circumstances, find out about Benjamin being his child. Ever."

She stares at me. Once again, I see the pieces clicking into place. "Because you think he killed Emily."

"And he might come for Benjamin if he knows," I confirm.

She wheezes out a breath and drops unceremoniously down into the chair next to me. Her legs flop like they're filled with sand instead of bones. She looks as exhausted as I feel. "Rodion really has no idea?"

"None."

"Does anyone know?" she asks, peeking over at me.

"Me," I tell her. "And now, you."

She blows out another breath. "Wow. Okay."

"I need to know I can trust you to be discreet. Or else—"

She grabs my hands and shakes her head. "No 'or else,' okay? I don't need one. Benjamin would be in danger. That's enough for me. You have my word. I'll never tell a soul."

I could kiss her right now.

I could do a lot more than kiss her right now.

Before I can make that mistake again, the door opens.

74

PIPER

I drop Timofey's hand like it's on fire.

If the nurse notices, she doesn't say anything. Her face is a horrifying mask of neutrality. The kind of expression that says, *"Don't panic, but also don't get your hopes up."* I've seen it on the face of too many social workers to count during my life. Hell, I've worn that mask myself.

Ironically, it only ever opens a deep well of panic up at the very center of me.

Today is no different.

"Do you know anything?" I plead.

My breathless question is drowned out by Timofey's command. "Tell me what is going on."

The woman's face sharpens slightly at his tone, but she's ever the professional. "You were both right to bring Benjamin in tonight."

"We don't need a gold star," Timofey growls. "Tell us what's wrong with him."

Her eyes narrow, but she continues on, voice gentle. "We ran some tests and it looks like Benjamin has a congenital heart defect."

"It's his heart?" I gasp, clasping my hands over my mouth. "I felt his heart tonight. I'm no doctor, but, I mean… it felt fine."

"As far as defects go, it's minor," she says.

"But as far as organs go, it's major," Timofey says. "If something is wrong with it, then that can't be good."

She nods. "You're right, Mr. Viktorov. It is not good. What is good, however, is that you came to a place where we are more than capable of taking care of your son. We have a pediatric cardiac surgeon on staff. We can have Benjamin prepped and in the operating room by sunrise tomorrow morning."

"Surgery." I drop down into the chair, my hand pressed to my own heart. "He needs heart surgery?"

The thought of Benjamin's tiny body lying on a cold operating table, his chest opened wide… I squeeze my eyes closed to block out the mental image.

I feel a weight settle into me. I think it might be Timofey, but then a pair of cold, unfamiliar hands close over mine.

"It isn't anything as serious as what you're picturing," the nurse reassures me. "With this particular defect, we just need to make some incisions in the right side of his chest between the ribs. The surgeon will be able to do what needs to be done that way. As far as heart surgeries go, it'll be an in-and-out kind of thing."

"Then we don't need to wait until tomorrow morning for the surgery," Timofey says. "I want Benjamin in as soon as possible."

The nurse glances at the clock on the wall. It's almost midnight. "Tomorrow morning is as soon as possible."

"Don't tell me what you can't do; tell me what you need to get it done," Timofey booms. "Does the hospital need a new pediatric wing? Updated equipment? I have the money to make any of that happen. Get the surgeon in tonight, and it's yours."

The nurse sighs. "That is beyond my pay grade, Mr. Viktorov. What I can tell you is that the surgeon is sleeping right now. The last thing you'd want is a half-asleep surgeon performing heart surgery on your son."

Timofey doesn't look happy about the prospect of waiting, but the woman's logic is sound.

"I'll page the surgeon tonight," she continues. "Your son will be on the schedule bright and early."

Timofey blows out a breath. "Fine. I want to see him."

"He's in the NICU for the night." She holds up her hands before either of us can say anything. "I know that sounds scary, but he's stable. He just needs to be monitored until the surgery. For tonight, he's intubated. You can see him before you leave, but you can't stay in the NICU overnight."

"I'm not going to leave my child here alone until morning."

"He won't be alone. He's going to be taken care of by a whole team of nurses." The woman reaches out to lend some kind of comfort to Timofey, but seems to think differently of it at the last second. She pulls her hand back and offers a tight smile instead. "Like I said, he's intubated. He'll be asleep all night, so if I were you, I'd go get some sleep yourself and be back tomorrow morning. After the surgery is when you'll want to be around and rested."

Timofey's jaw works back and forth as he considers. Then he turns to the nurse. "You'll be here all night?"

"I get off in three hours, actually. But the rest of the nurses are—"

Before she can finish, Timofey whips out a wad of cash and waves it in front of her face. "I asked, will you be here with him all night?"

Her eyes widen. The calm professional she's been portraying falls away. She glances over her shoulder nervously and then back to Timofey. "Tips aren't allowed."

"It's not a tip. It's a bribe."

She smooths a hand across her cheek. "Well, I'm not supposed to accept that, either."

"Then don't tell anyone," Timofey says evenly. "Just take the money and watch my son."

I can see the war she's waging inside. Timofey can, too, because he pulls out another fold of bills and adds it to the stack.

Whatever willpower the nurse had crumbles. She plucks the money out of his hand and shoves it into the pocket of her pale purple scrubs.

"I'll be here," she says. "All night."

Timofey nods curtly. "Good."

The woman slips back into the hallway. As soon as she's gone, Timofey is on the move. He spins around, grabs his jacket, and fishes out his phone.

"I'll call Akim to come and pick you up. He's the only one home right now who can drive the motorcycle."

"But we drove here together."

"In a car," he points out. "I don't assume you'll want to ride in that back home."

I frown. "I don't know. I didn't really… I guess I didn't notice on the way here."

"You were slightly distracted."

"I guess so." Truthfully, I think the fact I was with Timofey has something to do with me being able to stay calm. "But I'll be okay for the drive back. I mean, we're going to the same place. It feels like a waste for someone to come get me."

"I'm not going home."

"But the nurse said to rest."

"I'm going to a penthouse I own nearby," he says. "So I'm close by in case anything changes with Benjamin."

I press my lips together and try to hold in the question burning inside of me.

Can I come with you?

I want to be close by in case anything happens to Benjamin. I want to be back here in the morning for his surgery.

But Timofey didn't ask me to come with him. Maybe he doesn't want me there.

I follow him quietly out of the hospital room and into the hall. Timofey pulls out his phone, and I assume he's texting Akim to come get me.

He starts tapping out a message, and I try to accept my fate. I'm going to go home while Timofey handles things with Benjamin on his own. He's going to go to his penthouse in the city and be alone. Or maybe… not alone.

He wouldn't call a woman to come be with him tonight, right? No, of course he wouldn't. I know that.

The animal part of my brain doesn't, though. *Timofey is getting rid of me so he can be with someone else. That's why he's pawning me off on Akim,* it says. Petty, traitorous little bitch.

I glance over at his phone screen. I can't read it, but the message is long. Before I can stop myself, I grab his wrist and yank him towards me.

"What the fuck?" He scowls, twisting to make sure his phone doesn't clatter to the hard tile floor.

"Take me with you." There's a broken, pleading edge to my voice. "I want to—I want to be close to Benjamin."

I want to be close to you, too.

Timofey's blue eyes are washed-out pastels in the hospital fluorescents. He stares down at me, and with every passing second, I feel smaller.

He's uncertain and that is answer enough. I shouldn't go with him. I'm being stupid. Desperate.

I start to say so, shaking my head and backing away from him, when I bump into a passing nurse. "Excuse me," I mumble.

The woman utters a similar apology before she stops and turns back. "Piper?"

I look up and a frigid panic slips down my spine. I know this woman. "Oh. Hi. Hello. Good to see you."

It's not good to see her. The last thing this moment needs is a witness.

"It's been a while." Her smile falters, confusion creasing her kind face. "It's after visiting hours. How did you get back here?"

My mouth opens with the hopes that an explanation will start to pour out, but it's late and there is too much going on. I don't know how to tell this nurse that I'm here with my employer-slash-kidnapper and the son that is legally not his because he has a congenital heart defect that he may or may not have inherited from his parents, whose origins and whereabouts are both unknown.

Thankfully, she waves away the question. "It doesn't matter. Your dad has been asking about you."

I can't turn around to look at Timofey, but I can feel his eyes boring into the back of me.

The other last thing this night needs? *My dad.*

75

PIPER

"Oh no, you don't have to do that," I say as politely as I can. "I'm sure he's sleeping now."

"He's a night owl, you know that," she says with a laugh. "And if you're with me, no one will boot you out. Come on. I'll get you in to see him."

Again, I try to come up with the words to end this experience, but I can't summon anything. How do I tell this woman that I do not want to visit my own father while he's sick in the hospital?

She pulls ahead, walking through the halls with a confidence I don't possess, and Timofey falls into stride with me. "Your father?"

I groan. "Cirrhosis of the liver. He's back in the hospital right now. I… forgot."

"No, you didn't."

My mouth pulls into an exhausted grimace. Why does this man have to be privy to every thought in my mind?

"You're right. I didn't," I admit. "But I wanted to forget. I didn't want to think about him tonight."

"And yet now, we're going to visit." He gestures to the back of the nurse leading us to him. "You know her?"

"I think her name is Pam. I saw her the few times I visited."

Timofey lofts a brow. "You visited him 'a few times.'"

It isn't a question, which makes it even worse. It's a judgment. And a fair one, too.

"He… called," I say weakly. "He was lonely. He just wanted someone to talk to."

He wanted money, actually.

"There's nothing left in the coffers, Piper," Dad said through watery hacks when I last saw him. *"When they shit me out of here with the bill, I'll be up a creek."*

I told him he wouldn't be up a creek, and we both knew what that meant. *I'd* foot the bill. *I'd* pay his rent. *I'd* make sure he didn't starve in a gutter like he probably deserved.

I haven't seen him since.

Now, I'm walking towards his hospital room with Timofey Viktorov in tow.

"Actually, you can go home—er, to your penthouse," I tell him quickly. "I'll be fine here. Akim can pick me up."

He arches a dark brow. "I thought you wanted to come with me."

"I just didn't want you to be alone. During this trying time." My face burns with the lie. "But you want to be alone. I can tell. So go ahead. I can handle this."

"I'm not going to abandon you to see your father on your own."

For a moment, my hopes soar. Timofey cares. He wants to be here for me. He wants to support me.

"It would look bad in front of the nurses," he continues. "If we're a couple, I should be here with you."

"Optics. Right." I nod, trying to hide how crestfallen I am. "But you can wait outside."

"No."

The sharp tone surprises me, but when I look over, Timofey's expression is flat. I know there will be no arguing with him.

Whether I like it or not, it's time to meet the parents.

76

PIPER

The lights are dimmed and the curtains are drawn. The television in the corner is the main source of brightness, splashing color across the room. It's some late night host playing a game where celebrities have to identify objects while blindfolded. A blonde woman I don't recognize is stroking the handle of a golf club like she's on the set of a porn movie.

My dad laughs, and I snap my attention to the bed.

He's reclined back in the same position he was when I last saw him. His gown is loose around his shoulders so I can see too much of his too-prominent collarbone. His chin rests on his chest, making it look like he doesn't have a neck.

I want to reverse back into the hallway and drag Timofey away from here. I don't want them to see each other. I don't want the two spheres of my life to turn into a Venn diagram. No overlapping.

But then my dad turns and sees me, and it's too late.

"Pip?" My nickname is a greeting and a question at the same time. He looks at the clock. "Late for a visit. Am I dying or something? Did they call you to say your goodbyes?"

"I was just… in the neighborhood."

"Huh. How 'bout that." He glances at Timofey but doesn't acknowledge him. "You haven't been in the neighborhood in a while. I figured you were done with me."

"I've just been busy."

"Too busy for your dad," he says. He pshaws and waves his hands. "No, no, I get it. You have a life and I'm not a part of it. What young girl has time for a sick old man?"

"I'm here, aren't I?" I protest, even though I wouldn't be here if the nurse hadn't forced me.

If I'm honest with myself, I may have never come back.

If I'm *really* honest with myself, I knew I'd be back. That's the worst truth of all.

"You are. A random late night visit, but hey, that's great. The bare minimum is all I can expect." He hits the button on the side of his bed and it rattles and groans as it tilts him up to a seated position.

I almost sit down in the armchair next to his bed, but that feels too permanent. I don't want to put down any more roots in this room than I have to.

So instead, I stand halfway between the door and his bed, floating in the awkward expanse with my hands folded behind my back. "How are you doing?"

"My liver is shot to fuck, but I'm not dying today. I don't think," he adds with a phlegmy chuckle. "My heart isn't doing too good, neither. They think I might need some fancy procedure to get it beating right, but with my liver the way it is, I might not be worth the insurance company's time. That's a belief the two of you have in common."

"Oh." I don't know what else to say. I clear my throat and add in a, "Sorry."

He snorts. "You'll be happy to be done with me. You can say it."

"Dad! I would never say that."

"I know. That's why I'm giving you permission." He laughs again. When he looks at me, I see the spark of meanness in his eyes. Looks like I caught him in rare form tonight. Lucky me. "You quit paying for my phone, so I know you don't want to call me no more."

I know Timofey is standing behind me, but I have to pretend he's not. Talking to my dad is hard enough without processing everything through the filter of Timofey.

What must he think of me right now? I'm pathetic and weak. I can't stand up to my own father. I let him walk all over me.

I shake my head and focus on my father. "You told me you were going to take over that payment."

"Sure, but I figured you'd give it a month or six before you pulled out," he complains. "I didn't have all the financing lined up yet. Now, I'm behind and I owe fees for letting my contract lapse. I can't afford to get it going again."

I should've known his burst of independence was a fluke. He'll never do anything for himself if I'm willing to do it for him.

Apparently, I'm always willing.

I nod. "I'll—I'll call them tomorrow, okay? I can get that stuff waived; you just have to know how to ask."

"I know how to ask," he snaps. "I'm not stupid."

"That isn't what I said."

He rolls his eyes. There's meanness in his smile now, too. It's spreading like a cancer through him. "It's what you meant. I know you think I'm worthless, but I still deserve basic respect, goddammit."

Frustrated tears burn the backs of my eyes, but I refuse to let myself cry in front of my father or Timofey. I swallow down the emotion and square my shoulders. "I don't think you're stupid. I respect you, Dad. I—"

"You show up here with your boyfriend like you need a bodyguard," he hisses, gesturing to Timofey for the first time. "Like you have some reason to be scared of me? Then you don't call or visit. That isn't respect."

"I'm sorry." I look down at my feet, unable to meet my father's eyes.

I should turn around and stomp out of here. I should have stared that nurse in the face and told her that I hate my dad and she could tell him I'll never visit him again.

But for some reason, I can't seem to sever this connection. This biological tie to the family that could have been. To the life that could have been mine if things had been different. If *he* had been different.

I guess I keep hoping he'll change.

Even as I know for a fact he won't.

"I know you are," Dad says uncharacteristically gently. "You're a sweet girl, Pip. That's why you take care of me."

I give him a weak smile, all the fight drained out of me. I want to end on good terms, so I take a step back towards the door. "Well, Dad, we better—"

"You have more important things to do." He waves us towards the door. "I know. Thanks for the brief drive-by. It's better than nothin'."

Everything he says comes with a barb. It's exhausting.

I wave and send my love, but by the time I step into the hallway I barely remember what I said. I feel like I've been hit by a truck.

Then I turn and see Timofey watching me. And the truck shifts into reverse and flattens me again.

77

TIMOFEY

"So that's your father." My voice sounds calm enough, but rage has been simmering under the surface since the moment we walked through that door.

I already hated Piper's dad based on what she's told me. Then to see the way he looked at her, like he was a snake and a fresh mouse had just been dropped in his cage… I wanted to strangle him with his own IV cord.

"Yeah, that's him." Piper tries to smile, but it's thin. Almost as thin as her father's sweat-soaked hospital gown. "Charming, isn't he?"

"No," I correct. "He's fucking scum."

I expect her to nod in agreement. Instead, she spins towards me, jaw set. "Your father employs a hitman. A hitman who tried to kill you! I don't think you should be the authority on what makes a good father."

I step back, taking in all of her at once. Her tense shoulders and narrowed eyes.

Even though I rushed Benjamin through town like a Formula fucking 1 driver, I'll never be a good enough father in Piper's eyes.

Even though I took him in off my own fucking doorstep, I'll never be good enough.

No matter what I do, how far I go, how much I spend or how hard I fight to make the world safe and pure for him—to her, I'll never be good enough.

"It isn't—" she starts quickly, blowing out a frustrated breath. "I didn't mean—We both have shitty parents, okay? That's been confirmed. We don't need to dwell on it. That's all I meant."

"Except we do need to dwell, if you're going to keep footing the bill for him to treat you like shit."

"It's none of your business!"

"*You* are my business!"

Without meaning to, we both started to yell. I look down the hall and see two nurses moving towards us at a quick clip.

I grab Piper's shoulder and steer her towards the elevators.

"Don't touch me!" She tries to squirm away.

"If you'd like to be let back in the building tomorrow for Benjamin's surgery, I suggest you hurry. We're about to have security called on us." I gesture to the nurses hot on our heels and Piper lets me lead her into a waiting elevator.

The doors close when the nurses are still half a hallway away. Then we're alone in a confined box.

Which might be worse.

"My relationship with my father has nothing to do with you," Piper says, picking up where we left off. "If I want to take care of the people in my life, you don't get to tell me I'm wrong."

"I can if you let useless people who aren't worth your time or money suck you dry."

"Useless." She shakes her head. "I didn't know a human being could be 'useless.'"

I grit my teeth so hard my molars groan under the pressure. "He isn't the least bit grateful, Piper. He's manipulating you."

"You're no stranger to that concept, are you?" she fires back.

"What exactly have I manipulated you into, Piper? Because I seem to recall you begging me to show you what you wanted just a few nights ago."

Her cheeks turn pink and she stretches onto her toes to close the distance between us. "You remind me a lot of my dad. Have I ever told you that? The hot and cold, the push and pull. Every good thing you do comes with a price tag. It's why I can never, ever trust you."

The words are a slap in the face, but I don't flinch.

Instead, I take a step closer, forcing her down to her normal height and then back against the wood-paneled wall. I can see in her face as she realizes how small this space is, how weak and feeble she is, how not those things I am. "Your father is a drain on society. He is a helpless, thankless leech who has no issue taking his fill without ever offering anything useful in return. I've worked hard to get to where I am. I've earned my place and the luxuries I have, and while he wants to suck you dry, I want to give you everything. If you'd just stop being too fucking stubborn to let me."

Piper's eyes widen at my confession, but there isn't any time to process it.

The doors open. Outside, there are people waiting to get on the elevator.

Piper politely maneuvers around the small crowd, but I stay perfectly still.

She's through the doors when she turns to look for me. I wave to her from inside the elevator. "One of my men will pick you up out front."

She frowns. "But where are you—"

The doors close before she can ask. Not that I would have told her the truth anyway.

I go back up and retrace our steps until I'm standing in the doorway of the hospital room again. The television is still on, flickering in the dark, but Piper's father is asleep now. Dreaming the peaceful dreams of someone without a single regret.

I march into the room and press the button on the side of his bed.

The machine groans and clicks him slowly into a sitting position, but he jolts like he's woken up to find himself on a rollercoaster.

"What the shit is—what's wrong with this bed?" he hollers. "The fucking thing is taking me away! I—"

"Shut up," I growl.

He looks up at me. If possible, he looks even more frightened.

Good.

"Wh-what are you doing back here?" he asks. His voice trembles ever so slightly.

"We never got a chance to properly meet."

He scans me from head to toe and seems to relax slightly, though his face is still a ruddy color. "If you're here to ask for my blessing or some shit like that, then this ain't a good first impression."

I actually laugh. "If you believe I give a single fuck what you think of me, then you're even stupider than you look. Which I'm not sure is possible."

"Then why are you here?"

"So that Piper never has to be again."

He frowns. "You're tryin' to keep my Pip from me?"

I want to reach for his neck, but I manage to hold off. "Strangling you would set off all these machines you're connected to and alert the nurses, so from this point on, refrain from ever calling her *yours* again. She does not belong to you."

Based on the increasingly rapid beeps of his heart monitor, the nurses might be joining us in here in a few minutes regardless.

I'd better wrap things up.

"Piper deserved better than you as a child, and she sure as hell deserves better than you now," I tell him. "If she can't see that for herself, then I'll make sure you're gone for good."

The man scrambles up the bed like he has a chance of escaping me. "Are—are you going to kill me?"

"As good as," I confirm. "Because once I leave this room, you are never going to contact Piper again. Not for money, not for a chat. You aren't going to so much as send her flowers on her birthday, if you even know when that is."

"And why would I do that?"

It's a fair question. He clearly doesn't have much to live for. Without Piper, he doesn't have anything at all save for a mountain of debt.

She's not his daughter; she's his piggy bank.

That's a burden I'm all too happy to bear if it means she'll never have to stand in a dark room like this one again and be berated by a man who doesn't deserve to breathe the same air as her.

"Because I'm going to offer you a fuck ton of money to do exactly as I say."

How much money is enough to give up Piper Quinn? I consider the question and draw a blank. No one could hand me a check big enough.

Then I look at the light in her father's eyes, and I realize I won't have to reach nearly as high as I might think. This man has no clue how priceless his daughter is.

Piper was so wrong: he and I are nothing at all alike.

"How much?" he asks, licking his lower lip.

"Fifty grand."

It's paltry. Nothing. Pitiful crumbs compared to what Piper is worth. But her father's heart monitor ticks along faster and faster, registering every beat of his excitement.

Still, he tries to play it cool, as if the truth isn't blaring in the background. "That's not much to cut my daughter out of my life."

"The correct answer would have been that there isn't enough money in the world to cut your daughter out of your life," I growl. "Which is why it's as high as I'm going to go. Take it or leave it."

His flabby jaw works back and forth.

Part of me wants him to refuse. I'd kill him, of course. Anything to keep him out of Piper's life. But at least he'd die with a shred of my respect.

In the end, he does exactly what I knew he would.

"Deal." He holds out his hand to shake. I just let it hang there. Eventually, he withdraws it. After a few seconds, he shifts in his squeaky bed. "How do I know you're good for it?"

"Check your bank account tomorrow morning. It will be in there."

He frowns. "You can't get into my account."

"I can do anything I fucking want. Which is why you should know that if you break our deal, you'll be dead before the day is done. If you reach out to Piper or contact her in any way—if you ask her for a single penny—then I will give myself the privilege of wringing your last breath from your miserable, rotten lungs. Do you understand?"

He's shaking as I leave. I take it as a yes.

I ride the same elevator down to the lobby, and I feel Piper's absence like a dark cloud hanging low over my head.

She and Akim are probably halfway back to the house by now. And if Akim makes even one crack to me about how Piper wrapped her arms around him on the ride, I'll shatter his right arm. Let's see him try to cook without the use of his strong hand.

The next few hours stretch out in front of me, empty and anxious.

I'm half-tempted to threaten one of the nurses into letting me sleep in the NICU with Benjamin after all. That would be better than my solitary penthouse.

Then the elevator doors open.

And there she is.

Piper is standing in front of a wall of windows, her back towards me. It's so dark outside that I can see her reflection in the glass. Her arms are folded over her chest, her brow lowered in concentration.

Is Akim running late? Did he not show up?

Suddenly, I want to kill him for a new reason. How dare he leave her waiting?

I walk towards her. When she spies me in the glass, her body tenses. She spins around with a frown on her face. It matches the one I left her with a few minutes ago.

Apparently, our fight is picking up where we left off.

"I told Akim to go back home. I'm coming with you," she blurts before I can say anything. She shuffles nervously and then stands tall and confident. Her green eyes meet mine. "I want to—I want to be here for Benjamin, too. I'm coming to the penthouse with you."

"Okay."

Piper was ready for a fight. She didn't expect my easy acceptance.

Her brows knit together and then smooth out. She crosses her arms and uncrosses them.

I walk past her, and she follows me through the front doors and into the parking lot. My phone buzzes. I pull it out. The screen glows in the darkness, Akim's name flashing with a new message.

Have fun at your slumber party, he texts. Followed by a string of increasingly sexual emojis.

Then I hear the familiar rumble of my motorcycle and look up as he tears out of the parking lot for the main road.

78

PIPER

I want to give you everything.

Timofey's voice echoes through my head as I stare out over the city below. The view of the skyline from his penthouse is as close to having "everything" as I've ever been.

Cars weave through the snarled tangle of city streets. In glimpses between the buildings across from us, I can see moonlight sparkling off the surface of the river. It's late, but the city is so alive.

And yet, even with all that to be seen, the better view is from the outside looking in.

High ceilings, arched doorways, warm wood floors, and plush white carpets—Timofey's penthouse is a full-blown palace. I never want to leave.

I want to give you everything.

"Water?" Timofey appears next to me, two tall glasses of water in his hand.

I smile up at him as I grab the glass, our fingers brushing. "Thanks." I take a long drink, trying to swallow some of my desperation along with it. "This view is incredible."

"It's not quite a mountaintop, but it's as close as we can get in the city." He looks at me from the corner of his eyes. "I thought you'd enjoy it."

I'm fully clothed, but the tattoo on my hip tingles as if he's running his fingers over the delicate lines.

I want to give you everything.

He said that. I heard it with my own two ears. While I can usually be accused of harboring more than my fair share of inconvenient, unrealistic hopes, I'm not actually delusional. Yet.

Timofey looked me in the eyes and told me that he wants to give me everything.

I think through the different interpretations of those words. He wants to give me everything professionally? Emotionally? Sexually?

Yes to all three. Sign me up.

No matter how I slice it, it seems like a good thing.

Which is a very, very bad thing.

I need to get away from Timofey Viktorov. That should be my goal. To put distance between us, to sever this connection and escape.

And yet…

I turn to him, a smile on my face. "You thought I'd like the view, but you were going to send me with Akim?"

"I never said I was going to show it to you. Just that I thought you'd like it."

I snort. "So you were going to hold out on me? Not nice."

"I've warned you about that already," he says, voice low. "I'm not nice."

I take another drink of water, draining my glass. Timofey plucks the empty cup from my hand, and I curl my arms around myself to fight off the shiver that wants to race through me.

Every step of the way, Timofey has told me who he is. He's been honest about it from the start. So I'm not sure why I'm standing here instead of back in my room at his mansion.

I should have gone with Akim. I should have gotten on that bike and ridden off into the night, as far away from Timofey as I could get. But here I am.

I want to give you everything.

"Shower," I blurt.

Timofey places our glasses in the sink and turns around, eyebrow arched. "Pardon?"

"I mean, could I use your shower?" I ask, stumbling my way towards the socially normal way to ask that question. "Hospitals make me feel clammy and gross."

He turns down the long hallway that leads towards the back of the house. "Follow me."

"I can find it. You just point the way and I'll figure it out."

"I saw the shower at your apartment," he says, looking back over his shoulder. "I highly doubt you'd figure mine out."

I ignore the subtle dig and ask the obvious. "When were you in my shower?"

"You're a heavy sleeper. Before I woke you up that night I broke in, I glanced around."

He says it with the same ease someone else would say they perused someone's bookshelves. Except he was doing it in the middle of the night while I was asleep, right before he came to threaten me into submission.

I'm not nearly as bothered by the thought of Timofey in my shower as I should be.

I shake my head. "I had no idea you were such a freak."

He chuckles as he leads me through a pocket door into a dark room. Suddenly, he stops and spins around. I nearly crash into his chest, but he steadies me with a hand on my lower back. Instinctively, I bend, molding to his touch.

"Yes," he rasps, "you did."

Before I can catch my breath, Timofey sets me right and turns to flip on the light. Then my breath is stolen for an entirely new reason.

"*This* is your bathroom?" I gasp.

The room is wide with black marble floors and cream cabinets. A wooden vanity runs along the left wall with a framed mirror above it. But the showstopper is on the actual, literal stage at the back. Three black marble steps lead up to the largest tub I've ever seen.

"Is that a bathtub or a swimming pool?"

Timofey smirks. "Anything can be a swimming pool if you put your mind to it, I suppose. I call it an appropriate-sized tub."

"Only if you need to lay out end to end in the bottom of it!" I yelp, gesturing to him. "This is massive, even for your ridiculous standards."

He opens a panel in the wall and presses a series of buttons. Water begins flowing into the tub from half a dozen hidden faucets. "What if two people want to lay end to end in it?"

My face burns and it's not from the steam rising off the surface of the water. I nod. "I guess if you… Well, if you have guests in the water with you, then you might need one this size."

My shower head is barely tall enough for little old me to fit under it, let alone a fully grown man. But of course Timofey has a tub big enough for him and a harem of women. I don't know why I'm surprised.

Jealousy I have no right to feel singes my already frayed nerves. I sit on the top step next to the tub and swirl my hand in the water. It's the perfect temperature, and a vanilla scent fills the air.

"Well, I can definitely figure it out from here," I tell him. "Thank you."

Timofey's massive silhouette lurks in my peripherals, but I refuse to look at him. I can't. Not without hearing what he said in the elevator. I can't look at him without wanting what I very much know I should not want.

"We'll have to agree to disagree there," he murmurs.

I snap my attention to him.

I want to give you everything.

I shake the words out of my brain, wondering if I'll ever stop hearing that refrain. "What are you talking about?"

"The nurse said we should relax," he reminds me. "That isn't your strong suit."

I want to argue with him, but my body is taut as a bowstring right now. "And what? You're going to give me some pointers?"

"One or two," he says, holding up two fingers together. He smirks and adds a third. "Maybe three, if that's not enough to get the job done."

Holy shit. I swallow audibly and dry my hand on my jeans. "I can relax on my own just fine."

Timofey's smile spreads wide. "That's fine, too. I'll watch."

My entire body is burning now. I want that, exactly the thing he's promising and/or teasing me. I want him to watch. I want him to touch me. I want it all.

I want to give you everything.

Timofey closes the distance between us and kneels on the step in front of me. He's so tall that we're still at eye level as his hands smooth down my outer thighs. "Relax, Piper. Doctor's orders."

He gently slides my jeans down my legs, and I let him. Wordlessly, I lift my hips and part my knees as Timofey undresses me from the waist down.

Slowly, he slides the same two fingers from earlier across my heat. He curls his calloused skin against my wet opening, and I can't bite back my moan.

"Is your mind made up?" he whispers. "Do you want my help or would you still rather take care of yourself?"

The thought of losing his touch makes me want to cry. "You," I breathe. "I want you."

As promised, Timofey slides his two fingers into my ready opening. "Good girl."

In gentle strokes, he stokes the flames growing in my core. I grip the edge of the tub and spread my knees. Timofey uses the improved access to dip his head and press a kiss to the inside of my thigh.

Slowly, his kisses trail closer and closer to where I want them. Where I need them.

I curl my hand in his silky hair just as his lips circle around my clit. "Tim—oh, fuck."

He growls, and the vibration arches through me. I hook one knee over his shoulder and roll my hips against his mouth.

He sucks and flicks while his fingers stroke me at a slow, relentless pace until I'm shaking.

"Please," I whimper. "I need... I want..."

Without a word, Timofey slides a third finger into me—and I break.

My body clamps down on his hand while I grab a fistful of his hair. Every muscle in my body clenches and holds, trying to keep him with me for as long as possible. Trying to draw out every blissful second of this orgasm. I never want it to end.

For a long time, it doesn't.

Until, eventually, it does. The waves flow and ripple away until I'm a sagging, breathless mess on the edge of the tub.

Timofey stands up and swipes a hand across the back of his lips, shiny with my desire.

"Oh my god," I breathe. "That was… You are…"

"It seems full sentences are beyond you tonight." He draws me to my feet. "That's fine. We don't need to talk."

I want to give you everything.

We need to talk about that. About what he said and what it means.

But then Timofey is pulling my shirt over my head, slipping my bra off just as quickly. I'm completely naked in front of him, and I forget all about talking. There aren't enough words in the English language to describe what it feels like to have his eyes on my body. To know that I'm the one turning his blue eyes black with desire.

I reach for the waistband of his pants, and he makes quick work of his own shirt. His skin glows bronze in the warm bathroom lighting. His muscles flex and pull as he lifts me into his arms and then lowers us both into the Olympic-sized tub.

"There's a bench in here! And it smells like vanilla."

"So you appreciate my trip into your shower, then?"

I frown. "I don't know what you—"

"Vanilla shampoo, vanilla conditioner," he says, ticking off his fingers one by one. "There was a vanilla body scrub in there, too."

"You… you made your tub smell like vanilla because of me?"

He presses his nose to my hair and inhales deeply. Then his mouth trails down my neck. "I like the way you smell."

I guess that's all the explanation I'm going to get. But it's all the explanation I need when Timofey hooks his arms under my thighs and wraps my legs around his waist.

We slide together easily. Inch by inch he pushes into me, and I sigh when he's fully seated.

He pulses into me with slow, gentle thrusts that are so tender I can feel my heart breaking. This isn't like the night in the garage where we crashed together on the hood of the car, pounding and screaming out. This is something else entirely. Something that has me wrapping my arms around his neck and burying my face in his chest to hide the tears welling in my eyes.

There is no striving or straining for release. The orgasm flows through me as naturally as breathing.

"I'm coming," I whisper, digging my teeth into his muscled shoulder. "You feel so good."

Timofey pushes into me and then steps backward, lowering himself onto the bench that rings the tub. His arms stretch out on either side of the rim, and his intention is clear enough. I rise onto my knees and slide down his length.

Before, my face was buried in his chest or his face was buried between my legs. Now, we stare into each other's eyes.

In rolling strokes, I work myself onto him again and again while Timofey stares at me.

Eventually, he grips my waist with one hand. Then, a few seconds later, the second joins. As his breathing grows more ragged, he thrusts into me with sharp, purposeful movements.

As I stare back into his blue eyes, his expression breaks.

"Fuck, Piper," he groans. His brow creases and his jaw clicks.

I want to close my eyes and ride him to the finish line. I want to steal the pleasure and leave the rest behind, but I can't close my eyes to this. To the feelings growing between us.

So I press my forehead to his, look deep into his blue eyes, and come on his cock for the third time.

"Timofey," I gasp, curling my fingers behind his ears, clinging to him with my quivering thighs.

He holds me to him, pulsing inside of me as he breathes my name in ragged gasps. "Piper. Piper. Piper…"

I can't lie about this moment. Later on, I won't be able to tell myself I didn't know. I won't be able to say I was powerless to stop it.

I could have walked away from Timofey Viktorov. I could have kept my legs and heart closed, but I opened myself to him willingly. Happily.

Whatever comes next, I have to face that truth, ugly as it may be.

When it came time to choose, I chose *him*.

79

PIPER

"I think the doctor meant we should sleep," I say, pushing pasta around my plate.

"Could you go to sleep right now?" Timofey asks.

"No. Definitely not."

What happened in the bathtub relaxed me, but now, I feel wired. Adrenaline courses through my veins. I've never been more awake.

"Me neither," he says. "But I am starving. I think a doctor would recommend both of us refuel and rehydrate."

I shove a bite of pasta in my mouth so I don't have to find the words to respond to that.

It's only been half an hour since we climbed out of the warm water and got dressed, but it already feels like another world. Like some hazy, lust-fueled dream.

The bubble really burst when Timofey ordered us food.

"What do you want?" he asked, the phone wedged between his stubbled jawline and shoulder.

I shook my head. "I'm not actually very hungry."

"She'll take the pasta," Timofey said without hesitation. "The cheesiest one you have."

He was already ignoring me and making decisions on my behalf. Sure, his decision was the right one because I'm now famished and this is the most delicious pasta I've ever tasted. But still.

"What time is it, anyway?" I pat my back pocket, but my phone isn't there. A surge of panic sends me lunging for the couch, sliding my hand between the leather cushions.

"Late."

"It was late when we got here," I say. "It might technically be 'early' now."

"Why does it matter? It's the middle of the night. No one else is up. Enjoy the peace."

Peace. I guess, in some ways, I'm one step closer to peace.

By five this morning, Ashley and Gram should be on their way to the airport to board their flight to Mexico. A few more hours, and they'll be beyond Timofey's immediate reach.

The irony of me drawing closer to Timofey while I try to get my family and friends away from him is not lost on me.

The truth is, I'm worried Timofey might hurt Ashley or Gram. I'm worried for Noelle. But I don't worry for myself. Timofey has done so much for me, despite the many times he could have taken me out of the equation. Too much probably. More than I could ever repay.

I trust him. Even if I shouldn't.

"Is that why you have this place?" I ask. "For the peace and quiet?"

"Everyone needs a place to go when the shit hits the fan."

"What does that mean for you? Like, during a Bratva war or something?"

He nods. "Yeah. Or when Sergey decides he'd like his Bratva back and kicks me to the curb."

"Could he do that?"

"Now?" He shakes his head. "No. But at one point, maybe. When I was young. I bought this place with the first real paycheck I ever earned."

My eyes nearly bug out of my head. "You bought *this* with your first paycheck?"

"It didn't look like this," he chuckles. "It was down to the studs. The tenants before me trashed the place. I got it on the cheap. The relative cheap."

"Still… I think I bought cigarettes with my first paycheck."

"No shit," he says. "You were a smoker?"

"I haven't always been so prim and proper."

He smiles at me and my insides flip and roll. "Yes, you have. Deep down, you're a good girl, Piper."

"Fine," I admit. "I am. What about you?"

"Am I a good girl, you mean?" He bats his lashes at me, and I stifle a laugh.

"Are you as bad as you seem?"

I ask the question easily enough, but as it settles between us, layers of meaning pile on. His smile slips away and mine follows.

"I didn't really have a choice. Someone had to take care of the house. It wasn't going to be my mom."

I see the path we're heading towards. The dark trail of our shared traumas. Emotional vulnerability. Bonding. As quickly as possible, I take the fork in the road.

"Was it all bad?"

He looks up, surprised. "What? My childhood?"

"Yeah. What's a good memory? I want to hear something happy."

"You checked out the wrong book if you want happy stories," he snorts.

"Come on, Timofey. There has to be a good time. Tell me about it."

For a second, it looks like he might not answer. He pushes his food around his plate, his brow pinched together. Then he inhales. "There was one time."

I lean forward to the edge of my seat. "Yeah?"

"It was after… Emily and I were living together in this youth hostel. It was an absolute piece of shit. Fly-by-night dump at its worst. The building was damn near abandoned and the owner accepted payment in whatever form they came in. Cash, coins, drugs, sexual favors—"

"I said a *happy* memory," I remind him. "So far, this sounds terrible."

"Just wait. I'm getting to the good part."

His blue eyes are alive with an excitement I haven't seen in them… maybe ever. He looks ten years younger. I wave him on, and he slides back into the story.

"Emily and I were sharing a room. A bed, actually. It was a twin, so I let her have the mattress while I slept on the floor."

It's hard to imagine Timofey being the gentleman. Lying on the floor while a woman took the bed from him. It's a testament to how much he cared about Emily that he did that.

Would he do the same for me? It shouldn't matter, but the question burrows in my mind, taking up space and meaning. I want him to care about me that much.

"We stayed there for a while before the money ran low," he continues. "I was just a kid, so finding work was a mess. Emily had it even worse. A young girl walking the streets and begging for money is only asking one thing in a lot of men's minds."

I wince. "Did she ever—"

"No," he says quickly. "I worked hard to make sure it wasn't necessary. But then we got behind, and the piece of shit who ran the hostel came knocking. He took one look at Emily and decided how we should repay our debts."

"I hate to repeat myself, but this isn't a happy memory, Timofey."

He gestures for me to wait and keeps going. "Well, he propositioned Emily and told her she better be in his room by the end of the night or we'd be out on our asses."

"What did you do?"

Timofey's expression twists into dark amusement. "Well, I wasn't quite as strapping as I am now, so I slipped into Emily's sweater and stocking cap."

I slap a hand over my mouth. "You didn't."

"Then I pulled the hat low and walked into the motherfucker's room," he chuckles.

"To do what? I can tell you from experience, he would have figured out you weren't Emily pretty freaking fast."

"Oh, he did," Timofey says. "Almost immediately. I made it through the door and halfway across the room before he started ranting and yelling for me to leave. It probably had something to do with the fact that he was already 'ready,' if you know what I mean."

I hold up a stiff finger. "*Ready* ready?"

Timofey nods. "I caught him with his pants down in a real way, and he didn't love it. He told me to get the fuck out, but I wanted to talk. Especially since I had the upper hand. Except, I didn't really. Because I had no idea that he had a gun stashed in his bedside drawer."

My eyes go wide. Timofey is sitting in front of me whole and well, but I'm terrified for the teenage version of him. "He shot you?!"

"He tried," he admits. "But he was lying down and, like I said, there was a certain part of his body between the two of us.

Somehow, the guy whipped his gun around, pulled the trigger, and managed to hit that very small target."

I inhale so sharply I almost choke. "He shot his own—"

"Grazed," Timofey corrects, barely stifling a laugh. "It was a graze. But based on the way he screamed, you'd think he blew the thing off. He called the ambulance and spent the night in the hospital. Cried like a bitch the whole time."

I toss my head back and laugh. But after a second, I look back at him. "I love an adult male predator getting his dose of karma as much as the next person, but that still isn't a happy memory exactly."

"No, that part isn't happy. But the asshole spent the night in the emergency room," Timofey said. "So his room was empty... His room, which was furnished with a double bed and a fridge full of food and beer. He also had the only television in the entire building."

"You kept the place warm for him?" I guess.

"Well, we didn't want all of that food to go bad." He smirks and his eyes go glassy, reliving the old memory. "We ate enough day-old Chinese food and frozen ice cream bars to make ourselves sick. Then we watched some cheesy horror movie and fell asleep in the big bed. It was still a dump, but compared to what we'd been living in, it felt like a palace."

I smile sadly. "Memories from childhood are like that. I had an old lace curtain that hung around my bed like a canopy. It was moth-eaten and stained, but it felt so magical."

"Emily said the same thing that night. She said it was like a fairytale." His chest hitches with a breathy laugh, and I can hear the fondness he had for Emily. The fondness he still has for her.

"Okay, fine. That's a happy memory," I admit. "But what happened when he came back?"

Timofey shrugs. "We left early the next morning. We knew we weren't going to be welcomed back. But last I heard, the place was shut down, then torn down. Just an empty lot now. It's gone. All of it."

Including Emily.

He doesn't need to say it. I can hear the words in his somber tone.

Whatever temporary moment of levity the happy memory brought him, the payment seems to be a reminder of how many unhappy moments have come since then.

"I bet Emily was grateful," I say, trying to swing the pendulum back to the positive. "Things could have been a lot worse if you hadn't been there to protect her."

His brows knit together. Something unsaid passes over his face and a chill settles over the moment that leaves the hairs on my arms standing tall. I've never been one to believe in ghosts, but I believe in them now.

Emily may be dead, but she's in this room.

Timofey can see her, too.

"You protected her as well as you could." I want to comfort him, but this particular coin has two sides. I can't help but flip it. "Didn't you?"

Timofey snaps his attention to me. His eyes are a searing shade of blue. "I've answered that question, Piper."

"I didn't mean—I mean, I wasn't saying—"

"You were doing everything but say it," he growls. "Still, after everything, you want to know if I killed her."

Yes. Tell me the truth. Please.

"I know you loved her," I say. "You took care of her like a sister. You're taking care of her son now. But…you had a falling out. I could understand if something changed. If you had no other choice."

There is always another choice when murder is on the table. Still, I tell the lie because the truth would be too hard to fathom.

Timofey killing someone he once loved and saw as family would shatter the image I have of him. What we did—what I let him do to me—in the bathroom would become twisted and sick.

His fork clatters against the table, and he grips the edges of the coffee table with white-knuckled ferocity. "I'm a selfish man, Piper. I look out for myself. I take care of myself."

My heart lurches into my throat. Is this it? Is he confessing? He had to kill Emily to look out for himself?

I can feel the walls of this fantasy world I've created melting around me under the heat of his almost-confession.

"I know what it feels like to lose a family member," he continues. "I wouldn't willingly put myself through that again."

I lift my eyes to his, searching his face. "You mean your mother?"

His jaw sets. It's as much of a confirmation as I'm going to get.

"I've killed plenty of people, Piper. But I did not kill Emily. It would have been like killing a part of myself."

The clamp around my chest loosens. Maybe a life with Timofey is still possible. Maybe there is a way forward for the two of us.

And maybe I'm a naive sap who falls for a beautifully-wrapped box of lies.

There's only one way to find out.

I lay my hand over his. "Okay, Timofey. I believe you."

80

TIMOFEY

"It's a fucking furnace in here." I grimace, swiping my hand over the back of my damp neck.

The NICU is a balmy seventy-five degrees at least. My clothes stick to my skin, and I would give anything to dive into another bath. Preferably with a naked Piper waiting beneath the surface.

I glance over. The hair at her temples is curling in the humidity. The sheen across her skin reminds me of the dewy glow she had post-orgasm.

"Well, Benjamin can't really wear clothes with all of this going on," she says, gesturing to his tiny body. "They want to keep him comfortable."

Her words send the dirty thoughts scuttling to the dark corners of my mind where they belong. Benjamin is wearing nothing but a diaper, a huge white bandage, and a maze of wires and tubes. They crisscross over his sleeping body and connect to a half-dozen different machines beeping around his bassinet.

He looks impossibly small next to all of the equipment.

And fragile. So fucking fragile.

"He doesn't look comfortable."

Piper lays a hand on my shoulder. I almost pull away on instinct. But the feel of her next to me is a surprising comfort.

She's been here the entire time. All night at the penthouse. During the three-hour surgery. For the last hour while we've waited to talk to the doctor.

Knowing your child is under some surgeon's knife and there's nothing you can do to help is an emotion I'd be fine never experiencing again.

"He looks good," she says softly. "Look how pink his skin is. When we brought him in, he looked gray."

"His lips were blue. I remember."

Piper's hand tightens on my arm. When she speaks, her voice wavers. "He was so sick, Timofey. But look at him now."

His chest rises and falls in deep, strong breaths. His lips are a pale rose color. He gets his mouth from his mom. Emily's lips were the exact same, deeply bowed in the middle and upturned at the corners.

I'm about to thank Piper for checking on Benjamin last night. For calling me and getting him to the hospital so fast. But before I can, the door opens.

"Knock, knock." A man in a white coat strolls into the room, an easy smile on his face. "You're the parents of this little champion, I presume?"

He says "little champion" the way people say "buddy" or "old chap." A placeholder when you can't remember someone's name.

"How did Benjamin do?" I ask. "What's his prognosis?"

He gestures to the bassinet casually. "Look at him. He's pink and healthy as a baby can be. Things went well."

"Define 'well.' I'd like specifics."

His smile tightens, but he nods. "Of course. Everything went exactly as we hoped. We kept it minimally invasive and were in and out in an hour."

"And that's all he needed?" Piper asks. "One surgery and he's cured?"

The surgeon nods. "For now, yes."

A red flag waves in my mind. "What does that mean, 'for now?' Will he need more surgeries?"

"Potentially," the doctor says, like it's no big deal. "There will be appointments to check in and make sure everything is healing the way we want. Especially over the next few years. But if all goes well, he'll be just like any other kid."

Will he be just like any other don*, though?* I hear Sergey's voice in the back of my head. *You know the answer. He can't handle the stress of this life. His enemies will take advantage of every weakness, up to and including his broken heart.*

"You're saying he'll be average."

The doctor frowns. I can tell he's trying to decide if I think that's a good thing or not.

"Well," he answers, smoothing the lapel of his white coat, "you shouldn't notice any issues."

"I don't want to just not notice issues; I want there to be no issues to notice. What do we need to do to make sure there are none of those?"

Piper's warm hand circles around my wrist. "He'll be exceptional." I look down at her, and her eyes are glassy with sincerity. "If anything goes wrong down the line, we'll take care of it. He'll be perfect."

He's already perfect, I think. *He's always been perfect.*

He was perfect with blue lips and gray skin. He was perfect when I found him swaddled in a flannel receiving blanket on my porch.

Heart condition or not, nothing will change that.

"He's perfect." I nod in agreement and then hold my hand out for the surgeon. "Thank you, Doctor."

The man's chest puffs out and he shakes my hand. "Of course. The nurses will be in and out to talk with you about his care, but he'll be drowsy for a few more hours. Rest up, eat, relax. Your boy is fine."

The doctor leaves, but his voice echoes in my head.

Your boy.

My boy.

My heart swells with pride, and fuck if I'm not turning into a sap.

The woman responsible for my transition sniffles at my side. I turn just as she swipes at her eyes and darts into the en-suite bathroom. "I'll be right back."

I follow behind her and knock on the door. "Piper."

"Just a second!" She tries to sound cheery, but I can hear the tears in her voice.

"Piper, open the door."

She clears her throat. "Just a second. I'll be out in—"

"Open the fucking door before I break it down," I growl.

There's a beat of silence before the lock turns and the door cracks open. I push it the rest of the way and find Piper leaning against the back wall, her eyes red and puffy, hot tears streaming down her face.

"We were talking to the same doctor back there, right?" I hitch my thumb over my shoulder towards the room. "Middle-aged guy, dark hair, good news. This ringing bells for you?"

She gives me a watery smile and nods. "Yeah. I was there. I just—he's fine."

I narrow my eyes in confusion. "Yes. Benjamin is fine. Hence all the not-crying I'm doing."

"Please," she snorts. "I doubt you're even capable of crying."

"And clearly, you're too capable. You should be happy right now. We're celebrating."

"I know. I am happy!" she insists as she swipes more tears from her cheeks. "I guess it just hit me how close we were to…to losing him."

The newfound sap in me clings to the word *we*. Piper and myself. The two of us.

We've been pretending to be Benjamin's parents at the hospital, but the line between reality and fantasy is getting blurrier by the second.

"This is hindsight crying, then. You're realizing how much more you should have been crying before and you're catching up."

She laughs. "Yeah, I guess so. Because when I should have been crying, I was…taking a bath."

"Is 'taking a bath' our new euphemism for having multiple orgasms?"

Her face flushes. I like when it does that.

I step fully into the room and close the door behind me. The artificial light over the sink casts us both in a soft yellow light. As I close in on Piper, she shrinks into my shadow.

"What are you doing?" Her voice is soft enough that I know she knows exactly what I'm doing.

I slip my hand under the hem of her shirt and grip her narrow waist. Her skin is impossibly soft. "I want to make sure you celebrate properly."

Her back bends and she arches into my touch. "In a bathroom?"

I unbutton her jeans and curl my fingers around the warmest part of her. She gasps when I stroke her slit over her panties.

"I don't mind celebrating in front of a crowd, but I thought you might like privacy." I press my lips to the soft place beneath her ear. After hours of sterile hospital smells and latex, it feels like a miracle to catch a whiff of vanilla floating off of her skin.

Piper lolls her head back and purrs as my fingers work across her pussy, coaxing her legs apart and drawing moisture between her thighs.

"Someone could come," she whimpers, shuddering as I circle her clit.

"That's the idea."

She chuckles softly, her forehead falling against my shoulder. "Into the room, I mean. Someone could come in to talk to us and—"

"And they can wait until I'm done."

81

TIMOFEY

I slide my middle finger into her waiting warmth, and curl it against her walls. I pulse one finger and then two into her, working rhythmically until she's rolling onto my hand, seeking out my touch.

"Timofey," she gasps, arching as a mild orgasm trembles through her.

It's not enough to satiate, but it is enough to light her fuse. When Piper opens her eyes, her pupils are blown wide. She's half-crazed with the new need coursing through her.

She plants her palms on my chest and pushes me back against the door. I let her, keeping my hands at my sides as she drops to her knees in front of me and undoes my pants.

The instant my cock is free, Piper takes me into her mouth. She swirls her tongue around my head and then plunges deep until I feel the vibration of her moan against my tip.

"Fuck," I growl, fisting a handful of her hair.

She follows this rhythm, licking and sucking before practically swallowing me. By the third or fourth pass, I'm aching to explode.

But I want more than this. I want all of her.

I pull her off of me with a pop and grab her around her waist.

"Wait. Timofey. I want to—"

"And I want you," I growl, placing her on the edge of the sink. "Take off your pants."

In a matter of seconds, her pants are on the floor and her bare thighs are wrapped around my waist.

"You're so soft." I drag my hands up to her hips, marveling at the way we look together. My scarred, calloused fingers against her porcelain skin.

Then her hand slips between us and drags roughly down my length. "And you're so hard."

I nip at her jawline. It's a playful bite, but Piper moans. Her hand tightens around me, and then I'm pressed against her entrance.

"Fuck me until I can't think anymore, Timofey," she whispers. Her lips brush against my cheek with every word. "Please. Fuck me until I can't worry."

It's the filthiest thing I've ever heard from the most beautiful mouth I've ever seen. And I want to give her every single thing she asks. Especially this.

I press into her slowly, delighting in the way she stretches around me. I don't stop until I'm deep inside of her, as connected as we can be. Still, it doesn't seem to be enough for Piper. She hooks her legs around my lower back and holds tight.

"I want to stay like this. Just like this. Forever."

I kiss her neck and lick the pulse in her neck. "Typical Piper."

"What?"

I smirk. "Once again, I have to show you what you really want."

She starts to frown, but then I slide out of her. The friction parts her lips in a sigh that turns into a moan as I fill her once again.

"Okay, yes. That," she says, clawing at my back. "Yes. Do that."

I take her ass in my hands and fill her over and over again until we're a panting, writhing mass of limbs.

"I'm close." Piper smooths her hands over my chest and loops them around my neck. She presses her lips to my jawline. "Come with me."

She doesn't need to ask me twice.

I lift her fully off the sink, balancing her weight on my hips. Piper leans back, and we hit a new angle that forces her to bite down on her lower lip to keep from screaming.

I feel her deepest muscles contracting around me, and I release the pent-up ball of heat in my core.

Together, we ride the wave, cresting and falling in sync. I stumble forward so she is wedged between my chest and the wall, and we stay together until the last twitches of pleasure ease. Until there's no sound except the contented sound of our breathing.

Piper turns her head and kisses my neck and my jaw. She strokes her hands over me like she's worried I might not be real.

"I can't believe…" She chuckles softly and shakes her head.

"How I keep making you come again and again?"

She rolls her eyes and smiles. It's so easy and familiar. It shoots straight to the heart of me, branding me with the goodness that is Piper Quinn.

A *good* girl. With a man like me. Who would have ever thought?

"No," she continues. "I can't believe I'm not having a panic attack. I mean…look at this room."

There isn't much to look at. One glance over my shoulder and I've seen all there is to say. Hell, I could stretch one arm back and be touching both walls. It's microscopic.

Then it hits me.

"Oh, shit. You're claustrophobic."

"Unless I'm with you, I guess." She shrugs.

"I'm honored."

She immediately waves a finger at me. "No, no. Don't do that. Don't get a big head."

"How can I not? My dick is the cure for claustrophobia."

A laugh bursts from between pursed lips. She slaps a hand over her mouth to quiet herself. "That is *not* what is happening here."

"It's definitely what's happening here," I say. "Are you part of a support group or something? Do you have any young, single women in the class who are desperate for a cure? It's now my duty to spread this cure as wide and far as possible."

Her brow arches dangerously, but she's still smiling at me. "Wow. How selfless you are."

"With great power," I say, gesturing to my still-hard dick, "comes great responsibility."

Piper slaps my chest, and I snatch her hand and press her fingers to my mouth. It's a surprisingly intimate gesture, and she freezes. Her green eyes scan my face and where our hands are twined together.

Something is shifting between us. We both feel it.

I drop her hand like a hot coal and snatch her pants off the floor. She takes them gratefully and we slip back into a version of the roles we've been playing since we met.

Acquaintances. Reluctant employer and employee. Even more reluctant friends.

"Well, if you feel yourself growing panicked and need my assistance, I'm only a phone call away."

Piper laughs, and now, I agree with her: I want to stay here forever, too. This bathroom is the only place in the world where we can be like this.

Whatever "this" is.

Then I hear footsteps, followed by the prim voice of a nurse. "Mr. Viktorov? Are you in there, sir?"

I should've guessed we'd be interrupted. I know better than most that fantasies don't last.

The real world always comes knocking.

82

PIPER

The rehearsal dinner for the wedding feels like a dress rehearsal in more ways than one.

The dinner is being held in Timofey's formal dining room with Akim serving food from the newly-remodeled kitchen. There won't be any press, but this is still the first time I have to pretend to be Timofey's girlfriend in front of other people who matter.

I'm not sure I'm ready.

I smooth my hands over the dress he chose for me and try to calm my nerves. That has been an impossible feat the last week. Ever since we stepped out of that hospital bathroom, something has been different.

I'm supposed to be working to get away from Timofey. To protect Benjamin from his influence and get him sent to prison.

And yet, I've spent every spare moment tangled in his sheets and wrapped in his arms.

I fist the green velvet fabric of my dress and breathe through the butterflies erupting in my stomach. I can still feel what he did to me last night. My body seems to have permanently molded around the shape of him. When he isn't inside of me, I ache for him.

"Get it together," I mutter, squeezing my eyes closed. "Focus."

I can't be the woman drooling all over Timofey and falling to pieces at his every glance. I need to appear as his wife-to-be. His equal. I need to look like someone he would believably choose as his partner.

The thought of it is enough to send another bolt of anxiety through me.

Not because it doesn't feel possible, but because it feels all too real.

This last week has felt like sitting in a trash compactor as the walls slowly close in. Falling for Timofey is an inevitable kind of doom in that way. It presses in from every direction until I'm not sure which way is up or how to get out.

He has me in a stranglehold, and I'm afraid pretending to love him will be one crush too far.

How long until the dinner? I need to know how many minutes I have to get my shit together.

I grab my phone from the vanity to check the time, but I'm distracted by the message icon flashing in the top left corner. It must have gone off while I was meticulously curling my hair for the last hour. I tap the message and Noelle's name fills the screen.

Before I can scan what she wrote, I lock the screen and it goes black. I hold the phone like it might spontaneously catch on fire.

I haven't heard from Noelle since she told me about Emily's murder. Does she have more information? Did she uncover something incriminating?

More importantly, *do I still want to hear it?*

I drum my fingers nervously on the screen, weighing my options. I could dismiss the message and pretend I never saw it. But Noelle won't give up. She does not take well to being ignored, especially now that she knows I've received and opened the message.

"So I have to read it," I mumble, my thumb hovering over the button to unlock the screen.

Except, if I read the message and it does have incriminating information about Timofey, I have to deal with that.

I've killed plenty of people, Piper. I'm not a good man.

Timofey has been honest with me from the beginning about who he is. Still, I've shoved down my reservations and thrown myself into whatever this thing between us is.

I can be okay with the fact that he didn't kill Emily. But there is still blood on his hands. If I find out more, I won't be able to hide from the truth. I won't be able to live in denial.

Before I can make a decision one way or the other, my phone starts to ring. On instinct, I answer it.

"There you are," Noelle says. "You never texted me back."

"I never read your message," I say honestly.

"Yes, you did. It says 'Read.' I know you saw it."

"Well, I saw it," I quickly explain. "But I've been busy and I didn't read it. I was going to. Later."

Maybe. Maybe not.

She makes a disapproving noise in the back of her throat. "What have you been busy doing?"

Timofey. The stupid joke rises up in me, and I swat it down. "There is this party—er, a work function tonight. I'm getting ready."

"Wow, what a depressing party that must be. A bunch of social workers from CPS huddled around a sweaty cheese tray? No thanks."

I'm slightly offended by Noelle's assessment of what an actual work party would look like for me, but only because it's accurate. Our Christmas party last year was just carols played on Andrea's tinny phone speakers for the last thirty minutes of the work day. James made hot chocolate in the break room microwave and it tasted like burnt popcorn.

"Not for that job," I explain. "My other job. With Timofey."

There is a long stretch of silence before Noelle speaks again. "You still work for him?"

"Last I checked." I try to laugh, but it doesn't sound genuine. "It's just a dinner."

"But you're supposed to be getting away from him. That's why I did all of that research, right? He's not a good guy."

"I know. I asked you to look into that stuff—"

"A murder," Noelle interrupts. "Not 'stuff.' A murder."

"Right. I asked you to look into that, but it's all a lot more complicated than we thought. Timofey didn't do it."

"Because he got his hitman to do it for him!" Noelle hisses.

"I thought that, too. At first. But I talked to him, and—"

"Fuck's sake, Piper."

Noelle has a way of sounding like a scolding mom sometimes. It makes you want to please her. I chew on my lower lip, but can't bring myself to say anything. I don't know how to explain my decision to myself, let alone to Noelle.

"Fuck," she says again, almost to herself. "He sucked you in. I knew he would."

"Excuse me? He hasn't sucked me anywhere."

Obviously, my word choice leaves a little bit to be desired. My cheeks go red hot.

"Are you having sex?" The question is blunt and clinical. It makes everything Timofey and I have done in the last week feel wrong.

"That doesn't have anything to do with anything. I'm capable of making rational choices regardless of—"

"You are," she accuses. "You're fucking him, and now, you're going to get yourself killed."

Whatever guilt I feel is washed away by the condescension in her tone. "Stop it, Noelle. You are so—so judgmental sometimes."

She gasps in surprise. Usually, Ashley is the one levying that accusation against her. She doesn't expect it from me.

"Only because I care about you. I don't want you getting hurt!"

"Well, luckily, I don't think this thousand-dollar gown I'm wearing is going to hurt me," I snap.

"Is he buying you clothes now?"

I groan. "No. Well, yes. Just this one dress. But it's for the event."

She laughs cruelly. "I'm sure it's a tax write-off for him. *One dress for this month's booty call.* Fucking you is a business expense."

I stand up and pace across the room, too angry to stay seated. "It's not like that! Don't make this something it isn't."

"Last I knew, this was a rescue mission," Noelle says. "You were there to save a little kid from a bad guy. Now, you're playing House with a killer and acting like nothing is wrong. So maybe you're the one making this something it isn't, Piper."

Her words ring a little too true, but I don't have the capacity to deal with this on top of my first public outing with Timofey in less than twenty minutes.

"If you called to insult me then you'll just have to wait. I'm busy, and I have to—"

"I'm sorry," Noelle blurts. She sighs, and I can imagine her pinching the bridge of her nose, the rings on her fingers slipping around her thin fingers. "I'm sorry. You're right, I'm being judgmental. I'm sorry."

I'm not quite ready to forgive her yet, but I don't want to look like an asshole. "Thanks. Thanks for saying that. I'm sorry, too."

Sorry for what, though? For falling onto Timofey's dick and forgetting about the task at hand?

"You know I love you, Piper. I would hate it if anything bad happened to you."

"Nothing bad is going to happen to me." I can't say that with any certainty, but I try to sound as sincere as I can.

"You don't know that. This thing you're going to tonight… Do you know what it is?"

"It's just a party."

"What kind of party?" she asks. "Do you know who will be there?"

Timofey gave me the rundown last night, right after he gave my body a rundown in his shower.

"It's going to be the bride and groom and their families," he explained. "Then some shared friends, some Bratva and some civilian."

"A mix of people," I tell Noelle. "It's going to be a stuffy, boring dinner. Nothing wild."

"Piper." Noelle's voice breaks and it sounds like she is about to cry. "Get out of there."

"I will. Eventually. But tonight, I—"

"Just grab Benjamin and get out of there," she continues. "You have no idea who this guy is. Every day you spend with him is another day where you could get hurt. Just cut your losses and leave while he's distracted with the party."

Not so long ago, I would have thought of that idea myself. While Timofey was going over party planning details and welcoming guests, I would have been planning my great escape. The fact that running away hasn't even crossed my mind all week feels like a bucket of ice water over my head.

He *has* sucked me in. Noelle is right.

"I can't leave," I whimper to her. "He notices everything. He won't let me go."

"Try, Piper. Please promise me you'll try."

I hate lying to my friends, but I hate worrying them even more. "I'll try."

My bedroom door creaks open, and I turn just as Timofey steps inside. He's decked out in a tux with green detailing that matches my dress, and when I see the familiar shape of him, my stomach flips.

His blue eyes take me in from head to toe and swallow me whole. I'm drawn to his gaze like a minnow trapped in a whirlpool, helpless to escape. Without consciously choosing to, I walk towards him.

"… know I just want what's best for you," Noelle is saying on the phone. "I love you."

With my eyes on Timofey, I respond, "I love you, too."

83

PIPER

"Should I be worried?" Timofey asks the moment I hang up with Noelle.

My heart thunders against my chest. *How much did he overhear?*

"Worried about what?" My voice comes out a bit too high and unnatural.

He closes my door and moves closer, his gaze slipping up and down my body on an endless loop. "That you're wearing this dress and telling someone else you love them. I'm not an insecure man, but when you look like this…" He shakes his head. "It's bringing out my possessive side."

"Possessive is the only side you have," I tease.

"No." He bites his lower lip. It's the single sexiest thing I've ever seen in my life. "That was me wanting you close. Wanting you here with me for my own devious purposes. But this…*this* is me wanting to kick every single one of the forty guests waiting for me downstairs out of my house so I can fuck you until your throat is sore from screaming my name."

His words are dirty, and I can barely catch my breath with how much I want them to come true. Then Timofey grips my waist, and I might as well be a puddle at his feet. His hands are the only thing holding me upright.

"Right now, I want to possess every single part of you."

He spins me around so we're looking into the mirror. This close, it's clear that his tux was designed with my dress in mind. The velvet sheen of my gown is mirrored in the veridian piping down the sides of his pants and around his lapels. His pocket square matches the lace overlay from my bodice.

We're a perfect pair.

He leans in close, a blue-eyed devil whispering temptations in my ear. "I want to rip you out of this dress stitch by stitch and fuck you on it," he growls. "I want to fill you until you scream my name and every person in attendance tonight knows, without a doubt, that you belong to me and me alone."

I swallow down the desire pulsing through me. "That's… um… pretty possessive."

He slides his hands from my shoulders to my waist. "It's only because you look so beautiful. Have I said that?" he asks, his nose buried in my hair. "Have I said how stunning you look?"

It's taking every ounce of self-control in my body to stand here and not spin around and leap into his arms. I want the dirty promises he made. I want them again and again and again.

And again, and again, and again, and again.

"Not in so many words. But I got the general idea."

He kisses the junction of my neck and shoulder and smiles at our reflection. "Good. Because you look fucking incredible. No one is going to wonder what Timofey Viktorov is doing with a social worker when they see you in this. No one will doubt our relationship for a second."

All at once, I remember this isn't real. I'm not his girlfriend, I'm pretending.

I step away from him and smooth down the folds of the skirt. "You did a great job with the dress."

"I had it custom made for you. All those dresses I ordered were shit. You needed something that would suit you."

"Plenty of those dresses suited just fine," I tell him. "Most of them were more than my monthly rent."

He rolls his eyes. "Let's not get started on your rent. The dresses were a disaster, end of story."

"They were not! That purple one was super pretty. I loved it."

It doesn't matter, but arguing about dresses is a nice distraction from the fact that I'm spiraling.

I want to be Timofey's girlfriend, even though he is a killer and a criminal. Instead, I'm pretending to be his girlfriend while I'm supposed to be trying to get away from him so I can potentially get him sent to prison.

The web of lies and deceit I've woven is too tangled even for me to pick apart.

Timofey shakes his head. "The purple dress made your skin look yellow, whereas this shade of green brings out your naturally pink blush points here," he says, pointing to my cheeks. Then his hand slips down to my collarbone. "And here."

I blink at him, dumbfounded that he is paying *any* attention to me, let alone this much.

"Speaking of here," he says, running his finger along my collarbone to my breastbone. "This square neckline and tapered waist highlight your incredible curves and show off your bone structure."

"What do you know about bone structure?"

"In general? Nothing. But yours?" He lowers his chin, his eyes deathly serious. "Everything. You're a fucking dream, Piper. You have a heart-shaped face, petite shoulders, and hips that make me want to do filthy things all of the time. So I told the seamstress to make you look like my worst nightmare: a fucking fairytale princess."

"You mean 'a fuckable fairytale princess'?"

He laughs and pulls me close again, looping his arms around my lower back. "A fairytale princess shouldn't have such a dirty mouth."

"Maybe you'll have to punish me," I say with doe eyes and an exaggerated porn star voice. "Teach me how to be a good girl, Timofey."

He growls and dips his head, nipping at my earlobe. "Keep it up and I really will have you screaming my name until all the guests can hear."

Guests.

Dinner guests.

As in, Timofey's friends and acquaintances and Bratva connections who are all waiting downstairs for me to play the part of his perfect new girlfriend.

All while Noelle wants me to try and escape into the night with a tiny infant baby.

Not to mention, *this isn't real.* With his arms around me, I can almost forget everything else.

Almost.

But the weight of expectation settles over me as gracefully as a piano falling on my head, and I take a shaky inhale.

Timofey notices. Because of course he does. "Relax," he murmurs. "You look the part, Piper. You're ready."

He sounds sincere. I believe him.

The question is: *Ready for what, exactly?*

84

PIPER

Being on Timofey's arm as he leads me from senator to CEO and veteran to billionaire feels like hurtling around on an amusement park ride. I'm floating through a scene that doesn't feel real. I'm not supposed to breathe the same air as these people, let alone shake hands and trade polite compliments with them.

Yet, here I am.

And somehow, Timofey makes it all make sense.

"I'm not surprised Timofey found himself a generous woman like you," the senator's wife says. I don't know her name, and she doesn't offer it up, probably assuming I ought to recognize her. It doesn't really matter—her double-looped string of pearls and glossy blonde hair is enough of an introduction. "He himself was very generous with my husband's last campaign."

I nod and smile. "Oh. How nice."

I have no clue what to say to that. Politics has never been on my radar. There's no room for it when you're too worried about buying groceries, making rent, and not losing my job.

The woman seems to take this as me playing hard-to-get.

"You and I will have to get together sometime." She pinches my elbow conspiratorially and gives me a wink. "Good friends are hard to find. We have to stick together."

This woman and I are barely acquaintances, let alone friends. But I have a feeling her interest lies more in the connection she and her husband could have to Timofey than it has anything to do with me. She doesn't exactly seem down for a pajama party with Noelle and Ashley.

Timofey finishes his conversation with the woman's husband and loops his arm around my waist. "Piper will have to talk with you more later, Margaret," he says. "Right now, she's running defense for me."

The woman—Margaret, apparently—actually giggles. "Good of you to practice. You'll need a solid defense at the wedding."

"Should I be expecting trouble?" he rumbles.

"Heaps of it," Margaret says with a grin. "When word got out you were off the market, there were a lot of broken hearts. Those women might not take as kindly to Piper as I have."

Timofey spreads his hand across my hip. My skin practically sizzles at his touch. "Once they meet her, they'll love her as much as I do."

Not real. Not real. Not real.

If I keep repeating the words to myself, maybe they will stick. Maybe my heart will stop beating out of my chest every time

Timofey looks my way over the crowd.

Maybe.

But probably not.

The party is meant to be a rehearsal dinner, but as the bride and groom move through the room, everyone's eyes are on Timofey. He commands attention even when he isn't trying.

But while everyone is watching him, he is watching me.

"Do you need a drink?" His lips brush the shell of my ear when he leans in to whisper.

I fight off a shiver. "I'm okay. Thanks."

"Just tell me what you need." He brushes a strand of hair over my shoulder and smooths it down my back. "I'll take care of it for you."

I need some air. I need distance. The closer Timofey and I are, the harder it is to keep my head clear.

But the closer we are, the less I want to pull away from him.

Is this what it would be like to be truly his? He's attentive and gentle. I feel like the only woman in the universe. It's intoxicating in a way nothing else ever has been. I don't want to let this high go.

"All of these people respect you," I whisper.

He snorts. "I'd fucking hope so. I built most of their careers."

"You introduced me to a neurosurgeon earlier. Did you build his career?"

"He's a talent and will be a great surgeon in his own right. But he has the promise of a new research hospital to thank for his residency."

Whiskey Poison 541

I gape at him. "Are you talking about the cancer research hospital by the river?"

Timofey takes a smug sip from his champagne glass.

"Timofey! That was like... a huge fucking deal." I clap a hand over my mouth and look around to make sure no one overheard me. Not only should I know which hospitals my boyfriend has funded, I also need to be a proper lady. Proper ladies don't swear.

"Most things I do are a huge fucking deal."

"I remember hearing about it because the 'anonymous' donation that paid for it freed up a lot of other funds. Our department was awarded some of the money."

It was used to buy an air conditioner unit for the temporary overnight room where kids can stay between foster placements, along with an official transport van. The A/C fried itself within six months. The van was broken into and totaled within a year.

"Then you're very welcome," he says with a shallow, mocking bow.

"I don't assume you made that donation from the goodness of your heart."

He pretends to be offended. "How dare you suggest I am not a Good Samaritan, bettering the world for the sake of it?" I arch a brow, and he smiles mischievously. "Dr. Brainiac comes from a long line of influential people. His daddy is a D.A. I worked up a way for all of us to benefit from our friendship."

A district attorney, a senator, a brain surgeon, a police officer —Timofey has his own personal *Guess Who?* board. Is there any spot in this city where Timofey doesn't have a connection? Is there any place he can't reach?

"I guess I should feel lucky you only had me thrown in jail for a day and not locked away for life." I laugh weakly.

But when I look up at Timofey, he isn't laughing.

He's staring straight ahead, his expression stony. Whatever warmth I felt a moment ago is gone. A chill moves up my spine as panic sets in.

"I'm sorry," I blurt quickly. "I didn't mean—It was a joke and—I know this isn't the time or place, so I—"

Timofey squeezes my hand and pulls me closer to him. His breath is warm against my temple. "Stay close to me."

"Why?"

I'm staring up at him, trying to read his expression. But Timofey narrows his eyes towards the door. "Don't look at me, Piper."

My face flushes with embarrassment. He caught me staring. He probably thinks I'm as obsessed with him as I really am. But before I can spiral into shame, I catch sight of someone new standing in the doorway.

Timofey wasn't telling me not to look at him. He was telling me to look around.

"We've got company," he mutters, downing the rest of his drink. "Let's go greet our uninvited guest."

Then he pulls me across the room towards Rodion.

85

TIMOFEY

I keep a tight grip on Piper's hand.

In an ideal world, I'd get her as far away from Rodion and half the people in this godforsaken room as possible. Especially Senator Gracen and his repulsive wife.

My "donation" to his last campaign helped him afford a slew of sexual assault settlements. The moment he passes the legislation he and I worked up together, I'll toss him to the social justice wolves and let them feast.

But this isn't an ideal world. I'm the only one I can trust with Piper's safety, and I don't want her out of my sight.

Rodion sees us moving towards him, and he squares his shoulders. I know that glint in his eye. It looks like we're in for a fight.

I snatch a champagne flute off of a passing server's tray and seamlessly offer it to him as I approach. "Here. A drink for the road."

"Ah, a warm dismissal," he says, taking a sip. "I'd prefer a warm welcome, but beggars can't be choosers."

"Especially when I should shoot the beggar on sight."

He holds up a hand in a subtle surrender. "Things got a little tense the last time we spoke. I'm here to rectify that."

"You chose an inconvenient time. I'm busy."

He nods. "I thought I might fare better with more witnesses."

"Everyone in this room knows who I am, whether they admit it publicly or not. I could kill you right now and your death wouldn't even make a ripple in the morning news. Half the people here would testify they've never seen you in their lives. The other half would help me dig the grave."

Piper's hand slides more firmly into mine. I'm not sure if she's trying to rein me in or show her support. Either way, the feel of her skin against mine strokes some deeper part of me that wants nothing more than to protect her.

From Rodion.

From the world.

From every bad thing that might wipe the smile off of her face.

Forget Rodion; I'd torch this entire room if it meant she'd be happy.

"There's no need for dramatics," Rodion says coolly. "Just give me five minutes. I want to talk to you alone."

"You want to be alone with the person who just threatened your life?" Piper asks.

Rodion turns to her. His eyes narrow in on where our hands are intertwined. "This is a shiny glass house you're living in. I wouldn't throw stones if I were you."

"If you want to continue breathing, don't say another word to her," I warn.

Rodion averts his eyes quickly and nods. "I'm sorry. I'm not here to—I want to explain, Timofey. Everything. Please."

I've known Rodion a long time, and the man has never struck me as especially sincere. Certainly not contrite.

Right now, he's both.

I'm not going to be fooled by some little act, but I am intrigued. That alone is reason enough for me to agree.

Another reason is that it will be much easier to kill him in private and then return to the party.

I hold up my other hand, fingers spread wide. "Five minutes. That's what you get."

He gives a half-gracious, half-mocking bow. "It's all I need."

"We're going to my office." I gesture to the door. "You lead the way. And keep your hands where I can see them."

Rodion walks in front of us with his hands loose and open at his sides. I should pat him down, but it doesn't matter. If he so much as flinches towards his pocket, I'll kill him.

Piper is a ball of tension against me. "Are you sure this is safe?"

"You're safe. I'll protect you, Piper."

"I don't mean for me," she whispers, her arm looping around mine. "What about you?"

If she is playing the role of my loving girlfriend, she's doing a thorough job. There's no one around and she is still pretending to be worried about me.

But I'm not pretending. I haven't been for a while.

And I have no clue how to tell her that I would put myself in danger one thousand times over if it meant making sure she was safe.

86

TIMOFEY

In my office, Rodion looks much less relaxed than he did when we were surrounded by witnesses. I can see a sheen of sweat on his forehead.

I shut the door behind me and check my watch. "Your five minutes have started."

"Right. Okay." He takes a deep breath. "I had this all planned out, but now, I'm not really sure where to start."

"The beginning is a good place."

He chuckles and runs a hand over his neck. "You'd think, but... I'll start with the most recent thing first. I know you didn't try to have me killed."

I can't help but roll my eyes. "I already told you that."

"I should have listened when I showed up that night and you said you didn't know about it," he says. "I was just so fucking mad. The guy told me you sent him, and I believed him. It was a good setup."

I shake my head. "It wasn't that good. Someone wanted you dead. If that failed, they wanted to turn us against each other. It was transparent to me."

"Because you knew the truth. You knew you didn't do it. I didn't know that." He glances sidelong at me. "Kind of like the way you still think I might have killed Emily, even though I didn't."

I grit my teeth. "Four minutes."

"Shit," he mutters. "Okay. So, yeah, I'm sorry I accused you of trying to kill me. I know it wasn't you, but I've been trying to figure out who it was."

"If you find them, give them my number. I might be in the market for a new hitman in three minutes and counting."

He chuckles nervously. "I'm also here to tell you, firmly and finally, that I did not kill Emily."

I hold up a hand to stop him. "Go talk to Sergey about this if you want someone to listen. He's your little cheerleader. I'm fucking tired of talking about it. The truth will come out eventually. When it does—"

"You'll realize I'm telling the truth," Rodion says. "I still have three minutes, right?"

"Two and a half."

"Then please let me use them." He waits for my response. When I say nothing, he continues. "My mom died a year ago. It really tore me up, you know?"

I do know. It's the one and only time I've ever seen Rodion close to tears.

His mother was young. She had him when she was a teenager, so her death was unexpected. I could sympathize with how he was feeling. He sent money back home to her every month like clockwork. She'd just bought a new car.

"Emily tried to be there for me, but I couldn't hear it," he continues. "I needed space, so we broke up. I went to Russia to try and deal with my family shit, and she stayed here."

"It's a convenient alibi, being out of the country. I'd commend the planning if it hadn't resulted in the murder of my sister."

He sighs, but tries to carry on like I didn't say anything. He doesn't want to waste a second of the time he has left.

"When I was in Russia, Emily and I reconnected. She reached out and we started talking. There had been some weirdness between us the last few months, even before my mom died, and she wanted to explain everything and fix it. Fix us. So I was going to come back and we would sort through our shit."

"What 'shit' was that?" Piper asks.

I glance over. She's hyperfocused on Rodion. Aside from the occasional squeeze of her hand in mine, I almost forgot she was here.

Rodion shrugs, careful not to look her way any longer than necessary. "I don't know. She told me she wanted to tell me in person. By the time my plane landed on American soil, she was dead."

I snort. "How convenient. You two were making up and then she is murdered on the same day you are back in the country? It's pretty coincidental. And I don't believe in coincidences."

"Neither do I," he says. "I think someone knew Emily and I were reconnecting. Someone knew we were getting back together and they didn't want that to happen. Maybe it has something to do with what she wanted to tell me, but I… I don't know."

Rodion drags a hand through his hair, sending the ends spiking up in every direction. "I've been tracking down leads in my free time. My biggest theory is the Albanians, of course. But so far, no one has given me any useful information."

"If an Albanian did this, I'd know about it," I tell him. "None of my contacts have said anything to that effect."

He shrugs, his arms hanging limp at his sides. "I don't know, Timofey. I wish I did, but I—I'm telling you what I do know. I didn't do it."

All of the restraint I've managed to draw on until now goes slack all at once. I lunge forward, smoke practically pouring out of my ears. "You're fucking lying. You know how I know? Because Emily *told* me you threatened her."

Rodion shrinks back against the wall, and Piper pulls gently on my hand. She's just reminding me that she's there.

And it works.

If I do decide to kill Rodion, I'll make sure she's out of the room first.

I retreat back next to Piper, eyes still narrowed on Rodion. "Emily told me about every single time you swore she'd end up as one of the dots tattooed on your arm."

He nods. "I did that. I have never claimed to be a good boyfriend, a good man, anything like that. I'm as fucked-up as they come. And when she threatened to leave me, I fucking lost it. But I never, *ever* hurt her. Not physically. If I had, she would have told you."

"At one point, maybe. But we weren't on good terms at the end," I retort. *"Because of you.* The moment you two got together, I knew Emily deserved better. When she said you threatened her, I swore to her I'd kill you if you ever laid a hand on her. Then, slowly, she pulled away. Probably because she was tangled in your web and didn't want me to slit your throat when she showed up with a black eye."

"There was never a black eye! I swear." He glances at the clock on the wall, and I have no idea how much time he has left. I've lost count. "I loved her, Timofey. I did. But I had no clue how to love her until it was too late. I wasted years being jealous and controlling. Now, she's gone, and I—I'll never forgive myself."

In his words, I hear a warning.

Since the moment I met Piper, she has been a means to an end. Even as my feelings for her have grown and expanded, I've rammed them down into the box I've fit her into. With a promise to myself all along: once I get what I want from her, I'll toss her aside.

But things have changed.

If I follow through with that plan, I know I'll live to regret it. One day, I'll have the same pained, desperate look on my face as Rodion does now.

It's that expression that, more than anything else he has said, makes me believe him.

"His time is up," Piper says quietly.

I look back, and she's glaring past me at Rodion. She doesn't believe him. She still thinks he's responsible.

"So what's it going to be?" Rodion asks, resignation in his voice.

I hesitate. Suddenly, the air itself feels heavy on my shoulders. Then I let out a long sigh that does nothing to lighten it. "For now, you're going to walk out of here alive."

He visibly sags in relief. "You believe me, then?"

"I didn't say that," I snarl. "I have guests waiting for me. I don't have time to clean blood out from under my fingernails."

Piper wraps both hands around mine, and she is all but dragging me to the door. But I don't budge. Not yet.

"I'll make you a deal, Rodion."

"Anything," he says eagerly. "Name it and it's yours."

"Bring me the Albanian responsible for Emily's death, and I'll believe your story. I'll welcome you back into the Bratva and my good graces without another question."

Enthusiasm drains out of him. "But I—I've talked to the Albanians. I've tortured men to death. There isn't anything to find there."

I nod. "Fine. Then I'll kill you with my own hands. Payback for Emily's death. No less than you deserve."

He is stuck between a rock and a hard place and he knows it. But the rock is instant death and the hard place lets him maintain a heartbeat. Wisely, Rodion accepts the offer.

"I'll find out whatever I can. I'll bring you proof I didn't do this," he says.

"Good. But in the meantime," I point to the door, "get out of my fucking house."

Rodion doesn't hesitate. He bows his head one last time and then hurries around us, giving Piper a wide berth.

87

PIPER

Once, I dreamed I was living in my dentist's office and went to swim lessons in the lobby. The receptionist was my mom and she had wings like an angel.

Stepping out of Timofey's office and back into the party feels a lot like that. Like moving through the incoherent stages of a dream. Nothing makes any sense, but I'm expected to smile and wave at guests after spending the last five minutes talking to a potential murderer.

"If you don't get some color in your cheeks, people are going to think you're scared of me." Timofey pulls me into his chest as the music shifts into a slow song, almost as if he timed it this way. I wouldn't be surprised if he did.

"Maybe I am."

A frown pinches his brows together. His blue eyes are sapphire tonight, shimmering in the light from the candles that have been placed in the center of all the tables. "I told you I'd protect you."

"There are lots of different reasons to be scared," I say softly.

I'm terrified of what I feel when Timofey is touching me.

I'm terrified that a man like Rodion might try to make a move against him.

Most of all, I'm terrified that this is all fake. That the way he is looking at me now, with adoration and warmth, is all a facade. I'm terrified that the clock will strike midnight and this moment will shatter into a million, irreconcilable pieces.

Timofey cups my face in his hand and strokes my cheekbone. "Turn off your brain. Be here with me for a few minutes. You're in a stunning dress, I'm in a tux—"

"Also stunning," I say, smoothing my hand down his sleeve. I can feel the flex and pull of his muscles as he molds our bodies together.

"Agreed. So let's be two incredibly stunning people at a stunning event," he says with a smirk. "For a minute, forget everything else and just be here with me."

For reasons I can't fully explain, tears spring into my eyes. Before he can see them, I press my cheek against his chest and sway with the music.

I promised Noelle I'd try to get away tonight. I told her I'd try to escape.

Does this look like escape?

I think not. If anything, I'm even deeper into this mess now than I was two hours ago.

"You're tense." He squeezes my arms and then forces them around his waist. "Do I need to help you relax?"

The sultry tone of his voice mixed with the way the words vibrate through his chest does strange things to my heart. I could stay here all night.

I could stay here forever.

The thought is like a lightning bolt through me. The vulnerability has me feeling fragile, and I go stiff. If he squeezes too hard, I'm sure I'll shatter.

His palm glides down my exposed spine. "We can sneak away for a few minutes if we need to."

"A few minutes?" I try to sound casual, but the words squeal out of me like I'm a balloon with a leak. "Is that all you can offer me?"

He laughs low and slow. "Don't tempt me. I'll clear this room out and show you exactly what I have to offer."

I almost tell him to go for it. In the end, he doesn't need to.

The gunshots clear the room for him.

88

PIPER

Timofey moves impossibly fast. I don't have time to react to the *pop-pop-pop* before I'm huddled under his arm and he's herding me across the room full of screaming people.

"What the—What is going on?" I gasp, ducking my head under his chest and doing my best not to trip over my own feet.

He doesn't respond. He's too busy cutting through the crowd. It's only when we step through a side door and into a dark hallway that Timofey presses me flat against the wall and peeks back through the door.

"Arber," he growls, pulling out his phone.

"Who is that? Is it—is this the Albanians?"

The dark sides of Timofey's world have always felt so far away. I logically understood it was dangerous, but I never expected it to come this close to me.

Now, it's here, and I am out of my depth.

Timofey calls someone, but he curses when they don't answer. He dials another number and takes my hand. We jog down the hallway.

"Akim. Stay out of the ballroom. Get to the security by the—" He pauses as he listens. "The guards never would have let him in. They're dead. I'm sure of it."

"Dead?"

Timofey barks out an order to Akim that I don't hear and then hangs up. At each intersection of the hallway, he stops and checks both ways before we continue.

"Are we running away?" I ask. "What about your guests? Who is going to take care of them?"

He told Rodion that a death at his party wouldn't crack into tomorrow's big headlines, but I can't imagine shots fired in the middle of a gaudy wedding rehearsal dinner won't appear in the papers.

I gasp, remembering all the faces I've seen and smiled at over the last hour. "The bride and groom! The senator! The-the… surgeon! Are they okay?"

Timofey isn't responding. His blue eyes are narrowed as he plunges deeper into the house. I'm not even sure if he can hear me.

"Timofey!" I try to pull my hand out of his iron grip, but it's useless. "Timofey, listen to me. We can't run. People are hurt back there. Your—*our* guests. We have to help them. We have to—"

All at once, he stops and turns. I slam into his chest, and he hauls me off of my feet, pinning me against the broad expanse of him. "I have to make sure you and Benjamin are safe. *That* is my priority."

I swallow. "But everyone else—"

"Can fucking bleed," he growls. "Let me take care of you. Let me make sure you are okay. Then I'll deal with everyone else."

I want to argue with him, but I also can't imagine navigating the maze-like hallways of this house without him while there are gunmen inside.

I nod. "Okay."

He lowers me to the floor and we take off at a jog, side by side.

"Do you know who is responsible?"

"Arber Kreshnik." The way he growls the name makes me feel bad for the owner of it. Clearly, the man is in for a brutal death.

"Does he know the bride and groom? Is he here for them or is this about—"

"He's here for you," Timofey says.

I must have misunderstood him. I shake my head. "No, he's not here for me. I don't even know him."

Timofey stops outside of Benjamin's room, his hand on the doorknob. When he looks back at me, there's something vulnerable in his eyes. It's a sliver of his soul I've never seen before. It's tender and warm, and I want to curl up there and hide away from every dark thing in his life.

"Arber is here to destroy me, Piper," Timofey explains. "What better way to do that than to destroy you first?"

I'm not sure what killing me has to do with hurting Timofey, but he says it with enough sincerity that I believe him.

Timofey pushes open Benjamin's door. I almost cry with relief when I see him sleeping in his crib, still swaddled and perfect like we left him.

The night nurse Timofey hired for the event stands up, surprised by our intrusion. But before the woman can get a word out, Timofey orders her out. "Get to the basement and hide there. We're under attack."

The woman, to her credit, isn't half as confused as I am. She nods and leaves the room at a brisk pace.

"Should I go with her?" I ask. "Benjamin and I can go with her while you—"

I can't finish that sentence.

While you walk into a gunfight that you might not walk out of again.

Timofey pulls Benjamin out of his crib with gentle hands, presses a kiss to his little head, and then hands him to me. Benjamin's eyelids flutter, but he quickly settles back into his deep, even breathing.

"You're not going to the basement with my staff." Timofey spins towards the closet and wrenches the doors open. He slides all of the infant-sized hangers to each side of the closet, and for the first time, I notice a panel built into the back wall of the closet.

Just looking at the narrow door, my claustrophobia rears its ugly head.

"Wh-where are we going?" I stammer.

He opens a hidden panel that is flush with the drywall and punches in a number. There is the hiss of some kind of hydraulic hinge, and then a door swings open, revealing a closet within a closet.

Timofey steps to the side and ushers me in. "It's a safe room. Each bedroom is equipped with one. It has its own ducts that don't connect to the rest of the house and it's resistant to fire, bullets, and just about anything else someone might try to throw at it."

"Air?" I rasp. "Is there air in there? It looks small. Maybe the Albanians are gone already. I haven't heard anything. Maybe I'll stay in the closet and go in there if I see anyone coming. Maybe we don't have to go—"

"Piper." Timofey draws close and grips my chin. His nose brushes against the tip of mine, and my eyes flutter closed of their own accord. "I need you to do this for me. I know, *I fucking know*, it's going to be hard for you. But this is the only way I'll know you're safe."

"We haven't seen anyone on this side of the house. Maybe Benjamin and I will be fine if we turn off the lights and—"

"'Maybe' isn't good enough for me," he says. "I won't be able to focus if I'm not sure you're safe. And I need to be focused. I need to go."

I shake my head, terror choking me out. "Stay with me, Timofey. Don't go. You have soldiers. Let them handle it."

"If my men are willing to die for me, I have to be willing to fight for them." He shakes his head gently. "I'll force you in there if I have to, but I want you to choose it. Please, Piper. For me."

Distantly, I hear another gunshot.

The threat is still here. It might even be moving closer. Benjamin is nestled in my arms, safe for the moment. But I have to do what's best for him. What's best for Timofey. What's best for myself.

I blow out a breath that feels like it might be my last and nod. "Okay."

Quick as a hummingbird, Timofey presses his lips to mine. It's so fast that I almost don't believe it happened. Then I'm stepping into the dark, narrow closet while Timofey pushes the door closed.

"I'll be back as soon as I can," he says through the crack. "I'll always come back for you, Piper. I'll never leave you."

When the door closes, I think I might have imagined his words of comfort. Still, I cling to them as I slide down the back wall with Benjamin in my arms.

"We'll be okay," I whisper to the still sleeping baby. "Timofey will come back for us. He'll take care of us."

I hope to God I'm telling him the truth.

89

PIPER

I hear Timofey's voice in my head.

Breathe, Piper.

Inhale.

Exhale.

Over and over again, I fill my lungs and release, hoping some of the tightness in my chest will ease. But it gets worse.

There isn't enough oxygen in here. Every deep breath is stealing what little there is for the two of us, and if I hog it all, Benjamin will suffocate.

I take short, shallow breaths until darkness creeps into the edges of my vision. Until I squeeze my eyes closed and lose track of where I am.

Noises come to me, muffled and distant. Is that a gunshot or a car backfiring? Did Benjamin whimper or is someone moaning?

"It's okay," I whisper to myself. "You'll get out. This will end. You'll get out."

The words echo back to me, but they're in a child's voice. My own voice, decades younger.

I can smell the dusty upholstery of the rusted-out car's trunk. When I open my eyes, I think I see a flash in the corner, the red glow of a taillight viewed from the inside. I feel the warm putter of the engine clunking along somewhere in the guts of the vehicle.

I shouldn't be in here. I'll die in here.

"I'm not in the trunk anymore; I'm in Timofey's house. I'm not a little girl anymore; I'm grown. I'm okay. I'm okay. I'm okay."

The words beat against the door of my logical mind, but trauma has slid the bolt home. There's no getting through.

So the memory opens its jaws and swallows me whole.

I'm ten years old again, huddled in the trunk of a car. I can hear voices a foot away, maybe less. But the sounds are lost somewhere in the cushion of the backseat between me and them.

I feel the swaying, though. The rocking that always makes me seasick. Like I'm trapped below deck on a ship, sailing out into the endless expanse of the ocean. Never to be seen again.

My arms tighten around myself, but there's something in my arms.

I blink and I'm holding a baby.

A baby.

I have to make sure you and Benjamin are safe. Timofey's voice is a baritone siren song. I reach for it, desperate to ground myself on something real, something solid. *I'll always come back for you, Piper. I'll never leave you.*

"Now," I plead, tears rolling down my cheeks. "Come back now."

No one responds, and I gently bang my head back against the wall of the panic room. The pain is better than feeling unmoored. It's better than floating through a river of muddled memories.

"Timofey. Please." I swallow back a sob.

There's a soft bang and a hissing noise. The world seems to split and crack wide, light pouring into the dark. I blink against the brightness with tears in my eyes, struggling to see.

"Piper." His voice is dry land after years at sea. He's the lighthouse in the storm, and I throw myself forward and into the warmth.

He wraps strong arms around both of us and nuzzles my head under his chin. "I'm sorry. I'm so sorry."

"Sorry for what?" I hiccup. "You saved me."

90

PIPER

I take another drink of ice water and then fold my hands around the glass. The night is warm and condensation drips down the cup, pooling in my palms. But I don't mind. I'd dive headfirst into the pond behind me if I thought Timofey wouldn't have me committed to an insane asylum for it.

"Take another drink," he orders, nudging my hands. "You look pale."

I listen. Drinking is easier than arguing, and I barely have the energy for either as it is.

"You were right," I tell him, wiping my mouth with the back of my hand. "Fresh air is helping. I can breathe out here."

Even the mention of breathing makes my chest seize up. The fear is wound so deeply inside of me that I'm not sure I'll ever disentangle it.

"Security is everywhere," he assures me. "You're safe, inside or out."

He's already explained it twice, but I still want to hear what happened again.

"Everyone from the party was okay?"

"Shaken up, but alive," he confirms. "Arber was here looking for me, no one else. I got you out of the room so fast that Arber never even saw us."

"I'm not surprised. I mean, I didn't even have time to react before you were dragging me out of the room." I can still feel his arm around my back. The pounding of his heart against my rib cage.

He shrugs. "Yeah, well, it was a Bratva rehearsal dinner. A gun had to come out at some point."

I frown. "You don't mean that, do you? This isn't… Stuff like this doesn't always happen, does it?"

His warm hand wraps around my knee and squeezes. "No. It's been a long time since anyone dared to challenge me at my own home."

"Rodion tried, too." Then an idea hits me. I turn to Timofey. "Do you think Rodion—"

"No." He drags a hand through his hair, pushing the silky strands into wild disarray on top of his head. "Rodion showed up tonight just before the attack, but it doesn't make any sense. What would be the point of getting me alone and then sending men in to attack the entire party?"

"If Rodion was involved, why not attack us when we were in your office?" I say, thinking out loud.

"Exactly." He nods and then curses under his breath. "I shouldn't have taken you to that meeting. I should have left you—"

"Alone in the ballroom where gunmen entered three minutes later?" I arch a brow, challenging him. "If you hadn't been there with me, I'd be dead, Timofey."

His jaw clenches. "Don't say that."

"It's true."

"No. No, it's—" His knuckles go white on my knee and he lets go quickly before he crushes my leg. "You would have gotten out. I'll make sure you know the codes to the safe rooms so if anything like this happens again, you can get Benjamin and yourself to safety."

I'm in the middle of a garden with no walls in sight, but I feel the air around me condense and press from all sides. Quickly, I take a sip of water to try and clear my airway.

Timofey sees it and presses a hand to my back. "It's okay, Piper. You're safe now. The gunmen are dead and Arber won't try to attack again so soon."

"It's not that. I don't know if I can go in that room again," I admit. Embarrassment warms my cheeks, and I stare down at my feet. "You were fighting with intruders and protecting your house, and here I am, scared of a stupid closet. I know it's ridiculous, but—"

"It's not."

"Don't lie," I say with a humorless laugh. "It's embarrassing. I should be beyond horrified that I was almost shot, but all I can think about is how it felt when you closed the door to that safe room. It was like being buried alive. I thought I was going to…" My voice trails off, my throat too tight with emotion to squeeze the words out.

"What happened?"

I shake my head. "Nothing. Benjamin and I just sat there until you came back. There wasn't room to do anything else."

"Not tonight," he says gently. "What happened that made you so afraid of small spaces?"

"It's just a fear. Some people are born with them. I don't know."

The lie is clumsy and my execution is even worse. Tears burn in my eyes, and I blink them back.

He slides closer, his knee brushing against mine. "When I opened that door, your eyes were glazed over, Piper. You didn't know where you were. You were somewhere else. You were fucking terrified."

The truth expands inside of me, steam searching for a release valve. I try to hold it all in, but when Timofey uses his knuckle to catch a tear falling down my cheek, I break.

"It was my mom," I gasp. "She—she put me in the trunk sometimes. When she couldn't leave me at home."

His face creases in horror. As it should. "She locked you in a trunk?"

His voice is a threat. If she wasn't already dead, I'm positive Timofey would hunt her down.

"She was deep in her addiction," I explain. "Her life was about getting high and figuring out how to get high. I wasn't an asset to either of those goals."

"You were a child. You didn't need to be a goddamn *asset*."

I snort tearily. "If only you'd been around to explain that to my mom. She left me at home a lot, but occasionally, someone would report her to Child Protective Services for abandoning me. When she got spooked, she'd take me with her."

He huffs out an angry laugh. "Locking you in a trunk isn't better than leaving you home alone."

I take a shaky breath. "That's because you don't know the other option."

Timofey watches me, waiting for my explanation. But I don't feel pressured. I can tell there is no rush. He's here with me as long as it takes. The ease I feel brings the truth rising to the surface.

"I guess between locking me in the trunk or letting me watch her get paid to have sex with random men, locking me in the trunk won out."

It's not my shame to carry; I know that. Still, I keep my eyes on the ground. I dig the pointed ends of my high heels into the dirt.

Then Timofey wraps an arm around my back.

I look over, and his expression is stony. "You undersold your parents, Piper. 'Shitty' isn't a strong enough descriptor."

I lean my head into the crook of his arm as more disgusting truth dribbles out of me like snot. "Occasionally, the man she hooked up with paid her in drugs. She'd get high and forget about me. So I'd be in there for a while."

His arm tightens around me. "I wouldn't have left you in that safe room if I knew."

"You did the right thing, Timofey. We were safe in there. Benjamin is safe." I glance over my shoulder at the house as if I can somehow see through the walls and see him sleeping soundly in his crib. "I'd go in there again if it meant keeping him safe."

I'd do it for you, too, I almost say. But that truth stays buried down deep.

"I hope it won't come to that, but I don't know. We both have to be prepared for anything."

"You really think he'll try again?" I ask.

Timofey nods. "If he doesn't, someone else will."

There's a solemn resignation in his voice. This is the life Timofey leads, and he has accepted it.

As for me? I'm not there yet.

Noelle's warnings ring in my ears. She told me to leave tonight. If I'd listened… well, I don't know what would have happened. Maybe Timofey would have been spotted by Arber and killed on sight. Or maybe he would have taken Arber out and ended all of this.

It's impossible to know.

The only thing I know for sure is that having Timofey in my life makes things infinitely more complicated.

91

TIMOFEY

"Arber is dead," Pavel says. His voice crackles, the cell signal failing to reach him in whatever warehouse or cement dungeon he's in, but his message is clear.

I duck out of the living room into the hallway. The penthouse is significantly smaller than the mansion, so getting out of earshot of Piper isn't possible. Still, the less she knows, the better.

"Confirmed?" I ask.

"What's the survival rate of your head being separated from your body? It's gotta be zero percent, right?"

I chuckle darkly. "I suppose that counts for confirmation."

"Rodion probably would have shredded him." He makes the crack before he remembers Rodion isn't on good terms with the Bratva at the moment. He clears his throat. "Anyway, I'm absolutely positive he's dead. What should we do with him now?"

"Wrap him up. Let's send Kreshnik a little gift."

It's as good as a formal declaration of war. Then again, Arber declared the same thing when he walked into my house with a gun. He signed his own death warrant.

There's a pause before Pavel laughs. "Fuck. That's brutal."

"Brutality for brutality. I think it's a fair trade."

"Do you want to make the delivery personally, or—"

"You do it," I interrupt. "I trust you to handle things."

Usually, I'd be all over this. If the Albanians are going to make a move on me, I want to head the charge to retaliate. But usually, I'm the only person I have to worry about.

Now, there's Benjamin and Piper. I don't want to leave them alone. Not after everything they've been through tonight.

After helping Piper calm down from being locked in the safe room, I then had to convince her to get into a car and drive across town with me. Having Benjamin in the backseat with her helped, but she's still on edge. I can't leave her alone.

"Okay," Pavel says excitedly. "I can absolutely handle things."

"Message me when it's done."

"You got it, Don. I'll take care of everything."

I shove the phone in my pocket and flex my hands. I physically itch to get into the mix. It's the same feeling I had as I guided Piper through the house to the safe room. I knew I was making the right choice. Getting her as far away from the gunfire as possible and protecting Benjamin was the only thing that mattered.

Still, that didn't quiet the instinctual part of me that wanted to turn around and wring Arber's neck. I wanted to be the one to watch the life drain out of him.

But watching him die can't compete with making sure Piper and Benjamin live.

When I walk back into the sitting room, Piper is peering over the side of Benjamin's travel crib, watching him sleep. I can hear the soft lilt of whatever lullaby she's singing to him.

"I'm glad at least one of us can sleep," I say, announcing myself.

Piper stands up and moves closer to my side of the room. She drops down into the deep, L-shaped sofa. "Not me. I think my body is running on pure adrenaline right now. He didn't even need me to sing to him, but I couldn't sit still."

The thought of calling Pavel back and telling him that, actually, I'm going to deliver Arber's head to his father's doorstep rises up in me. "I'm right there with you."

"Who was that on the phone?" As soon as she asks, she shakes her head. "Sorry. That's your business. I don't need to know. I just feel like I'm in a bubble, you know? Something crazy happened to me and now, no one is talking about it. I checked the news, and you were right. Not a peep."

She's talking faster than I can keep up, but I understand enough.

"The man responsible for what happened tonight is dead," I tell her.

Her mouth falls open. "You…you killed him?"

"Personally? No. I've been with you all night."

She shakes her head in embarrassment. "Right. Obviously."

"But I ordered him to be killed," I continue, answering the question she was really asking. "It had to be done. He was a threat to the Bratva. And to you and Benjamin."

"Because we're dating." It's a statement, not a question. Though, when she looks up at me, I see a world of questions in her eyes.

"It's one of the perks of your job. You get to be under lock and key all the time so my enemies can't get to you. I could have sworn I mentioned that."

She laughs weakly. "You might have left that bit out of the initial pitch."

"It's usually what I lead with. Around-the-clock security, my massive fortune, and my massive—"

"Ew." She tosses a throw pillow at me, biting back a laugh. "Don't finish that sentence."

I slide the pillow behind my head and relax back against the arm of the couch. Piper stretches her legs out close enough to graze me with her toes.

It feels like we're a normal couple. Just two people relaxing during a night in, cuddled up on the sofa. I never imagined myself as that type, but I'll take Piper pressed against me in whatever form it comes.

"I was going to say my massive heart," I joke.

"Sure you were."

She smiles at me, but as the silence stretches, the moment of good humor passes. I can feel the events of the night gathering over us like a dark cloud. I'm just not sure how to dispel it.

"We're safest here at the penthouse," I announce suddenly. "The mansion is being repaired and the security system is being upgraded. But the penthouse has always been my most lowkey home."

"Only you could say a five thousand square foot luxury penthouse is 'lowkey.'"

"I've only told a handful of people I even own it. Even fewer have been here."

She arches her brows. "Wow. I guess I should feel flattered."

"I'd rather you feel safe."

She runs her green eyes over my face and then looks down at her lap, picking idly at the hem of her oversized sweatshirt with nervous fingers. "I'm starting to wonder whether anyone can be safe in your world. Gunmen showed up at a wedding rehearsal tonight. Rodion tried to kill you last week. Emily was murdered."

I know the dangers that come with my life. Hearing Piper read the receipts still doesn't feel great.

"There's always a risk of violence in life. You were attacked in an alley the night we met."

"Yeah, but you were there to save me," she says, nudging my thigh with her foot. "I guess that means I'm safe as long as you're around."

"That wasn't true for Emily," I mutter.

As soon as the words are out of my mouth, I want to reel them back in. But it's too late. Piper leans forward, her face creased in worry. "What happened to Emily wasn't your fault."

I don't point out that this opinion is a far cry from the last time we were in the penthouse together and she accused me of murdering her myself.

"No, maybe not," I agree. "But the only reason Emily was part of my world at all is because I hired her."

"To get her off the street."

"Off the street and into the underworld. That's out of the frying pan and into the fire. Most people will tell you which one is better." I shake my head. "She met Rodion the first month she worked for me. Just like you, she showed up at my house and there he was."

Piper wrinkles her nose. "Did he show her the tattoo on his forearm? Maybe she would have felt the way I do about him if he led with the number of people he'd killed."

"The tattoo was smaller back then. Even if he had shown it to her, Emily might have liked that." Piper looks horrified, and I feel the need to defend who Emily was. "You have to understand, she'd been on her own for most of her life. Rodion is someone who... well, if you're his friend, he'll take care of you. I think Emily wanted that from someone."

"It doesn't sound like he took care of her, though. Tonight, he made it sound like he was a terrible boyfriend. He threatened her."

"A lot of people put up with less than they deserve. It's not like she had any good male role models to look up to."

"She had you," Piper says quickly.

I snort. "Are you sure you didn't hit your head in that safe room or something? It almost seems like you just said I was a good man."

"Well, you took care of Emily when she needed you to." She shrugs. "You dressed in her clothes and fought off a pervy landlord. You gave her a job and got her off of the street. She even left you her son to take care of. Clearly, she trusted you."

"Fuck knows why," I murmur beneath my breath.

"Do you know why?" Piper asks softly. "It's a serious question. You must have some idea why she trusted you. Especially after you said the two of you had a falling out. Why would she leave you her son if the two of you weren't even talking?"

"It's… complicated."

She rests her cheek against the back of the couch and curls her legs against mine. "I have time for a story."

She may have the time, but I'm not sure I have the desire to tell it.

I sigh. "The short version is that I never thought Rodion was good enough for Emily. I wanted the two of them to break up, but I didn't want to order them apart. Emily was stubborn. If I'd forced her to end things with Rodion, she never would have listened. Then things between them got bad and—"

"You threatened to kill him," Piper finishes. "Sorry, but that's what you told Rodion tonight. You were going to protect Emily from him."

I run a hand through my hair. "I was going to try. Then Emily pulled away from me. We would go weeks at a time or longer with no contact. I could have tracked her down, but I didn't want to force her to talk to me if she didn't want to. Not after I'd introduced her to Rodion and then pushed her away by trying to break them up. In a lot of ways, it made sense that she wouldn't want to see me."

Piper shakes her head. "No. It doesn't make sense. She was just in a toxic relationship. She probably couldn't see her way out and it was easier to blame you than it was to break through her own denial."

"Well, she managed to break through it a little. Because right before she died, she showed up at my house with Benjamin."

Piper's green eyes widen in shock. "You—but wait, you said she left the baby on your doorstep. I assumed she did it because she knew she would be killed. Or maybe someone else brought him to you. But… you spoke to her that night?"

"At length," I nod. "Emily showed up and begged me to take care of Benjamin and raise him as my own."

"Why?" she asks, fully engrossed in the story.

I haven't told anyone these details, but if I'm going to rope Piper into this life the same way I did Emily, she deserves to know everything.

"Honestly, she didn't have very many options. I was the best choice out of a lineup of bad, worse, and terrifying."

"Rodion was one of those?" Piper guesses.

I nod. "She knew she was pregnant when she and Rodion broke up, but she kept it from him. She didn't trust him to be a good father."

"But Rodion said the two of them were going to get back together once he came back from Russia." Her eyes scroll back and forth like she's piecing together the timeline in her head. She gasps. "The day she came to you with Benjamin is the same day Rodion was coming back into town! It's the day she was murdered."

"It was."

"So did she know she was going to be murdered?"

"I've asked myself that a million times. But I don't think she did."

Piper blows out a breath. "So she was planning to leave Benjamin with you and then go get back together with Rodion? And then what? Just keep Benjamin a secret?"

I shrug. "That's what she seemed to think."

"I've seen a lot of toxic relationships in my day, but that would take the cake."

"Emily told me she didn't think a woman who had never had actual parents and a hitman would make good parents."

It was a fair point. She and I knew better than most what bad parents could do to a kid's life. But it's not as if I was a major upgrade.

"And you think I would make a good parent?" I asked Emily at the time. "I'm the don of a fucking Bratva, Em. I've killed people, too."

She grabbed my hand and looked deep in my eyes. "But you're a good man, Timofey. Under everything—your title, the things you've done—you are a good man."

"If you can't say the same thing about Rodion, you shouldn't be with him," I told her.

She gave me a sad smile. "You say that like I have another option."

I blink, and the memory dissipates like smoke. Piper is watching me, and I have the feeling she was reading my thoughts.

"She was right to choose you over Rodion," Piper says softly.

"Are you sure? You know the rest of the story. It was written up in my case file."

She frowns, thinking. I see the moment her memory picks up the plot. "You took Benjamin to the hospital. You were going to abandon him there."

"Rodion probably wouldn't have done that," I say bitterly. "But I thought Emily was insane. She refused to take Benjamin with her, and what the fuck do I know about babies? I'd never even held one before that night. So I dropped him off and figured he'd end up where he was supposed to. And then…"

Piper presses her hand to my thigh. Her fingers tense. "She died."

"I went back to the hospital as soon as I heard she was gone. I was out of my mind with… everything. Every emotion imaginable."

"You'd just lost one of your oldest friends," Piper says. "It makes sense."

"The doctor wouldn't give Benjamin back to me, and I fucking decked him. I was going to die before I left that hospital without him. It was—" I take a deep breath. Vulnerability isn't one of my strengths. I have to force my way through it. "It was the last way I could take care of Emily. Raising Benjamin was the last thing I would ever be able to do for her, aside from catching her killer. And I would rather have died than fail her again."

I cast my eyes down for a few seconds. But when I finally look up, Piper is wiping tears away. "Oh, Timofey... You didn't fail Emily. You did everything you could for her. Absolutely everything. You have to see that."

"It wasn't enough."

She shifts to her knees and crawls over me, settling on my lap. Her hands on my face are gentle. "You are enough, Timofey. You're—You're more than enough. But even you can't save someone who doesn't want to be saved."

I try to hold her words lightly in my hands. Maybe if I'm gentle enough, they won't shatter under the weight of my guilt.

Piper leans forward and presses her lips to my cheek. She touches her nose to mine and looks deep into my eyes. "You're a good man, Timofey. No matter what has happened, I know you're a good man capable of great things."

Emily's words all those months ago echo beneath Piper's. Piper is giving me a gift. In the same way Emily gave me Benjamin, Piper is giving me the gift of a new beginning. All I have to do is let go of the past and accept it.

I'm not sure it's possible, but when she's touching me like this, I desperately want to try.

I grab her face and kiss her properly. I kiss her until my head is clear and my body is on fire.

The kiss shifts quickly from tender to scorching. Piper is wearing a tiny pair of pajama shorts and an oversized sweatshirt that I make quick work of ripping off of her and tossing to the floor.

"There are no security cameras in here, right?" she pants, rolling her hips over me as I slide my hands up the curve of her waist.

"No. But I almost wish there were." I bite the strap of her bra and pull it down her arm. Her breast pops free, and I circle her nipple with my tongue. "I'd watch this back."

She throws her head back, a moan parting her lips. "We'll just have to reenact it. Frequently."

She reaches around and unclasps her bra as I slide my hand between her legs. She's already wet, and my fingers glide into her with no resistance.

Piper works herself onto my hand in slow strokes at first that quickly grow more frantic. She rocks and arches into me until she's panting against my neck, begging for relief.

I circle my thumb over her clit, and it's like an explosion goes off inside of her.

She arches above me, her face twisted in exquisite torture. "T-Timofey…"

The sound of my name on her lips has me wild for her. She's still pulsing around my fingers when I wrap an arm around her waist and flip us both over. She yelps, but the sound melds into a moan. I stroke my fingers in and out of her, coaxing her down from her high.

"Holy…" She covers her face with her hands, smothering a delirious giggle. "How is it this good every time?"

I pull her hands away and kiss her jawline and cheekbones. A humming sound vibrates through her chest, almost like a purr. "You've been setting your bar too low, Piper."

"Is that right?"

She lifts her hips as I slide her panties down. "Yes. You deserve so much more."

Her fingers work over my abs and up my chest before she tugs my shirt over my head and tosses it to the floor with the rest of our clothes.

"What do I deserve?"

She's laid out beneath me, her auburn hair a halo around her head. She's an angel. A fucking angel.

"You deserve everything," I growl.

I slide into her all at once, and then we are moving together. Piper grips my shoulder blades, and I drag her hips against me again and again.

It's not especially graceful, but there's an undercurrent of desperation. It's a kind of passion I've never experienced before. The need I feel goes beyond the fiery knot in my stomach.

I need this woman to never stop looking at me the way she is right now. Like there is no one on the planet she'd rather be with. Like there isn't a single other person she'd rather be holding.

I need to pour myself into her and have some quiet, broken part of myself filled in return.

"Timofey," Piper breathes, repeating my name like a prayer. "Timofey, I'm coming again. I can't—I have to—I—"

I capture her words with my lips and fall with her.

92

PIPER

When I open my eyes, there's only more darkness.

I blink a few times. When the darkness doesn't fade, I start to panic. "Timofey," I breathe, reaching across the bed for him.

My hand lands on a familiar, muscular thigh.

"Relax. It's a blindfold," he says. I hear the amusement in his voice, which is the only reason I don't start freaking out.

"You know it is extremely not socially acceptable to wake people up with blindfolds, right?"

"What society does and does not accept is the least of my worries, Piper."

He is not wrong there. Being the leader of a Bratva is probably pretty high on the list of things polite society would hold against him.

Briefly, I wonder what it says about me that I'm thrilled he's in bed next to me. Or what it says about me that we did *a lot* more than sleep in this bed last night.

But before I can fall into that shame spiral, I shove it away. "I know letting someone see you in a less than perfect state might be hard for you, but your bed head can't be this bad," I tease. "Take this blindfold off and we'll comb out your tangles together."

I can practically hear him roll his eyes. "Keep making jokes and I'm not going to show you the surprise."

I perk up. "Surprise? What kind of surprise? Is it for me?"

"Come with me and you'll find out."

He takes my hand and coaxes me out of bed. I follow along reluctantly, bumbling against him as we leave the room like a newborn fawn with legs that don't work yet.

I sigh. "I'd ask you where we're going, but on second thought, I think I'll save my breath. I know you well enough to know you aren't going to answer my questions until you're good and ready."

"Took you long enough to catch on."

We step onto the elevator together and it's only as the doors are closing that I panic and lunge for the "doors open" button.

Timofey snatches me around the waist, pulling me back. "What in the hell are you doing?"

"Benjamin!" I gasp. "I can't believe I—Who is watching him? Where is he?"

Timofey might have literally fucked the sense out of me last night. How on earth could I forget we have a baby upstairs who needs our attention?

"Oh, wow. You're right," Timofey says calmly. "I completely forgot about him. I'm sure he'll be fine up there, though. Right? He's sleeping, so—"

I swat around blindly until I make contact with his muscular torso, then I thwack him hard a few times as I screech, "Are you insane? He is a baby! He can't be left alone. Especially after last night. Someone needs to be there in case he wakes up or is hungry or…or…or if there is a fire…" My voice trails off and then I slap him again. "You jerk! You're messing with me! I thought you were serious."

He chuckles just as the elevator stops. "Akim is watching Benjamin. He woke up an hour ago, but I let you sleep in."

As my heart returns to its normal rhythm, I can once again be excited about the surprise. "Stay still," he orders. He undoes the clasp of the blindfold and takes it off of me. We step out into…

An entirely empty parking garage.

I frown as I look around. "Where are all of the other cars? Isn't this the garage for the entire building?"

He shakes his head. "Not at present. It's safer this way."

Right. Because there could still be gunmen coming after us. So much for a return to my resting heart rate.

"You cleared out a level of a parking garage for me? But when did you—" I stop, putting the pieces together. "Wow. This is a *surprise* surprise. You planned this out."

"It's not a *plan*." He says it like a dirty word. "It's just something I arranged."

I nod. "Yeah. A plan. You cleared out this floor of the garage; you asked Akim to come over and watch Benjamin. That's a plan in my book."

"It's not that big of a deal. Lower your expectations."

"Considering I expect absolutely nothing from you, that will be pretty hard to do."

His jaw clenches, a line forming between his eyes. He looks…*hurt*. That's the only real word for it.

"I didn't mean I expect nothing from you. I meant I don't expect anything from you." I sigh. "Ugh. That sounded like the same thing. I just mean, you didn't have to do anything for me. You've already done more than enough."

His blue eyes peer over at me, and I instantly go from worrying I've offended him to worrying that I've said something far too vulnerable.

Thankfully, he doesn't dwell.

Timofey grabs my shoulders and steers me down the center of the garage towards one of the tile-wrapped cement pillars.

I'm about to ask if he carved our names into the concrete like it was a tree, when we turn the corner of the pillar—and I lose the ability to speak.

Parked behind the pillar is a champagne-colored motorcycle with shimmery handles and the prettiest caramel leather seat I've ever seen in my life. Everything about it is chic and well-designed. I have no idea how much motorcycles cost, but there is no way this one was sitting in a lot somewhere. It was specifically designed this way.

But for who? That is the question.

"Well?" Timofey prods.

"Well, what?"

"Do I need to draw a map for you? This is the surprise."

Lower your expectations. That's what he said. So that is what I'm going to try to do.

"Someone is letting me borrow it?"

He screws up his face, confused and a little disappointed. "Someone is letting you *own* it."

"But I can't afford that." Actually, that isn't entirely true now that I'm Benjamin's nanny. Timofey has come through in a real way in that department. He's paying me five times what I ever could have made as a social worker.

He pulls his hand through his hair, sending the dark strands twisting up in every direction. The early morning light shimmers through the back of the parking garage, creating a golden halo around his head.

Timofey moves in front of me and places his hands gently on my shoulders. "This," he says, pointing aggressively up and down the length of the motorcycle, "is for you. It is a gift. You do not need to pay for it. You just need to accept it."

I blink at him. "This isn't funny."

"That's because it's a gift, not a joke."

The information starts to click into place. I peek around him at the bike and then back up to him, my brow creased. "That is for me? Like… forever?"

"Yes, it's yours, Piper. Forever." He gives me a small smile. "Do you like it?"

I open my mouth to respond…and burst into tears.

93

PIPER

It's not as if I've never been given a nice gift before.

I got a jewelry box from Gram when I was eight that I still keep old love letters and jewelry in.

Ashley and Noelle pitched in and bought me tickets to a Broadway show a few years ago. They were nosebleeds and the play was so bad they canceled it after a month, but it was still fun.

And my father knew how to absolutely love-bomb me. After he manipulated me into giving him money or screamed at me for being "useless" and "a disappointment," he would inevitably show up with flowers and gifts.

Once, he took me out for dinner. I found out later he paid for it with his new boss's credit card. When his boss disputed the seventy-five dollar charge and fired him, Dad showed up at my door.

"It's your fault I got fired," he said. "You guilted me into paying for your food. You made me feel pathetic for not being able to afford it, even though the only reason I can't afford it is because your mother got pregnant with you."

Every gift would finally show up after I was forced into helping him again and again and again. Just when I'd consider cutting ties and setting boundaries, there he'd come with a smile and a nice gesture. Then I'd live to regret ever accepting them, which usually didn't take very long.

But this…

"I can't accept this," I say for the fifth time, my shoulders still shaking. "It's too much."

"I'll show you my bank account if you think this is too much. It's nothing, Piper."

On anyone else's lips, that line would make me roll my eyes. Who could call a gift like this "nothing"? But Timofey genuinely means it. To him, this gift is a drop in the bucket. God knows he has more than enough money for a fleet of motorcycles.

The thing is, the money isn't the problem for me.

It's the time he put into it. The effort.

Whether he admits it or not, he had a plan. A plan that went into place well before we had sex last night.

"But you cleared out the parking garage. Akim is upstairs." I dab at my eyes, grateful I didn't bother putting on any mascara before we left. It would be pouring down my cheeks in thick black streaks. "You went to this trouble for me, and I… I…"

"You what?" Timofey grabs my face, his thumbs brushing the tears from my cheeks. "If your answer is anything other than 'I love and accept it,' then shut up."

"I love it. So much. It's the most beautiful bike I've ever seen." The champagne paint sparkles in the sunlight, and I can already imagine the wind through my hair. The freedom. I look back to him and shake my head. "But I can't accept it. I don't know how."

He narrows his eyes, searching my face for an answer that I'm not even sure I can give. "Explain."

"No one has ever given me something like this without wanting something in return." I'm finding the answer as I go, stumbling through the truth in hopes we'll end up at some explanation for why I'm weeping instead of doing wheelies in this parking garage. "I'm usually the one giving people what they need. My dad, Gram, Ashley, even Noelle. I just… I don't know how to accept something this big."

Timofey scowls, his hands curling around my neck and tangling in my hair. "Those leeches have sucked the life out of you, Piper. You give everything you have to everyone—your family, your friends, the kids you work with. But there has to be something left for you at the end of the day."

The words are simple, but they bring a fresh wave of tears.

"Stop crying," he orders, a hopeless kind of laugh laced in his words.

"Stop saying that," I counter. "You're making it worse."

My dad typically took me crying as a sign of success. Once I was in tears, he had what he wanted. The fact Timofey wants me to stop only makes me like him more.

Maybe he's right. Maybe I should figure out how to pull back on all the assistance I offer the people in my life.

Timofey throws up his hands. "You are a fucking mystery, woman. What are you thinking?"

"I'm thinking that if I grew up with a parent who made sure someone was around to watch me when they left the house," I say, gesturing up to where Benjamin is happily playing with Akim many floors above our heads, "or a parent who gave me even one thoughtful gift in my entire life that I didn't have to work tooth and nail to earn... that maybe things would have turned out differently for me."

"Are you saying I'm like the father you never had?"

I pretend to gag and he laughs.

"No! God no. Absolutely not. But if I had even one person in my life who loved me the way—" *The way you do.* "The way you love Benjamin," I say instead. "Or took care of me the way you have... Well, things could have been different."

Timofey's blue eyes peer into my soul, and I'm positive he can see the vulnerable words tucked away there. The ones I'm trying to save for myself, because I'm afraid that they'll shatter like dropped porcelain if I give them to him.

"Instead," I continue, "here I am, crying in the face of a lovely gift because I have no experience receiving something like this. I'm overwhelmed."

"In a good way," Timofey says, confirming what he already knows.

I wipe at my eyes again and nod. "In a very good way."

He smiles in satisfaction. "Okay. Good. Now, if I explain myself, will you promise not to burst into tears again?"

"I can't make any guarantees."

He guides me over to the bike again and places my hand on the handlebars. The grip is supple against my palms. The speedometer and other gauges are ringed in rose gold.

"I wanted to get you a pretty motorcycle because it was enjoyable for me to design it. And why the fuck should I have all this money if I'm not going to spend it?" he says. "But more than that, I wanted you to have this motorcycle for your own safety."

"Most people would say motorcycles are less safe."

He nods. "For most people, yeah. But you aren't most people. I can't have you depending on your pedal bike to outrun enemies."

The excitement wanes in the face of his scary rationale. "Do you think I'm going to be running from enemies?"

"I hope not," he says sincerely. "But with your claustrophobia, I need to know you have a way to escape that is fast and won't send you spiraling into an attack."

My face flushes. I look down at my sneakers and nod. "It's embarrassing that even in an emergency, I might not be able to overcome my fear."

Timofey grips my chin and forces my face up to his. "It's not embarrassing, Piper. Nothing about you overcoming your childhood and becoming a hardworking, decent person is embarrassing. It would be surprising if you didn't have some baggage from all the shit you've been through."

I meet his eyes and swallow hard. "That's a Weeping Warning, for sure."

He nods and drops his hand. "I didn't get this for you because you're weak; I got this for you because I want you to be free. Whether I'm there with you or not."

His final words hang in the air between us, and I want to ask what they mean.

Like, if he *temporarily* isn't there with me? Or if he is no longer part of my life at all?

Only a couple weeks ago, I wished for Timofey Viktorov to be nothing more than a bad dream. I wanted to forget he ever existed and move on with my life. But now... I can't imagine moving forward without him.

I love him.

The truth of it sits in my stomach like a bowling ball. I swallow down a fresh wave of tears, willing myself not to dissolve into hysterics again.

"Okay, here we go." Timofey grabs my waist and hoists me up onto the bike in one seamless movement. It's like I weigh no more than a carton of eggs to him. "Time to make use of this empty parking garage while I still have it for the next hour."

"You rented it out?"

His hands are still on my hips when he nods. "I wanted you to get some practice in where it would be safe."

I place my hands over his, slowly dragging my fingers up the twining muscles of his arms. "Thank you, Timofey."

He squeezes my waist and draws in closer, dipping his head. "Actions speak louder than words, Piper Quinn."

I smile and stretch up to press my lips to his. It's a quick kiss, but it gets a very different kind of engine rumbling inside of me.

Maybe this thing with Timofey does have a deadline. It might even be sooner rather than later.

But when he holds me like this, I could care less.

He's worth every piece of my shattered heart.

94

PIPER

It's the fifth time I've called my dad in as many days. This time, he finally picks up the phone.

"What do you want?" he barks.

His voice still sounds weak. I have no clue if he's still in the hospital or not. I haven't been to visit him since the night Timofey and I were there with Benjamin. If I have it my way, I never will again.

I brace myself for the begging and pleading he'll do when I tell him I'm cutting him off. It's not going to be pretty, but it's necessary. Finally, I'm going to do what Timofey has been encouraging me to do from the beginning: I'm going to look out for myself.

"I want to talk," I tell him. "It will only take a minute."

"I'm not even supposed to give you a second."

I frown. "Is the hospital limiting your calls or something?"

"What?" he barks. "No. They can't—no, it's not the hospital. You know damn fucking well who I'm talking about."

I'm used to my dad's crude language and surly attitude, but I'm not accustomed to him making zero sense. Does the hospital have him on medication that is making him delirious? I want to ask, but I can't imagine I'd get a straight answer out of him, anyway.

"I don't, actually. But it doesn't matter, Dad. Because I'm calling to tell you I'm done—"

"Your boyfriend came to see me. He made it clear that we weren't supposed to be talking anymore."

"My boyfriend? I don't have a boyfriend." Even when I did, I never introduced them to Dad. That would have been a surefire way to end a relationship. Though, in most cases, that would have been to my benefit. I haven't had many men in my life worth keeping around.

Until now.

He snorts and the effort sends him into a flurry of hacking and coughing.

"Don't pretend you aren't giving it up to that man you brought to my fucking deathbed. You take after your mother that way." He mutters something along the lines of *just another no-good whore spreading it* before I cut him off.

"Are you talking about Timofey?"

"Hell if I know his name! There wasn't a lot of time for chitchat. He marched in here after the two of you left and told me to leave you alone."

The last two weeks have been a blur. Getting Benjamin to the hospital, surgeries, arranging nurses to care for him at home, the shooting, the motorcycle. It's been one thing to the next, and the days have all run together.

But I remember that night.

Timofey stood in the elevator and told me he wanted to give me everything.

Then he took the elevator back upstairs.

When he returned, I was so anxious to tell him I was coming with him to the penthouse that I didn't even consider where he'd been. I didn't care.

"He just walked into your room and told you to stay away from me? And you listened?"

There's hesitation on his end. I can tell, because Dad has never been shy about spouting off the first vile thought that crosses his mind. If he's pausing now, it's for a good reason.

"Dad!" I snap. "Tell me what happened. Now."

"Well, he threatened me within an inch of my life, that's what happened! He walked into my room and scared your poor, sick dad nearly to death, kiddo."

I press my hand to my face and squeeze my eyes. *Kiddo.* He's putting on his "poor, pitiful me" act. He's trying to guilt me into forgiving him for whatever is coming next.

"Dad," I say more gently. If he thinks I'm already angry, he'll clam up. I have to ease it out of him. "What did he say?"

He sniffles like he might actually have a heart soft enough to cry. "He told me he'd kill me unless I accepted his deal. He didn't give me no damn choice."

"What was the deal?"

"I was in the hospital bed. I was weak," he says. "He came in here and there were no nurses—not that they could have stopped him. He's a big man."

I don't respond. Waiting.

Finally, he sighs. "He told me if I stayed away, some money would find its way into my account. I don't know how he got into my bank, but the next day, I opened the account and there it—"

"How much?" I grit the words out between clenched teeth.

It doesn't matter how much. I can imagine my father jumping at the chance to trade me in for a few hundred. And Timofey is good for a lot more than that. He gave me a motorcycle worth God knows how much and called it "nothing."

How much does Timofey think I'm worth? *Hopefully more than nothing.*

"Fifty thousand," he admits at last. "But we can still talk in secret. I need you, Piper. You're all I have left. Fifty thousand doesn't get a man far in this day and age. I need—"

I hang up before he can finish.

I don't care what he needs. The only thing that matters now is what I need.

Timofey was right. No one is going to take care of me if I don't take care of myself.

Not even him.

95

PIPER

I'm in the living room with Benjamin when Timofey gets back to the penthouse.

"Piper!" he calls.

There's a familiarity to the way he says my name. There's an expectation. He knew I'd be here waiting for him. A few hours ago, that would have meant everything to me.

Now, there's a dark undertone.

Of course he expects me to be here—he arranged it that way. He's severed my lifelines one by one until there's only one person left I can rely on.

Him.

I snuggle Benjamin to my chest and move to the hallway. Timofey's expression opens up when he sees me. He doesn't smile, but there's a lightness in his blue eyes that wasn't there before. He looks… happy.

Fuck me, he looks so fucking happy.

"The upgrades on the mansion are done, so we can move back in whenever you're ready."

I press a finger to my lips and motion to Benjamin. "I'm going to put him to sleep."

He waves me on and kicks his boots off by the door.

Timofey in socks. It's so domestic I want to cry. Instead, I turn away and move into Benjamin's makeshift nursery.

He's already asleep, but I sing him song after song because working up the courage to walk out of this room and face Timofey is taking longer than I expected.

When I finally ease out of his room and close the door, Timofey is waiting in the hallway.

"I was about to come check on you," he teases. "I thought you might have fallen asleep in there with him."

I can't even fake a smile. I plow past him and walk towards the living room. We can't have this discussion in the hallway. I need more space. More room to breathe. Taking in oxygen is difficult enough as it is right now.

"Piper," he says. "Stop."

I spin around once I reach the sofa. "Is that an order? What do I get if I obey?"

He stares at me, refusing to respond until he understands what is going on here. I hate that I know that about him. I hate that I know so many small, intricate details about his personality, yet I still didn't see this coming.

"Fifty thousand dollars seems to be the going rate," I add.

Understanding dawns across his face. His jaw clenches, but he still doesn't say anything.

I grab a pillow and chuck it at his head. He deftly swats it out of the air. "Who told you?"

"Not you!" I cry out. "Were you just going to keep it a secret?"

"Your father hasn't talked to you in weeks and you didn't notice. Did you miss him? Were you sad the greedy bastard hadn't reached out?"

No and no. The last two weeks have been amazing. But I can't tell him that. Not now.

"That doesn't matter. What matters is that you lied to me."

He rolls his eyes. "I didn't lie."

"You kept information from me. You interfered in my life as if my opinion didn't matter."

"Because your opinion would be to move him into the mansion when he got sick," he snorts. "Or you'd want me to pay for the hospital bills he drank himself into."

Shame slices through me so sharply I'm surprised I don't fall to the floor in two distinct pieces. "So you paid off my dad because you thought I was only here to use you and your money to take care of him?"

He sighs. "You wouldn't be in my house if I thought—"

"First of all, you're the manipulative one here, not me," I interrupt, jabbing a finger in his direction. "Second, when you *forced* me to come work for you, you said you'd pay me enough to make all of my debts disappear. That includes my dad's medical bills. If I did ask you to pay those, it would be because you offered that up. Even then, I wouldn't ask you to do that!"

"I just meant that you don't know how to refuse him, Piper." He moves towards me cautiously. "If you wanted money to help your dad, I'd give it to you without a second thought. But the man has his hooks in you. He knows how to play you, and I didn't want to see you get used by him again."

I tip my head back and laugh. It's a cruel, bitter sound. "Because you want to be the only one using me, right?"

"I didn't hear you complaining when I gave you that motorcycle."

More than anything else, those words stop me dead.

Before he can even start to regret them, I reach into my pocket and throw the keys onto the coffee table. "Take it back then. I was under the impression it was a gift. *'All you have to do is accept it.'* But if there are conditions, I don't want it."

"You're being ridiculous," he growls. "Pick those keys up. The bike is yours."

"Only so long as I do what you want. As soon as I step out of line, you're gonna throw it back in my face."

Timofey drags his large hand down his face. "How the fuck am I the bad guy here? Your own father accepted fifty thousand dollars as adequate payment to never see you again."

"Because you offered it to him!"

"That doesn't—" He roars in frustration and throws his arms wide. "There isn't enough money in the world someone could offer me to make me give you up. If your dad had a single clue how amazing you are, he'd feel the same way."

My throat tightens with tears, but I swallow them down. *Not now. Not here.*

"You told me you were nothing like my father. You said you cared about me more than he did, but then you went behind my back and manipulated me."

"I helped you," he argues, his teeth clenched.

"Instead of letting me make my own choices, you forced me into one. That is the exact kind of thing my dad would do."

"I did it for your benefit."

I shake my head. "No, you did it for yourself. You interfered in my relationship with my father because he was inconvenient to you. It's why you've separated me from everyone in my life. You don't want me to have anyone to depend on except for you."

"I don't want everyone in your life depending on you," he snaps. "There is a difference. I'm trying to make sure that you can focus on taking care of yourself instead of everyone else."

"That's my decision to make!" I close my hands into tight fists and take a deep breath. "I am capable of making my own choices, Timofey. I don't need you to control my life. And I certainly don't need you to use me and my circumstances for your own benefit."

"What benefit?" he scoffs. "What do I get out of having you around?"

Of all the things I thought he would say, that one never crossed my mind.

I'm his nanny, for one thing. Not to mention the caseworker assigned to Benjamin's welfare. I'm one of the people responsible for deciding whether he can keep Benjamin or not. Those are two notable benefits right there.

But more than that, I thought that we had formed a real relationship under the guise of the fake one. I thought spending time with me, talking to me, being with me… I thought that might be a benefit to him. I thought it meant something.

Apparently, I thought wrong.

It feels like he ripped my weakly beating heart out of my chest and gave it one final stomp.

"Exactly," I say, fighting back tears. "You said you'd keep me around so long as I'm useful. I guess I'm not useful anymore. So I'd say it's time for me to go."

He squeezes his eyes closed for a second. When they open, there's a desperate tinge to the electric blue. "You have to see that I had your best interests at heart."

"What heart?" His eyes narrow, and I hold up a hand. "I'm— I'm sorry. This is actually my fault. I never should have expected anything different from you."

"Because the man who has saved your life more times than you can count is obviously awful. What a monster," he says, voice thick with sarcasm.

"I'd rather die on my own terms than live under yours."

He nods, his mouth working angrily from one side to the other. "Glad to know being with me is worse than death."

"And I'm glad to know you think I'm so incompetent that you have to make decisions for me. I guess we both learned something." I blow out a long breath and step away from him. "Benjamin will need a bottle when he wakes up. He's almost out of diapers, so you'll need to get more before tomorrow. He's—"

"He's my son," Timofey snarls. "I fucking know how to take care of him."

I'm not sure how I thought this conversation would go, but I never imagined feeling like this.

Hollow. Empty. Drained to the core.

I turn and walk towards the door. Each step is a struggle. I don't know where I'm going; I just know I can't stay here.

Before I reach the door, I hear the scrape of keys against a table. I turn just as Timofey tosses me the keys to my motorcycle.

"Consider it severance," he says, his voice cold and merciless.

I want to argue. I want to lie and tell him I don't need his charity and I can get around fine on my own. But I don't have my bike here, and I can't imagine stuffing myself and all of the emotions clouded around me into a taxi. So I shove the keys in my back pocket and hurry out of the penthouse before I can do something stupid.

Like throw myself in Timofey's arms and beg for him to fight for me.

PIPER

"Put that card away." Noelle swats at my wallet as I try to pull my debit card out. "The food is on me."

"I can afford a sandwich and some sweet potato fries, Noey."

Does everyone in my life think I'm utterly helpless?

"I know you can. But you don't have to." She widens her eyes, giving me her scary *I-mean-business* look.

I hold up my hands and step away from the café counter. I suppose, out of the two of us, I am the one who is jobless and homeless. Maybe it's fair that she pays for dinner.

Noelle chooses a booth at the very back of the hip sandwich shop. We're underneath a stuffed deer head mounted to the wall and next to a jukebox that only plays Cher songs.

It's a weird post-breakup dinner spot, but it's close to Noelle's work and I wanted to meet as soon as possible.

She slides a tray in front of me with my food piled on top. It's been spray painted gold and the napkins have "SILF" written on them.

I hold one up and point to the acronym. "What is that?"

"'Sandwich I'd Like to Fuck.'"

"Ew." I wrinkle my nose and crush the napkin in my hand. "Who would want to fuck a sandwich?"

Noelle gives me an apologetic shrug. "This used to be a Mexican place, but they closed down last year. A couple twenty-somethings own the place now. It's weird, but they have a good Italian sub."

I roll my eyes. "How can twenty-somethings afford to start a restaurant? I thought our generation was united in our struggle against capitalism."

"Piper." Noelle gently unfurls my fingers and forces me to drop the napkin. "Normally, you'd love this place. You'd laugh at the napkins and you'd be admiring all of the art. I mean, have you even seen the painting of the off-brand Miss Piggy posed like Rose from *Titanic*?"

I look across the aisle at the oil painting, but can't muster even a smile. "That is single-handedly ruining my already ruined childhood."

Noelle groans. "You've been a sad sack since you called me. You have got to tell me what is going on. Is everything okay? Is it Ashley? I've been busy, so I haven't heard much from her, but—"

"She's in Mexico."

Noelle's eyes widen. "She's *what*?"

"She and Gram are in Mexico." I sigh. "I bought them tickets and gave them some money to get started. I wanted them to be safe from Timofey."

How bizarre is it that I was sending my loved ones to other countries to escape Timofey, and now, I'm mourning the loss of him myself? The world is too weird sometimes.

I take a bite of my sandwich and chew while Noelle gawks at me, too shocked to speak.

"You're right," I tell her, dabbing oil off of my mouth. "The Italian sub is really good."

She holds up both hands. "Pause. Rewind. You sent Ashley and Gram to Mexico?"

"They're doing fine. This isn't about them."

She blinks. "Okay. But why did you—"

"I'm upset because Timofey paid my dad fifty thousand dollars for him to stay away from me."

Without breaking eye contact, Noelle grabs her drink and takes a long pull of her soda. When she's done, she blows out a breath. "Okay. This is a lot to process. But I think the most important thing is: you aren't with Timofey anymore?"

"I was never with him," I explain. "I worked for him. But it was complicated and—"

"Are you or are you not currently planning to have sex with him?"

My cheeks flush, and I shake my head. "No. I'm not currently planning to do anything with him. Sexual or otherwise."

Noelle pauses for a brief moment, letting the news sink in. Then she grins and claps her hands. "Thank fucking God, Piper. That's amazing!"

"Yeah, except for the part where I don't have a job and I'm homeless."

"You still have your job at CPS."

"Maybe. I've been sick most of the last two weeks. James has been calling my phone, but I've been texting back. I didn't know how to explain to him that I couldn't come into work because I was afraid someone might shoot up our office to take me out."

Noelle winces. "I told you to get Benjamin and leave before that party. I had a bad feeling about it."

"There wasn't an opportunity. It's not like I could have waltzed through the front doors without Timofey noticing."

"Do you think you could get to Benjamin now?" Noelle muses. "Clearly, Timofey isn't watching you anymore. If he let you leave, it must mean he doesn't care about keeping you under surveillance."

The reminder that Timofey doesn't care about me doesn't feel as positive as Noelle is making it sound. I brush off the hurt that settles over me like a heavy blanket and pick at my sandwich.

"I went into this wanting to protect Benjamin, but I don't know if I can sacrifice my own life—the lives of the people I care about—to get him away from Timofey," I admit. "It's so much riskier than I originally thought."

Plus, in a lot of ways, Timofey has proven himself to be a good father. Even if he has no idea how to be someone's partner, I think he'll do his best to keep Benjamin safe. That's more than a lot of kids get.

"But if you get Benjamin out of there, maybe you could use him to explain to your boss why you've been MIA the last couple weeks, yeah?" Noelle says. She's talking fast, the words pouring out of her like water from a hose that has recently been un-kinked. "You could tell him that you had to go undercover to get a kid out of a dangerous situation. You'd be a CPS hero."

I chuckle. "Maybe if my life was an action movie, I'd give that a try."

Noelle just stares back at me, confused.

"Are you serious?" I ask. "You really think I should break into a Bratva don's house and try to steal his son?"

"That's why you were staying with him in the first place, is it not?"

I can't believe these words are coming from the more level-headed, more rational of my two best friends.

"I was staying with him because I thought I could gather enough information on him to have him thrown in prison. I was going to let the authorities deal with him. Plus, he was paying me enough money to pay off my debts at the same time," I admit. "But I was also only there because he threatened you and Ashley and my family. I would have left a lot sooner if I knew he wasn't going to hurt you all."

"But he is!" Noelle spits.

"What do you mean?"

She shakes her head. "It's nothing. I'm just saying... I think you should consider making another try for Benjamin. That was the goal. He isn't safe there."

"I really think he is. I know Timofey's world is dangerous, but he has so many resources. Benjamin is going to be really well taken care of there."

"Well, that makes one of us," Noelle blurts. She slams her drink down on the table so hard a bit of soda shoots out of the straw.

The girl working the front counter glances our way, and I smile back at her before I duck my head and hiss at Noelle. "What is going on with you? I was the one who wanted to meet and vent, but you're acting weird. Is something wrong with—"

"Everything is great." She shoves her half-eaten sandwich to the edge of the table and grabs her purse. "Everything is amazing. I'm peachy."

She slides out of the booth, and I just watch her for a few stunned seconds. I haven't eaten all day, and I really don't want to leave my sandwich here. But I also can't let Noelle storm out like this without figuring out what is going on.

I toss a five-dollar tip on the table and hurry after her. I run halfway down the block before I can grab her arm and pull her to a stop.

"Noelle," I gasp, breathing heavily, "slow down. Where are you going?"

"Home. While I still have one."

"What does that mean?"

She holds up a hand to quiet me. "Nothing, Piper. I'm just disappointed. I thought you were going to do the right thing and try to get that innocent little boy away from that monster you were shacking up with. But you must have Stockholm Syndrome or something. Because you are going to abandon him there."

The words coming out of Noelle's mouth are so absurd that I have to laugh. "Are you—You're serious. I can tell you're serious. But this doesn't make any sense. You do understand I could die if I go back into Timofey's house and try to kidnap his son, right?" I lean forward to catch Noelle's eye, but she crosses her arms and looks away from me. "He could kill me. Literally, not figuratively. The fact that you don't seem to care is honestly beyond me. I'm not sure when you started caring more about some baby you don't know more than your own friend, but—"

"Around the time that my 'friend' ruined my life!" she yells.

The moment her anger peaks, it dissolves. She drops her face into her hands. Her shoulders shake with sobs.

I lay a hand on her shoulder. "Noelle? Noey, talk to me. What's going on?"

When she looks up, her eyes are dry, but she looks haggard. I'm not sure how I didn't see it before. She isn't sporting her usual cat eyeliner and her hair is greasy. It looks like she hasn't had a good night's sleep in days.

"Wayne and I are in a lot of trouble, Piper. A lot of trouble. And… it's kind of your fault."

97

PIPER

And it's kind of your fault.

I'm baffled. "How did I get you and your boyfriend in trouble?"

"Because you got involved with Timofey Viktorov," she explains. "You popped up in his life and his enemies started trying to figure out how to get to him."

"The Albanians?" I guess with a creeping sense of dread.

"I don't know," she says, shrugging. "Maybe. One of them was some guy named 'Arber.' He showed up at my front door and said he was there because you led him to me."

I flatten my palm over my beating heart. "I did not lead anyone to you, Noelle. I swear. I've been working to keep you and Ashley out of all of this!"

"Not like that. They found me because they wanted to break into Timofey's inner circle. His men are apparently very loyal. And Timofey wasn't letting anyone near you. So they thought they'd get to you through me." She crosses her arms over her chest, and she looks thinner than I remember. "Or they wanted me to get to you for them, I guess. They wanted me to turn you against Timofey and try to get Benjamin away from him."

I take a step away from my friend. Suddenly, I realize how exposed I am here, standing on the open street. We should have had this meeting in a more secluded location.

"And what did you tell them?" I ask, fearing I already know the answer.

Tears well in her eyes. "I didn't have a choice, Piper. They were going to send me to prison."

I remember my own afternoon spent in a jail cell. If Timofey had that power, I'm sure the Albanians do, too.

"I would have fought for you. I still will," I say. "They can't lock you away on false charges and get away with it. We can fight back and—"

"You don't understand." Her voice breaks around the words. "They aren't false charges, Piper."

"What did you do? It can't have been that bad. People don't go to prison for jaywalking or stealing a pack of gum. You have to—"

"You never asked how I met Wayne."

The change in subject is abrupt. "Yes, I did. You said you met him at work."

"Yeah. I met him at work," she repeats. "When he was there investigating my company for fraud."

I stare at her, the ability to speak having momentarily escaped me.

"I did some bad stuff, Piper. Faked some numbers. Swept some stuff under the rug. Then the FBI came and I was sure it was over for me. But... we hit it off, Wayne and I, and he helped me hide some of my involvement." Noelle puts her hands on her head, almost as if she's trying to shove the truth back into her skull. "But the Albanians dug all of it back up. If I don't do what they say, they are going to make sure Wayne and I are ruined. At best, we'll be fired. At worst, we'll go to prison. I didn't have a choice, Piper. I can't go to prison."

So this is what it feels like, I think. *This is what it feels like to have everything you think you know about the world shatter in front of you.*

"You're the good one," I whisper.

"What?"

"Ashley is the fucked-up one," I say a little louder. "She is the one who calls me for bail money and cancels plans with me to go get beat up by her shitty ex instead. You... you are supposed to be the one I can count on."

Her face screws up in anger. "And you're supposed to be the one who is always there to lend a helping hand. Yet when I need you most, you don't seem to care! I called and told you exactly what you needed to do, but you screwed me on that, too."

I don't understand what she means, but then it hits me.

"The wedding rehearsal." I clap a hand over my mouth, the words coming out muffled. "You called and told me to get out. You said it would be dangerous. I thought you were worried, but that's not it, is it? *You knew what the Albanians had planned.*"

The way her mouth puckers tells me I'm right.

I thought Rodion might have been the rat because he showed up just before the shooting.

But it was Noelle all along.

"I could have *died*," I hiss. "All you had to do was tell me on the phone what was going on, and I would have left. Instead, you risked my life so you wouldn't have to go to prison."

"I thought you would listen to me!" she argues. "I made you promise you'd try to escape."

Some small part of me wants to give her the benefit of the doubt. Noelle was trying to protect herself, Wayne, and me all at the same time. I can't fault her for not doing it flawlessly. She tried her best.

But another part of me—a part that seems to be growing bigger everyday—is tired of accepting whatever scraps are left over once everyone has served their own needs.

I'm worth more than that.

"I am not responsible for the trouble you're in, Noelle. I didn't make you commit fraud at work. I didn't force you to ask Wayne to help you cover it up. If you go to prison, it will be because you put yourself there," I tell her. "But I don't deserve to die to keep you out of a jail cell. My life is worth more than your freedom."

Noelle gasps. "That's rich coming from the don's girlfriend. Or did his dick give you amnesia? Timofey has committed plenty of crimes, and I don't see you trying to send him to prison."

"That's different because—"

Because Timofey would do anything for me.

Because he never would have betrayed me to protect himself.

I walked away from Timofey because he paid my dad off to stay out of my life, but in a lot of ways, he was just doing for me what I've always done for other people: he was taking care of me, even though I didn't ask. He was sacrificing for my benefit, expecting nothing in return.

I take a deep breath. "No one in my life has ever treated me the way I deserve to be treated. I'm always the doormat, the open wallet. But there is only one person who has offered me anything resembling a safe place to land… and I walked away from him."

"Don't tell me you're talking about Timofey," Noelle says in disbelief. "He is way worse than I am!"

I shake my head. "No. No, he isn't. The world isn't black and white, Noelle. There is a lot of gray. Sometimes, good people do terrible things for a very good reason. But you don't have any excuse. You did it because you're selfish."

Noelle snorts. "You are so fucking brainwashed. You are—"

"Done here." I wave. "I'm done with this and with you. Goodbye."

I turn away before Noelle can try to reel me back in. When I glance back, I realize there was no reason to worry. She didn't even try.

She's gone.

Before I get on my motorcycle, I call Timofey. He needs to know what the Albanians are up to. He needs to know that he can't trust anyone in my life, especially Noelle.

The phone rings and rings and rings.

He never answers.

98

TIMOFEY

My phone buzzes in my pocket, but I ignore it. My hands are a little full at the moment.

I don't want to say Benjamin can sense Piper is gone and is now protesting, but there's nothing else that can explain the last six hours.

Nonstop screaming and crying. Refusing naps. Hurling food the second he gets his hands on it.

I have never touched so many bodily fluids in such a short amount of time in my life. And that's coming from a man who has scooped up human brains with my own bare hands.

"The food doesn't do any good if you don't keep it inside," I grit out, tossing another ruined onesie over my shoulder in the general direction of the hamper. It's buried under a mountain of shit-stained sheets and clothes.

The maids worked hard to make the house as clean as new before we moved back in, but Benjamin has seen to it that his room is a disaster.

Akim offered to watch him for the afternoon. I refused solely because I knew why he offered.

"I'll take Benjamin," he said. "You know, if you need… some time."

"I don't need anything."

He nodded. "Right. Obviously. But if you want to, I dunno, get shit-faced or something…"

"I don't need to eat a pint of ice cream and cry over a romantic movie. My nanny quit. That's all."

"Yeah, I know. I'm just saying that I'm happy to take care of him."

"I can take care of my own son," I gritted out.

"I know that. But—"

"But nothing," I growled. "I don't need you. I don't need her. I don't need anyone."

He sulked off after that. If he's heard Benjamin's endless wailing and the string of curses I've let fly every time he spits up all over another one of my shirts, then he's wisely chosen to keep his distance.

I hold Benjamin up, keeping an arm's distance in case he decides to erupt again. He's in a blue thermal romper and the smallest pair of sweats I've ever seen. "There you are. Good as new."

For the first time in hours, he isn't crying. He just stares at me, his wide eyes curious. They flick from me to the ceiling and back again. He's taking it all in: his room, his world.

His not-quite-dad.

"Between you and me, I don't know if I'm cut out for this gig," I whisper. "*Dad*. It feels wrong. Father? Maybe. Guardian? Sure. But being someone's dad feels like a step too far. I'm not even sure if I've had one of those."

His lips purse, and I think he's about to let more body fluids fly. Instead, he screws his face up and then lets loose a wide-mouthed yawn.

"All that projectile vomiting finally worn you out?" I tuck him against my chest.

After a few laps around his room and two lullabies that I butcher all of the lyrics to, he's sleeping soundly. I settle him into his crib and creep into the hallway.

Piper tried to give me some tips on what Benjamin would need before she left, but I couldn't hear it. I didn't want to hear anything she had to say. Least of all about all the ways I remind her of her deadbeat father.

I wouldn't mind talking to her now, though.

She'd hide a laugh behind her hand if I could tell her about Benjamin waiting until he was diaperless to finally shit for the first time all day. She'd laugh even harder if I told her I couldn't find the clean diapers and temporarily had him strapped into an upside down onesie, which he promptly peed through.

I've faced enemy armies and the hail of gunfire, but nothing brings you to your knees quite like an infant.

I pull out my phone to check the time—to see if I can run to the kitchen and grab something to eat before Benjamin wakes up—when I see Piper's name on my screen.

I forgot about the vibration from earlier. She called almost forty minutes ago.

Maybe she's calmed down and is ready to hear my explanation for what happened with her dad. She probably understands why I did it now. We can talk it out and make up…vigorously…several times.

I'm about to call her back when the doorbell rings.

"Always something," I mutter.

Usually, I'd let a maid handle it, but we're operating with a reduced staff since Arber's attack on the house. I've allocated more resources to security and cut down on the number of people in non-essential roles. They would just be more bodies if the Albanians chose to attack again.

Whoever is at the door, they made it through security without me being alerted. That must mean no one believes they are a threat.

The hope that it is Piper rises up in me so swiftly that I don't have a chance to bat it down. She called, I didn't answer, and now, she's here. Right?

Maybe our reconciliation will happen even sooner than I thought. Preferably right on the tile floor of the entryway.

I check my shoulder for any lingering spit-up and then pull the door open. My hopes immediately dash against the rocks of reality.

"Hi, Timofey."

Piper's best friend is her opposite in so many ways. Where Piper is short and curvy, Noelle is tall and lean. Where Piper greets everyone with a nervous smile, Noelle eyes me with open disdain.

It's that last one that has me already closing the door.

"Piper can come talk to me herself if she has something to say," I start. "I'm not in the mood to be set upon by her flying monkeys. Tell her—"

Noelle catches the door with her hand. "This isn't about Piper."

"Why else would you be here?"

Without Piper, there is no world where Noelle's interests overlap with mine.

"Just let me in," she presses. "Please. It's important."

After a beat of hesitation, I hold open the door and usher her in. "Make it quick."

99

TIMOFEY

Noelle is still glaring at me, even as she shifts nervously from foot to foot in the foyer. "I don't want to be here," she announces.

"What a coincidence. I don't want you to be here, either."

She narrows her eyes. "I'm the only one with a good reason to dislike you. You don't even know me."

"I know enough," I snap. "You are here to slap my wrist for hurting your friend even though none of you have done a thing to take care of Piper the entire time you've known her. At least I've been trying to help her out."

Noelle looks down at the floor for a moment. Is that contrition? I wouldn't have expected anything I said to break through to her, but she looks genuinely guilty.

As soon as it flashes across her face, it's gone again. "I told you, this isn't about Piper. It's about Emily."

The words are so unexpected that I actually take a step back. "You don't know a thing about Emily."

"Piper told me about her. She asked me to—"

"Piper may have asked you to type some things into a search bar, but that isn't the same as an actual investigation."

"What about the FBI?" she asks, eyebrow arched. "Is that an official enough investigation for you?"

"You're not in the FBI."

"No. But my boyfriend is." She reaches into her pocket and pulls out a piece of paper. "And he uncovered something."

I want to tear the paper from her hands right now. But I've lived long enough in this world to know you should never show your cards.

"Why the fuck should I care? It won't bring her back."

Noelle sighs "Listen, I'm sure you're used to people in your life leveraging information against you. You've been betrayed and blackmailed. Well, that isn't what I'm here to do."

I cross my arms. "Then why are you here?"

"Because…" She shrugs. "Because Piper came to care about you. I have no idea why, but she really cared about you."

I ignore her use of the past tense. The possibility that Piper doesn't care anymore is harder to take than I'd like to admit.

Noelle holds the note out to me. "She would want you to have this."

"What is it?" I ask, already reaching for the note.

But the second I unfold the bottom third, I know.

It's Emily's handwriting.

The letter looks like it is a photocopy of a taped together piece of paper. But the sloppy print letters and heart over the "i" in her name tells me it's legit.

"The note was found in her apartment after she died," Noelle explains. "My boyfriend, Wayne, looked into the case after I asked him to. A colleague told him about the letter. I had to do some not-quite-legal things to get my hands on that, but…well, everyone deserves closure. Even murderous, manipulative bastards like you."

"Manipulative, eh?" I roll my eyes. "Looks like you've talked to Piper recently."

She frowns. "I have. Have you?"

I can feel my phone burning a hole in my pocket. I was going to call her before Noelle knocked. I will later.

But for now, I can't take my eyes off of Emily's note.

I ignore Noelle's question and open the letter fully.

Dear Benjamin,

One day, I hope you'll read this. You might be upset with me. I would be if I were you. But I know I'm doing what is best for you. It's not safe for people to know who your father is. I love him… but he isn't fit to be a father, anyway. Fuck knows I'm not fit to be a mother. (See? I just cursed in a letter to you.) I'm a mess. But Timofey isn't.

I inhale sharply. If I were to close my eyes, I'm sure I'd feel Emily reading over my shoulder.

She would've laughed and pointed to the curse word. "Do you think he'll laugh at that? Maybe he'll have my sense of humor."

I'm aware Noelle is still in the room with me, though. So I clench my teeth and keep reading.

If I thought for even a second that I could keep you safe, I would. But Timofey is the only reason I'm alive. He's the only reason I survived long enough to have you. I trust him with my life, and I trust him with yours. I hope you come to love him even half as much as I do.

You might be tempted to come look for me or your biological dad one day. But... don't. In another world, I'd love nothing more, but it's not safe for you. Don't try to find us, and don't look into either of our lineages. Some secrets are better left buried. One day, maybe, I'll be able to come to you. I'll get to know you. But not until a few important things happen.

"What important things?" I growl, clenching the edges of the paper in my fists. I want to shake it as if I might be able to shake an explanation out of Emily.

Rodion is an asshole. I know why she wouldn't want him to raise Benjamin, but even he wouldn't hurt his own son.

I love you, Benjamin. Please know that. I don't regret a single thing that has led up to you. I'd do it all exactly the same so long as it meant that you existed. No matter who your father is... or your grandfather is... you are my son. I'm so proud of you.

I reread the last few lines again and again.

Emily doesn't know her parents. Rodion doesn't either, as far as I know. Which grandfather is she talking about?

Noelle clears her throat. "Wayne told me they think Emily knew who Rodion's father was."

I look up at her, and she's watching me closely. "Who?"

"I don't know." She holds up both hands. "I swear I don't."

Emily never told me anything. Rodion didn't, either. Sergey took Rodion in as a favor to his mother. He gave him a job and a purpose because he felt bad for him. If Sergey knew who Rodion's father was, he would have told me... right?

I read the letter again.

It's not safe for people to know who your father is.

Don't look into either of our lineages. Some secrets are better left buried.

"No," I breathe as pieces of a puzzle I didn't know I was solving start to come together. "It's not—That isn't possible."

Even as the thought solidifies in my mind, I'm sure it's not possible. There is no way.

Noelle takes a step back. "Maybe I should—should I go?"

I ignore her and move into the sitting room. I pull my phone from my pocket.

Piper's missed call is still on the screen, and I swipe it away. Instead, I call Sergey. Even in my phone, I have him listed under his first name.

"I need to talk to you," I bark into the line. "Come to the mansion now."

"Are you ordering me around now?" he scoffs.

"It's about the Bratva. It's important."

He'll come if he thinks it has something to do with work. He's always felt more like my boss than my father.

Maybe that's for a good reason.

Maybe it's because he *already had a son.*

100

TIMOFEY

I stop pacing across the kitchen when I hear the front door open.

"Well?" Sergey calls. His voice echoes through the rooms that feel emptier now than ever before. I never noticed it before Piper—how abandoned the place feels without her. She brought warmth with her when she lived here. Now, it's cold and lifeless.

It doesn't help that I have no fucking idea who I can trust.

"In here." I move to the kitchen doorway.

Sergey walks past me, claiming a seat at the new island. "What's so important it couldn't wait until the morning?"

"It's about Emily."

The moment the words are out of my mouth, he shakes his head and stands right back up. "Not this again, Timofey."

"I told you I was going to look into her murder."

"And I told you to let sleeping dogs lie!"

"Emily's murder never made any sense to me," I continue coolly. "Why would someone go after her and not me or you? The only person who ever made sense as her killer was Rodion."

"Who was in Russia at the time," he finishes, waving a hand in the air. "I'm leaving. We've talked about all of this endlessly."

"But we haven't talked about why you've been defending him so fiercely."

"Because he was in Russia," he repeats. "Rodion is a good hitman, but even he can't take a sniper shot from half a world away."

"He could have hired someone to do it for him," I offer up.

"He didn't."

I nod. "You're probably right."

Sergey looks over his shoulder at me. "Is this you finally seeing reason?"

"I think I finally am. I mean, why would Rodion hire a hitman to take Emily out the day he was set to return from Russia? If he wanted to make sure he was in the clear, he would have done it in the middle of his trip. He wouldn't have waited until the last minute. It's almost like someone wanted to make sure Emily was dead before he could come back and talk to her."

My adopted father goes perfectly still. Apparently, I'm not seeing the reason he hoped.

After a few seconds, he shrugs. "Maybe. But we've looked into it, Timofey."

"Rodion has tortured countless Albanians in search of her killer. I've kicked down the doors of all of our enemies. None of the usual suspects seem to be at fault."

"Because there is nothing to be found."

"I wouldn't say that." I walk through the connected sitting room and move into the entryway, blocking Sergey's path to the exit. "The problem is that I've been kicking down doors… when the killer was in my house all along."

Sergey stares at me. His expression is neutral, but that in and of itself is a clue. He should be curious. He should be asking me to explain myself.

Instead, he's waiting. Like a man expecting the other shoe to drop.

"You killed her, Sergey. Didn't you?"

He scoffs, waving me away with both hands. "You have fucking lost it. I know she was like a sister to you, but your obsession with her death has become concerning."

"She *was* a sister to me," I snap. "You wouldn't adopt her because you didn't see her value, but Emily was the only true family I've ever had."

He gestures wildly at the ceiling and floors. "I give you this mansion and I'm not family? Goes to show how fucking ungrateful you are. If you're going to accuse me of this, then maybe I'll rescind my blessing. The men won't treat you as their don if I don't approve."

"You're too old to lead. That's why you passed things on to me. The Bratva was failing under you. I'm the one who has given it new life."

"You aren't the only choice to lead," he spits. "I have other options."

I didn't hear the footsteps moving down the hallway until they got close, so I know Sergey didn't, either. It's why he jolts when Rodion's voice echoes through the room.

"How about your true biological son?" Rodion asks. "Is he an option?"

101

TIMOFEY

Sergey turns just as Rodion comes to a stop in the arched doorway.

Framed as he is in the threshold, he looks like a medieval painting. Chin raised, hands on his hips.

In this light, he also looks a whole hell of a lot like Sergey.

I'm not sure how I didn't see it before. The resemblance between them is subtle, but obvious. They have the same square hairline and the same brawny legs. Rodion's features are more elongated, but now that I'm looking for the similarities, I can see they have the same bushy brows and thin upper lips.

"My true son is the conniving bastard standing behind me," Sergey says, hitching a thumb over his shoulder. "What the fuck are *you* doing here?"

"I called him right after I called you," I explain before Rodion can answer.

Rodion didn't hesitate to drop what he was doing and meet me at the mansion. When I presented him with my theory, the pieces fit together for him, too.

"When I asked why you hired an orphaned kid like me, you told me not to look a gift horse in the mouth," Rodion says. "My mother never would tell me who my father was. She acted like she was scared of him. I couldn't even find the answer hidden in the belongings she left behind. I always guessed he threatened her. Now… I'm sure he did."

"You didn't want anyone to know Rodion was your son," I say to Sergey. "Why?"

Sergey laughs, but it's a sharp, angry sound. "He isn't my son. That's why."

"It's because I was sick. I was born with a heart defect. The doctors didn't think I'd survive childhood," Rodion adds. "But I did. The small hole healed on its own."

I think of Benjamin and his heart defect. The nurse suspected it could be genetic. It makes so much sense.

"Would you abandon your own child because of a health condition, Sergey?" I muse.

Sergey spins around, spittle flying. "He isn't my son! You are my son—or you were. Not anymore."

"I always knew I existed on thin ice. I guess I had no idea how thin." I shake my head. "You abandoned your own child and adopted another, healthier one to continue your lineage. What kind of sick fuck—"

"The same kind of sick fuck who kills a woman so she won't reveal his secret." Rodion's nostrils flare. He takes a dangerous step forward. I can see his hands shaking. "You killed Emily because she was going to tell me the truth. When I talked to her last, she told me she had something to tell me. Something important. But you didn't give her the chance."

Sergey leans in, his voice eerily calm. "I warned you about looking in the gift horse's mouth, Rodion. You're fired. You are no longer my soldier. Just as you are not and have never been my son."

I'm about to remind Sergey that Rodion is *my* soldier. Before I can, Rodion lets out a primal roar and charges towards Sergey.

It's a second. Maybe two.

But it's enough.

Enough for Sergey to pull the loaded gun from his holster and pull the trigger.

Enough for the bullet to hit Rodion square between the eyes.

He cracks against the tile floor at Sergey's feet with no resistance. Blood pools around his head, spilling out of him in rhythmic bursts that grow slower by the second.

Sergey blows out a breath and steps carefully over the puddle. When he turns to me, there is a faraway smile on his face. "I don't know why I didn't do that the day he was born. It sure would have saved me some trouble."

I've seen Sergey kill men in cold blood. But this feels different.

"You taught me to never betray the family," I rasp.

"Rodion isn't my fucking family. How many times do I need to explain it?"

"The Bratva is a family," I clarify. "All of us. If I could have killed Rodion because he annoys me, I would've done it years ago. But we can't. Because—"

"Because *nothing*," Sergey cuts in. "I'll let you in on a little secret: you can do whatever the hell you want. Who is going to stop you?" He chuckles to himself. "Well, I am now. Because you don't know when to keep your head down and your mouth shut."

"Rodion was your biological son."

He rolls his eyes. "Fine. Yes. But that doesn't matter. He was a sick boy. No one expected him to make it past toddlerhood. When he did, I knew he didn't have it in him to lead. He was impulsive and angry and reckless. So I gave him a job that suited his talents. I did right by him."

"You did—" I almost choke on a laugh. "You turned your son into a murderer. Rodion has been shot at, stabbed, and thrown into more dangerous situations than almost anyone else. It's like you've been trying to kill him for years."

"Him dying would guarantee no one contested your position as don." Sergey shrugs. "When I adopted you and made you the next in line to leadership, plenty of men grumbled about your legitimacy. Some of them even wanted Rodion to lead."

I know that. I heard plenty of men who were mad that I wasn't born into this world. They didn't think I could handle it.

I showed them otherwise.

"Imagine if it ever got out that he had a blood connection to me." Sergey shakes his head. "There would have been a coup."

"No, there wouldn't have been. Because I've earned my place. The men trust me."

Rodion's blood has spread even further and Sergey has to move closer to me to avoid getting any on his shoes. "This is why you need my guidance, son. The Bratva is built on tradition. You think you're safe now that you're at the top, but you have to fight to stay there. Everyone wants to take you down. Every man in your employ wants to be you, which means they'll gladly watch you die and try to take your place. You can't give them an excuse."

"If you were so worried about Rodion taking over, why not kill him?" I snarl. "Why did you go after Emily?"

Part of me wants him to deny it. I want him to say, *Rodion is my son, but I never killed Emily. I would never do that to you. I would never do that to her.*

Instead, he shrugs weakly. "Rodion is the best hitman I've ever had. I didn't want to get rid of him."

I try to blink through the rush of anger that courses through me, but all I see is red. "Emily wasn't as useful to you as Rodion… So you murdered her."

"She was bringing you down. The girl was headed nowhere fast. Why the fuck do you think she ended up with Rodion, after all? She was looking for trouble, and you were spending too much time and energy keeping her alive. I did you a favor. Both of you."

I hear the echo of my words to Piper. I want to deny the similarity between me and my adopted father, but there it is.

He got rid of a woman who was family to me, supposedly for my own benefit.

Is that what I did to Piper when I paid off her father?

"She was snooping where she shouldn't have been, and I found out about it," Sergey continues. "When I realized she was going to get back with Rodion, I knew I couldn't let her live. So I killed her. You're welcome."

The bubble inside of me bursts. Without thinking, I charge at Sergey.

Once again, he lifts his gun. But unlike Rodion, I dodge.

The bullet buries itself in the wall behind me. Gunpowder clouds the air in front of my face. Still, I drive my shoulder into Sergey's stomach and tackle him backward.

He huffs as I knock the wind out of him and huffs again when he hits the floor. His head smacks against the tile, and his hands go limp from the impact.

I scramble to grab the gun off the ground and stand up, towering over my prone father.

"You're the one who taught me not to waste time monologuing," I say, cocking the weapon. "You were distracted. Now, I'm going to kill you."

His eyes are glassy from a probable concussion, but he smiles. "No, you won't. Without me, you have nothing."

"With you, I have nothing," I grit out. "You've never been a father to me. You've never taken care of me the way you should have."

The way I take care of Benjamin, I think.

"I saved you from dying in a gutter somewhere," he spits. "With me alive, you might hold onto the throne. But if you kill me, you will be the illegitimate son of a don you murdered when he was unarmed on the ground. You'll look weak. The men will turn on you."

I don't want to believe him, but what he's saying isn't unfounded. There have been mutinies within Bratva ranks before. And for a lot less.

I hesitate. And it's just long enough for Akim to sprint into the room.

"Benjamin is gone!" He looks from Rodion's body, to me, to Sergey on the ground. A thousand questions flicker across his face, but he doesn't ask any of them. None of them are as important as what he is telling me right now. "Benjamin isn't in his room. He isn't—he's gone."

My mind rejects what he's saying. It's impossible. "I laid him in his crib. I put him to bed. He's—"

"Gone," Akim repeats, his eyes pleading with me.

"Where did he go? When did you check on him?"

"I heard the gunshot," Akim says. "I went to the nursery to get Benjamin into the safe room, but he wasn't there."

"A nurse grabbed him." *Please let one of the nurses have grabbed him.*

"None of them are on duty, Timofey. And no one else would go in his room."

The answer is immediately obvious.

Noelle.

Noelle was here.

Distantly, I hear movement. But I'm too focused on the next steps. On whom to call and where to turn. I don't even look up until the front door is slamming closed.

"Sergey is getting away!" Akim cries out, scrambling after him.

I shove him hard in the chest, forcing him away from the door. "Fuck him. Find Benjamin. Now."

Akim calls down to the security department to check the cameras and see who could have taken Benjamin. But I already know.

I head down the hall to his room. I need to see it for myself. I need to kill the small speck of hope that exists in my chest if I'm going to be able to do what has to happen next.

Over the last few weeks, I thought I could have it all. The Bratva and a family. Duty and love.

And in a matter of minutes, it has all come crashing down.

Sergey lied to me—has been lying to me—for my entire life. I gave him my obedience, my time, my energy; all he gave me in return were hollow lies and a paper throne.

Piper made me believe there could be more to life. It only served to make me weak.

Benjamin gave me hope. I can feel its absence before I even step into his room.

The sound machine is still humming. The curtains are still drawn. So much is the same, but the air feels stale.

His crib is empty. The indent of his body is still warm.

Akim steps into the doorway, his shadow casting across the room. I grip the edge of the crib with white knuckles.

"Find Piper," I say without looking.

"Will she know where he is?" Akim asks.

Betrayal scorches through me, burning away my newly-softened edges. What remains is vengeance, tempered and sharp. Along with the ache to wield it.

"She'll know," I growl. "Piper will know exactly where Benjamin is. Because she is the one who took him."

TO BE CONTINUED

Timofey and Piper's story concludes in Book 2 of the Viktorov Bratva Duet, **WHISKEY PAIN.**

CLICK HERE TO START READING

Printed in Great Britain
by Amazon